The author was born in London, and attended school in Watford having moved there with his family when he was aged eight. After spending some years working in the retail sector, and in sales, he returned to education as a mature student, obtaining a BA (Hons). Following a spell working in theatre, in lighting and stage management, he qualified as a secondary school teacher. An alumni of The Central School of Speech and Drama Richard, now lives in Northumberland with his wife, Hilary, and two cars.

This book is dedicated to the love of my life, my best friend and wife, Hilary. Thank for the best years of my life. This is for you and because of you.

Richard Abbott-Brailey

# AZARIAS TOR:
# THE HISTORY MAKER

AUSTIN MACAULEY
PUBLISHERS LTD.

A CIP catalogue record for this title is available from the British Library.

ISBN 9781786933638 (Paperback)
ISBN 9781786933645 (E-Book)

www.austinmacauley.com

First Published (2017)
Austin Macauley Publishers Ltd.
25 Canada Square
Canary Wharf
London
E14 5LQ

Acknowledgements go to those friends, including my wife, who afforded me the opportunity to sound out my ideas, and test my plot and themes on an audience, and for taking time to read the manuscript, providing feedback and encouragement – including Ian, Joanne, Judy, Stephen, Geoff and Lesley, Derek and Dorothy. "D 'n' D – how could I ever forget you?" Finally, acknowledgements also go to the Spanish Armada, H.G. Wells, and CERN, for providing some of the inspiration.

# Prologue

History! *'Do we make history or does history make us what we are? Are our lives influenced by all those who have been there before us, the ancestors we have superseded, attempting to improve the 'lot' of every generation as we produce progeny? Or, do we accept our 'lot'? "It was good enough for your grandparents and your parents, why should you choose to rise above your station in life? Is there then a problem with that expectation – my grandfather went down the 'pit', worked in the shipyards, so it is my birthright – why should any government take that away and destroy communities? To that end, do we allow our lives to be dictated by history or do we attempt to make our history the 'new' future; do we have an impact in history, and the future, or do we allow ourselves to be the 'victims' of the impact of history upon us, having the future shaped for us by others?*

Imagine, then – it is not so difficult – that there are people out there, many of whom we have never met, who will make us part of their history, and make their future our future; world leaders, governments, terrorists, freedom fighters, artists, authors, playwrights, scientists, and so on; all those extraordinary gifted and talented people. But what of the ordinary people – those people living next door, in the neighbourhood, or that person, alone in their car, passing you on the A19, as you prepare to enter the southbound toll at the Tyne tunnel and the impact that they might have on your future? Is that person, the one that you have given a cursory glance – singing along with the radio, CD player, or iPod – going to *'make history'* and have a marked effect on your future? How can you be sure? What if that person, driving that British Racing Green coloured car, alongside you, has secrets that you could not even begin to comprehend? And what if that person, an average tutor at an average college of further education, with the less ordinary name of Azarias, had secrets that even he was not aware of, secrets that could have a major impact on the lives of everyone, throughout the whole of time?

# Chapter 1

*'TFI Friday'!* The thoughts of an ordinary man, driving south on the A19 from the fairly ordinary Northumberland town of Cramlington, leading up to a potentially ordinary weekend, just like any other weekend; at least that was what Azarias might have expected. He was certainly not prepared for what was about to happen but, then, we do not always expect the unexpected, the totally unexpected.

"Prat," he spat at the windscreen of his Rover 75 Club SE, as the old battered weather worn Vauxhall Astra cut across the path of his trajectory, moving from right to left at the southern end of the Tyne Tunnel. The driver of the car with the severely corroded bodywork careered across Azarias's field of vision, causing him to brake sharply, even though he was travelling no faster than 30 mph as he exited the tunnel. There was a female passenger, with jet black hair, who was so close to him that he was momentarily transfixed by the emerald eyes set in an almost white face. He even took time to process that image, reflecting that she possibly resembled the romantic image of Cleopatra, offered up in various history books, art, and movies – not unlike a young

Elizabeth Taylor in the role, he mused. Yet another thought entered his mind – *'Do I know you?'*

She was looking directly at him, almost through him, deep into his eyes, maybe into his soul – perhaps taunting him – as the vehicle swerved off the A19 in the direction of Jarrow and South Shields. Cleopatra appeared to be holding a mobile phone, or small digital camera, up to her face. Maybe this was some new game – carve up another motorist, then capture their reaction on film or, even worse, video that reaction, upload to the net, and, before you can say Bill Gates, it goes viral. His reaction, though, was somewhat muted. *"Yeah, get your Vauxhall shit bucket to the tip,"* Aazrias uttered in the direction of the offending vehicle, as it curved away towards the roundabout above the tunnel exit. Then, they were gone; she was gone, almost forgotten, having been considered insignificant in the greater scheme of things.

Radio 2 invaded the inside of the car, as thoughts of the minor motoring infraction faded. Dean Martin and Helen O'Connell sang, *"How do you like your eggs in the morning"* which cut off at the point where the toddler, echoing in a bathroom, recorded by a very proud parent, shouts *"Kiss-er, kiss-er."* Same time, same place. Azarias was a creature of habit, a few points from being diagnosed with OCD; not that he had ever sought a diagnosis. But he was usually somewhere just south of the Tyne Tunnel on a week day when this section of the breakfast show hit the airwaves. Somewhere between the tunnel and Testos roundabout. That was usual. At this point the tail lights of vehicles approaching the roundabout, piled back from that point like red dominoes falling, causing Azarias to dab his brakes a few times,

12

continuing that domino effect for following drivers. For a while the traffic remained stationary, as motorists waited for the lights to change at the roundabout. And it was during that time, thinking time, those thoughts danced around in his head. The woman, that woman in that car – he thought he had seen her somewhere before. Her face was strangely familiar, '*but why?*'

"No," he said to his eyes in the interior mirror. "No. You're imagining things. Not possible."

A trick of the mind, he thought, trying to dismiss the idea from his head, which he shook vigorously. But he could not shake the image of her face from his mind, nor dismiss the thought that he had seen her somewhere before. He reached the roundabout as the lights flashed from amber to red, giving him pole position when they next changed to green. The face of the Cleopatra woman came into focus again, in his mind's eye. Where had he seen her before?

Azarias had a memory for faces, placing names to faces. He used to rely on that skill, in a previous life, when he was in the force. Another life, another world, another Azarias. He was certain, though, that he had seen that woman before, and not just in passing. She was not one of those faces passed in a crowd, at a station, an airport, or in a bar, which perhaps becomes embedded in the sub-conscious but someone with whom he had had close contact. '*But where and when?*' A deep intermittent foghorn-like sound shook him from the shackles of deepest thought. The lights were on green. The driver to his rear, in the white van, with the ladder on the roof, was punching his horn impatiently. Azarias waved an apologetic back-hand wave and pushed his foot to the accelerator, and moved around the nearside of the roundabout, continuing his journey south, using choice words to curse his own lapse of concentration – though that was the problem – he was concentrating; deeply, just not on his driving.

The ladder van pulled out and began to pass on the right, the driver and his passenger, in paint-spattered overalls, giving Azarias their best hard-man evil stares. Azarias nodded his apology, but with the skill of a ventriloquist, through clenched teeth and a sarcastic smile he hissed, *"In your dreams, fuck-wits, in your dreams,"* and allowed another two vehicles to pass, before signalling his intention to pull out and pass the traffic that was slowing on the approach to 'Nissan' junction.

As he ascended the A19 towards the A690 junction, the index finger of his left hand gently slid the S/E switch into sport, increasing acceleration up the hill causing him to roar past the 'ladder van'. The early morning Radio 2 banter was disturbing his train of thought, as he tried to focus on the woman's face, and where he had seen her before. Where? Azarias pressed the CD button in the console – he had no further need of the radio broadcast – particularly the traffic news. Mario Caribe started strumming his double bass, spilling jazz sounds into his ears. And then he remembered where he had seen that face – in his dreams. *'No. Just coincidence. Trick of the mind'.*

Many of his dreams were vivid, and had been for as long as he could remember. It was as if he was really there, in whatever the place was, in the dream. In his dreams he had noted he was always looking out, never at himself – though there had been occasions when he had caught glimpse of his reflection in a mirror or a window. Those were the dreams he most likely recalled to mind the next morning. Sometimes he would awaken feeling exhausted as if he needed more sleep.

A colleague had suggested that he might be suffering with depression, with regard to his tiredness and the vivid dreams, though didn't really believe that to be the case. He was just dreaming, and had a good strong imagination. But now he was in doubt, now that he had seen her face – twice – in his dream the previous night, then staring right at him – as close to him as the driver of the Volkswagen Polo he was overtaking on the A19. As double bass, guitar, saxophone and keyboards melded harmonically, Azarias brought to mind that dream. He remembered the cool breeze on his face and the feel of sand between his toes as he walked along the beach – where, he did not know. *'Was it really her?'*

\*\*\*

Azarias surmised he was somewhere in the west, wherever that somewhere was, judging by the position of the sun in the sky and the prevailing wind with the sea to his left, he concluded that he was heading north, beneath rugged, ragged high cliffs. The sea lapped calmly, almost still, at the land, glistening in the clear light as the water foamed, bubbled and soaked into the sand, with each returning wave. Seabirds wheeled and whirred, circling above the cliffs and calling to wind. It all felt and sounded so real. And then there was the smell – the smell of death.

Feeling his way around a promontory the rock face damp and cool to the touch, he discovered the source of the sickly stench, a smell he remembered; a smell that had once played a part in his working day – death and decay. Ahead of him stretched a long broad belt of sand, peppered with rocks, overshadowed and cradled by an almost perfect sight before him – a semi-circle of cliff tops, maybe 50 metres high. What he initially took to be seals soaking in the warmth of the sun, showed them to be beached, bloated bodies – 25, no 27, a quick count revealed.

Strange, he thought, that he could smell their decay – so real – and that the gulls, gannets and those big black birds – carrion – he could never tell one from the other, crow, rook or raven, refused to give up their bounty, their feast. The birds pecked at exposed fleshy parts of the puffy, wrinkled discoloured faces – blue lips, purple and white blotches set against sea-ravished, tanned leathery skin. Hispanic, maybe even some Arabic he thought, on closer examination taking into account the style of clothing, the sea soaked sun-dried linen shirts, the moleskin breeches, long tousled hair, the odd gold hooped earring here and there, and bearded faces, Azarias wondered if it was a 'Pirates of the Caribbean' tribute party; perhaps one of those stag parties that goes horribly wrong. Hire a yacht, then discover that there is more to sailing than first meets the eye – dashed against the rocks, then drowned. Then he took a closer look at one of the faces.

The cawing carrion challenged Azarias, flapping wings and hopping wildly, in a bid to prevent him from invading that territory and stealing the cadaver they had secured which would surely supply a good number of feeds and easy pickings. Azarias flapped his arms and growled at them, *"This is my dream. Go on – bog off."* A sort of a 'Mexican stand-off' developed – the birds refused to give up their gains, and Azarias ignored the threats of their pecking weapons – it was only a dream, after all. A weird dream; but a dream! Or, was it?

Leaning forwards, taking note that he was on this beach in his pyjamas – very strange – Azarias peered into the glassy chestnut bloodshot eyes, which stared lifelessly at the white puffs of cloud, drifting across the blue sky, disappearing over the cliff. There was little doubt that he, and the other men had drowned. The drowned man wore a gold hoop in each ear, and an angry red scar on his right cheek. *"That must have smarted! Who are you? What are you doing here?"*

The man's open mouth gaped at Azarias, but no answer was given. His teeth mostly consisted of rotten black and grey stumps with only two complete teeth to the left and right. A piece of seaweed hanging in the corner of the mouth suddenly twitched, causing Azarias to start, as if the dead man was about to sit up and speak. 'A dream, but anything can happen in dreams'. Instead, a small crab pulled its way up the seaweed and out of the cavernous mouth, dropping onto the sand and scurrying sideways along the sand, flicking small grains of yellow sand from the ends of the pointed legs. Azarias gagged, turning away from the bloated blotchy face, and that was when a small leather pouch, wedged beneath a rock, caught his attention.

Azarias stooped to collect the pouch, which fitted in the palm of his left hand. There was something inside, tied in with leather string. He shook the small, purse-shaped bag, and then held it still. A solitary object rattled inside. He just wanted to be sure that it didn't feel as if there was something living lurking inside – another small scuttling crab perhaps. But there was no reaction. He shook it again. '*Nothing'*. An inanimate object, then.

He pulled at the leather knot, swollen with salty sea water, which resisted attempts from his large fingers and thumbs to reveal the contents. Azarias thought about using his teeth to loosen the knot, reconsidering that idea when he surveyed the beached bodies – he did not want to be contaminated by death. '*No, not a good idea!*' A body, less than a metre away, appeared to have a knife in a sheath, which was held at the waist with a crude leather belt of sorts. '*That will do the job.*'

Using a flattish rock as a cutting board, the knife sliced through the top of the pouch with ease. '*Wow that is sharp!*' He stabbed the blade into the sand then turned the purse inside out. A gold coin fell into his right hand. Azarias stood up and walked towards the sea, avoiding outstretched arms of the dead, in case they should grab him and drag him down to their hell. Studying the coin, and surveying the sorry scene, he reasoned that this was not a 'Pirates of the Caribbean' stag party after all. Azarias was trying to make sense of the relief on the coin, a head, and etched words – foreign – perhaps Latin, he thought – when he heard a noise. *A voice?* Shouting, calling, but unintelligible.

He had reached the point of the beach where the frothing sea stained the flat sand to caramel colour, where small bubbles appeared at the edge of the tide as it tracked back towards the vast expansive horizon. The water was cold on his bare feet, and his toes spread and clawed into the wet sand – amazing but peculiar dream. Very odd! Looking back, around the beach, expecting a body to be sitting up, calling and waving, Azarias saw nothing but the scene resembling an open top cemetery, where the dead are left out to be eaten by nature and the elements. Again, he heard a voice – no two, maybe three voices – calling, screeching like the gulls into the breeze.

A flash of light dazzled his eyes – light reflected from a source above him, on the cliff tops. Illuminated in the sunlight, now dipping down to the western horizon, he spotted glints of red, gold then silver. Four, five, then six men – very strange, but then dreams are strange; *'do we have such a capacity to remember faces and places, or even invent people and places we have never seen?'* – seemingly part of some civil war re-enactment society, assembled along the ridge of the cliff.

First the stag party, that probably wasn't a stag party, and now this – frightening but interesting – men dressed in red, with gold braid, wearing metallic looking helmets. And each of them carried a sword, in a scabbard, suspended from a belt which ran diagonally from the right shoulder to the left hip. They were shouting and waving, so Azarias waved back. Perhaps

19

they had been sent to collect the bodies. There again, maybe not, and maybe they were not waving at him.

Another man, similarly dressed, though wearing somewhat flamboyant large black headgear, accentuated with a huge white feather, appeared in their midst, close to the edge of the cliff, and stabbed into the soft grass a long shaft-like stick, topped with a 'V' shape, like an angler might use to rest the fishing rod. Into the 'V' he rested something resembling a long telescope – perhaps to get a closer look at Azarias, or the bodies on the beach. Then the man removed his floppy hat and seemingly a wig, and handed these to one of the other men.

The man, now bald, looked along the length of his telescope – not through it – strange, but then dreams can be strange. Suddenly it dawned on Azarias that the telescope was in fact a musket, and he was in the line of fire – the target. *"So what, it can't hurt, it's a dream."* He would wake up, or the dream would just finish. *"Do dreams just finish or do we make them finish?"* Anyway, if he ran about on the beach, the rifleman would not be able to get a clear shot – he would have to keep moving his musket. Azarias was in control of his dream – he thought.

Three more men appeared on the cliff, each of them armed, so it seemed, with a loaded crossbow. The rifleman appeared to give them orders – he must be in charge – as they spread out to form a triangle, with Azarias at the apex. One musket and three crossbows now focused on Azarias. A point had been reached where he wanted the dream to end – this was a nightmare, a bad trip. *"Wake up. Move. Fly. Something. It's a dream."* He was about 200 metres from the cliff base, and out in the open, nowhere to run, nowhere to hide.

He heard two successive cracks – a sort of 'thwack' – as two bolts were released, under immense pressure, from the crossbows high above. The first plunged deep into the wet sand close to him, and the next fell short of the intended target, and thudded into the bulging gut of a corpse, causing a spurting, farting sound to erupt as pent-up gases were released. Azarias found himself fixed to the spot, almost hypnotised. He'd had some dreams, but this one – it was becoming dangerous, and crazy, but intriguing.

More shouting from the cliff top. The man with the 'V' shaped stick disappeared behind a white cloud and red flash of flame. Azarias felt a thud in his left side, causing him to stumble a few metres to his right, and heard a loud echoing boom, a 'whoosh' and 'whizz', followed by a 'splash' as a projectile from the musket narrowly missed his head, splashing into the sea. But what had hit him just below the rib cage?

"Don't just stand there. Move! Start running, find some cover," a female voice to his left shouted.

There was little doubt that the crowd on the cliff were reloading, preparing to take more shots at Azarias. These people had been there all along, pretty much throughout this dream. But where had this person, somewhere to his left, appeared from? *'Things like that happen in dreams.'* People can appear from anywhere,

21

and change into other people, even disappear. Anything can happen in dreams.

Like the woman appearing to his left, her right foot still lowering from the kick she had delivered which had helped to push him out of the line of fire of the musket. Azarias turned to look at her – *"Wow, where did you come from? Who are you?"* She was not much shorter than him, willowy and slim, with narrow hips and small breasts, tightly clad in a lilac coloured one piece. Her jet black straight cut hair, with fringe, framed her pale skin and emerald eyes. She reminded Azarias of images of Cleopatra he had seen in any number of books. She was not unlike Elizabeth Taylor in the movie Antony and Cleopatra.

\*\*\*

Two thoughts immediately fired up in Azarias's mind. The first, he had been so lost in thought he had nearly missed his turn-off from the A19. The second thought – the woman in the car that had carved him up at the tunnel, was the same woman in that dream. That was where he had seen her before. It had to be her. *'How was that possible? No. Can't be.'* Perhaps he had met her somewhere before; a face in a crowd, retained in his subconscious amongst the thousands of others stored by the brain, yet not instantly recognisable. Pure coincidence, and not worthy of much thought.

Though the dream had been unusual; and not the first because he had had many dreams similar before this one, there had never been a dream quite as potentially life-threatening, in the sense that people seemed intent on trying to kill him. *"Was it really possible that if you died in a dream, you died in real life?"* Maybe he just had a vivid imagination, and a memory for faces. He had already thought that through. In his life before this one, that skill – the memory for faces, with his precise recollection of dates and events had proven to be an integral part of his work in another life, the life before the death of his wife. He shook the thought from his mind. There were some things he did not want to replay, so returned his thoughts to the dream.

\*\*\*

She had appeared from nowhere. But things like that happen in dreams, when events from the real world are replayed, mixed together, or when our subconscious digs into our deeply buried fears and aspirations. This dream was different, though – different from his ordinary dreams. Azarias had two categories of dreams – 'absurd' and 'ordinary'. This one, without doubt, fell into the 'absurd' category. And more so, *'because of that woman – the one with the emerald eyes.'*

She had spoken to him – Azarias had heard her, for sure. She had kicked him – he had felt that, definitely. She had approached him; he had smelled her scent – clean, warm, inviting, with an undertone of lavender – perhaps a hint of vanilla. Azarias had wanted to reach out and touch her. *"Where had she come from? Who was she?"*

He had asked, *"Who are you?"*

*"Your guide,"* she had answered,

*"I need a guide?"* he had asked.

She had answered, *"You will soon."*

Emerald Eyes had extended her right hand towards him, palm upwards, as if offering a gift. *"Curiosity killed the cat."*

But he had felt compelled to take a look and had leaned forward. There was nothing in her hand, but a nozzle, beneath the sleeve of the one-piece suit, ejected a fine aerosol spray, which formed a small cloud, around his nostrils and mouth. Azarias swatted at the puff of vapour, like he might an annoying insect, and swayed, drunkenly as his limbs and head began to feel as if they were made from wet clay. As he began to stagger, two other people appeared – from nowhere. *"But things like that happen in dreams."*

Dressed from head to foot in polar white one-piece jumpsuits, boots and gloves, and wearing a motorcycle full-face helmet, with black-tinted visors, these two appeared to melt out of the air, having oozed through invisible cracks in – in his dream. *"Wow!"* Azarias tried to escape from their clutching hands but he couldn't move, his legs feeling as if they were wading through thick treacle. *'Dreams can be like that. Unable to run. Incapable of throwing a punch with any force. Finding it impossible to fly again, once you have landed.'*

Something grabbed his left ankle – the outstretched hand of a corpse caught him, and Azarias began to fall, slowly, into a spiralling blackness. His head was spinning, as he floated down through pitch-black, aware of something, someone, gripping his arms. He thought he could hear voices, mumbling, droning, in slow motion, as he drifted down into the dark depths of his sleep.

Azarias awoke with a start, gasping for a breath, as he appeared to reach an abrupt end to his spinning and falling, floating through the dark void. As he tried to focus his eyes, in the gloom, there was still a sense that his head was spinning. He began to focus – no, it was the room that was spinning. When it stopped, when his head and the room had ceased spinning, when that sense of falling ended with a gentle jolt, he found himself on the floor of his bedroom, staring up at the ceiling, with his quilt pulled over his body, with his left leg on the bed, tangled in the top sheet, and there was that feeling of holding something in his hand; a coin, but nothing was there, on close examination.

He dragged himself and the quilt, back on to the bed, untangling his left foot from the sheet. Rearranging the bed linen, Azarias searched in the dark for the time – the digital radio alarm clock at 03.30, glowed green in the dark. There was at least another two hours before Azarias would need to be out of bed, readying himself for the day ahead. Resting his right cheek into the pillow, and pulling the cover over his foetal shaped body, he muttered to himself *"Not there. Not that dream again,"* and drifted back to sleep, and did not go there again.

Having driven around the one-way system of the college car park, Azarias came to rest in his preferred parking area. Of which there were four spaces he was happy to use – a little OCD maybe, but certainly a creature of habit. Repetition! So many things he did the same each day. Why, he did not know; perhaps did not want to know why. Then he placed the gear shift in 'park', pulled up the handbrake, switched off the ignition, pulled his 'BlackBerry' from his left trouser pocket, and did the same thing he had done every day, for many a year – in this life, and his previous life. Azarias thumbed the ball of his 'old Pearl', until he reached the 'address book', opened it, then scrolled down until he reached *'Theresa'*.

Clicking on the ball revealed the name, *'Theresa'*, a home phone number, mobile phone number, home address, and a birthday. Another click of the ball opened a page, with numerous options, and again scrolled down, selecting 'SMS Theresa'. Another click of the ball, 'SMS which number?' Azarias selected 'mobile', and then typed *'Arrived. Love you always. X'*. Just as he had done all of his married life – only his wife Theresa had been dead for over four years.

And then, he pressed 'Send'.

# Chapter 2

In a large white, square room, with minimal white furniture – not so that anyone might avoid bumping into a desk, or banging a knee on a cabinet such was the camouflage effect; not necessarily deliberate, but clean, efficient and hygienic. To make matters worse – to play cruel tricks on the eye – a man dressed in white with white goatee beard and moustache and matching long white hair tied back in a ponytail, sat behind an empty white desk in a white high-backed chair. Due to the pale colour of his face, at first glance, a person might initially notice only the green eyes and the thin red line of his lips, and they might appear to float in space, detached, without any physical connection – almost an abstract work of art.

There is no obvious light source, no windows in the room. The white walls seem to glow, and emanate light, as if particles in the paint, or materials from which the walls are made, are capable of conducting electricity, or are made up of tiny light emitting diodes. And the same could be said of the floor – whiter than a freshly polished and smoothed skating rink, yet emitting a cool light, like natural daylight, without windows.

White bearded man raised his left arm, and peeled back the white sleeve of his one-piece suit, with his right thumb and forefinger, to reveal a wide, gauntlet-style bracelet consisting of three crystal glass screens – one on the top of the forearm adjacent to the back of his hand, and the other two either side – akin to a triptych of flexible wrist-sized mobile phone/watches wrapped around the arm, though in a smooth curve, clasped at the bottom by a switch in the shape of a DNA helix. *'Technology! Never still. In a state of constant flux. Ever-changing. New. Obsolete. New. Nothing lasts forever.'*

His grandfather would have been amazed, impressed, just how much things have changed, moved on, in the last forty years, thirty years even. He had visited the Museum of Modern Antiquities with his grandfather and marvelled at the quaintness of emerging technologies from a bygone era, when a person would have to type numbers and letters on an old fashioned 'qwerty-style' keyboard in order to send messages or speak to someone, using their mobile devices. Things improved, marginally with touch-screen, and then voice-activated technology. *'But now? How times have changed – technology has moved on'.*

A life-time contract is taken out, effectively from birth, for the uRAPP (utility Rapid Accelerometer Photonic Processor); from Mobile Personal Genetic Telecommunications, a subsidiary company of Geneticorp. Once the appropriate package is chosen, in accordance with status, qualifications, profession, and 'potential' – which allows for upgrades – two microchips; individually, genetically, manufactured chips – are inserted painlessly beneath the skin; one under the left wrist, the other behind the right ear. From that point on, all technologies used, as part of the lifetime guarantee, are matched to the individual's genetic make-up – upgraded as per requirements and personal allowances.

He had heard the stories and was aware of theft of mobile telecommunication devices, many moons ago, yet that never happened any more. No point. All technology is individually designed to match a person's genetic make-up, and any attachments will not operate unless in contact with the individual. In the extreme a thief could cut off a person's arm and head, but he doubted they would benefit much from that, especially as his own uRAPP informed him, regularly, that he was alive – reporting current vital signs and oxygen levels in the blood, amongst other things, acting as a utility device containing a variety of tools; weapons depending upon security clearance.

The man with the white beard, had never really given it much thought until then, but perhaps that was part of the lifetime guarantee – that once you ceased to live, the uRAPP switched you off, or your death switched them off, releasing you from the lifetime contract, though it was most likely not the case for himself and his team, as he and they could find themselves in places where the uRAPP signal didn't even exist. Of course, he and his team had 'access all areas' contracts. *'Easy to forget, just how important you really are!'* Suddenly, the device sounded an alarm, pinging three notes running down a musical scale – G, F#, E, which repeated three times, before the middle screen illuminated, showing the time – 14.41.

At that precise moment the air in the white room crackled with static electricity. Even the hairs in his white beard rose, like iron filings drawn towards a magnet. He stood, and moved from behind his desk, walking around the furniture, leaning his hindquarters against the desk, waiting in anticipation of some events though still camouflaged against the backdrop. Suddenly three figures, people, emerged from nowhere, from thin air, as if squeezed through cracks in the air that seemingly had an invisible link to some other place.

They just melted out of thin air into the room, the woman and two men, perhaps. Difficult to tell them apart at first glance; all about the same height – approx. 1.80m – willowy and lean, though the woman with jet black hair and emerald eyes, had the semblance of breasts and hips, small and boyish though they were. She stepped forward from the other two, dressed in a lilac-coloured one-piece close-fitting jumpsuit, with matching boots and thin tailored gloves. The other two removed their white full-face helmets, with tinted black visors, and held them under one arm, against the sides of their polar-white one-piece jumpsuits, in such a way as to make them appear as matching bookends. Both wore close-cut chestnut hair, sported pale complexions, aquiline noses, square, clean-shaven jawlines, then pink lips and emerald green eyes. They could have been twins – expressionless; but twins nonetheless.

The man with the white beard moved forward, pushing himself away from his desk, and raised both arms in a greeting.

"My daughter," he rasped, his voice almost a hoarse whisper. "Saluki. Punctual as always."

Her pale cheeks flushed as she hissed, conspiratorially "Father! How many times? Please. When I am on duty, when I am working, treat me as you would all rank and file. Please."

"Apologies. You are right, of course," he replied, lowering his arms, making a triangle with his hands, beneath his chin, as if he was about to pray. "Saluki. Commandant. Tell me. Please tell."

With an accent hinting that the languages of Europe, though spoken in English, had melded; leaning slightly towards the east of the continent, Saluki began to prepare her report, peeling back her left sleeve, and giving spoken instructions to her uRAPP.

"Filename. Azarias Tor. Image. A-T one."

The pure white room began to fill with colour, and the walls, floor and ceiling dimmed a little, as a holographic image, a metre square, formed in the air. Particles in the air took on various colours, tones and shades, forming the features of a man, glaring through the windscreen of an automobile, lips pursed, as if uttering some expletive directed at the person who had captured the candid shot. More detail became apparent as the millions upon millions of airborne pixels formed and picked out the individual hairs in his thick luxurious dark waves and eyebrows, and the few minor imperfections on the weather-toned, suntanned skin, though few they were. Large almond-shaped hazel-coloured eyes stared accusingly into the room.

"Azarias Tor," Saluki announced, walking through the photograph, waving an introductory right hand up and down the length of the face, suspended in the air.

"Azarias Tor," she repeated, for effect, perhaps in case those assembled had not been listening, and were in danger of missing the person profile that was about to be delivered.

Saluki Damarov continued, "Age. 42 years old. Born 1972 in London. An only child. Raised by his mother. No record of the father. Moved away from London when he was 8 years old. To a town called Watford."

"An interesting name," her father interjected.

"Watford?" Saluki queried, a little surprised by the seemingly pointless interruption.

"No, no, no," he rasped stoically. "Azarias is an interesting name. Azarias. I wonder what inspired his mother to give him that name."

"I have no idea. May I—"

A loud electronic buzzing sound cut Saluki off in mid-sentence, and another image appeared in mid-air, though this time it was a moving image – a video of a man, possibly in his forties, with almost white hair, white eyebrows, pink complexion, and glassy green eyes. He appeared to be leaning forward, as if peering into the lens of a camera. His tone was brusque, his speech clipped and precise, and his British accent very 'home-counties' with emphasis on the Received Pronunciation.

"Good day Superus Gabriel Damarov," he began, giving the man with the white beard his full title, thus establishing his role and level of importance in the overall scheme of things. Very few people hold higher office and status, than that of someone who has risen through the ranks to reach the heady heights of 'Superus'; a person beyond and above the law, and only fourth in line in the hierarchy to President General. A great position – non-executive but with a finger on the pulse of power, with a mouth close to the ears of the 'puppeteers', and those who really run the show.

"Apologies for my tardiness," he continued, "A matter of some urgency required my attention."

Superus Gabriel Damarov spoke in reassuring tones to the suspended image, saying, "Nevertheless, Vice-Superus Raphael Antinori, you are here now. And most welcome." The 'pecking order' established and reinforced! Damarov's tone of voice became more authoritarian as he gave an order, not to anyone but to the room - *"Command. Open door."*

The video call, suspended in the air, folded and vanished. A section of wall, about 3 metres square, at the far end of the room, opposite where Damarov stood, and beyond the white *'bookends'* with helmets under their arms, appeared to dissolve, revealing a long corridor. Vice Superus Raphael Antinori entered the room through the gap. The officers stood to attention as did Saluki, acknowledging their superior with a salute; which involved bowing slightly at the waist, and tipping the head so the chin touched the chest. Raphael, in turn, deferred in the same manner, to his superior, Superus Gabriel Damarov.

"It's so good to see you," said Damarov, perhaps a little lacking in sincerity, raising his arms as if about to hug the Vice-Superus. He pulled short of a proper man-hug, clasping Raphael at the sides of both shoulders. "So very good to see you," he continued, the shoulder-grasping potentially more 'power-play' than camaraderie.

"Of course. I am here. As you requested." Raphael returned. "To hear the report of your..." He was cut short by a look from Damarov, and a dismissive conspiratorial shake of the head.

"Yes. Of course," the Vice-Superus gathered his thoughts, "To hear the report of your – our Commandant Saluki Damarov."

"Do you have any objections, Commandant?" Gabriel Damarov asked of his daughter, "To Vice-Superus Antinori being present at this de-briefing?"

"Of course not," she replied. "I had not anticipated such, but it will be an honour to share my report with the Vice-Superus. First though, I would like to give my team leave."

Saluki turned to her two subordinates, speaking to them in hushed tones, inaudible to her father and the Vice-Superus. The two men bowed their heads, turning together, and marching from the room like overgrown clockwork toys, into the corridor from which Raphael had entered, and as the two men marched along the dimly lit corridor, a tunnel of light illuminated in their wake, before Gabriel Damarov gave the command "Close!" The wall reappeared, like skin on custard melding over the gap, leaving no evidence, crack or sign that there might be a door.

The Superus then made four very precise taps on the centre screen of his uRAPP with the middle finger of his right hand. This action appeared to have an immediate impact on the surroundings, as three white chairs, shaped like hollowed-out half eggs, supported on a single leg, emerged from the floor. They did not just rise up from the ground but were formed from the very material, the atoms that made the floor, as if there were enough extra molecules and particles, which had replicated themselves, to mould furniture from the very fabric of the room.

Gabriel Damarov ushered the other two towards the vacant seats, which were set out like the vertices of a triangle. Saluki declined, wishing to remain standing, for potential maximum impact, while the Vice-Superus eased his slim frame into the chair, the cushioning moulding around his rear and his thighs. Damarov offered a beverage and both declined. He took a seat and the Commandant continued with her interrupted report.

She tapped and stroked the central monitor of the uRAPP, and a silver screen appeared, floating in the air, half a metre from her, about head height. Text moved on the screen like a prompt utilised in the event that the interruption might have caused a lapse of memory, or that important information may be omitted from the report. Her green eyes flashed from side to side and her black curtain-like hair swished back and forth with the movements of her head, like velvet drapes, as she followed the text, speaking with an obvious acerbic sarcastic tone – a protest aimed silently, at those who would dare to waste her time.

"If I may continue. Azarias Tor. 42. Born in London. Lived most of his formative years in a town called Watford. This was in the old county of Hertfordshire, in the English Territories. Educated at an independent school in the town."

Gabriel raised the index finger of his right hand and did not wait for acknowledgement, and, once again, someone or something cut a swathe through her attempts to deliver the report.

"Question," he said. "Would you be so kind as to explain this independent school education?"

Saluki, once again tapped the central screen of the uRAPP on her left wrist, and a newsreader type voice, from Speakapaedia filled the room, giving an historical explanation of independent schools in the 1980s –

*'An independent school is a school that is independent in its finances and governance; it is not dependent upon national or local government for financing its operations, nor reliant on taxpayer contributions, and is instead funded by a combination of tuition charges, donations, and in some cases the investment yield of an endowment. It is governed by a board of directors that is elected by an independent means and a system of governance that ensures its*

*independent operation. It may receive government funds. However, its board must be independent.*

*The terms independent school and private school are often synonymous in popular usage outside the United Kingdom. Independent schools may have a religious affiliation, but the more precise usage of the term excludes parochial and other schools if there is a financial dependence upon or governance subordinate to outside organizations. These definitions generally apply equally to primary education, secondary education, and tertiary education institutions' ...*

Gabriel snapped the thumb and forefinger of his right hand. "Enough," he clucked. "I have heard enough. How times have changed. People used to leave their homes to receive an education? Teachers? I have read about them. A job carried out by robots and computers. Anyway. No more interruptions. I promise."

Saluki tapped her device once and the voice ceased, and the Speakapaedia screen vanished. She continued with her version of events, her report and her screen, using her notes.

"A high achiever. Straight As throughout his early academic career. Played rugby and football for the county. Major in English with a minor in history at Durham University. Graduated with first class honours. Worked in the hotel George in a place called Keswick, for about 18 months before applying to join the police in the Northumbria constabulary."

At this juncture, the Vice-Superus interjected "I apologise, Commandant, for this interruption. Why did he not return home? Did he not spend time with his mother?"

"It seems that he took a liking to the northern counties of the English Territories. He walked in the hills and used a bicycle to explore the area. Accepted into the police, he proved to be a high-flier. He settled in a town called Cramlington. Have you heard of it?"

Both men nodded affirmatively. Damarov added, "It is a well-visited holiday resort on the coast."

"Now it is," Saluki stated, with the confidence of sound research to support her appraisal. "Then, it was inland. Perhaps 8 kilometres from the coast."

Saluki waved her right hand over the text, which was still hanging in from of her face, and the words shifted, changed, making room for the image of a woman.

"Iona," she gestured with her left hand. "His mother. An artisan. Artist of sorts. She won money guessing the results of football matches. More than enough to enable her to work for herself, to fund her son's education, and buy her home. She was very comfortable."

Gabriel Damarov examined the fingernails of his right hand, the way a woman does, fingers stretched outwards, away from him, and then the way a man does, curling his fingers towards the palm of the hand and then uttered "Perfect."

"That is what I would have thought. Perfect. And then I uncovered this report in a local newspaper." Saluki once again waved her left hand over the image and the text, hovering in the air. "Death through misadventure. Not suicide, though the coroner's report

38

intimated that her death was brought about by an accidental overdose."

"Though it is not what you are investigating, Commandant, is it?" the Superus grumbled, "Please focus on your task."

"As you wish," she deferred. "I had just considered her death relevant to my report. With regards to *his* inheritance. The purchase of *his* home."

"It is not. Of little interest. Of no consequence. Please continue," he ordered.

Sensing a strained atmosphere between daughter and father, serving officer and superior, Raphael interceded with a question, uncertain, and confused, as to why Gabriel appeared agitated.

"What is his current status?"

The questioning technique had the desired effect, pulling focus from the issue causing friction between the Damarovs, whatever the cause was. Something regarding Gabriel's over-reaction to references to the mother of Azarias Tor concerned the Vice Supcrus. Why did he react so vehemently at the mention of the mother, and her death? He seemed to take it personally. Why? Saluki suddenly cut through the fog of thought in his mind, with the answer to his question.

"He is an Emergent," she proffered.

"Not Established yet, then?" Raphael queried, assuming control over a seemingly inflammatory situation. Why the over-reaction? The thought echoed inside his skull. "He doesn't yet know?" he continued.

"No. To both," she answered. "He is not yet established and he does not yet know. He is not yet aware. Soon, though."

"How soon?" her father asked, having regained his composure.

"Very soon." Saluki declared. "Very soon. He has seen me. More than once, in different times. In his own time, so now he will be confused. How is it possible to see me in his world, when he thinks he has seen me in his dreams? When he makes another leap. After that, I will make contact."

Damarov and Antinori expressed an interest in hearing more history about Azarias Tor – his career, achievements, personal life and traits. This pleased Saluki, as she had gone to great lengths to research the list of this man, and welcomed the opportunity to show off her skills as a detective. She proceeded to give some more in-depth details, as if her career depended on these revelations.

Saluki informed them that Azarias had purchased a property in Cramlington, which she had attempted to mention before, and that he had enrolled with the Northumbria Constabulary, where he rose quickly through the ranks, soaking up all challenges like a sponge – becoming an expert driver; a crack shot with firearms, and was seconded as a trainer to the academy where he also taught hand-to-hand combat skills. Azarias moved to C.I.D., where he moved rapidly through the ranks to become a Detective Inspector, receiving numerous commendations. He married the sister of his best friend, and colleague – Saluki raised her hand towards the image of a handsome, olive-skinned man , in his mid to late thirties, with jet black hair, amber-brown eyes, and a look of the Hispanic – 'Luciano Flores'.

"And this is where it gets very interesting," she enthused, continuing unabated in spite of being reminded, occasionally, of repetition. "Azarias and Luciano were assigned to go undercover in another police force area, to detect corruption within that force, and links to drug-running and money laundering. There were arrests, but no convictions, and Azarias and Luciano were caught up in a warehouse fire, and explosion, which was part of a stake-out. Luciano died in the resulting fire yet Azarias was found outside, concussed but otherwise unharmed."

Damarov nodded his head sagely, "It is known to manifest in times of stress…"

"This," interrupted his daughter, "would explain why he was not in the automobile crash in which his wife was killed. They had been forced off the road. This happened after the fire. They were returning from her brother's funeral. The other car was found burned out but no one was ever arrested. Azarias was found again, concussed, yet unharmed on the grass at the top of a cliff. The vehicle had plunged about 60 metres to the rocks below. He was found at the top. He hadn't opened the door and jumped. An eyewitness account said that he was driving, and was heading over the cliff. He was fighting against the other automobile when it went over the edge, yet the witness stated that he just saw his body appear on the grass from nowhere. His wife died at the scene."

"Yet he is still an Emergent," Raphael muttered. "He has no idea of his true potential."

Gabriel rose from his seat, stroked and pulled at his white beard, letting his right hand slide to the end before clasping both hands behind his back. There was a long pause, a heavy silence as he walked across the room to walk to the left of his desk and announced – *"Command. Window."* A large rectangular window appeared, formed from the wall itself; either that or the wall had vanished, to be replaced by the vast quadrilateral of triple glazing, set in a thick black frame, so as to create a stark contrast with the wall – a giant picture frame.

He raised his right hand, as if the very action would push Saluki's pause button. Damarov was thinking, processing the information, while he stared through the picture frame. Not that there was much to see outside, from the 180th floor of the 1500 metre, 200 storey high Pan Genetikos Towers, home to Geneticorp and subsidiary companies and government. A polarised blue sky, with a few white strands daubed aimlessly across the backdrop. Leaning forward, he squinted his eyes to view the map-like world far below in the haze, and, on the distant horizon, the thick sulphur-yellow curtain separating the land from the sky. The pan-pipe shadows of the seven stepped ascending structures cast a long afternoon shadow over the landscape, a sundial of Brobdingnagian proportions.

"Death," his tongue hissed through his teeth. He turned to face the others, "Death is not a stranger to him. And he is a survivor with survivor guilt. That gives me some cause for concern." The Vice-Superus and the

Commandant looked at him with questioning eyes, and Damarov duly supplied an answer before either of them spoke. "If you had the power, what wouldn't you do to save…no, save is not the word." He slapped the back of his right hand in the palm of his left, a few times, as if this stimulated flow of blood to his brain, enhancing thought processes. Damarov moved away from the window, his gesticulating hands beginning to relay these thought processes, as he circled Raphael and Saluki, as might a shark before moving in to kill its prey. Then he spiralled into the centre of chairs, where he completed his journey, looking from one to the other.

"Preserve," he announced. "Preserve is the word. And my point? Death. The death of loved ones. Lovers. Wives. Husbands. Comrades. Family. And my point. If you had the power, what wouldn't you do to preserve the lives of those loved ones? Or, to put it another way, what if you learned you had the power to go back and prevent that death from ever having happened?"

# Chapter 3

The youth wearing the beer bottle-bottomed spectacles turned away from the wall, adjacent to the classroom door, announcing that he had placed his three Post-it notes on the posters on the appropriate posters – two with 'things learned today' and the other containing 'something I need to learn'. The magnification of the glass made his eyes appear huge, almost like the joke eyes that fall away from the face on springs. Two other lads, heads down, scribbled on their Post-it pads, while one pulled on his casual jacket, and another fiddled with his mobile phone, which he hid beneath the desk.

"What's the date today?" asked one of those still completing the Post-it pad exercise for the plenary. His sallow-skinned face looked up- from his efforts to feign interest in the learning experience, the functional skills, in which he saw no point– he would rather be somewhere else; anywhere but in this lesson. The watery, grey, cold eyes and the huge dark bags sagging beneath the heavy lids and cloudy pools, reflected his lack of sleep, perhaps late nights playing on the X-Box 360, just as the scabbing in the corners of his mouth, potentially show a propensity for glue-sniffing, or other solvent abuse. Not that Azarias was, in any way, shape or form, judgemental – he just knew, and understood, these young men. Azarias had met them before, those with similar tales to tell, in his previous life – a world and a time he had known before this one – and he had helped some of them improve their life chances, and choices.

"The date is written on the board," Azarias replied, vaguely pointing in that general direction with his right hand

"Seventeenth of May?" the lad enquired, having looked at the board; every question, and interaction guaranteeing him attention – a major improvement on the early days, back in January, when he had often sought attention through picking fights with other students or by being abusive towards teaching staff. Attention seeking, for one reason or another. Reasons aside, the important thing had been avoiding confrontation with the youth, Kyle. Avoiding confrontation with any of the young people, seeking a reaction through provocation – provocation plus reaction equals attention, albeit attention for negative reasons.

Azarias had been patient, and persistent, and had shown them that they were rewarded for positive behaviour. They would get the attention they desired, and they felt as if they were treated with respect; like young adults, not children. The young adults, then, responded accordingly, and did so because it was their idea!

Humour played a major part in the educational philosophy of Azarias Tor, which was implicitly embedded into schemes of work, and lesson plans, when teaching functional English and Maths. School had not been a bundle of laughs, where too many of these young people had been failed by a 'league table' driven educational system, yet the young people were made to feel like the failures – not that the system had failed them. With a chip on each shoulder, and a negative experience of education, they were then pushed from pillar to post, into further education, perhaps to pursue a vocational course, yet the government sets out criteria for a level of functionality in English and Maths, which the young people need to achieve, before being accepted onto an apprenticeship, or considered employable.

And then the government, as it is wont to do, changes its mind, only it doesn't just move the goal posts – it digs up the whole playing field, moves it somewhere else, and writes a new set of rules for the game. No wonder that these young males fall into the category for highest incidences of suicide. *'Too much pressure to succeed and too many opportunities to fail.'* Azarias did what he could to make a difference, just as he had done in his previous incarnation, when it was often too late, when the frustration and anger had exploded into violence, or young minds had been corrupted, turned to a life of crime because there was nothing else left. He had probably seen gallons of blood spilled, and mopped up, over the years, and delivered the bad news to too many mothers, girlfriends, or wives, and in many cases, justice was not always delivered.

But that was in his previous life, in another world – a different time and place. Nobody knew about that part of his life and they didn't need to know. Azarias had developed a good relationship with his students, and they trusted him. The truth could erode the trust he had earned, if ever they discovered that he once represented the authority they so despised. It was a secret, best kept, between the management and him – a lie that hurt no-one.

Kyle made an effort, took his turn to stick his Post-it notes on the posters, and then started on his favourite subject – the most favourite part of his anatomy. The lad's penis had been a topic for discussion in the past, when Azarias first took over the teaching of the group, because another lecturer could not manage the behaviour in the classroom. Many of the behaviour issues had blown up around Kyle, who often challenged someone else in the room to a fight.

The first time Azarias was in the company of the group, Kyle had challenged another lad to a fight, for reasons unknown, through the phrase, *"Outside now, you and me, let's sort this out once and for all,"* was used. Someone else in the room had suggested that Kyle *"Drop it"* as he was *"not man enough."* What Kyle did drop was his trousers and his pants, whereupon he had pointed at his genitals declaring his manhood and that he was *"all man."* And, if part of this declaration of manhood had involved provoking and 'testing' the new lecturer, the response probably wasn't what he had expected. Azarias had calmly and drily, but audibly muttered *"Thank you for reminding me. Fishing bait. I need some maggots."*

Everyone had howled with laughter, even the marginally embarrassed Kyle, who, having hitched up his underwear and trousers, realised the joke was on him, could do nothing more than laugh. It had diffused the situation, though, and the trouser-dropping incident had remained 'in the room'. There had been no reason to report it, or turn it into a formal complaint. Kyle's behaviour changed, for the better, though there were still occasions when he could not help himself – he had 'foot and mouth' Azarias thought, as there were times when he opened his mouth and put his foot right in it! He will learn, though, through the 'school of hard knocks', and he was about to learn again.

Kyle stalked back to his desk, and announced that he *'had had sex last weekend'*. To be precise, he had *had a 'shag'!*

"Bet no-one else in this room had a shag last weekend" he stated. "I did. I've had more shags than anyone in this room. How many shags have you had?" he asked of the youth Kyle had been sitting next to. That youth, with the scruffy part-grown facial hair, Elliott, shrugged his shoulders and muttered, "Two."

"And you," Kyle asked of the lad wearing the beer bottle-bottomed spectacles, "How many shags have you had?"

He didn't give him a chance to answer before pointing at the lad fiddling with his mobile phone under the desk. "You haven't had any," Kyle said, before turning his attention on Azarias. "And I bet you haven't had a shag for ten years."

Azarias let the comment slide, like water off a duck's back. *'Actually,'* he thought *'More like four years.'* Since his wife had died he had not touched another woman, nor even flirted, or talked to another female in such a way as to express any interest or desire, to enter into any kind of relationship. *'Four years,'* he mused, but no-one needed to know that, nor that it was because he was a 'young' widower. To announce that would only, likely, make Kyle feel 'shit' – the lad was not without feeling, having lost an uncle in recent months. That was not the way to deal with the situation, but a retort flitted through this mind, and timing and delivery would be crucial.

"I've had more shags than anyone in this room," Kyle repeated. "I've had seven shags."

And then the timing and delivery were executed with perfection, as Azarias muttered, seemingly absent-mindedly, though audible to everyone in the room "Isn't sheep worrying illegal in these parts?"

Everyone in the room, with the exception of the lad playing with the mobile phone under the desk, hooted and barked their approval of the retort. The lad with the mobile phone looked up and asked *"What did he say?"* Scruffy facial hair youth replayed the incident and the lad laughed so hard that he dropped his mobile phone on the floor, causing the back to break away from the front, and the battery to pop out. *"Shit!"*

Kyle had to laugh, with a deliberately forced, "Ha ha!" to emphasise his awareness of having been outwitted. In reality he was probably enjoying being the centre of attention. The hilarity was interrupted by a light rapping on the heavy door, and the aluminium handle tilted some forty five degrees towards the floor.

As the door opened the head of a male, possibly in his late fifties, poked into the room.

The round face and beaky nose gave him the appearance of an owl. As for the hairstyle, if there was style, it gave him the look of a stereotypical wacky professor. To look at it another way, his bald pate had hair growing up from the sides in such a way as to give him the appearance of an area of the Amazon forest stripped clear with trees growing either side of the bare patch. He pushed the door open, almost by way of an apology, and edged his way into the room. His navy blue suit was rumpled, and the pale blue open-necked shirt un-ironed. Azarias ushered him into the room.

"Right, you lot," Azarias boomed. "I'll take a look at your Post-it notes, and we'll incorporate them into the start of the next lesson. Now, clear off."

Kyle and the scruffy facial hair youth were the first off the starting blocks, and out of the room. The others didn't need telling a second time. Given the choice they would rather be elsewhere, other than in a functional skills lesson – they were not there through choice. *'Broken mobile phone'* lad left the room last of all, grumbling about the damage to his 'hardware', sliding slowly across the floor like a slug, his focus and concentration on reassembling the separate parts.

"And what have you learned today?" Azarias asked of the lad, as he reached the door. He was the only one not to have placed any Post-it notes of the charts.

"Not to be holding my phone when you tell one of your jokes," he mumbled, then left the room, leaving the door open.

"I read your email," the owl-faced man said, sucking excess saliva through his teeth. "You wanted a word?"

"Please Alan," Azarias replied. "If you can spare a few minutes, I'd like to pick your brains," he continued, closing the door, before perching himself on a desk in the middle of the room.

"Okay. I hope my brains are up to picking," Alan offered, finding himself a similar perch on a desk, facing Azarias, causing his rumpled trousers to rise up and expose a massive gulf between trouser hem and scuffed unpolished shoe. He wore long brown woollen socks, and his ankles were thin, shoes loose at the top.

"Psychology," Azarias said, breaking the momentary uncomfortable silence, tearing himself from his deep reverie. "You teach 'A' level psychology." A statement, not a question. He was not one for asking a question if he already knew the answer. Alan answered "I do," like someone completing their marriage vows.

"And more? I mean, are you a psychologist? Do you practise?" Azarias enquired.

Again, Alan answered "I do. I lecture here part-time, and run my practise part-time, also. Why do you ask?"

There was a long pause while Azarias composed his thoughts into a reply. He slid from the desk and walked over to a window. The weather was looking good for the weekend – some broken cloud, and warm sunshine. Looking down to his right, Azarias observed small groups of students gathering on the steps to the college, the steps leading to the main drag into town. Kyle and 'scruffy' appeared down there, popping out of the building like spermatozoa in an ejaculate. Beyond the boundary fence they lit up cigarettes, inhaling their addiction, their craving. On the road, an Arriva bus trundled, and juddered, from left to right, towards the A19, probably heading towards Newcastle. On the school playing field opposite the college, a lone tractor lawn mower, caretaker atop, cut dark and light green stripes on a football pitch.

"I need to talk," he spouted, turning away from the window, "I need to work through some stuff. Can you help? Can you spare the time? I'll pay the going rate."

"One thing at a time," Alan said, placing his hands down on the desk upon which he was sitting, and gripping the edge with his fingers. "When? And where?"

"Not immediately," Azarias replied. "I'm going to the caravan straight from work today. Perhaps some time next week."

"You have a caravan?" Alan queried, following up with a question regarding the location of the said caravan.

Azarias then went to pains to make it clear that it was not technically a caravan.

*"It was a static; a mobile home – holiday home and holiday retreat. Home from home. Two bedrooms with gas central heating and double glazing. Not really a caravan. Located in the Eden valley, between Appleby and Penrith. Beautiful countryside. No clubhouse,*

*nothing like that, not even lights on the site. Quiet, except for the sounds of arcadia – the sheep, cows, birds, and the occasional owl at night. A pub close by, about 10 minutes' walk, up the hill in the village."*

"And you go there a lot?" Alan asked, pushing himself down from the desk, and pulling out a chair from under the desk to sit upon. He crossed his legs, right over left, and clasped his hands in front of his chest, thumbs up, and tapping against each other. "To escape?"

"Escape?" Azarias repeated the question. "To escape. Yes. Sometimes. But too many memories. Maybe I go there for the memories."

"Tuesday or Thursday?" Alan interjected, sensing the depth of potential issues to be raised in any forthcoming sessions with Azarias. "After college of course. Tuesday or Thursday would suit me," Alan continued.

"Either, or, is good for me. Tuesday would be better. I go to the gym on Mondays, I'm busy on Wednesdays and some Thursdays," Azarias stated.

"Busy social life?" was the response.

"Not a social life, necessarily. Busy, yes. I keep myself busy. If I have too much time on my hands I think too much."

"And you don't want to think?" Alan queried, cocking his head to his left. Sensing a slightly awkward silence developing, when Azarias did not respond immediately and, instead, turned away to look out of the window again, Alan suggested meeting at his practice, at his home, on Tuesday evening; he had an office in his home.

Azarias turned and paced slowly and thoughtfully to his desk, and sank himself into the cushioned swivel chair. He said nothing but reached for his shoulder bag, rummaging inside, before lifting out his black Filofax, placing this on the desk and opening up at the appropriate place. Releasing the brushed stainless steel ball pen from the loop which held it in place, Azarias placed the tip on a page, ready to write.

"Where is your office?" Azarias requested, glancing at the time on the gold Geneve watch, worn on his left wrist.

Alan furnished him with the necessary information, an address in South Shields, and a time of 6.30 p.m. Azarias scratched the details onto the paper before closing the book, clicking it shut with the press stud clasp. A handy place, South Shields, as it was on the way home, and Azarias knew the geography of the area, well enough to find his way around. An appointment made, and agreed, Azarias then requested that anything discussed in any session, or sessions, remain secret, even though that was his expectation of a professional psychologist.

"Of course, that goes without saying. Client confidentiality is guaranteed. Professional courtesy," the man in the rumpled suit concurred. "Drawing up a contact regarding the work, conditions, expectations, and so on, would be part of the first session And, is there anything particular you want to discuss at the first session?" he added.

"Dreams, to start with," Azarias said.

Alan stood up, and began walking around the room, as if the activity aided his thought processes, before speaking again.

"Okay. Here's what I am going to ask you to do. Write down anything about any dreams you want to talk about. Keep a record of any dreams you have between now and your first session," Alan proposed, before finishing with, "And think about anything else you might wish to discuss related to this topic."

Azarias pressed his hands down on the desk, pushing the whole of his weight upwards. He moved away from the chair, placing his hands behind his back, walking towards the windows. A pause, before turning, looking directly at Alan, and clasping his hands under his chin, and then said, "That's easy. Any other discussion? Easy. There are times when I cannot tell the difference between reality and dreams."

# Chapter 4

Those words *"What if you had the power to go back and prevent the death from ever having happened?"* reverberated in this ears of Saluki and Raphael. The words penetrated their minds, tore into the very depths of their souls. Massive implications for their own well-being, the establishment, and stability of everything they knew and understood, the very substance and essence of their world. If someone made changes to the past, the damage could be substantial. And that was their role, to prevent such from happening.

Raphael stroked his smooth chin, thoughtfully, with the forefinger and thumb of his left hand, staring into the distance, far beyond the window, and the heat of the blue sky afternoon. There was a long silence, imposed by that question, "What if you learned you had the power to go back and prevent death?"

"The paradox. The anomaly," Raphael barked, breaking the contemplative silence, then continuing, having grasped the attention of the other two; "If a person could go back and prevent the death of another, what would be the impact on time? Would that act of resurrection change history, or make history?"

"But," Saluki cut in, before Raphael had a chance to reach the destination with his train of thought, "You said yourself he is still an Emergent. He has no idea of his true potential." And then she rose to her feet, and began to pace around the triangular seating arrangement, whilst almost muttering to herself, "I am sure that if I know the answer, you know the answer. You tell me. Is it his mistake? No. Our job is to investigate. Yes? You have to agree. He doesn't know what is happening to him. The answer is in his education."

"And you think you are the person for that job?" Damarov enquired, in a tone that reasserted his authority, "To educate him?"

She answered with supreme confidence, "I don't think I am. I know I am."

"Good answer," said Raphael.

"Correct answer," said Damarov. "Any other answer would have been unacceptable. It is a matter of duty." He paused, "As for a team, resources, what will you require?"

Saluki ceased her pacing around the room, close to the window, slightly to the side, so as not to create a silhouette for Raphael and Damarov, looking into the light, or an obvious target for an assassin, such had been part of her training. At that height above sea level though, any would-be assassin would have to be flying. As for a team, she required the services of, and trusted, the two men who had earlier taken leave of their company – Augustin Le Feuvre and Tyrell Helling. With regards to resources, apart from the usual, their uRAPPs;

each of them would need a 'chameleon suit' to enable them to blend in with their surroundings, and access to available satellites, and sentinels, to maintain contact with headquarters, and allow freedom of movement. That was all she would require to accomplish the mission.

Damarov asserted his authority, moving behind his desk, pressing a button and giving a command to 'ordnance', stating that Commandant Saluki Damarov was to have immediate access to anything she required. He would act as signatory, and all requisitions should be assigned to his office. Command executed, Gabriel returned to the seating area, ushering his daughter to join him and Raphael, requesting that Saluki conclude her report, without any further interruption. The main focus of interest, and where, and when Saluki had made contact with Azarias Tor, and, more importantly, who did she think he was – how had he come to be?

The Commandant painted for Raphael and Damarov a verbal and mental picture of the west Coast of Ireland in 1558, and the fleeing Spanish Armada, wrecked by storms, and dashed upon the rugged rocks. She delivered a brief history lesson, giving reasons as to why the Armada found itself in such a position, with particular reference to the bodies washed up along the coastline – some survived, settling within the Irish communities, but most died, drowned, washed up with the incoming tide.

This was what Azarias Tor had stumbled across, having experienced an unexplained 'time lapse event' during his sleep – and this was not the first occasion that such a 'time lapse event' had happened. The major concern was, why? Azarias Tor was, though, unaware of what was happening to him. Which brought them back to the most important question – how had he come to be? And, are there others? Any investigation would likely reveal who was responsible – who had broken the rules, and might face charges of corruption. Who was responsible for Azarias Tor? Responsible for his very existence?

Saluki explained that Azarias had collected a gold coin from a leather pouch, and had been unaware of the English soldiers on the cliff top. They had opened fire with their muskets, and he could have been killed. His disappearance would have been difficult to explain, though in the sixteenth century his body would have likely been treated the same as any of the Spanish or Moors washed up on the beaches of Ireland.

"He thought he was in a dream," she continued, "We had to intervene, sedate him, and place him in his bedroom. Without the coin, obviously. That might have been difficult to explain. We tried to make it look like he had woken from a dream. And then I let him see me, in the automobile. The same morning. Cut him off on his way to work. Our first real contact. He may find it a bit confusing. To start with. I will tread carefully."

The Vice-Superus offered his support, agreeing that "It is time to bring him in. He needs to become *Established.* And we need to discover the truth. About him. And how he came to be."

"We are in agreement then," Damarov interjected, steering the meeting towards a conclusion. "Educate him. Control him. If there are problems, or if he breaks the rules, we will have to eradicate him. Eradicate all evidence of him. Now, Commandant, if you would be so good as to commence the planning, I have other business with the Vice-Superus. But please, keep us informed of your progress."

Saluki took that as her cue to leave. She stood to attention, and bowed at the waist, tipping her head so that her chin touched the top of her chest. Having made good the salute to her superiors, Saluki turned, without making eye contact, and headed towards that section of wall that melted away, to reveal the corridor. Once in the corridor, she looked back over her left shoulder, and watched the Nano-particles of the fabric knit and meld together to form something resembling large glass doors, set in an oak-panelled wall. To complete the effect the image, shapes of figures, people, appeared to move, and work in an office on the other side of the fake frosted glass. 'all for effect, and without purpose'.

There was also the name – Superus Gabriel Damarov, Head of Operations for Genetikos Orological Defence Systems, etched into the imaginary glass. To the right of the door, the observer's right, a large rectangular emblem, an azure flag containing a circle of twelve gold stars. Above the flag, in half metre high upper case ITC Didi font letters, the same colour gold as used in the stars on the flag 'EFRON'. Beneath the flag, in the same font and colour, in size 48, the words 'European Federal Republic of Nations'. Further to the viewer's right, a plaque, reaching from ceiling to floor, containing the flags and emblems of the 40 member states of EFRON.

Saluki turned her view from the offices of her father, and started to walk along the corridor, each progressive step illuminating her path from dim to bright. To her right, and left, behind frosted glass, workers, like bees in a hive, buzzed and chattered with their information technology, researchers, secretaries, interns seeking to impress, innovators, auditors, assessors, trainers, government officials and office clerks. As she made her way towards the bank of four elevator doors, Saluki shook her black curtain of hair, and exclaimed to herself, with a touch of irony, "Educate or eradicate!"

# Chapter 5

5 a.m. Saturday morning. *'A good night – no unusual dreams'.* Just a normal sleep, with a couple of work-related dreams, and this type of dream usually involved the inability to meet a deadline to provide some form of data related to the education of his learners. Often than not, the data appeared to be more important than the education. The most annoying thing, was the repetition of the same data, and having to reproduce data that Azarias had already prepared, being proactive, only to discover that some *'person with petty power'* collating such data, required it to be entered into a spreadsheet of their making, rather than accept the presentation in a similarly designed spreadsheet. People with petty positions of power! But it was the weekend, and Azarias was an expert when it came to organising his work/life balance.

The country retreat, the mobile home – a Swift Moselle – had been their escape from 'the world' for seven years, though the past four years it had only been his escape. Or was it a prison – a prison of his own making – refusing to let go of the past, and move forward? Maybe he was moving forward, slowly, and he was dealing with the pain, the loss, and the guilt, the way only he knew suited him best, torturing and punishing him, like some form of religious and ritualistic self-flagellation. Everything had just about been left the way it was since the day she died…, *'no, not died, went away'*. She went away, left him. Death is so final. The end! To hang on to the belief that she had gone away, left him, intimated at 'an' ending, and the possibility that she was out there, somewhere, alive. And, that she might return some day. Something to cling to, a life raft when ditched at seas – a hope that maybe, it was all just a bad dream.

Not everything had stayed the same, both here, and at home. There were new flat screen HDTV televisions, and the veranda had been painted and treated, at least twice since the day *she went away*. And, Azarias had replaced the old tablecloth, and he had purchased new kitchen implements. He still liked to cook, experimenting with recipes and flavours, if only for himself. Also, there were a few new herb plants on the veranda – the winter of 2012 had killed many of them. So, there had been some progress but many things remained the same. Some things never change, like the need to cling to that life raft when ditched at sea, clinging to the hope that the bad things had never really happened. It had all just been a dream!

A creature of habit, though probably not even borderline OCD, Azarias changed the date on the calendar, which sat on the middle glass shelf of the inset shelving unit, just as he had every morning he had risen at the holiday home. The calendar, shaped like a surreal cow, sitting upwards, head tilted upwards, legs dangling over the edge of the shelf, and hanging at the sides of the

63

body, has a square hollowed out, in which two cube, dice-shaped objects sat on top of thick matchsticks. The two cubes, dun in colour, had raised, cream painted numbers, rearranged accordingly to represent the date, while the matchstick objects had the months of the year etched on them. The month, May, was already in place, so Azarias had only to rearrange the numbers to read 18 – May 18th.

Alongside the cow calendar, on the shelf above, and below, a range of ornaments – sheep, cows, owls – were reflecting *tastefully*, with a touch of irony, life in this rural idyll. At least, reflecting their view of the world they had shared during holidays and weekends in that place. And then one day, it had changed. Nothing was ever the same, yet Azarias kept the memories alive – a living shrine to his dead wife.

And then, the photograph – one of the 'reportage' snaps, captured long after all the pre-arranged posed-for wedding album shots, usually when most people were well oiled and caught unawares during the course of the celebrations. One of the favourite images, dressed in a gold-coloured and chrome frame, sat in the left corner on the bottom shelf of the sand-coloured mantel, above the built-in gas fire. In the photograph, a much younger couple – he, 28 years old, and she 24, hair tied up in a Grecian knot, with hanging curls by her ears. Dressed in a white flowery lace Grecian-style, scallop-necked, wedding dress, Theresa is leaning onto Azarias, her long, naked arms hooked around his shoulders.

Her amber brown eyes, posing for the camera, expressed the joy of the moment, and full dark pink lips

64

stretched in a chasm of a smile, exposing the ivory of a piano keyboard, spoke volumes – it doesn't get much better than this. His arms, wrapped around her waist, appeared to steady Theresa, preventing them from collapsing into a heap on the floor, and the somewhat lecherous, perhaps drunken grin on his face said the same – *'it doesn't get much better than this.'* And, it didn't get much better than that – than them, as a couple, as a team. Nothing was better, and nothing is better. How could anything be better? It was perfect. Life was perfect. Then, one day things changed, and nothing was the same again – ever!

A deep, tremoring sigh, rose from his diaphragm, and was expelled through trembling lips. It was all he could do to prevent the stinging tears from welling up in his eyes, and spilling down his cheeks. A few gulps of air – *'get this under control, stop feeling sorry for yourself!'* But that wasn't really what this was about – loss, yes, but the loss of all those years that she should have had. The loss of her potential, someone so special, who touched so many lives, who meant so much to so many people, and not just his personal loss. But, oh, how that hurt – every day.

Some things never change, and don't get better, and he had lost the light of his life, his joy, and his reason for being, for living. And, yet, he carried on, as best as he could. But it hurt every day, and he scourged himself because he felt he was to blame. If only he had known then – but that didn't make it any better – he couldn't go back and change things, whatever the level of his current knowledge. But, if he could turn the clock back, there would be a lot of things that he would do differently. He

65

sniffed back the memories in an attempt to regain a little composure. Did he feel any better? Probably not and maybe he would never feel any better. Why should he? But then he spoke to the photograph, to his wife, just as he always had done, since that day that everything had changed – even though some things always remain the same.

As he fixed the light-gold coloured curtains to the tie-backs, in the bay-shaped window, stretching across and kneeling on one of the sofas, Azarias spoke to his wife, as if she were there with him, perhaps on a Skype call, or on the phone. With the curtains tied back, the promise of a glorious day flooded into the caravan, and he began his heartfelt description of his solo world, outlining his plans – Theresa might as well have been on a business trip, somewhere in the world, and not of this world.

"No other cars up this end. No neighbours," he began, moving back towards the dining table, which was always set for two people, where he leaned across to look out of the window, facing out across the fields at the rear of the caravan. He continued his soliloquy.

"Cows in the field. Plenty of young ones. Must have moved in recently. The grass is very long. Lots of yellow buttercups. There's the bull. A handsome lad. Look at the muscle on him. A Limousin, I think. I topped up the food on the bird feeding station when I arrived. It's a busy restaurant. The rooks muscle in and chase the others away, but they pick at everything in the tray, and on the ground. Their beak is too big to pick at the nut-feeder and seed dispenser. It is a beautiful morning.

Some cloud. More than enough blue sky to make a few sailor suits."

Azarias pushed his weight against the dining table, adjacent to the window, and levered himself upright. Walking around the table, and into the U-shaped kitchen, which was open to the lounge, in such way that anyone cooking could converse with anyone relaxing on either of the sofas, he picked up a box of eggs, opened the lid and selected the two largest. These he set down by the left of the gas hob, built into a corner, with oven beneath and extractor above. There the eggs rested, in a space between the hob and the chrome of the draining board beneath the kitchen window, whilst he sought out a copper-bottomed saucepan with lid. He filled the pan with cold water from the tap over the kitchen sink and placed it upon the front right ring, and ignited the flame.

"The usual," he said, seeking a large plate, and two spring-shaped egg cups from the cupboards, supported by chrome columns above the floor units, which separated the kitchen from the lounge. "Eggs from the farm on the corner. Toasted soldiers. Just the way you like them. A la Delia. Bring the water to the boil. Gently, though. Put the eggs in the water. One minute. Take them off the heat, lid on. Leave for another six minutes in the pan. Perfecto. I still haven't taken a photograph of one with its head chopped off. Yellow runny yolk set in the gelatinous white. Your favourite breakfast. Apart from the bacon butties, the fried egg sandwich and the full Monty."

Azarias paused, gathered his thoughts and placed two slices of bread in the toaster. He then filled the electric kettle, and set that away to boil, before picking up his BlackBerry from the dining table, he did the same thing he had always done, when he was not with Theresa – he thumbed the ball of his trusty old 'Pearl' until he reached the 'Address Book', opened that, then scrolled down until he reached the name Theresa. He then followed the motions appropriate for sending an SMS. Then he typed, *'Up early – made the effort. Got my arse out of bed. Going to fulfil that promise, to go to the river at dawn. Catch a photograph of a kingfisher. Said I would, one day. I am doing it today. Wish you were here. Miss you.' And he signed it with XXX'.* Azarias then walked into the middle of the lounge, pressed *'Send'* and held the phone high in the air, as the signal tended to fluctuate, and watched as the 'circle' turned to a 'tick', with 'D' – the message had been sent, delivered and received.

# Chapter 6

Saluki studied her surroundings, carefully turning a complete 360° on the spot. She stood in the middle of a narrow tarmac lane, in a valley, where the winding black ribbon dropped steeply to cross a ford, ascending sharply the other side of the slow, shallow, lazy river, through a sunlit dappled tunnel of green foliage. Completing her revolution Saluki stood facing the river, where a myriad of tiny lights flickered in the gentle warming air of the early morning. A smaller cloud of insects gathered above her head, causing Saluki to make an attempt at swatting them away, resulting in a brief parting of the swarm before re-forming to continue the manic aerial dance.

A few metres to her right, a short stretch of dirt track bordered by long grass and cow parsley, stopped at 'cedar' painted wooden double gates, for vehicles, and a pedestrian access to a footpath by the river. Beyond the gates, to the footpath, a white stucco rendered cottage nestled beneath 20 metre high crags, but there was no obvious sign of life, other than a few rapacious rabbits, chewing at grass, the fleeting dust nebulae of midges, and the occasional sploosh in the river as fish leapt from the water to snack on fork-tailed mayfly. She walked to the single gate, opening it softly, with only a breath of sound – not even enough to disturb the wildlife – as the greased hinges swivelled with little friction.

Saluki made a deliberate point of leaving the gate open, before turning left and heading towards a footbridge, barely wide enough to push a bicycle across, should anyone fear pedalling across the ford. Stepping up onto the bridge her right foot splashed in a small puddle, creating spatters and spots of orange-brown mud to appear on her white shoes, and on the hem of the slacks of her two-piece suit, of the same colour. By the time Saluki had reached the centre of the bridge, the bio-Nano-tech fibres forming the different material of shoes and slacks visibly moved, erasing all evidence of contact with the puddles.

When Saluki found herself at the approximate centre of the bridge she stopped, leaned on the rail with both hands, looking in the direction in which the river flowed, and pondered on the ramifications of the task that lay ahead of her. In about five minutes, Azarias Tor would come through the gate she had deliberately left open, if for no other reason than to arouse his suspicions – she suspected that it would be normal for persons passing this way to close the gate, any gate, after them. Above all, she didn't just anticipate the arrival of Azarias Tor, she expected it – that very moment had happened before, many times, she had seen it before. Saluki knew where he would be, before he knew.

Turning around, facing the ford, her eyes soaked in the colours of green, reflected in the mirror-glass river, and she breathed in the clean morning air, suddenly starting at the sight of her own reflection in the water.

Saluki had forgotten to blend in with her surroundings. She had neglected to alter her image and adapt, and adopt camouflage to suit the habitat. Though she did want her target to make visual contact, Saluki desired to look as if she belonged – dressed in the two-piece white outfit, at this time of day, in the Cumbrian countryside, she appeared somewhat alien. Saluki had momentarily forgotten one of the first rules, set in stone, for this type of mission – blend in with the surroundings as soon as possible.

Exposing the 'wrap-around' on her left wrist, her uRAPP, Saluki noted the lack of a reference point – an image of a woman wearing appropriate clothing, which she could capture and process, so as to enable the 'chameleon clothing' to change to suit the place in which she found herself. Tapping the device on the central screen, and typing in the words *'outdoor clothing'*, Saluki selected, and surveyed, photographs of models on the Rohan website. Finding an image which she found pleasing, she touched the model, described as wearing 'Driftwood' colour Roamers, a black Aura jacket, and un-named black walking boots, then swiped the words *'select'*, *'process'* and *'fabricate'* in that order. Then there followed a dull flash, like someone had taken a photograph indoors, in a bar, or a restaurant, when persons not involved in taking the snap are sort of aware of the single strobe effect.

During the following ten to twenty seconds a shimmering halo of fine glowing white dust flickered and throbbed around Saluki. The fabric of the two-piece suit glimmered, colours and hues blending, creating a two-tone effect, as the Nano-particles absorbed and processed the information fed from the device on her wrist, analysed by the artificial microscopic intelligence. As the bright halo subsided, the light dimming, the outfit began to resemble that worn by the online catalogue model, right down to the boots. When the desired effect had been achieved, Saluki relaxed, resting her arms on the rail of the bridge. Not long to wait but enough time to file a report, so she pressed a button on the left side of her uRAPP, and spoke.

"Start report. Commandant Saluki Damarov. Open file, operation Cassandra. Sub-file Azarias Tor. Fifteen, zero six, twenty one, ninety eight. Mission update. Target Azarias Tor will pass this way in a matter of minutes. The plan, agreed with Helling and Le Feuvre, is to move the target from the status of Emergent to that of Established within the next seven days."

She paused, looking skyward at the large white X in the stratosphere, vapour trails from two long-haul flights whose paths appeared to have crossed at around 11,600 metres – the large X forming the cross-hairs of the sight of a sniper's rifle, with Saluki the target. She shook her head, continuing the report.

"Seven of his days. From Emergent to Established in seven of his days. I will make initial contact, with the intention to educate and not eradicate. At his point, I wish to make it known that I have concerns. There have been quality issues before, mostly ending in eradication of the target, but this is different. The main issue is not 'who he is' but 'why he is'. Who is responsible for his existence? Who is responsible for him? Save sub-file,

Azarias Tor. Close file, operation Cassandra. Close all attachments."

Saluki rolled the cuff of her left sleeve over her utility device, and returned her gaze to the fading white cross in the cool blue morning sky. She shivered slightly, her body adapted to warmer climes, and waited.

# Chapter 7

Such was the promise of good weather, and the already warm, calm, morning, that Azarias had chosen to wear a pair of khaki shorts, his black Berghaus boots, with Rohan socks folded over the tops, and a dark green T-shirt. Just in case it did turn out to be a cruel trick of nature he had tied his Tibetan Red fleece at his waist, the sleeves knotted at his lower abdomen. His trouser belt held a flask of coffee in an attached holster, at his right hip, and his Lowepro backpack contained his Canon 600D, lenses, and other photographic equipment. He was on a mission – to shoot, and capture, wildlife, using his camera.

Azarias had set off at a brisk pace, turning right out of the site, heading uphill towards the centre of the village, which housed one public house, a village hall, a Methodist chapel and little more than 100 inhabitants. The timber yard to his right, now empty with planning permission for the development of nine residences. He had read the planning notice, and was aware of the inclusion that a number of the residences had to be made available to young local people, at affordable prices. This was a farming community, steeped in tradition, which relied on the younger generations to maintain the inheritance. Azarias had always made an effort to support the community, shopping locally, rather than purchase his food in Cramlington or thereabouts, and probably put more into the coffers of Cumbria than Northumberland during 'the season', which commenced at the start of March and finished at the beginning of January – the closed season only lasting two months.

His eyes were drawn to the almost cloudless French sky blue canopy, where two vapour trails of long haul flights formed a spreading cross, as if some giant hand had marked a huge X on a map, indicating where treasure might be buried or perhaps raising the alarm – *'there be dragons in these parts'*. Crossing the road, to the left, the view over the dry stone wall winged over open countryside, which dropped towards the Lyvennet, rising again towards the dark ridges on the horizon, where a few cauliflower clouds sprouted above Blencathra – a good day on the tops.

At the junction of Welltree Brow, adjacent to the gravel car park, stone bus shelter, and the village hall, Azarias turned left and headed downhill towards the ford, which crosses the Lyvennet. All along the sides of the narrow lane, on the descent, an abundance of May – a white haze against a backdrop of varying shades of green calmed the stresses of modern life; the birdsong sonata complementing the complete meditation package. Then, the gentle tinkle of the river crawling across the ford, cool water tickling stones and pebbles, a soft caress on his ears – *heaven is a place on earth!*

Some three metres or so from the ford, a public footpath sign, and foliage, blocked the view of the bridge, as he turned towards the white cottage, and the path alongside the river. The double gates were closed, as usual, but the single wooden gate, with galvanised steel catch, was open – wide open, and that was unusual. People don't leave gates open – not around these parts. *'No livestock to escape but that was not the point'* – people close the gates behind them. *'Unusual. At this time of the morning'.*

Azarias glanced at his gold watch worn on his left wrist – 6.13 a.m. You can take the man out of the police force, but you can't take the police out of the man. His curiosity was aroused, and his suspicions were suddenly confirmed, as he quickly scanned the immediate surroundings, eyes finally resting on a lone figure leaning on the handrail of the footbridge. A woman, hair the colour of jet. That woman – Cleopatra, Elizabeth Taylor lookalike. *'Not possible. She was not real – a dream. Don't lose it. Get a grip. A brain tumour? Must be something wrong in my head,'* he thought, making a point of not looking at the figure on the bridge, as he carefully closed the gate, only turning around once the latch had clicked shut firmly.

But, the bridge was empty. She was no longer there. *'Was she ever there?'*

Within a few, long, quick strides he reached the middle of the bridge, where his imagination had created the image. *'But why? Why the same face?'* Perhaps someone he had once met – the memory is fantastic for storing faces. *'Might have been a face in a crowd. Perhaps when I was in the job,'* he brooded, searching for any sign of human life, in and around the river.

'*Nothing*'. Not on the bridge, or near the bridge. '*A trick of the mind*'. No-one could have moved that quickly. He sniffed at the air, like a predator downwind of its prey – nothing.

"You need help," he muttered to himself, returning to the east side of the river, affording the bridge a final glance over his left shoulder, before heading north into the lush, thick foliage bordering the Lyvennet. Azarias shook his head, chuntering "You are losing it, mate. Big time." And then continued on his way.

# Chapter 8

Superus Damarov stroked his white beard, as he was often wont to do, whether for effect, or because he was lost in thought, and paced to and fro, behind his white desk, in his white office, wearing his white robes. No window to the outside world, just bare, clinical, spotless walls. He was not alone, though. A lean, lithe, tall figure dressed in a polar white two-piece suit, with matching shoes, androgynous in appearance, and still wearing a white helmet, with tinted visor, stood to attention. Whoever it was, they had just appeared in the room, seemingly walking out of thin air.

"Better to keep your headwear on," Damarov commanded, waving the forefinger of his right hand, in a circular motion, whilst pointing at his own head. "It is not necessary for anyone to recognise you leaving the office, and it would not be advisable to make an unregistered leap from my office. Such things are recorded. This meeting is between us, and no one else. You do understand that?" Damarov enquired; a conspiratorial edge to his voice.

His co-conspirator, subordinate, nodded the crash-helmeted head in affirmation but did not speak.

"You show great potential," Damarov confided. "Your loyalty will not go unrewarded. There will be a position of importance for someone of your calibre in the organisation. But I need your assurances that these meetings remain confidential between us, that no one else is involved. I have your assurances?" he probed.

Again, not a word was spoken, as the crash helmet nodded agreement with the developing plan which Damarov was plotting, unfolding as he began walking in large circles around the figure, standing at attention in the middle of the room.

"This is a great responsibility I am giving to you," he effused to the silent white-suited adjuvant. "It is a great responsibility. And you must not reveal your mission to anyone. Yes. Mission. For that is what it is, a mission. This is a mission of great importance. You know what you have to do. I will clear your travel. No one will stand in your way. And you will be above any suspicion. I will await your reports, as we arranged, but, should it prove necessary, you have the authority to eradicate Azarias Tor. We cannot allow him to interfere in matters. Keep a close eye on him and the Commandant. I have grave concerns. Use your discretion. Silence the three of them, if necessary. Raphael, the Commandant, and the Emergent."

The white lean figure appeared to flinch slightly, stretching the neck in a semi-circular motion, as if flexing muscles and bone at the very thought of the consequences of undertaking such a mission, but still said nothing – nothing at all. He acceded to Damarov's cursory wave of the right hand, which signalled the end of the meeting. The crash helmet dipped in acknowledgement, and the heels clicked together as a salute. Every Nano-particle responded to the command of the Superus, re-shaping to form an opening in the wall, to act as a door, allowing egress for the figure in white, who turned and headed out into the corridor.

The wall closed behind Damarov's 'lieutenant', blocking the Superus from view, but there was no looking back. There appeared to be a focus on reaching the elevator, making it to lower levels, mingling with the others, and blending in with the crowds. *'Above suspicion. With a secret, and on a mission. Alone and undercover. Great potential. Position of importance.'* Motivation, but with great risk. Onward. Unrecognised. Unseen.

Except the fast-moving figure wearing the helmet, had not noticed Raphael Antinori step out from within one of the frosted glass 'honeycomb' offices, which lined the corridor from the offices of the Head of Operations for Genetikos Orological Defence Systems to the elevators. Raphael Antinori, though, had noticed the fast-moving figure when he stepped out from the office, hidden behind frosted glass. Raphael was ignored and offended, as the unknown officer failed to acknowledge the 'superior' in the corridor. Into an elevator, turned around, still wearing the helmet and visor, and then was lost as the doors slid silently shut. Gone, but not forgotten.

Raphael watched the figure disappear from his vision, and then turned his head towards the fake frosted glass, of the imaginary door to the office of Gabriel

Damarov. His eyes rested on the blue flag, with its circle of twelve golden stars. Etched into the glass, the imaginary frosted glass, the name – Superus Gabriel Damarov, Head of Operations for Genetikos Orological Defence Systems. Adjacent from ceiling to floor, the states of the European Federal Republic of Nations. The Vice-Superus stroked his smooth jaw four times, thoughtfully, with a questioning visage.

"Lamont?" The Vice-Superus questioned in a calm, but inquisitive tone, throwing his voice behind him to person, or persons, in the office, beyond the frosted glass. The sound of another voice registered in the entrance, reaching Raphael's ears, though just about audible to him.

"Remind me, Lamont," he continued, rolling his eyes back in his head, as if that might indicate the direction of his conversation, "What is the protocol regarding wearing helmets and visors within the confines of Genetikos?"

Following a pause, a reply heard only by Raphael, whose body blocked the voice from escaping into the corridor, buzzed like a bluebottle skittering against the glass of a window.

"Exactly what I thought. No helmets or masks to be worn within the complex. Of course. Security being imperative. Strange, then, that I have just witnessed an officer in this corridor wearing a helmet and visor, coming from the direction of the office of Superus Damarov."

Again, the voice in the office buzzed – this time, like a wasp, diving in and out of the room, and around the head of the Vice-Superus. Rather than swat at the insect, he took heed of the concern expressed, responded accordingly.

"I hear what you are saying. I will go and pay a visit to his office. There might be no cause for alarm. If you don't hear from me in ten minutes then, by all means, take appropriate action. It is probably nothing. Sit tight."

And then, Raphael turned left, away from the small, insignificant, yet important office – one cog helping to drive the many wheels of Genetikos Orological Defence Systems – and towards the office of his superior and his friend, Gabriel Damarov. The wall opened to allow access to the highest office within the corporation, and as Raphael entered, the imaginary fake frosted glass closed behind him.

# Chapter 9

Azarias had poured himself a bottle of Black Sheep Ale into a pint glass, etched with the words 'White Horse Beer Festival, 2010' and an image of a horse. Straight from the fridge, slightly cooled, it was refreshing. As he took a sip, memories of the vision on the bridge, which had given him some cause for concern, flooded into his mind. He spoke directly to that photograph on the inset shelf, the one captured on the day of their wedding, when life was so different – when they were so happy.

"I really am losing it," he said, placing his glass of ale on a square coaster, which had images of sheep and a collie dog on it on the coffee table. "I don't know what to do. And it is not just the dreams. I'm seeing things. People that are there one minute, then gone the next. And that same person lives inside my head. In my dreams."

He ceased chatting to the photograph, to himself, and knelt before the corner media unit, as if it were an altar, and reached underneath the top shelf, to the wall, where he flicked the switch down on the mains plug socket. A small illuminated red light appeared at the right hand bottom corner of the Samsung flat screen television, which sat on top of the corner unit. Pushing himself up from his haunches, Azarias stepped back, clutching the remote, and selected *'718 Smooth Radio'*, in the middle of a commercial break for *'confused.com'*.

Settling in the very corner where the two sofas met, one along the wall, the other backing onto the kitchen floor and ceiling cupboards, and worktops, he picked up his glass and swallowed a few small gulps of ale, relaxing into the upholstery as he did so. Returning the ale to the coaster upon which a wet ring had formed, due to the condensation running down the side of the glass – he knew he should have placed a square of absorbent paper on the mat to prevent it sticking to the bottom of his drinking vessel the next time he lifted it to his lips.

Without introduction, following the adverts on Smooth Radio, Roberta Flack began singing *'The first time ever I saw your face''* and Azarias reflected on his early morning walk by the river. Not what he had anticipated. Yet, while he tried to gather his thoughts, the words of the song filtered through, reminding him of the first date he had with Theresa, though not the first time he had seen her face, when he waited for her beneath The Monument on that Friday morning in November 1999.

That first date had been arranged by Luciano, Theresa's brother, and his colleague – 'partner in crime', the standing joke. If truth be known, it hadn't been the first time they had met. Azarias had been welcomed in the heart of the Flores family; Luciano's Spanish parents treated Azarias as if he was another son. If Azarias had ever been polite enough to knock at the front door, or ring the bell, he would be chastised by Mrs Flores,

Amparo, who would remind him that no one knocks at the door of their own home. He was part of the family, and proud in that knowledge. In that case, Theresa was like a sister to him. Only, it turned out, she didn't want to be treated like a sister.

"Are you sure you trust me with your sister?" Azarias had asked when the date had been arranged.

"Man. I trust you with my life, don't I?" he had replied.

Yet both of them were dead, and he blamed himself. And his own mother was dead. And, Mario Flores? Theresa's father. The death of his daughter had destroyed him. Azarias was certain that his father-in-law had died of a broken heart, though was not sure if such a cause was available to a coroner, when writing a report. And, Amparo, her mother – dementia! But what was the cause? It was obvious. He knew. A family torn apart by grief, and Azarias saw him as a common denominator – everything had happened because of him. It was his fault. If only he could go back, and do things differently – if only. If only!

Shaking the guilt from his thoughts, Azarias returned his focus to the events of earlier, by the river. Someone had left that gate open – that was strange, for these parts, but could have meant nothing, except for the woman, that woman, on the bridge. There but not there. Clear as day but no trace, whatsoever. *'Is the human mind capable of creating such visions?'*

He switched his train of thought, again, onto another track, and pondered on the missed photographic opportunities. The deer had been too far away, and had bolted the moment it had got wind of Azarias, and the camera was still in the backpack when the two red squirrels chased each other around the tree in an upward spiral. Sitting on the bench, near the deep pool, where white water cascaded musically over small ledges of rock, he had poured himself coffee from his flask into a plastic cup, and lost some two and a half hours, absorbing the sounds, the scents, and the sights.

It was still early, with respect to the ale on the coffee table, 10.15, but he had surmised that the sun was over the yard arm somewhere in the world. Aware, once again, of his surroundings – sitting in the corner where the two sofas were pushed together – he picked up his glass, took a few more sips, and placing it on the mat, muttered to himself, "Plenty to talk about on Tuesday."

Then he sat back, stretching his arms out, either side of the corner, in a crucifix fashion. The last thing he heard, as he descended into darkness, unable to stop his lids from falling over his eyes, was the voice of George Michael singing *'A Different Corner'*. Deeper and deeper he drifted to the dark pit, spinning as he was dragged down into a heavy sleep, unable to fight against the rapid decline.

# Chapter 10

"Welcome. Please, come in," Damarov ushered, with a sweep of his right hand. "It is good to see you, as always. This is an unexpected, unplanned and unrecorded meeting. Is there something on your mind?"

The Vice-Superus responded, casually, walking towards the wall, far right to the entrance. "I much prefer to see the window here," and created an imaginary opening to the outside world with his arms. We spend so much time inside," he sighed, "and we should let the outside inside, more often. Don't you agree?"

"Perhaps we should venture outside more often," Damarov retorted, "But our lot in life, our mission, which brings with it such responsibility, does, unfortunately, mean that we must while away our hours within the confines of these walls. With great power comes great responsibility."

Gabriel glided towards Raphael, commanding the picture window to open. The ever deep blue sunlit sky, without a white wisp of cloud, was revealed, altering the balance of natural light in the room – all artificial light reacted, dimming slightly.

"It is there, any time you want it," Damarov snarled impatiently, "But that is not why you are here, is it? Is there something on your mind?" He uttered the question in a more staccato fashion, slower than the first time he had asked the same question, emphasising every syllable.

"What can I do for you? He asked in a softer tone, fearing that he was revealing a loss of control, and that the loss of control might reveal more than he wished.

"To salve my curiosity, perhaps," Raphael offered.

"And how might I do that?" was the increasingly impatient retort.

"Answer me one question, that's how."

"And the question?"

There was a tension building between them, which had been brewing for some time. Raphael had developed a mistrust for his superior, though could not pinpoint anything in particular, no evidence, just a gut feeling, and it was highly likely that Damarov sensed this, or was just protective of his position. And what followed was a game of wits – a kind of verbal fencing, which Raphael continued, with a parry of the wits, and a thrust, with 'the question'.

"Have you had any visitors recently?"

Damarov responded rapidly, "I have many visitors. It is part of every day."

"When I say recently," the Vice-Superus probed further, "I mean, in the last few minutes. Any visitors in the last few minutes?"

"Why do you ask?"

*'Answering questions with questions. Avoiding the real answer',* the Vice-Superus pondered.

"As I said before, to salve my curiosity," he repeated, hoping for an answer and not another question. "I will phrase it another way. What is the protocol for officers wearing their helmets and visors around the corridors of Geneticorp and Genetikos?"

There was a long, deep, thoughtful pause, during which time Gabriel stroked his beard with his right hand, piercing emerald eyes searching the face of Raphael for a sign as to where the line of questioning was leading. The Vice-Superus maintained a neutral expression, remaining impassive throughout, choosing not to speak until the question received an answer.

*'He who blinks first.'*

Gabriel Damarov began to sound more irritated, as he found himself forced to give an answer. They had known each other for years, even been friends, and had risen through the ranks together, but, now, all these questions. So much easier to look the other way. *'Why hadn't he looked the other way? Why was this so important to Raphael? What is he really after?'*

Damarov cut through the solid silence with an icy tone – "You know the answer to that question. As well as I do. Why do you ask if you know the answer, and I know the answer?"

"I had seen an officer, wearing helmet and visor, leaving your office," Raphael began offering a reason for his concern with this matter, "The behaviour of this officer roused my suspicion. Perhaps there had been a security breach, and you were in danger, or had suffered harm."

"As you can see," Gabriel stated, stretching his arms to form a living crucifix, "I am in one piece. Unharmed and intact. No one has entered my office and caused me any harm. Maybe you have seen someone who has found their way into the wrong corridor. Perhaps lost their way. Just happened to be outside my office, or close by, when you saw whoever it was. But you are right to raise the issue of uniform protocol within the confines of these corridors."

Damarov returned to a neutral pose, dropping his left arm to his side, but raising his right hand, as if he had more to offer, which was very much the case.

"Let me finish," he stated, aware that Raphael might attempt to explore this line of questioning if not thwarted. "I would like to express my thanks for your concern about my safety. It has been noted. You are also right to be concerned about officers dressed inappropriately, and in contravention of regulations when on these premises. I assure you that I will instigate an investigation and ensure that protocol is observed. Do not concern yourself with this. Your office is of too high status to deal with such trivial matters. Are we agreed? You have more important things on your mind, I am sure."

Before the Vice-Superus had a chance to utter a word, Gabriel concluded the meeting, asserting his authority, leaving no doubt in the mind of his deputy who was in control, and why he was the Superus.

"Good," he said, stepping forward, placing his right hand on the left shoulder of Raphael, bringing them face to face, "I am glad that we see eye to eye, and that we understand each other. There is no need for concern. You agree? Good. I will inform of the outcome of my investigation."

Out-manoeuvred, Raphael was turned around by Damarov, and led towards the wall, arm around shoulder, which opened to reveal the long corridor, lined with frosted glass offices.

"Do not concern yourself with these trivial matters," he said, ushering Raphael from his office, "You have more important business to fill your hours. True?"

Raphael could do little but agree, and turned to walk away from the office, stopping once the wall had closed, to reveal the pseudo frosted glass frontage.

*'What had just happened there?'* he queried in his mind.

Raphael's suspicions appeared to have been diluted, but not dispelled. He could not be certain that the officer had exited from Damarov's domain. Maybe the officer had been lost in the honeycomb of corridors, and levels, of the Pan Genetikos Towers, though that did not explain the breach of protocol.

*'What if the officer had come from Damarov's office? Why would he lie though?'*

The mistrust crept into his mind again, like a sea fret drifting inland, blocking out the light. Something was not right. No evidence, just a feeling. Corruption was rife. *'Power corrupts.'* That was part of the problem, part of the investigation involving any potential Emergent. The very fact that even one Emergent existed implicated some level of corruption, and an abuse of power. And, any Emergent was a potential threat to the balance of power, and life, as Raphael and his kind, in their time, knew it. Not that the Emergent was to blame – they had not corrupted the system, and were nothing more than an outcome of an abuse of power; the *'spawn of the devil',* the corrupt, with the potential to destroy and undermine the very foundations of society. *'But who was that devil?'*

Doubt, suspicion, and mistrust, melded into mild fear. If the officer had come from Damarov's office, Raphael had possibly exposed himself to scrutiny. Maybe he had played his hand wrong, revealed his true concerns too soon, and alerted Gabriel with his probing questions. It was the Superus in the end, who had grasped hold of the security issue and possibly, used that to bring their meeting to an end. *'Nothing to worry about. Do not concern yourself with this. I assure you that I will instigate an investigation. Ever the politician, who, if roused, could prove dangerous.'* Damarov had a reputation for being ruthless and, besides, tales were rife, regarding the corrupt and the punishment metered out to those who crossed their paths – many people had disappeared, in the past. Likewise, anyone who had dared to question authority often vanished, or had been silenced.

Raphael now felt he had some reason to fear for his own welfare and safety, though his overriding concern was to ensure that others were made aware of this thoughts surrounding. *'Probable grounds for an investigation into corruption – and not just that an officer had been observed wandering around the corridors of power wearing a helmet and visor. Not enough to go on'.* The Vice-Superus, though, doubted the morals and actions of his immediate superior, and he had inadvertently alerted Gabriel to this, and would need to pass on the baton, so to speak, in order that an investigation would, and should, continue in the event that he might 'vanish' or be silenced. Raphael returned to the office from which he had exited earlier.

Damarov viewed the image, suspended in the air, and listened to the dialogue between Raphael and his assistant, Lamont, who were oblivious to the fact that they were being spied upon.

"Any cause for concern?" Lamont enquired.

"Maybe," Raphael replied, deep in thought.

"How serious?"

"I may be activating a Code Five-Eleven, with a full report, and you could be a beneficiary," was the answer.

"That serious," was the exclamation from Lamont.

The Superus waved the image away with his right hand, causing Raphael and Lamont to vanish. He was talking to an unseen person, or persons, using his uRAPP.

"Don't talk. Just listen. We may have another slight problem. Possibly two problems. Meet me, as arranged, at twenty hundred hours. Don't greet me. Absolute discretion is imperative. If anyone is in the booth, use your position to move them. I will do the same. Not a word to anyone. There is an opportunity, here, for you to begin to realise your potential. Until then."

Conversation ended, Gabriel walked towards the window and stared skyward, hands behind his back.

"Damn!" he muttered angrily, "Damn you Raphael. Shame. A real shame."

# Chapter 11

In the hollow, expansive, resonating blackness Azarias Tor heard a familiar sound – music. The opening bars of a tune he recognised moved through the darkness towards him, increasing in volume, filling the void with a rhythmic booming bass – The Eurythmics.

*'Sweet dreams (are made of this),'*

Was he smiling inside his head, or grinning outwardly? Azarias couldn't be sure but the song gave him a warm feeling, reminding him of his student days – clubbing in Newcastle; and there were the parties – wild parties, a few of them, as remembered. He was an adolescent exploring a world away from his home, growing into a man. That song brought it back to him – the remix was a hit on the dance floors. Louder and louder, the sound grew, filling his ears. More memories flooded in, stimulating other senses, taste and smell.

In the darkness, his nostrils twitched as he breathed in cigarette and cigar smoke – a sensation he had not experienced for some years, since the law had been introduced banning smoking in bars, restaurants and public buildings. He had never smoked, other than passively when in the company of smokers, and he would avoid that, if possible. There had been times when he had removed his clothes, just inside his front door, and taken a shower to rid himself of that clinging, acrid odour.

There was something else tantalising his senses – more than an odour, competing with the smoke. He picked up a taste, and the smell, of stale beer in the air, trodden into carpets, and dripped, and poured, onto upholstery, over time. The music boomed, louder still, as if the sounds had been wheeled towards him from some distance. He heard other noises, mingling with the music, rising and dropping, chattering and screeching – talking, and laughter, and the clinking of glasses. And the music played on, and another sense he had not used was sight.

Azarias opened his left eye first, slowly, absorbing the surroundings. Gone was the light that flooded into the mobile home through the large windows – replaced by darkness. No, not exactly darkness, but subdued lighting. He opened the other eye and he focused on the brighter lights, and shadowy figures, moving, flashing, in his field of vision. To his left, beyond the bar, lights of blue, green and yellow colours flashed and throbbed, with the beat of the song, refracted in the sea of fog – a combination of cigarettes and smoke machine. Shaking, twisting, brightly clad bodies gyrated and bounced to the rhythm.

As he became more aware of his surroundings, touch finally played a part, as the palms of both hands rested on the cracked leather of the sofa, upon which he was seated. In front of him, on a low, heavy wooden table, two glasses, filled with some dark coloured fluid, and a bottle – possibly red wine. *'Two glasses?'* Looking up from the table, to his left, he saw an empty leather armchair. On his right, sitting next to Azarias, on the sofa, illuminated in the gloom by the light from the bar, and the one fluorescent tube above his head, a woman, whose face he immediately recognised, a face he had seen a few times in recent days.

"You!" he said to the woman with the jet black hair and emerald eyes.

"Me," she replied.

"Who are you? What are you?" Azarias asked. "A dream? Why are you in my head? Am I hallucinating? Is this a dream?"

The next time she spoke, in reassuring tones, he became aware of her accent – mild but European; perhaps French, Belgian or, maybe, Dutch, or an amalgam of northern European accents, but not English, or anything considered British, even though she was evidently fluent in the language.

"You have many questions," she began. "Many questions. Perhaps I am your worst nightmare. Are you dreaming? Do you think you are sleeping? Does this not appear real to you?"

*'Answering questions with questions. All questions and no answers. Why am I talking to her?'*

"Are you real?" Azarias enquired, reaching out to touch her, before pulling back when he realised that she had made eye contact with someone standing near the bar.

97

There were two men; emerald eyes and pale complexions, piercing the dark grey smoke-filled air. One stood at the end of the bar, nearest to them, and the other was perched on a stool at a corner. Both appeared somewhat intense, like wild cats ready to pounce on prey, but they both relaxed when she appeared to mouth the words *"It's okay,"* and held up her right hand, as a signal to 'stand down'.

"I might be losing touch with reality," he continued. "You are probably a figment of my imagination. A brain tumour, even. Or else, I am having a breakdown. Who are you? What is happening? Where am I?" He was beginning to sound frustrated, probably because nothing made sense.

*'I will wake up soon. I usually do. It's all a weird dream. But if I know that, why can't I take control? I will wake up soon.'*

One music track had moved seamlessly into another – The Eurythmics had changed into Marc Almond, *'Sweet Dreams'* into *'Tainted Love'*. It was then that Azarias realised they were doing that 'shouting over the disco talking', voices raised over the music to be heard, which usually involved much leaning forward, talking loudly directly into each other's ears. Embarrassing, when there is a break in the music, and people are left shouting in the ensuing silence. She leaned forward and continued with the shouting over the disco talking, into his right ear.

"Are you certain you know what reality is? What is reality? We create our own reality. As for me being a figment of your imagination, when we meet again you will know the truth. I promise you that. I told you before, I am your guide. I will be your guide. You will know me. I am not the product of a brain tumour. Look around you. Do you not recognise where you are? I will give you a hint. The year is 1991. We are in the city of Newcastle. Stage Door night club? Look again."

Azarias refocused his eyes, and peered into the multi-coloured flickering smog. This time he looked initially at the faces of the gyrating and bumping figures. Yes, the brain has an amazing capacity for storing and remembering faces, and it is more likely to see people remembered from years ago as they were the last time you set eyes on them, and that was what Azarias saw – faces of friends from his early university days, frozen in time. Young 'Turks' full of hope and promise for the future, and females with Pixie cuts, wearing 'baby dolls' and 'Doc Martens' and the familiar 'uniforms' for the fashion-conscious youth of yesteryear.

Azarias was knocked off course from his journey down memory lane by that woman who was shouting into his ear again – it occurred to him that he did not know her name. But was that important? How many dreams had there been, over the years, in which he had connected with people whom he swore he had never set eyes on before. A face in a crowd. He had thought this before – many faces photographed by the brain. Of course he had seen her on the A19 recently and had probably seen her commuting to work before that. She had become the face of his dreams, appearing in his waking hours, and haunting his dreams.

*'Why such clarity of thought? Can I control my dreams? Make the demons go away? If I can do that, I can wake up.'*

He couldn't hear clearly what she was saying over the sound of the music, and other background noise, so leaned closer, feeling her warm breath on his face. She was barely audible, a whisper. Azarias leaned in even closer, unaware that the men at the bar, her colleagues, were also moving closer.

"You will have the answers soon," she whispered, drawing Azarias so close that their heads were almost touching – his attention fully focused on her. He shook his head, having missed some of her words.

"I said, soon. You will understand."

Azarias looked at her, questioningly. "Understand what?"

"Everything," she hissed, before continuing, "I said, everything. Some things you are not yet ready for. I said, not ready. Soon." She appeared to be pouting, pursing her lips, as if to kiss him, but, in reality, it was just the shape the mouth had taken when pronouncing that last word – *"Soon."*

He couldn't lean any closer without getting intimate, and was oblivious to her left hand, now angled towards his face.

"I said, sweet dreams," and she blew a white mist from her hand into his nostrils, pulling away quickly as his head slumped to his chest.

In a moment, Helling and Le Feuvre moved forward, on either side of Azarias, hooking their arms under his armpits, lifting the limp body to its feet. They were facing in the opposite direction to Azarias, and Helling, to the left of Azarias, held out his left arm towards Saluki who was still seated. She lifted the cuff on the left sleeve of his checked shirt, revealing his uRAPP, and Saluki deftly prodded the central screen using the index finger and middle finger of her right hand.

"Coordinates set," she shouted above the noise, pressing some unseen button on the screen. "Catch you on the other side."

And they were gone, vanished into the décor and the furniture. No one had noticed, or paid any attention to the couple on the sofa and the two men at the bar. Staff had been too busy serving; customers busy being served and partying, and generally too imbibed with alcohol to take much notice. Saluki was alone on the sofa, and picked up the glass of red wine from the table. She held it up towards the light from the bar, studied it, lowered the glass, gently swirled the contents, and then took a sip.

She grimaced, muttering to herself "Piss water," before whispering, breathlessly, "Timing is everything."

At that very moment, to her left, an adolescent male, late teens, maybe early twenties, nudged his way to the corner of the bar. The seemingly confident young man , tall and lean, wearing a brown leather bomber jacket, slashed T shirt, and ripped jeans tucked into tan leather calf length pointed toe boots, sporting a dark Caesar cut hair style, pulled a ten pound note from the inside zipped pocket of the jacket, using his right hand. He raised the index finger of his left hand, smiled a broad, white, gleaming smile in a bid to attract the attention of the bar staff. A young brunette, wearing a short black skirt and a black top, which exposed her ample cleavage, returned the smile and headed in his direction. And then, above all the noise, he heard someone call his name.

"Azarias?" Saluki called during a brief lull in the music, in an almost questioning tone from the comfort of the leather sofa, "Azarias Tor?"

The young Azarias turned in the direction of the voice calling his name, and noted the woman with the jet black hair and emerald coloured eyes. He raised his left hand towards the young woman behind the bar, muttering, *"Just a minute please."* He turned away from the bar and walked towards the table where the woman sat alone on a sofa.

"I'm sorry," he said, bowing his head in an attempt to appear polite, "But did you call my name?"

"Are you Azarias Tor?" she asked, already aware of the answer.

"Do I know you?"

"Not yet," she replied, "But I know you."

"Is this a con? You know me. I don't know you. Is this some sort of a scam? Sorry if I sound a bit disrespectful, but I don't know you. What do you want?"

"Give me a few minutes of your time," she patted the empty space on the sofa with her left hand, pleading "Please. I have something very important to share with you. No con. No tricks. Just a few minutes of your time is all I require. In fact, I have something to give to you."

His shoulders dropped, as he let out a sigh, mouthed the word *"Okay,"* and sat himself next to her – it was not every day of the week that an attractive older woman asked you to sit next to her.

"Would you like some red wine?" Saluki asked, pointing to the glass, which had remained untouched.

"If you don't mind," he laughed, "I'll pass on that. The wine they serve here tastes like piss water. Excuse the language. Vinegar at the very best."

Saluki laughed, then Azarias enquired after what she intended to share with him. Moreover, what was she going to give him? And, *'who is she?'*

# Chapter 12

He felt as he was in a never-ending blackness; a feeling of falling, slowly, backwards and downwards – almost floating, similar to the sensation experienced when a jet airline starts to make its final approach towards its destination airport. He had experienced the feeling before, recently, he was sure; that moment when engines decelerate, when the aircraft if still some distance from landing, and that massive metal airbus appears to 'hover' as if supported by a cushion of air. *'Yes'*, he was certain – *'experienced the same sensation just the other night.'* Azarias drifted, like a snowflake dropping feather-like through his mind, and he became aware of sound – again, someone singing. What was it? Who was it? The words began to filter through…in rich, deep, masculine tones…

It became clear – by far the best version of *'The Greatest Love'* – in his opinion, anyway. Azarias opened his eyes slowly, and rubbed them with the palms of both hands, to assist with focusing. He felt a little woozy, dare he acknowledge the feeling – almost nauseous. The interior of the warm, sun-drenched mobile home filled his senses. Everything was in its place – the ornaments, that wedding photograph, the television, switched to

Smooth Radio, throbbing with the voice of George Benson.

*'A dream! Another of those dreams. Get a grip.'*

Everything was definitely in its place. Azarias stretched his arms and the muscles in his back. A dream, that was all, though these particular dreams, and visions, were beginning to trouble him. He was becoming more concerned though, that something wasn't quite right in his head – his brain, or his mind; could be either, or both, and he needed to discover just what was going on up there. And then he noticed that everything was definitely not in its place.

Something was not right. The first thought, when Azarias had finished surveying the scene, was that his glass of beer had been moved, and was not where it was before he had dropped off to sleep. On second thoughts, though, it dawned on him that it was he himself who had moved. Azarias drifted off to sleep sitting in the corner, where the two sofas conjoined, yet he had woken, sitting upright a little under a metre to his right, on the sofa against the wall of the caravan. How had that happened? Was he now acting out his dreams, experiencing a form of REM Behaviour Disorder? Furthermore, was that an indication, and affirmation, of some disturbance or disorder in his brain?

"

George Benson faded into a commercial break, with a David Jason Del Boy sound-alike shouting *"Delivery, delivery."* The point of the advertisement was lost on

Azarias – he had switched off from the radio. Collecting his BlackBerry from the ledge, adjacent to the kitchen unit, Azarias headed outside on to the veranda, to the corner at the front, near the TV aerial, where the mobile phone signal was the strongest.

He needed to make a call, urgently, to Alan, to bring forward that appointment. He was in need of some serious help, and counselling, and the sooner the better. Having exchanged numbers, in the event of being delayed or unable to make the appointment on Tuesday, Azarias opted to 'call' Alan's mobile, albeit the only number he had stored under his name.

"Hi. Alan? Azarias," he began, "Are you free to talk?" *A pause.* "I'm sorry to disturb you on the weekend." He listened to then response from Alan. "Thanks. You know the appointment we made for Tuesday?" *Another pause.* "I was wondering if we could bring it forward." Yet another pause while he listened to Alan, and followed the wavering fluttering flight of a woodpecker, which had departed from a neighbour's 'nut-feeder' and flown towards the tall trees, lining the back path – Hoggs Lane. "What about some time tomorrow afternoon? I know it is Sunday but I am happy to pay whatever you want." There was a further silence while Alan spoke to Azarias, before he continued talking. "Are you sure?" *An answer.* "I'm grateful. Some other stuff has come up. Since I last spoke to you. I need to talk." He listened to the voice on the other end. "I was thinking about 6 p.m. Is that okay with you?" Azarias listened to the response. "Thanks, mate. There have been some developments. I'll tell you more when I see you. Can I just check your address?" Again he listened for a while. "Okay... Got that." Listening, again, BlackBerry heating up his right ear. "I'll find it. If I get lost I'll give you a call." Listening again. "Thank you. See you then. Bye."

Azarias ended the conversation, sitting on the black painted metal bench beneath the large front windows, and staring into the cloudless sky. A family of collared doves fluttered across his field of vision. Azarias had learned something about the environment, the habits of the bird, and there appeared to be three of them – parents and offspring. Relaxing in the warmth of the sun, he stretched his legs out, and muttered to himself.

"Keep it together, man. Don't lose it. Keep it together."

# Chapter 13

The elevator glided to a gentle halt at the 120$^{th}$ floor of 'Le Tour Sant Amelia', also known as Saint Amelia's Tower. A display of illuminated red numerals had maintained a record of each floor passed during the rapid rise in the dimly lit space, and a female robotic voice announced arrival at the chosen destination, cutting in over the background music.

*"Floor one hundred and twenty. Welcome to Restaurante Galicio. Enjoy your visit."*

Double doors hissed as they opened effortlessly, allowing Gabriel to exit into the restaurant foyer. The only other person in the elevator, a dark-haired, brown-eyed, twenty-something male, wearing a burgundy, gold-trimmed bell-hop suit, kow-towed and pressed a button on the wall, causing the doors to slide shut. Another dark-haired, brown-eyed male, some twenty years the senior of the elevator attendant, wearing crisp white suit, black bow tie, and sharp-creased black trousers, lifted his head from the lectern, and welcomed his new customer, whom he immediately recognised, to the 'Passada Three Platinum Shield' awarded gastronomic experience.

"Good afternoon, Superus Damarov," the Maître d'
fawned, bowing his head and sweeping his right arm in
an exaggerated arc through the opening in the frosted
geometric patterned etched glass wall. "Your usual
booth is ready for you. Please follow me."

Gabriel was the epitome of style, in his two-piece
lilac-coloured suit, with Mandarin collar white shirt and
white shoes, and he moved between the restaurant tables
elegantly, and with confidence. Diners looked up at him
as he made his way to his favourite table, in a circular
booth, close to a window. Many of the admiring glances
were mainly due to the fact that most people were well
aware of Damarov's role, his position, and his power –
he was often reported and quoted in the media, and after
all, had access to the ears of those persons in high
government.

And during his graceful glide across the floor the
very important Superus did not make eye contact with
anyone; not even the person whom he had arranged to
meet – who was sitting in the booth behind his chosen
seat, where once settled one could not see anyone in
adjoining booths, as the backs of the lavishly upholstered
seats were tall and comfortable.

"The menu," the Maître d' offered two electronic
menus. "Would Sir like to order a drink? The wine
menu."

Following a quick scan of images on the wine menu,
Damarov demanded his favourite.

"A large glass of Henri Patrice Red. The vintage
'94," without a please or thank you, such was his

manner, and the expectations of high office. There were very few people to whom he had to apply such pleasantries, and everybody else just did his bidding or faced the consequences. Power!

The head waiter made a note of the order on a small palm-held electronic pad, and bowed his head, his clear brown eyes showing his eagerness to please. He then queried, politely, as to how much time he should leave before returning for his food order, in the knowledge that he himself would most likely be that person. Superus Damarov, after all, was considered a very important customer, who should not be subjected to any potential errors, or placed in any embarrassing situations.

Not that such issues occurred often, if at all, in a restaurant holding the much-coveted 'Three Platinum Shield' award – this was not given lightly, and Restaurante Galicio was only one of three restaurants in all the 40 member states of EFRON to have achieved this high level of recognition. In the role of Maître d' he played an important role in maintaining standards. An award like this was not just given for the food, or any one element alone – it was awarded for the whole collective experience. Also, should any staff stutter, or fumble, or commit a faux pas in front of such an important customer, albeit highly unlikely, not only might Alberto Galicio, owner and executive chef, stand to lose a shield, he might lose his hard-earned position of Maître d'. It would be more humiliating to be demoted than lose employment altogether. It was all about control – power! Though not quite with a capital P!

"Bring the wine," Damarov ordered, "Then allow me five minutes to consider the menu."

As the waiter departed, so the sommelier appeared, the message passed from one PDA to the other, their paths crossing at some point mid-way on the restaurant floor. He was as attentive, and as professional as his colleague, presenting the label of an unopened bottle of Henri Patrice Langstrath red wine. It would not be the 'done thing' to present someone as important as the Superus with an already open bottle, even if he should only require one glass. With hardly a glance, and a cursory nod, Gabriel initially accepted the wine – prior to any further testing.

A corkscrew was produced and the cork removed silently from the neck. Ensuring that not even the slightest drop dribbled down the bottle, to keep up appearances and avoid any embarrassment, not associated with those holding "Three Shields," the sommelier poured a small amount into the bowl-shaped glass, holding the bottle by the dimple at the base, between fingers and thumb, perfect balance and attention to detail.

Again, without eye contact, and without a word, Gabriel picked up the 'fish bowl' glass his right hand supporting the bowlfingers parted either side of the stem, and commenced a gentle circular motion, causing the wine to swirl around the sides of the vessel. When he ceased this motion Damarov lifted the wine towards his face, poked his slightly large and prominent nose inside the glass, and inhaled through his nostrils, sniffing rather than breathing Having completed this action, he lowered the glass to his lips and took a small sip, sucking wine and air through his teeth, with a loud slurping sound. And only on completion of this exercise did he speak.

"Good. You may pour," he said, again, without any eye contact, and then he commanded. "Leave the bottle. And allow me five minutes with the menu."

The sommelier did as he was commanded, effectively bowing as he backed away from the table, at least four steps, before turning on his heels, taking the wine menu with him. Damarov lifted the glass to his lips again and took a satisfying sip, before holding the glass above eye level, studying the opacity, and colour, against the artificial light.

"Some things are worth paying that little extra for," Gabriel said in a voice loud enough that his contact sitting directly behind him could hear, yet low enough so that no one else would hear what he was saying, and what he was about to say.

It was not unusual for the booths near the windows to remain vacant, in the event that a VIP or celebrity, arriving unexpectedly with a party in tow, or alone, for that matter. Damarov was such a VIP – his contact had to 'buy' the table, though no doubt be reimbursed at a later date, one way or another. *'Power, offerings, prospects and prizes,'* had been the promises made by Damarov, in return for operating beyond the call of duty, and covertly.

"Good wine," he said, continuing his monologue. "Excellent food. Pleasure, luxury and style. And all of these you are entitled to, as part of your birthright. I will help you climb the ladder to success."

Damarov took a long, slow sip of the wine, and then kept the glass close to his lips. A mix of paranoia and a need for confidentiality had led to this meeting, away from prying eyes and walls with ears. And, in the event of being recorded on any hidden CCTV cameras, lip-reading would prove difficult with a glass of red wine held in front of his mouth. He took another sip then held the glass, in that slightly awkward pose, in front of his face.

"Together we will do the right thing," he conspired. "Don't respond, or speak. Just listen. We bear the weight of a large responsibility on our shoulders. I believe that we may now be dealing with major corruption. It is possible that the Vice-Superus may be closely associated with the Emergent. Between us, I am confident that we will produce evidence. The truth is out there. If Raphael, his assistant, and the others, prove a threat to the security of EFRON, we may have to eliminate them, if necessary. The wheels of Justice are often very slow, and capable of being corrupted. Any removal of personnel should be seen as an opportunity for yourself. There will be a vacancy for the post of Vice-Superus. Other vacancies will be created by any upward movement. You will be in a good position, and you will have my full support. In the meantime, you will wait to hear from me, using the appropriate channels. Also, keep an eye on all of them. Anything suspicious, report it immediately. The more evidence we have, the more justification we have. Now, it is time for you to leave."

Gabriel sipped from the glass, again, and this time lowered it to the table, before beckoning the Maître d' with a wave of his right hand. As the waiter scurried to attend to the needs of the Superus, Damarov was aware of the movement and the shadow, of his contact vacating the adjacent booth. What he failed to observe, attention fixed on the menu, were the slender fingers of a left hand carefully unpicking a pin from the upholstery behind Gabriel's head – on the end of the pin, the aerial, a very tiny microphone, deftly secreted in the palm of the hand, under the curled fingers of his contact. And Damarov did not even afford the moving shadow, the figure, a glance as it left the restaurant. He was only interested in his self-gratification – 'good wine and excellent food', and all the other trappings that position and power afforded him.

"I will have the Mungtao salad," he ordered.

# Chapter 14

Alan ushered Azarias into the front room of the Edwardian terraced villa. Like the long entrance hall, with the stairs to the right, the floorboards had been stripped and varnished in a shade of pine. In fact every centimetre of wood in the room, skirting, picture rail, window ledges and frames, and the alcove inset bookshelves, had been varnished in varying shades of pine.

The walls above the picture rail were a 'plaster white', though the wall facing the door, below the rail was a rich burgundy, yet much of that was concealed by the mass of books on the shelves built in the alcoves, either side of the chimney breast, which in turn, housed an ornate black leaded fireplace surround, with mantel. The fireplace itself appeared to be decorated with 'mock-Edwardian' glazed and 'authentically cracked' tiles, painted with images of flowers. On the grate, a strategically places pyramid of logs, sawn ends facing into the room. Other walls, the front being taken up by the large floor to ceiling box-bay window, were decorated with delicate floral print wallpaper.

That bay window was probably the most striking feature beneath the high white ceiling. A box shape, tapering at a shallow angle towards the outermost section, each of the three sides housed large sash windows with all wooden parts, again, painted a shade of pine. As the bottom of the bay had been completed with box seating on the three sides, topped off with fern-green cushioned seating also fixed to the wall, there were no curtains – a shame to hide such a feature. Instead, each window was covered with teak-coloured louvered slatted blinds, and though these were down, the louvered slats were open, allowing layers of particle-filled laser beams of light to infiltrate the room. It was all a bit 'Laura Ashley'.

Azarias was invited to sit in one of the plush, elegant high-backed armchairs, with the roll-top arms. The chairs were placed to the right of the door, against the wall facing the window. There was about a metre between them, and in the space a small square pine table, upon which sat two slate coasters. Against the wall on the left, dividing the hall and the room, a modern light pine veneered desk and filing cabinet. On the desk sat a PC and a few box files and one brushed steel Parker ball pen. The high backed swivel chair on castors was turned away from the desk, suggesting that Alan may well have been sitting there when Azarias had knocked at the door.

"Were you waiting long?" Alan asked. "I keep meaning to get that bell fixed. Some people leave, never thinking to knock."

"No. When I didn't hear anything, I knocked." Azarias assured him. "When I was in the force we had a special police knock. A sort of 'scare the wits out of the occupants, police are at the door' knock."

116

"The policeman always knocks twice," Alan added.

"Something like that," Azarias laughed, adding, "No photographs!"

"Photographs?" Alan questioned.

Azarias scanned the room, the way he had scanned many rooms, upon entry, when he was in the force. Were there any clues about the occupant, a crime, and, moreover, were there any hidden surprises? On this occasion he had noted a lack of family photographs – he knew that Alan was married, with children. In fact, there were no photographs of any kind, a large round clock – a mock-up of the type that once adorned the wall of many a railway station waiting room, before the days of Doctor Beeching's cuts. Alan pointed out that it was, effectively, his office, his place of work, when Azarias mentioned these observations, and that he only held surgeries when his family were elsewhere, usually visiting family nearby.

"Your surgery," Azarias offered.

"I don't do enough to warrant another premises," Alan said. "Please. Please take a seat," he continued, offering the opportunity again.

Azarias took the seat nearer the door, so that the small pine table was to his right. He adjusted his seating, just enough to avoid leaving any of the slatted rays of light dazzling his retinas – at least for the meantime, until the light shifts as the sun sets. Before Alan took his place in the other chair he offered a variety of beverages, and water, to Azarias – all of which he declined. It was also made clear that no-one else was in the house, as his wife and two children were visiting his mother-in-law, causing Azarias to apologise for being responsible for breaking the family up on a Sunday afternoon.

"Not at all," Alan smirked, "We had planned to visit my mother-in-law, anyway. You've saved me from the one hour monologue that is my mother-in-law. I would not have been in a position to meet you had my family not been out. Like I said, they would usually visit family. Liz and the children visit with her sister on a Tuesday. Anyway, you sounded as if you needed to talk."

"There have been developments," Azarias mumbled. "I need help unravelling the tangle of string in my head."

"Before we start," Alan began, "First thing I should point out is that you can be assured of confidentiality with regards to our situation at work, amongst colleagues, family and friends. I should inform you, though, neither privacy nor confidentiality, however, are absolute rights, and there are fundamental exceptions, some involving ethical considerations and some involving legalities. You were in the police force. CID, wasn't it? I am sure you comprehend. Do you need me to clarify this?"

Azarias shook his head, indicating that he understood the implications, and that he was eager to continue.

"We need to produce a contract and consider the following," Alan continued. "What specific outcomes, goals or objectives do we expect to aim for in this therapy? How different orientations of therapy will vary in how precise and specific it is appropriate to be here. In other words, can I actually help you? But whatever your orientation, it is helpful to specify in advance what shared, negotiated outcome we are working towards together. This can of course be renegotiated as required, but one of the strongest predictors of good outcome and satisfaction with the process is for the client and therapist to agree on shared goals. We both have to agree on the outcomes. With that in mind what do you hope to achieve?"

"In the first place," Azarias started, "Like I said. I want to be able to unravel this tangle of string inside my head."

"Okay. Let's start there. String you call it. Why?" Alan asked.

He responded, describing his metaphorical string as unclear thoughts and memories which, though linked, wove a confused tangle. By unravelling the string, pulling the thoughts, memories to the fore, and creating a straight line, a link from the present to the past, he might see more clearly what it is that is haunting him – he expressed that view, that he felt haunted. Azarias was convinced this was a psychological issue and not a physical problem, and wanted to clarify that matter – that there was nothing sinister growing inside his brain.

"Okay," Alan started, slightly shifting his position so that he angled his body towards Azarias, attempting deliberately, to mirror his posture. "I wish to keep a record of this session. Now, I can write it up while you are talking but it would be easier to record, using this. If you do not object."

He produced a palm-size digital Dictaphone from within his front right trouser pocket, and placed it on the pine table, between them. Azarias saw no problem, having already been reassured of his 'patient' confidentiality. Alan then depressed the black button on the gadget, causing a small red light to be illuminated, and a line of green light to throb, pulse, elongate and shorten, with every sound it recorded. And then, the session began in earnest, with Alan making an introduction for purposes of filing and storing.

"Sunday, May nineteenth, twenty fourteen. The time is sixteen twenty one. Client and subject, Azarias Tor and..." he paused, his eyes rolled upward as if searching for something in his mind, and having found that answer returned his gaze to Azarias "And confused states of mind between sleep and wakefulness."

Alan then suggested to Azarias that he should talk freely about his concerns and any links to the past, however random those links, and any associated thoughts – like streams of consciousness, often connected but not necessarily linked in a logical fashion, or inappropriate order in the passing of time. Questions may be asked, perhaps when seeking clarification, but more to expand the current line of thought, and explore all the involved processes. Azarias agreed, and began to add his voice and innermost thoughts to the session, relaxing back into the sumptuous comfort of the armchair.

"I am more confused than ever. There is a woman, the same woman, who is in my dreams. Has been for a while. On Friday I thought I saw her in a car. At the exit to the tunnel. Southbound. I took notice because the car cut me up. But not just that. She looked straight at me. I think she took a snap of me, using a mobile phone. And now, I think I may be hallucinating. I thought I saw her on a footbridge. Saturday morning. Yesterday. Just standing there, leaning on the handrail. Looking at the river. I looked away. Only for a few seconds. When I turned around, nothing. She wasn't there."

Azarias was aware that Alan was motioning with a pen, as if he wanted to speak. He was taking notes, along with the digital recording, in order to write down his own thoughts, and questions. Alan wanted to intervene, yet Azarias was not quite finished. Alan ceased to attempt to interrupt, and leaned forward, showing interest, and nodded to Azarias to continue. He relaxed again, slumping back into the upholstery, linking his hands across his stomach, twiddling his thumbs in a circular fashion around each other. Closing his eyes, Azarias picked up where he had finished.

"Where was I? The footbridge. One minute I see her. Think I see her. Clear as day. And the she is not there. But if she was never there, and I am having hallucinations, I'm concerned that something may not be quite right upstairs. Might be looking at an MRI scan. Is that what they do? And then I had another dream. I was in a night club. And she was sitting next to me. Talking to me. I was asking her questions. *"Who are you? What are you? Why are you in my head?"* *"I am your guide."* She said. She has said that before. *"Do you recognise where you are?"* she said. And *"You will have the answers soon."* And then I woke up. But I was not exactly in the same place where I was when I dozed off.

I had moved, probably in my sleep. What is going on there? Wait, wait. The strange thing is I think that I might have met her. In that club. The one in my dream. But in the past. She is in my head. Why?"

Alan attempted to answer the final questions, calling upon his knowledge and experience, whilst considering a number of points he had penned in his notepad. He moved the Dictaphone slightly, arranging the position so that it was seemingly equidistant between them and continued recording the consultation.

"We take for granted the ability to recognise faces," Alan continued, running the fingers of his right hand through his hair, and then gently scratching his scalp, subconsciously, as he spoke.

"Faces that we may have seen once, and many years ago, remain within our memories."

He gestured and pointed to different parts of his head, and face, as he discussed the role played by the fusiform gyrus, in the temporal lobe, in dealing with facial recognition, and how this, in turn, interacts with the occipital lobe, where visual input is processed. The good news, then, was that part of the brain appeared to be in working order, in light of any fears concerning physical issues in the brain. There was no evidence of face blindness, though perhaps a slight worry about wakening up in a different place to that where he had fallen asleep – some medical and scientific research has shown that 'living out; dreams, moving excessively during sleep, regularly, may indicate physical illness, or damage in the brain, and may even point to the onset of dementia. Alan then stated that he was more interested in exploring matters of the mind.

"A question," Alan said. "This woman. The one in your dreams. You said that you think you may have met her before. When was that?"

Azarias rapped gently, with the knuckles of his right hand, on his forehead as he said, "It's like I have a new memory of her, yet at the same time, that memory is old. It's difficult to explain. I'm trying to remember when I met her. A long time ago, I think. I'm not sure. Is she real, or just a dream? Maybe I did meet her once. I can't say when, but it might have been in that club. The one in my dream. Maybe that was why I had that dream."

Alan observed Azarias closely, aware that he appeared to be stuck on a loop – always returning to the starting point, without any resolution to his concerns, or answers to his questions. Round and round in ever-decreasing circles! His sanity was potentially, unravelling, disintegrating; his mind appearing to lose touch with reality. Alan had a plan.

"I'm going to make a suggestion," he began, swivelling his armchair around so that it created a 90 degree angle with the front of the chair occupied by Azarias. "You have to be in full agreement with my idea for it to work."

"I'm open to suggestions," Azarias said, "Anything to sort this out in my head."

"Hypnotism!" he spluttered as he often did, sucking saliva through his teeth. "Hypnotism. Have you ever been subjected to hypnotism before?"

Azarias explained that he had been hypnotised, many years before, in a working men's club, where the headline cabaret had been a hypnotist. Purely for reasons of entertainment, of course, he had volunteered himself as a subject for the show. With complete and full agreement, Azarias followed instructions to prepare himself to be hypnotised – sitting upright, arms resting on the sides of the chair, and feet planted firmly on the ground, slightly apart. Alan Asked Azarias to focus on the light breaking through one of the gaps in the slats in the blinds. *'Is that why they are like that?'* "Focus on that light. Fix your gaze on that light and listen to my voice, there is nothing but my voice."

Alan spoke slowly in a monotone voice, using repetitive phrases, starting with breathing, suggesting *that "feet were feeling like lead and were being pulled into the ground by gravity, pulling the eyelids down. Muscles relaxing, rippling down the back. A feeling of falling, floating, hearing nothing but that one voice, into the darkness."* Over and again.

"At any time," Alan continued, "If you feel uncomfortable, or unable to proceed, you will be able to wake yourself. Now, relax. Focus on my voice, and my words. You are falling into a deep sleep. A deep sleep. Deeper and deeper. Listen only to my voice. Deeper and deeper. You feel the muscles slide down your back. You feel the second finger of your right hand twitch. Good. Good. Relax. You will hear my voice. Nothing else. Deeper and deeper. You are now in a deep sleep, but you hear my voice. You are able to talk to me from your deep sleep. Do you hear me?"

Following the involuntary twitch of the second finger of the right hand, which then returned to a relaxed resting position, there was a pause while the words filtered through the ears and into the subconscious, into the deepest recesses of his psyche. And then, slowly, almost drunkenly, he responded.

"I hear you," he mumbled, his chin resting on his chest.

Azarias was breathing deeply, and rhythmically, as he drifted in the hollow blackness of his mind. He imagined that he was walking in a dark cavern, in which a familiar voice boomed and echoed off the walls. The voice commanded him to walk further into the dark. Azarias thought he might have laughed, though couldn't be sure, as the expectation, the cliché, was to be encouraged to walk into the light. On this occasion he was being directed to walk into the darkness, and as he lost himself in the void the voice seemed to grow louder.

"Ahead of you, there is a chink of light," the voice of Alan said.

*'Ah, the light! I see it',* Azarias said in his mind.

"Walk towards the light," the distant voice ordered.

*'I wondered! Walk towards the light.'*

"The light is growing as you draw closer. You see that it is a tunnel, and that the light is coming from the other end of the tunnel. As you walk towards the light you travel back in time. You walk through your life. Look at the images on the walls. Follow your memories towards the end of the tunnel. When you reach the end of the tunnel I want you to tell me what you see."

In his mind's eye Azarias could see the white brick-tiled walls and ceiling of a vaulted tunnel, stretching off into the distance, towards the bright, which illuminated his surroundings. He turned to look back into the darkness, the hollow blackness of his mind, but Alan urged him to move forward. As he prepared to focus on the journey, Alan's disembodied head, and voice, filled the tunnel, imploring him to reach the end of the tunnel, explaining that, though he may see many images, facets, of his past life worth exploring, it was important to discover what was at the end of the journey. The head and voice, faded as he continued to move through the labyrinth of his mind.

On the walls of the tunnel, deep in the recesses of his mind, images of his life flashed, flickered, and faded, some like photographs, others like videos or movies. In certain instances, it was still difficult to determine the reality from the imagined, and the dream. Azarias even imagined himself rising from the armchair, in Alan's front room, walking towards the shards of light beaming through the gaps in the slatted blinds, before finding himself once again, in the tunnel, as the bay window dissolved in his path. And there she was – *'Green Eyes'*.

He was sitting next to her – in that club. She was talking in a low voice, almost inaudible over the background noise, the music and the chatter, drawing him in closer, and then she blew some powder, dust, from the palm of her hand into his face. And then, nothing – waking up on the sofa. *'Not fall for that one again!'* The image faded, and then she was on the footbridge, above the river, and then she wasn't there. Then she was a passenger in a car cutting across his path, as he exited the tunnel south of the Tyne. And she took the time, so it seemed, to take a photograph of him.

As the images came and went, Alan compelled Azarias not to dwell on the major issues, locked inside his head, which confronted him. Together, they would face his demons and his nightmares, but not yet. *'One thing at a time'.* Find a happy place first, where the tunnel ends. A place without fear, and free of danger. Start there, in the past, and then move through time to the present day. *'Deal with one thing at a time'.* And, so Azarias moved along the tunnel, gaining speed, bypassing haunted memories and shattered images of his tortured past.

*'Green Eyes'* must have been around before on the periphery, when he was out jogging or shopping, because Azarias saw her face at different points along the journey. And then, *the funeral* – his wife. Alan urged him on, beckoning from the mouth of the tunnel. *"Don't stop there. Later. Not now. Find the end of the tunnel."* Azarias moved on, passing the image of the wrecked vehicle at the base of the cliff. Then another funeral – the same people but his wife was there, dressed in black. Next, that warehouse – the explosion, and the raging inferno that followed. He was watching it from outside. Again, the voice – Alan – drawing him further back into the past. His 'passing out' parade, his mother's funeral, graduation from university and school days became a jumbled blur as he flew towards the end of the tunnel, or maybe the end of the tunnel came to meet him. But he was there, at the end of the tunnel, at last, and he stepped out into the light.

Alan could see that Azarias was in a deep hypnotic state, relaxed, and that he had reached the end of 'the tunnel'. The subject of this consultation no longer appeared agitated, disturbed by painful memories, but sounded happy, as he emitted an almost childish laugh; '*A good time for questions*'.

"Where are you?" Alan asked, softly, with sensitivity in his voice.

"In the garden," Azarias answered, following a brief pause.

Alan always allowed thinking time, having asked a question, and never pressured his clients, even if to just attempt to break the seemingly, potentially, awkward or uncomfortable silence. *Time to think, time to explore long since forgotten memories. Time to understand, and unlock closed links to the past.* Azarias was ready to open up, and Alan held the key, and entered into a dialogue with lost and stored memories.

"Whose garden?" he enquired.

"My garden."

"How old are you?"

"Five. I'm five years old. I am actually five and a quarter."

"Tell me what you can see," Alan prompted, and then fell silent.

Azarias described the surroundings, slowly, almost child-like, from deep within his hypnotic trance, his eyes moving behind the closed lids. He was in a walled garden of his London home, on a warm summer day.

Insects buzzed, and sparrows, wrens and chaffinches chirped and cheeped in the bushes, shrubbery, and on the bird feeders. A few pigeons, perhaps collared doves, cooed from nearby rooftops. The two and a half metre high white painted garden walls, on three sides, and stucco rear wall, of the large, terraced house of the large terraced house reflected the light and heat of the afternoon sun, warming the air by a few more degrees than the surrounding neighbourhood. He stepped down from a crazy-paved patio onto a well-maintained lawn, amidst an artist's palette of flowers and herbs, in beds and terracotta tubs and pots. And there were a few small fruit trees, though he couldn't name them.

"Are you alone?" Alan probed further, when Azarias had finished 'painting the picture'; of the urban oasis – the back garden of his north west London home, where he had lived with his mother for the first six years of his life.

In that instant Azarias was in his mind that five and a quarter year old boy and he could see, feel and touch the very fabric of his world. The scent of the garden filled his nostrils, as he pondered on how best to answer the question, put to him by the voice without a physical form.

"Of course not. Silly!" he began, with the exasperation of a five and a half year old who has been asked by an adult if pigs can fly. "I am not old enough to be left on my own. I would have to be at least six. Or seven. No. Eight, I think, to be left on my own. But not while I am five. I am really five and a quarter. Did I tell you?

"You did tell me," Alan responded warmly. "You did. Five and a quarter. And yes, I am silly. You are not old enough to be left alone. So, tell me who you are with."

"My mum. I am with my mum."

"That's nice. Is she in the garden?"

"Yes. On the bench. Near the trees."

"And what is she doing?" he asked.

"Drawing. She is always drawing," Azarias answered. "Or making things. And she sells some of the things she makes. And her drawings. And her paintings. She is very clever."

Alan urged Azarias to take a look at the drawing his mother was completing. The boy, in his mind, approached his mother, and smiled. She returned his smile. Her dark brown eyes, with large, coal-black discs for pupils, reflected the light, and shone with love and pride, as she lifted and turned her sketch pad so that the young boy might see her finished work. Masses of thick, wavy chestnut hair cascaded to her shoulders, like the rapids of a turbulent river tumbling over rocks, as she leaned forward with the work of art – a sketch of a man's face.

"It's a man's face," Azarias said, in his own voice, as if conscious that he was conversing with Alan.

"Do you recognise him?" Alan asked, rubbing his chin thoughtfully with his right hand.

Yet again, Azarias answered in this adult demeanour. "Yes. My mother sketched him, and painted him many times."

"Who is he?"

A long silence followed, and the lack of response appeared to give Alan some cause for concern. Azarias was breathing deeply, his chin still resting on his chest, but had not answered the question. *'Try a different approach. Stay calm.'*

The boy, aged five and a quarter, was transfixed by his mother's beauty – the adult had forgotten how he had tried, many times, to count the cloud of ginger freckles that formed a milky way beneath her eyes on the brow of her cheeks, across the bridge of her nose. She had always made him lose count, making him laugh hysterically, when she pretended to bite his 'counting' finger. *'Why did I ever stop trying to count them?'* And her cheeks! They were the colour of the red apples on the trees at the bottom of the garden. *'Why did I ever stop kissing the apples on her cheeks?'* And then the voice boomed around the garden, though his mother did not appear to hear it.

"Azarias?" Alan asked, searching shadows, and depths, of the hypnosis. "Are you still in the garden?"

"Yes."

*'A quicker response. All is well. The boy speaks'.*

"What is happening now?" Alan enquired, placing his hands together beneath his chin, as if in prayer.

"I am looking at the drawing," came the response, loud and clear in the room, and in the garden, in his mind.

His mother, wearing a red, gold-trimmed Moroccan-style, thigh length smock top, white linen pants and Scholl sandals, presented the sketch, which he examined closely. It was just of the head. Azarias had seen many similar sketches, and paintings of the same man. This was just a pencil sketch, but in paintings, in colour, he had green eyes – emerald green eyes. In the bottom right corner of the sketch she had written something – two names and the date: Raphael, Iona, and 5/7/77.

"Raphael," Azarias uttered through his breath, "Raphael. My father."

"Your father?" Alan asked, slightly startled by the statement. "And where is your father? Where is Raphael?"

"I don't know," the reply. "I don't know. Maybe he is in heaven. Mum said he was an angel. *"The Angel Raphael,"* she called him."

Another long silence followed and that was disturbed only by the sound of deep rhythmic breathing, and the distant sounds of the outside world, beyond the bay window and the slatted blinds. Far away in the garden, the boy shuffled on to the bench, next to his mother, his sandal-clad feet and bare legs, dangling towards the ground. He could feel the heat of the day reflected from the bench, through his shorts and his short-sleeved shirt. The young Azarias pointed at the sketch of Raphael, his father, and stole the very thought, let alone the question, from Alan.

"Tell me about him," the young boy, in his mind, urged. "Tell me about my father."

Alan was transfixed, listening to Azarias reveal the words spoken to the boy by his mother, in his mind, under hypnosis. And then he became aware of an oversight, and hissed and cursed, *"Shit!"* under his breath, suddenly realising that he had neglected to charge the battery in the digital recorder. Frustration nagged at him as the tiny red light winked angrily, a warning of a limited amount of time, perhaps a few minutes, before the device ceased to record the session. The last thing, then, that Alan wanted was to disturb Azarias in mid-flow. This was fascinating, something he had never encountered before – maybe a psychologist's dream – someone under hypnosis, interrogating someone else, inside their mind.

*'Was this a first?'* Nothing immediately sprang to the front of his memory to suggest that anything had even been written about such as occurrence, a state of being, such as the case he was witnessing. Alan was going to have to scratch notes with his biro into his notebook, in order to keep a complete record, rather than attempt to plug the digital device into the mains. *'Better to improvise,'* and then he began to write his form of shorthand, attempting to capture every word spoken by Azarias, from the world deep within his hypnosis.

Azarias repeated the words spoken by his mother, to the child, in his mind, whether this was a deep-seated memory, unlocked by hypnosis, pure fantasy, or

133

something far deeper and more mysterious. Raphael and his mother had first met in 1970, when Iona was attempting to sell some of her artwork and ceramics on a friend's stall, on the Portobello Road. She was a 20-year-old art student in London; working her way through college to help make ends meet, when a friend suggested that she try to promote her work. Another friend offered her the opportunity to take advantage of space on his bric-a-brac stall on the market. And that was where she first laid eyes on Raphael.

Iona described him, Azarias continuing to repeat the words he heard in his head, which Alan noted with his pen, the digital Dictaphone having finally stopped recording. Raphael was unlike any man she had met, most of those having been around the same age as herself and lacking any real sense of style or intellect and they were, generally, somewhat immature. Yet, on a Saturday morning, in the spring of 1970, there stood before her at this market stall, the most elegant, captivating and haunting man. He was tall, slender, his long blonde hair tied in a ponytail and he had the most magnificent, almost hypnotic, emerald green eyes. But he was probably in his late twenties/early thirties, sophisticated, and almost other-worldly. Why would he be interested in her? Yet, he seemed to take an interest in her work.

In the garden of his mind, the young Azarias stared at the image in the sketch book, while he listened intently to his mother as she talked of Raphael, the art collector and interior designer to the famous and the wealthy. He had purchased six pieces of her work – two paintings and four samples of her ceramics. A month later, he called at the flat she shared with two friends – Iona had never thought to question how he knew where she lived – and he had orders for the work, and art, from his clients in Italy, Switzerland, the south of France and California, and New York, in the USA. She was made, even before finishing college, and then Iona fell for his charm, wisdom and style.

"He was magic," Azarias said, streaming the words from Iona, deep in his trance. "Like an angel," he continued. "My angel Raphael. And, you were my gift from an angel."

Alan scribbled notes – points for further discussion. *'Relationship with father, Raphael. Memories. What do you remember from your early years? Father, a significant other? Relationship with Mother? Relationship between parents? Describe Father in three sentences. Ditto, Mother.'* Then he put his pen and notepad on the table – time to move on, to find the woman with the green eyes. *'She must be in there, somewhere.'* And then he spoke.

"Relax, Azarias, relax," he began. "Relax. Deeper and deeper. Breathe deeply and listen to my voice. Relax. Listen carefully to my voice."

In that garden of consciousness, the young Azarias fell into a sleep, resting his head upon his mother's lap. Gently, she teased his hair with her fingers, having placed her sketch pad on the ground at her feet. With the warmth of the afternoon sun on her face Iona found it difficult to keep her eyes open, and she too, drifted, twitching slightly as sleep crawled comfortably into her waking day. Soon, both slumbered peacefully, though

135

Azarias was about to be awakened by the voice calling to him again.

That familiar voice urged Azarias to leave his mother and walk into the house. The gaping black mouth of the door set in the white stucco wall, with brooding dark eyes of windows, either side, beckoned, as Alan repeated the command. As he drew closer to the house, Azarias turned to look back at his mother, or the memory of the way she once was, and saw himself, five and a quarter years old, curled up, feet on the garden bench, with his head resting on his mother's lap. Her right hand rested gently in the dark curls, on his head. Both appeared to be sleeping, both appeared contented, and at peace with the world. He had forgotten how that had felt, had even lost the memories, buried warm and comfortable moments of his childhood innocence, and the exuberance of his youth, beneath the trials and tribulations heaped upon him over the years – *'time is a cruel mistress'!*

He took one last lingering look before stepping from the sunlit patio into the gloom of a room, long since frequented by Azarias. The room, a dining room, began to form as his eyes adjusted to the change of light, but quickly dissolved before he had a chance to focus on the memories of this childhood home. Alan wanted him to move on, to explore the dark rooms within his mind, and search for that hidden corner, where the first meeting with *'Green Eyes'* might be found. *'Why does she haunt him? Who is she? Where, and when, did they meet?'* *'Time to find the answers, locked away inside, and to discover if she is real, or imagined,'* Alan cogitated.

"Breathe deeply. In. Hold. Out. Hold. Breathe," Alan suggested. "Imagine that in the winding corridors of your mind are the doors leading into different rooms. Each room contains a different memory. Look into these rooms, to find the memory of the first time you met, or dreamed, of the woman with the green eyes. Where is she?"

Azarias fumbled his way through darkened rooms, and along endless corridors, in his mind, searching for the memories of *'Green Eyes'*, In the distance, along once of these corridors, he detected the heavy booming bass of a familiar tune – *'Tainted Love'*. Following the sound, he suddenly found himself in a nightclub, dimly lit, and smoky, with flashing, throbbing lights. Young bodies jerked, twisted and gyrated in a variety of ways to the sound of Marc Almond. For some reason, unbeknown to him, Azarias felt compelled to cross the dance floor, weaving his way through the mass of swirling youth. As he passed a square, load-bearing pillar, clad with mirrored glass, he caught a glimpse of his reflection.

He was young, late teens, early twenties, yes, twenty, tall and lean, wearing a brown leather bomber jacket, a slashed white T-shirt and ripped jeans, tucked into tan-coloured calf-length boots. This younger version of Azarias was sporting a Caesar-cut, and he looked cool and confident – he felt confident. His right hand dipped into an inside zipped pocket of the jacket, fingers and thumb locking on a crumpled piece of paper, which he revealed as a ten pound note. *'Of course, the bar!'*

Azarias set his sights on the far end of the bar, just around the corner, where no-one was vying for attention, attempting to catch the eye of one of the bar staff. The soles of his boots were audible as each upward step peeled away from the sticky linoleum flooring surrounding the bar. Around the corner of the bar, set back against the dark wall, a quiet area – if such a thing is possible in a night club – with a few low tables, leather chairs and sofas sitting on a beer-sodden and wine-stained carpet.

Azarias thought he saw two men help another man, possibly drunk, to his feet near one of the sofas, while a dark-haired woman watched. He was momentarily distracted by an attractive young blonde, dressed like a ballerina, wearing a black bomber-jacket and Doctor Marten boots, who eyed him up and down, with a smile full of wanton promises. Azarias followed her gaze, returning the smile with his cheeky boy persona. While he looked back, towards the bar, the three men were no longer there, though the woman remained seated on the sofa. *Where had they gone?* He couldn't see them anywhere, and imagined that the two on either side of the limp body could not move him quickly. Perhaps they had taken him to the toilet to sober him up, and the toilets were down that end of the bar. Maybe he had just imagined it all, and it was a trick of the light. The woman, sitting alone, appeared unaffected, though she grimaced when she took a sip of red wine.

There was a strong compulsion for Azarias to live this memory, to see it to the end, and through the repetition of an event, which may remain unchanged, discover the truth. *'Is this real or is this imagined?'*

Perhaps there is a chance that the mind might play tricks and create false memories. In that case, nothing would be learned, but, still, he made his way to the bar, to catch the eye of the brunette in the short black skirt and black top, exposing ample cleavage, who would return his smile, just as she had done before. And then, above all the noise, during a lull in the music, he heard someone call his name.

"Azarias?" a woman's voice called from somewhere behind him, on one of the leather sofas, causing him to turn and look in the direction from the voice came.

"Azarias Tor?" she asked, as if questioning recognition, establishing eye contact.

Her teeth shone out from the dark corner as she beamed a welcoming, confidence-building smile. Large emerald green eyes, set above a pert turned up nose, painted on her small square-set face, almost gave her the appearance of a Persian cat – *'Cat woman?'* Azarias smiled at the woman behind the bar, raised his left hand, declining her offer of service, mouthing "Just a minute." Turning away from the bar, he approached the woman with the cat-like eyes, sitting alone on the sofa.

He stood before the stranger, bowing his head slightly – a show of respect – and clasping his hands in front of his crotch, like a footballer defending a direct free-kick; though more likely, he was protecting himself from this woman's gaze. Perhaps he was feeling a little insecure, uncertain of how to deal with the situation, unsure of himself, but he found his voice.

"I'm sorry," he said, bowing his head in an attempt to appear polite, "But did you call my name?"

"Are you Azarias Tor?" she asked, already aware of the answer.

"Do I know you?"

"Not yet," she replied, "But I know you."

"Is this a con? You know me. I don't know you. Is this some sort of a scam? Sorry if I sound a bit disrespectful, but I don't know you. What do you want?"

"Give me a few minutes of your time," she patted the empty space on the sofa with her left hand, pleading "Please. I have something very important to share with you. No con. No tricks. Just a few minutes of your time is all I require. In fact, I have something to give to you."

His shoulders dropped, as he let out a sigh, mouthed the word *"Okay,"* and sat himself next to her – it was not every day of the week that an attractive older woman asked you to sit next to her. *'An attractive, older woman, on the pull? Why not?'* Azarias had no trouble attracting young females – not unlike flies around shit, really, such was his popularity, his demeanour, style, and overall appearance. Older women had expressed interest, of this he was aware, and he had flirted with them, even with the aunt of a good friend. He knew what to say, how to charm, and had a mature, well-developed sense of humour.

"Would you like some red wine?" Saluki asked, pointing to the glass, which had remained untouched.

"If you don't mind," he laughed, "I'll pass on that. The wine they serve here tastes like piss water. Excuse the language. Vinegar at the very best."

The question reverberated in his mind – "Do I know you?"

"Not yet," 'Green Eyes' replied, shaking her head, causing her pitch-black fringe to swish back and forth across her forehead, like theatrical curtains, at the end of a performance.

"But I know you," she continued.

"Please," she whispered, nearly inaudible above the background noise and thumping disco.

"I have something very important to share with you," she asserted, raising her voice. "No con. No tricks. Just a few minutes. In fact, I have something to give to you."

Azarias sighed, and, in that brief moment, synapses in his brain fired off signals in a variety of directions, calculating a number of permutations and possible outcomes.

*'She knows him but he doesn't know her. Something to do with the university? Student union? No – a lecturer? Why? Why, in this club? A friend of a friend? A relative of a friend? A friend of his mother? No – probably not in the same age group? On the pull? Okay – older, but attractive. Wouldn't kick her out of bed. Prostitute? Probably couldn't afford a hand job! How does he know his name? Still, the same question. What was there to lose? What could possibly happen, in a busy nightclub?'*

Marc had merged, following a brief lull in the music, into Madonna, as the disco version of *'Tainted Love'* blended with *'Vogue'*. While the young hopefuls danced, and bounced, around the floor, Azarias settled on the sofa on the edge, leaning forward slightly, as if ready to flee in the event that this woman presented any threat to him. She, in turn, produced a metallic-looking object, the size of a matchbox, from within an inside pocket of her jacket, and held it out towards him, in her right hand. The silvery cuboid appeared to vibrate, and shake on the flat of the open palm of her hand, throbbing, glowing phosphorous white, capturing and holding the attention of the adolescent male – trapped in a trance, while she spoke, slowly, to the deepest parts of his subconscious.

"You will forget," she started. "You will forget everything I am about to say. You will forget what is about to happen. Do you understand?"

Azarias nodded, heavily and slowly, dazzled, though not blinded, by the bright light which held his gaze. His mind buzzed with the words that the green-eyed woman muttered. She repeated certain phrases, which, once heard, folded into the creases of his brain, stored in the long-term memory, forgotten in the short term. *'Witchcraft.'* No escape from her humming lips, the glare of her emerald stare.

"You will forget what is about to happen. You will take the gift. Always keep it safe. But you will forget. Until the time is right. Then, you will remember. When the time is right. You will remember. When the time is right. Only when the time is right."

The words *'the time is right'* resounded in his ears, and he felt as if he was spinning, floating in the air, away from *'Green Eyes'*. As she faded into the darkness, twisted and contorted faces, on the dance floor, appeared to taunt him, singing the words over and over, *'the time is right, the time is right,'* as their bodies convulsed the night away. Then there was darkness – a hollow blackness he had experienced before. The tunnel!

In the darkness he could hear heavy laboured breathing, and the sound of someone's heart beating, pumping fiercely and loudly, as if it might burst – perhaps his breathing and his heart. No – his breathing and his footsteps. In his mind, he was running back through the tunnel, his feet tip-tapping as he made his way towards some distant, growing light, breathing *'the time is right, the time is right.'* Through the darkness and into the light.

"The time is right," Azarias loudly announced, as his eyes snapped open, startling Alan, who physically jumped up in his chair.

"I hear you," Alan said, settling himself. "I heard you. You repeated the phrase. A few times. Are you okay? Let me…"

"I'm okay," Azarias cut in. "I'm fine. I'm good."

Alan expressed his concern at the way Azarias had 'snapped' out of the hypnotic state and wanted to observe him for a while. He also had a number of questions. *'The time is right' – what did that mean? Who was this woman? What did she want? What did she say to him?'*

But Azarias was restless, fidgeting, and was on his feet, fumbling for his car keys in his trouser pocket.

"I have to go," he said, somewhat excitedly, and started to move towards the door.

"Wait," Alan urged. "Tell me, what is happening? What has happened? What do you mean when you say *'the time is right'*?"

Alan was following Azarias out into the hallway who now had his keys in his right hand and appeared animated. He didn't want the session to finish this way – *'too many unanswered questions'*. On top of that, Alan was chewed up with curiosity – it had been a long time since a client, or case, had so roused his professional interest, or even reawakened a dormant passion for his vocation. Azarias, though, had other thoughts on his mind, and was not making himself available as a subject of study in a thesis, or paper, in the British Journal of Psychology – he was already opening the front door, his words trailing in his wake.

"I have to go home," he said, not even looking back, striding up the path to the garden gate. "I think I remember. Thanks to you."

"Remember what?" Alan asked, pursuing Azarias to the pavement, his front door closing shut behind him.

"I'll tell you tomorrow," he said, reaching the Rover, the indicator lights flickering as he pressed the open button on the remote. "Let me know how much I owe you."

The door of the car clunked shut as he slid the seatbelt across his shoulder, from right to left. Then the engine thrummed. Drive was selected and Azarias steered the vehicle carefully away from parked cars lining the Edwardian street. And then he was gone.

Alan turned back towards his home and pushed the front door. It was shut. He patted the pockets of his trousers – no keys, no mobile phone. He was locked out – "Shit!" His wife would be home soon though. Alan walked back to the garden gate, leaned on it with both elbows, and looked up and down the street on that quiet Sunday afternoon.

"Stuff always happens to others," he muttered quietly, in case anybody close to any window, in any nearby house might hear him. "I am always the observer."

# Chapter 15

The double doors of the elevator hissed as they slid smoothly open, and Raphael Antinori entered from lower level five, subterranean vehicle storage. Sensors surrounding the elevator had scanned Raphael on several different tiers; most of those methods involving biometric readings – retinae, palm print of the right hand, held aloft, facial measurements, and voice recognition. There were systems in place to read data on the two chips embedded beneath his skin.

The process was repeated, in the blink of an eye, unseen scanners sweeping from head to toe, when the doors closed behind him – no one gained access to the interior, or the inner sanctum of 'La Tour de la Croix' without high security clearance, and this was the building in which Raphael had purchased a penthouse apartment two years previously. The penthouse was on the fiftieth level, high above the resident's exclusive shopping mall, and leisure complex.

An invisible male salesman-like voice filled the cabin, before any decision was made regarding the required floor – *"Good afternoon Vice-Superus Antinori. I have the privilege of reminding you that you, as a resident, enjoy unlimited access to one of the best retail experiences throughout EFRON, with facilities providing entertainment for you and the other 4,500 residents in this exclusive complex."*

"I know," he snapped. "I do not need to be reminded every time I enter the elevator."

The voice cut short the patter, repeated when a resident, or one of the 1200 employees, working in the mall, and offices, sought to move between floors in the complex, but only because the system acknowledged a command from the Vice-Superus of Genetikos. A brief silence filled the black walled, gold trimmed, dimly lit cabin, before a softly spoken, reassuring, female sang – *"Welcome Vice-Superus Antinori. Please state your destination."*

"Penthouse suites," he responded, calm and clear. "Southern block."

*"Thank you Vice-Superus Antinori. This is the express non-stop service to level fifty. Penthouse suites. Southern block. Roof-top bar. Restaurant and swimming pool."*

The elevator moved effortlessly skyward, as if on a cushion of air – so smoothly that any occupant might be forgiven for thinking that it had not moved and was, to the senses, stationary. On the contrary, it was moving upwards at a speed of 20 metres per second; silently, except for the in-car music – *Percussion Concerto number 5 by the classical composer, Karim Krimskova.* As Raphael plummeted towards the heavens, colourful, bright, images appeared, flickered, danced, and vanished, to be replaced by more persuasive moving pictures, and stills, on the black gold-trimmed screens. Targeted advertising, reaching the desired audience.

This was something of a 'bone of contention' with Raphael Antinori – the invasion of privacy through the uRAPP, and embedded chips. Of course, there was the argument that crime was low – so much so, that even the smallest, insignificant, of crimes did not go without a mention on the national news. On the down side the data collected from every scanner – and scanners are everywhere – monitoring every movement, all retail purchases, leisure activities, and vacations, was then used to create this targeted advertising. If anyone else should happen to be in the elevator they would most likely experience different commercials, based on their personal retail and leisure activities – and only the targeted individual will hear their selected endorsements, all acceptable in law. The large corporations had the power, the wherewithal, to bypass firewalls, and other security devices, affording protection against cybercrime, and identity theft, so as promote their products, ensuring that all persuasive messages reached the eyes and ears of potentially interested parties.

Mercifully, travelling at 20 metres per second, though subjected to specifically targeted subliminal endorsements, the individual would have to endure no more than 30 seconds, or so, of the commercial brainwashing, if they resided in the penthouse suites – much less time, the lower the floor. That having been noted, the same targeted advertising preyed on the desires, wants and needs, of every individual in every public place; shopping malls, leisure facilities, public transport, and bars and restaurants, on screens, or in the shape of holograms, with the ability to reach a person, with different messages, through their identity microchips, which were embedded at birth. The proof of identity, existence – the passport to everything – which guaranteed the individual protection from crime, affording them access to all that made the world a safe place to live, was used to gather information and data, which was, in turn, utilised in such a way as to attempt to manipulate consumer choices; just the tip of the iceberg. *Mucho dinero!*

Raphael experienced a slight popping in his ears as the elevator glided to an abrupt, though gentle, halt at the fiftieth floor. The journey was not yet complete, though, as Antinori's choice of ingress, and egress, to and from the building was always at the western side of the complex, affording him direct access to the E500; traffic always being heavier on the southern approaches – particularly at peak times. The Vice-Superus was not one for wasting time, let alone spending valuable time sitting in traffic, when he could be dealing with matters of importance, directing policy and developing strategies to resolve problems, and plan for the future – and, there never appeared to be enough time. *'Time is not just money, time is everything.'*

The elevator car clicked lightly, but audibly, as it slid back on to rails which ran around in a completed circle, linking all points on the compass, connecting to, and accessing, all four tower blocks; north, east, south and west – forming the shape of a large Celtic cross, if seen from above, sitting on top a square box; this foundation being the 800,000 square metres of the shopping mall and the leisure complex. Moving at a jogging pace the car then traversed in an anti-clockwise direction; the shortest distance between the western tower and the southern block. Having reached its destination the car moved forward, clicking on to another rail, at which point the infernal advertising ceased. The voice inside his head, and the images on the black, gold trimmed screen were replaced by the time – 17:10 – and the outside temperature – 34°C. As the doors hissed open the female elevator voice addressed him in polite tones.

*'Level fifty. Penthouse suites. Rooftop bar and restaurant. Communal swimming pool and gym. You are reminded that maintenance and concierge services are available 24 hours a day, every day, should you require any assistance. Have an enjoyable evening.'*

"An enjoyable evening? If only. If only," he muttered to himself, with a sense of irony and foreboding, such was his belief that his suspicions were about to be confirmed – and it was not a question of 'if', but when. *'Soon',* he thought, stepping from the elevator on to the polished Terridian floor, which stretched out into the distance. The corridor was almost as long as the tower was high – 580 metres – at which far end was the door to his apartment.

Antinori walked with purpose, striding the 8 metres towards the travellator and escalators. The lobby resembled an airport terminal, not unlike those at Schiphol airport, easily as wide, and long, with five doors, leading to luxurious penthouse apartments, on either side – the distance between doors reflecting the huge spaces in the homes behind the exterior walls. Just as the travellators at an airport are accentuated by the occasional break, to allow access to departure gates, there were stop-gaps adjacent to each pairs of doors, facing one another across the wide chasm of the corridor. Two pairs of escalators, one set near the elevators, and the other mirrored pair, facing the door to Raphael's apartment, at the far end, accessed the rooftop amenities through an air-conditioned atrium, housing a bar.

Stepping on to the southbound travellator he waved a hand over a green 'plus' symbol, standing out from a white background, situated on a column to the right of the start of the moving walkway. This action caused the forward motion to increase in speed, and Raphael stood stiffly, a soldier on parade, facing the direction of travel, as he floated alongside the faux green jungle foliage, and artificial brightly multi-coloured tropical flowers, heading towards his home at the far end of the cathedral-like vaulted upper floor of the 580 metre high monolith. During the journey he had stepped off three travellators, walking the short distance between two of them and some three metres from the third to reach his entrance door. At that point security systems, similar to that elsewhere in the building, scanned his retinae, read the print on his upheld right palm, and referenced a variety of biometric calculations, verifying his genetic make-up, before allowing him access to the palatial apartment.

The penthouse suite was flooded with natural light, the complete width of the end of the tower, all three outer walls, of the open plan layout, made from Pilkington Twenty-Two triple glazed tempered glass. As the door swished closed behind him, the immediate view that greeted him, beyond the glass walls, the lazy blue of the late afternoon sky, smeared with white wisps of cloud – an ever-changing natural wallpaper and, far below, an expansive panorama.

On the plain white north wall, reflecting the incoming light, taking on the hues of the ever changing day and night, six large back-lit paintings, seemingly abstract at first glance, hung at slightly different levels from one end of the width of the room to the other, where another adorned the wall of the kitchen, nestled beneath the gallery mezzanine landing. Further inspection of the images revealed the art of the cosmos – distant galaxies captured by various telescopes orbiting the Earth, or other planets in the universe – an array of cosmic colours. These, along with two black, and two white, sculptures, of varying sizes – between that of a child and an adult human – were the only adornments in an otherwise minimalist setting; the limitations of the furnishings, perhaps, reflecting the true desire for company.

One black leather contemporary four seater sofa faced south across a large toughened glass low set table, a fossilised tree trunk for the base. This was flanked by two armchairs, similar in design to the sofa, opposing each other at either end of the table, resting upon a caramel rug. Upon the table, two coasters, and nothing else. This enclave, oasis of comfort, within the vast space, some 12 metres floor to ceiling, was set off-centre, not quite into the south-west corner, along with a glass six seater dining table, the only sign that the occupant took some time off to relax. The art of the universe and the sculptures would have looked as much at home in the reception lobby of any major corporation, or museum, such was the thought given over to

152

relaxation, and entertaining for the sake of entertainment.

To the left – the east – a rarely used black painted, and stainless steel, professional styled kitchen, with two ranges, three ovens, ample storage, and refrigeration, gleaming beneath the mezzanine gallery. Double width floating glass stairs, suspended by steel cables, led to the other floor, as did an open elevator, set in a glass tube, and this continued upwards, beyond the mezzanine, housing two bedrooms, both with en-suite facilities and walk in wardrobes, and a study, into a dark space in the five metre thick ceiling, to the roof terrace. Without hesitation Raphael headed towards the elevator. He checked the time – 17:16 – and stepped on to the elevator platform, pressing the button on the console – *Terrace.*

Machinery murmured softly as Raphael moved upwards, passing the mezzanine, through dark deep void between ceiling and roof, before emerging in an air-conditioned conservatory in the sky. Again, the limited furnishings, two easy chairs, one occasional table, reinforced the premise that this was a man who valued his privacy, was not one given to entertaining; to the vagaries of unprofitable socialising, and had bigger things on his mind. Moving from the platform towards the west side of the building, he waved his right hand across his face. This action caused a glass door to slide open, and Raphael stepped out onto the roof terrace, and out in to the 34°C late afternoon heat.

On the spacious terrace, a swimming pool, devoid of water, a glass enclosed, air-conditioned, gymnasium, equipment as yet unwrapped, changing rooms and showers, and an outdoor cooking range, with barbecue, all unused, expressed the lack of leisure time enjoyed by a man whose life was his work. At the same time, though, he displayed all the trappings of the elite and the powerful, and the wealthy. Vice-Superus Antinori fell into those three categories, being amongst the top five most influential people in the European Federal Republic of Nations, and many of the residents of 'La Tour de la Croix', fell into at least one of those categories, though none wielded as much power as the Vice-Superus – he was, effectively, four steps away, bar an election, from holding the office of the president of EFRON.

The complex was just over two years old, and though Raphael had purchased the penthouse when new, he had only occupied it for the last four weeks. At the end of every working day, if ever there was an end to his working day, during those four weeks, he had returned home at around the same time, heading straight to the roof, creating a repetitive pattern – the same actions, at the same time, in the same place, every day, as if deliberate drawing attention to himself. Once again he checked the time – 17:18 – and then headed towards the most southerly part of the building, where the structure curved to form the shape of the bow of a ship.

Behind him a two and a half metre high wall, the width of the apartment from east to west, afforded seclusion from the communal rooftop amenities, none of which he had ever entertained – the public swimming pool, the bar and restaurant, and the running and cycling tracks which circumnavigated the top of the entire complex, linking all four towers, on all points of the compass. Though there was access from the private terrace to all the shared facilities, this door, too, had never been used. Raphael came to a halt at the southern end of the complex, above his apartment and, resting his hands on the waist high rail, he peered out over the edge.

The bow shaped end of the terrace protruded beyond the apartments, creating a geometric pattern, where all balconies on all levels lined up beyond the edge of the leisure and shopping facilities at the base of the building. And there, lapping at the foundations of the south side, an artificial lake, some two kilometres wide, and eight kilometres long. Six lane highways, winding black ribbons, ran along either side of the water feature, 580 metres below Raphael's vantage point. From those major roads smaller roads, like veins from arteries, connected, via a twist of off-ramps, and junctions, to urbanisations, where villas and townhouses clustered together on the brown, yellow and caramel-coloured landscape, dotted with the green of conifers and palms. Hugging the lakeside, larger, imposing, villas, each with a mooring and landing stage, yachts present, or out sailing, indicated the wealth in this region.

Vice-Superus Antinori was afforded a 180 degree panorama, reaching some 80 kilometres in three directions – south, west and east – of the Territories and Provinces de la Belgique. In the foreground, some six kilometres further south of the lake, the town of Namur shimmered, and the La Meuse River glimmered in the sunlight and heat of the June afternoon. From this high point in Cortil-Wodon – the fifth tallest building in the territory – in the west, Raphael could clearly see Lille, on the coast, and the orange haze above the Chanel de

155

Europa. But for the obstruction created by the western tower block, Bruxelles, in the North West, would be visible on such a clear day, and Raphael would be able to pick out the pan-pipe shaped edifice housing the offices of Genetikos, and the political nerve centre of EFRON. To the east, on the western edge of Liege, the massive Hyperion power station, and, everywhere, far below, the glistening termite-like traffic, and the ant-like people, going about their day-to-day repetitive lives, moved in orderly fashion, in ordered lines, from one place to another, fulfilling their expectations. Raphael had his expectations and, again, checked the time – 17:26.

"Soon," he muttered into the air. "Soon."

He studied the horizon, to the south, as if searching for something, and then stood for another five minutes, staring into the distance. It was as if he was waiting for something, and he had waited this way every afternoon for four weeks – waiting for something, or someone. At 17:31 the waiting was over.

Behind him the air crackled, audibly – a bubble-wrap orchestra – and static electricity caused his hair to rise slightly, and his sense of smell picked up a hint of ozone in the air. And when the brief flurry of activity ceased the Vice-Superus turned away from the view.

"I've been expecting you," he said, eyeing the white-clad figure standing before him. "Yes. I have been expecting you."

An awkward silence followed, and neither person moved, for what seemed like an eternity, though it was, in reality, less than 15 seconds. Raphael spoke again, the visitor remaining silent behind the visor of the crash helmet.

"Okay. My turn again," he said, with a hint of sarcasm, hands clasped behind his back, taking one large step forward to close the metre gap between them.

"First question," he continued, raising his gaze to stare into his reflection in the gloss-black mirrored visor. "How did you breach security? Friends in very high places? Yes. Unfair. That is two questions. Take your time."

The silent white figure took a step backwards, yet Raphael remained fixed to the spot.

"So tell me," he demanded. "What happens now? Do me the honour of informing me of my fate. I think I have a right to know."

The helmeted head tilted a little to the right, a show of surprise at the words uttered by the Vice-Superus, a man seemingly so calm and collected in the face of potential adversity. Then the white-gloved hands of the spectral figure rose, clamping on either side of the helmet, and lifting it clear, exposed the face of Augustin Le Feuvre – there was little doubt of his intent, having revealed his identity.

"Thank you. Thank you, Monsieur Le Feuvre. Now my fate is clear. But why?"

"I have my orders," he answered, grasping his helmet in his right hand at his side. "You are seen as a threat to the natural order of things. You are not to be trusted."

"And you are right not to trust everybody. Doubt is good. Doubt is healthy ..."

"... Clever," Le Feuvre interrupted. "Don't play mind games. Please treat me with respect."

"Of course. Of course. I apologise. But answer me one final question. Would you be willing to listen to what I might offer you? Help me and I could be Superus. Would you consider changing your allegiance?"

A slight pause followed, somewhat less than 10 seconds this time, before Raphael spoke again.

"No. I thought not," he shrugged. "Well. Let's get this over and done with. Time to die," he yelped, throwing his arms out wide. "Time to die.."

Le Feuvre appeared somewhat confused and, again, a little surprised, by the reaction of this man to his pending fate – a man facing death; welcoming death. Suddenly, the Vice-Superus jumped forwarded, grabbing Augustin in a crab-like pincer grip, wrapping his arms around the prospective assassin. The crash helmet clattered on the surface of the roof terrace, skidding some distance behind Le Feuvre, as Raphael toe-punted it with his left foot. A brief wrestling match ensued, Antinori attempting to maintain the bear-hug on a trained soldier, and killer – a member of the Elite Guard, and both knew it was only a matter of time before the status quo was re-established.

Sure enough the stronger, fitter, younger man broke free of the hold, pushing Raphael backwards, until the older man came to rest, staggering slightly, near the safety rail. The soldier raised his left arm, pointing towards his quarry. Curling the fingers of left hand into a fist stimulated activity from his uRAPP – a silver pencil-shaped object protruded.

"I am sorry to have to do this," Le Feuvre mumbled. "Truly. I am sorry."

"No. Not like this," Antinori screamed, in the face of death, raising his arms above his head as a sign of surrender.

Augustin Le Feuvre hesitated, and did not immediately release the trigger on his sonic impulse weapon. In that moment Raphael placed his right hand over his left wrist, stepped backwards against the rail, tipping himself over the edge of the roof – a diver on a high board at a swimming pool, but with a 580 metre drop to the water below. The last Le Feuvre saw of the Vice-Superus were the soles of his shoes, as he disappeared from view.

"Mierde," Augustin barked. "Mierde"!

Momentarily, he appeared at a loss as what to do next – move forward and observe the fatal fall, perhaps, to be seen by anyone watching the body plunge towards the lake, or pick up his helmet and vacate the scene of the incident immediately?

'Target eliminated. One way or another. Objective achieved."

# Chapter 16

High above the ground, some 320 kilometres; that measure being taken from the centre of the Earth, not the equator, a geostationary satellite – Ptolemy ZX5412 – focused on events of particular interest, triggered by an illicit, unwarranted, undeclared quantum leap, and the complete shutdown of a life system. Both persons of interest were connected to, and recognised by, computer chips aboard the extra-terrestrial vehicle, due their importance in the order of things that mattered, in the region of EFRON monitored by ZX5412. The two events occurred in the same proximity, within a short time-frame – suspicious activity. A large telescopic lens adjusted focus, and zoomed in the on the rooftop of the Celtic cross shape complex, far below.

In lower Earth orbit ZX5412 had responsibility for surveying territories of EFRON from Apeldoom, in the north west of the Territories of Nederlandia, including the coastal conurbations/urbanisations of Utrecht, Tilburg, Turnhout, Antwerp, Ghent, and Ypres, to Saint-Quentin in the south, Maastricht and Nimegan in the east, and all territories and regions inside that perimeter. The powerful magic eye, the lens, focused on the signals being emitted from coordinates 50° 34' Nord 4° 56' Est, and recorded the data on two different pieces of software, and each piece of software had its own special agenda.

The unauthorised, unregistered, movement of Augustin Le Feuvre had been recorded by software installed on ZX 5412 by Genetikos Orological Defence Systems; only accessed by personnel subject to the highest security clearances; Level 1; – there being fewer than 10 people in the whole of EFRON with that privilege.

The software, aboard the satellite, opened a file – Save As: Le Feuvre. Augustin. ZX5412/ Genetikos Orological Defence Systems: L1c/ 20062198/ 17:31:32/ 17:37:12/ UQL.

The movements of the two men were being recorded, from the moment shortly after Le Feuvre had appeared on the roof terrace, until the other man tipped himself backward over the rail, yet the system did not have time to recognise the individual, due to lack of data, and his untimely death. Le Feuvre was then chronicled moving around in a figure of eight, as if confused, before collecting his helmet – placing that on his head, and then tapping instructions into the uRAPP, he vanished.

All the activity had been recorded, saved to file by ZX5412, on the Genetikos software. And then – *Error 606: File name: Le Feuvre. Augustin. ZX5412/ Genetikos Orological Defence Systems: L1c/ 20062198/ 17:31:32/ 17:37:12/ UQL: DELETED. System override. Data erased.* And, so, the incident was forgotten; the recording having been eradicated, even though such data may be retrieved by those who know what they are seeking, and where to look. To the untrained eye, though, the data no longer existed – some things are best kept secret – that was the plan; all illicit movement, subterfuge, and unregistered quantum movement, on the part of anyone working undercover on the instructions of the Superus, subsequently recorded, would be deleted, ignored, and the very existence of any inappropriate activity, and actions, denied.

But, the other piece of software, with a different agenda, had recorded, and filed, the same incident, albeit from a different perspective, and for other reasons, because the differences did not stop there – access to information denied to only those with the ultimate security clearance; Level 1AA, of which there are only three people living, privileged enough to receive such data, and two those afforded Level 1AA authorisation were not included on the list of the ten names given Level 1 clearance by Genetikos. That aside, two of the persons afforded the higher level clearance were not even aware of their status, nor the highly secretive unknown, unnamed organisation, consisting of one person, with one purpose in mind – to serve, and administer, Code Delta One-Five. The chosen two, potential recipients of secret data, were also unaware of their future place, and obligations, in the scheme of things.

There was yet another major difference in the way in which the two pieces of software performed their tasks. The Genetikos software responded to a specific incident, recording any unregistered quantum leaps, though not normally given to deleting the data it had recorded – such did not happen often; only in circumstances where those in positions of power dictated this order; most likely to protect their own interests. Corrupted software!

The other piece of software, unnamed, had been primed to serve Code Delta One-Five, a top secret, high security level, failsafe programme, and had been recording events on the roof terrace from around the same time in the afternoon, 17:17, and not just that day, for the past few weeks, immediately upon receiving the 'positional' signal from the uRAPP belonging to Raphael Antinori, every time he stepped out on to the roof. Nothing had happened on any of the previous afternoons, and the Vice-Superus had just stood, staring out at the surrounding countryside, for around 30 minutes, each day, as if he was waiting for something to happen – and he was patient. The software, also, was patient, and the patience was rewarded – an event worthy of recording.

From the moment Raphael had exited the elevator, on the roof terrace, to the point at which the shadowy figure disappeared beneath the ripples in the lake far below, at the base of the building, the software had recorded every movement, and every interaction between the two men, lacking only the ability to record the sound of the conversation; albeit capable of synthesising, and recording, lip-reading in 40 different languages, idioms, and dialects.

Another difference, separating the two pieces of software, was that the data related to Code Delta One-Five, having been recorded, analysed, and stored, was not deleted. Nothing was deleted, though information was disseminated with a view to the three recipients collecting data appropriate to their individual 'need to know basis', and level of trust, in view of the person in charge of the unnamed 'organisation of one', plus the two recruits – unaware of their role, and their fate, until such a time they would receive the time-delayed message, and only one would receive the complete unabridged first edition, containing the' anomaly'. All recipients, though, would share the same brief obituary:

*File: ZX541221052148. Vice-Superus Antinori, Raphael. EFRON. Life extinct: 20.06.2198/ 17:35:15 seconds. Anomaly. Evaluate. Anomaly. Error report. Anomaly. Investigate. Life extinct. 20.06.2198/ 17:35:18 seconds. Anomaly. Final report. Ground zero impact: 20.06.2198/ 17:35:48 seconds. Life extinct: 20.06.2198/ 17:35:48 seconds. Anomaly. Error report.*

And then each report was sent, with a time-receive delay, though each of the three recipients would read an interpretation of the report appertaining to their needs, and level of security clearance. Tasks completed, the system went into sleep mode, and Ptolemy ZX5412 continued in Low Earth Orbit, measuring pollution levels, and monitoring the weather, and the movement of traffic, for media reports, and fulfilling a range of marketing related tasks, bought and paid for, by a variety of consumers and corporative entities.

# Chapter 17

Azarias turned the key, silencing the engine – the instruments on the varnished dashboard remained illuminated, casting an eerie glow upon his face, and the headlights forged sinister shadows in the shrubs and trees, on the perimeter of the Snowy Owl Public inn. He had parked at the farthest end, away from the road and the entrance.

Car headlights swung into the car park, halting adjacent to the main entrance of the public house. Two people exited the building and entered the back of the stationary vehicle, each using a separate door. Those doors closed simultaneously, with a dull, night-time, clunk. A brief pause, for confirmation of destination, and the vehicle, a taxi-cab, reversed into an empty parking space, before pulling forward to the edge of the road, where the red tail-lights splashed a blood-red glow on the walls and windows of the inn and nearby parked cars – and then it was gone, turning left, disappearing in a small cloud of exhaust fumes.

Azarias noted the time on the small inset analogue clock – 11:42. He was early – time to think, to reflect on the events of the last 28 hours or so. Soon, he would make his way to the meeting place, in the darkness, alone. Yet he felt no fear, in spite of the curious sequence of affairs since the previous Sunday evening, when he had left the company of Alan in a rush, inert memories having been awakened. Noting the outside temperature – 10°C – he killed the lights, turned the key to the final notch, removing it from the ignition, and sat, contemplating the trail that had led him to this place. He had questions buzzing around in his head – many questions.

*'What is she playing at? Why is she doing this? Going to all this trouble? Yeah. Perhaps, because she can. Because she wants to. Toying with me. Why? Why am I here? Why, why, why, why?'*

Hypnosis, the session with Alan, had played a part in bringing long lost memories to the fore – new memories that had been locked away and lain dormant for years. *'Was the hypnosis a trigger, or was that a coincidence, and would those memories have surfaced anyway, when the time was right?'* If the hypnosis had played a part then those words, *"When the time is right,"* may have had a major role in catapulting him out of the chair in Alan's home, leading him to this place, at this time.

\*\*\*

Azarias had departed in a hurry, with very little comment, Alan following him to the garden gate. A memory, of which he had not previous recollection, had provided answers to some of the questions he had been asking himself – the main ones being, *'Who is she? What does she want with me?'* Suddenly, though, as if the knowledge had always been there, locked away deep inside, he knew some of the answers – he was aware that, at some point, in that disco-bar, she had given him a small box-like object. He knew that he had that box, somewhere, in his possession. It was weird. He felt that he had a new memory, of which he had no memory!

On the journey from South Shields, and Alan's home, to his home in Cramlington, Azarias had ignored every speed limit, criss-crossing the double white lines in the Tyne Tunnel as he passed slower moving 'Sunday drivers' during his race to reach his home, as if in fear that the newly remembered memory might fade, or be forgotten, before reaching his front door. In his excited state, and haste, he narrowly missed crashing through the up-and-over door of the garage, attached to the semi-detached property, stopping a few centimetres short of the white painted portal. And then Azarias had struggled with the key in the Yale lock, delaying access to his home, but once inside as strange series of events began to unfold.

Entering the key code, Azarias silenced the beeping sound the alarm made when the door was first opened; a limited time before disturbing the quiet of the neighbourhood, but he was not greeted with silence. *Ping, ping, ping* – a two beat pause – *ping, ping, ping* – same pause – *ping, ping, ping* – repetition – a regular spaced high pitched signal – *ping, ping, ping* – silence – *ping, ping, ping.* Coming from upstairs, the sound grew louder, yet muffled, as if the source was hidden – wrapped up in a bundle or secreted in a box. He thought he recognised the sound, yet was confused as to why –

167

that new remembered memory thing, again. And then he made his way up the varnished wooden staircase, leading from the open plan lounge/diner, heading in the direction of the sound.

The screaming rhythmic pulse appeared to be coming from the study – in reality, the third and smallest bedroom – and the sound was growing louder, more intense, and, potentially, penetrating the party wall of the 1970s built semi. Opening the door to the bedroom cum study his eyes scanned the bookshelves to his immediate right, then the large desk, with shelving and cupboards, to his left, with the scrutiny once employed in a previous life; when he was 'in the job', at the scene of a crime or searching for a suspect in a sea of faces. He knew where the sound was coming from – the built-in cupboard above the stairs.

His ears were beginning to hurt – the screaming, pinging, beeping, sound had reached the pain barrier; somewhere in the region of 125 decibels, at the moment Azarias opened the cupboard. A wave of sound, without pause, akin to standing close to the jet engine of a 747 at the moment of take-off, shook the hidden contents of the cupboard, the bookshelves and the desk, and rattled the window.

"Shit! Shit!" he hissed, pulling diverse objects from the knee-high mezzanine shelf, throwing the detritus of modern living onto a heap under the window, near the filing cabinet – all that ever changing technology, upgraded through purchases of the latest models – fads – and deleted by virtue of abandonment in a dark hole; a crypt or mausoleum to the obsolete, the least required objects potential fodder for landfill sites:

*Two Berghaus rucksacks, hardly used. Three compact digital cameras, still in the original boxes – Nikon, Samsung, Sony! One defunct laptop. An unused Acer Notebook. A laptop backpack – a good idea purchase at the time, though never used.* – Ears hurting, temples throbbing. *Then, the wedding photograph boxed set. A box containing the wedding shoes; slightly scuffed, with grass stains on the sides.* – Tears rolling from his eyes; pain, memories, or both? *Picnic rug, Picnic set. An unopened duvet set. 'Cuddly toy'. A selection of some twelve box files, containing the essays and dissertations of two university graduates; outdated, outmoded, and unneeded undergraduate pretensions – totally irrelevant all these many years after the event – yet, for some reason, saved for posterity.* All of it – everything – heaped on the floor. The cupboard, though, was not yet empty, but it was silent.

The sound had ceased. Silence fell, apart from the ringing in his ears, the barking of neighbourhood dogs, awakened by the unusual, loud, high-pitched intrusion, and the beating of his heart. Yet, there was something else, unseen, and almost imperceptible – a gentle buzz, and rattle, like a mobile phone vibrating on a solid metallic surface. And there it was, in the far right hard corner of the cupboard – a large Jacob's cracker tin; a possible relic from some Christmas past. The tin shook, and jumped a little, and Azarias imagined it was calling to him, the buzzing a song in his head; '*pick me up, open me up, look inside*', it sang to him.

Azarias obliged, first taking the tin in both hands, with the care of handling a new-born, transporting it to the main bedroom, where it stopped vibrating and rattling. Placing the tin on the king size bed he carefully removed the lid. A white throbbing light caused shadows to dance on his face, casting ghostly shadows around his eyes, and upon the ceiling. Though the sound had ceased, and the shaking had stopped, an almost blinding light flashed in time with the beating of his heart. In a corner of the cracker tin, on top of a pile of charcoal and pastel drawn sketches, Azarias noted a matchbox sized object, of some indeterminable solid matter, which emitted an unfeasible white incandescent pulsing glow.

Resisting the temptation to reach in and grab the object, Azarias touched all four sides of the tin with the back of his right hand, perhaps to detect the danger of potential burning. That being a cause for concern, surely, though, the sketch paper would, in the very least, scorch, if not ignite, and combust. Yet the brilliant white light produced no heat. The sides of the tin were cold – the only warmth being from his hands when he carried the tin from one room to the next. Lifting the cracker tin above his head Azarias even examined the underside of the container, as if he might find a switch, or some other mechanism, which controlled the light. *'What is it? How does it work?'* Nothing. No batteries. No switch. No wires. Absolutely nothing. When he looked inside again the 'disco light' had stopped – no sound, no movement, no light; just a dull lead-coloured cuboid, the size of a matchbox, atop a selection of sketches and portraits. *'Curious.'*

And then his Blackberry cried out for attention – twice – once to signal the receipt of an email, the second to signify the arrival of SMS. *'Coincidence? Pick this up or read the messages? Pick it up. Remember!'* It was cool to the touch. *'Unusually heavy. Dense.'* A solid mass, devoid of seams, gaps, or joins, which he examined closely, turning it around and around in his hands, holding it up to the light. The Blackberry called to him again, then again, again, and again, and again – email and SMS. Again, and again, and again, until he pressed the illuminated roller ball and called up the messages symbol. Again, and again, and again, he read the same message numerous times, in the emails and the SMS messages – *'Keep it with you at all times. Follow all future instructions. The time is right. Soon. Saluki.'*

"This?" he whispered, analysing the object at eye level.

His Blackberry signalled the arrival of other messages – another text and another email – each with the same content; one word – *'Yes.'* Azarias laughed.

"Ask a silly question," he muttered. "I'm guessing that you have hacked into my mobile, and that you can hear me."

Nothing, No more messages. Quiet. He stared at the phone for some thirty seconds, as if some latent psychic power, or mind control, might cause a response to that last comment. But there was nothing – no more messages.

Placing the mobile phone and the object on the bed, to the side of the cracker tin, he lifted out the sketches –

eight in all. Five were of him, captured at various stages during his formative years, dated and signed by his mother – *Iona* – the other three were of the same man; his father he had always assumed. Azarias had almost forgotten that the sketches existed, having been hidden from view at the back of the cupboard for many years. The sketches of Azarias, in charcoal, four of them slightly smudged, with rubbing against each other, were, mostly, of head and shoulders, two being full length, in school uniform and one wearing his favourite football kit, with ball under his right arm; the latter showing a date – *May 1984*. Though it was in monochrome he remembered well those days when he used to follow Watford football club – still does – and that year was peak of the Graham Taylor years. His team was due to meet Everton in the F.A. Cup final at Wembley. Azarias had not posed for the sketches but remembered the photographs from which the sketches had been copied.

"We were robbed," he mumbled, studying the footballer sketch. "That second goal should never have been allowed. Gray fouled Sherwood. Knocked the ball out of his hands. Referee! Turning point of the game. Aye. The glory days."

Dropping that sketch on to the bed he picked up the collection of other images, and this was all he had ever seen of the man he knew to be his father. He had never met him, not even seen photographs of him. The likenesses of the man who would be father were captured in charcoal on two of the drawings, and in colourful pastels on the other. The name *Raphael* had been scribed on each portrait. *Raphael.*

Azarias knew very little about him, and had suspected, across the years, that his father had been married, with a family, leading a double life, or had something else to hide – *'undercover cop, or subject to a witness protection scheme',* the previous world, in the job, voice inside his head whispered. His mother, in her later years, prior to her death, had referred to his father as an *'angel'* – a play on his name, perhaps; the angel Raphael who, not actually recognised in the Bible, is an archangel of Judaism, Christianity and Islam. *'Something to do with healing.'* Perhaps it had been as much to do with the effects of her mental condition, at that time – all that *angel* talk, and his father never appearing to age each time he visited, which he appeared to have done – visiting her, but not his son! He had never once set on eyes on the man his mother claimed was his father.

Examining the face, staring back at him from the paper, Azarias absorbed all the detail, much the way he did, way back, when he was in the job – that other life – looking at a sketch, or E-Fit, of a potential suspect, or that of a victim. Azarias noted the pale complexion, framed by the dark brown hair, which dropped down to the angular jawline, and the contrast between the thin red, tightly closed, lips, and the emerald green eyes, capped with the dark bushy brooding brows.

*'Those eyes. No! Coincidence. A lot of people share the same eye colouring. Don't they?'*

Azarias dismissed the thought, even though he imagined that he had seen those eyes somewhere before, and replaced all of the sketches in the Jacob's Cracker tin, firmly pushing the lid into place. Resting the tin carefully on the floor, and settling down upon the bed, head raised by four pillows, he placed the strange object on the bedside table, and kicked off his shoes. *'Fucking knackered!'* Relaxing on top of the quilt Azarias attempted to gather his butterfly thoughts, to settle his mind in one place, and decide which of the many messages on the Blackberry he was going to delete.

*'Curious,'* he thought, lifting the Blackberry to his face, as he began deleting the list of repetitive messages. *'Curiouser and Curiouser!'*

A few minutes later he drifted into a comfortable sleep, his heavy lids drooping, and chin on his chest, only to awaken with a start, to the sound of the pre-programmed early morning alarm call, blaring out from the Blackberry. Confused, disorientated, and drooling from the right side of his mouth, Azarias picked up the phone, placing it against his right ear, as if answering a call.

"Hello?" he mumbled, rubbing his eyes and squeezing his nostrils together with forefinger and thumb, suddenly realising his error. "Shit! Shit, shit, shit, fuckety shit," he exclaimed, recognising the fact that he was answering his early morning alarm call – *06:15* – he had slept right through. Silencing the alarm, he cursed himself once more before sitting up on the edge of the bed. "Fuck!"

***

A creature of habit – repetitive, anal, OCD, *whatever* – Azarias sat in his car, in the car park at the college, using his thumbs, he typed into his mobile phone: *'Arrived. Love you always. X'* just as he had done all of his married life, and every working day during the past four years, since the death of his wife. And, then, as always, he pressed *'Send'*, though Theresa had not responded to the messages from his Blackberry in a long time, but that did not deter Aazrias from attempting to communicate with the dead.

"Why do I do this? Why?" he asked himself, talking aloud. "Why am I doing this? You have been dead a long time. I'm sorry, but that's the truth. Why can't I move on? I'll tell you why. Guilt. That's why. My fault."

He looked at his reflection in the rear view mirror, his eyes accusing the image staring back at him.

"You. It's your fault. If not for you she would be alive today. And her brother. The common denominator? You. Fuckwit!"

Azarias slapped at the top of his head, in anger, with both hands, on both sides, cursing himself for being the only survivor – wife, brother-in-law, and mother, all dead. The knocking became audible – bang, bang, and bang – in his ears, and inside his head; but it was not inside his head. The knocking was coming from outside the car, a hammering on the driver's window. And there was Alan, his owl face peering through the glass, tap, tap, tapping with his knuckles, loud enough to awake Azarias from his self-pitying torpor. Releasing the ignition key, depressing the boot release mechanism, he then opened the car door, causing Alan to step sideways, and backwards, towards the rear passenger door.

"You had me worried," Alan started, before Azarias had even exited the Rover. "Taking off like that."

Following Azarias to the back of the car, where he collected his shoulder bag, and an armful of yellow exercise books, Alan sucked at his saliva as he continued expressing his point of view, and his concern.

"I was locked out of the house. Not your fault, of course. Had to wait for my wife," he mumbled, stumbling through his words, as they walked from the car park towards the college. "Anyway, that is not important. You left in a hurry. Unfinished business. I was concerned. What with you coming out from under the hypnosis like that. Very worried, to say the least. I was going to call you but you are ex-directory. And I seem to have misplaced your mobile number. Might have deleted it by mistake. At least you are safe. Are you okay? I was …"

"Alan," he cut in, "I'm okay. I'm fine. Absolutely fine. Got time for a coffee? I'll bring you up to speed. I owe you that."

Locating a table some distance away from students, colleagues, and prying ears, they sat opposite each other with their coffee – a large Americano for Azarias, a regular Cappuccino for Alan. The voice of Paloma Faith, singing *'Only Love can Hurt Like This'*, drifted across the airport terminal-like space of the refectory, booming from the LCD television, tuned to Century FM radio, as the tale of the previous evening unfolded, complete with apologies for appearing so ungrateful by running out like that.

"So, that's about it," Azarias said, sipping at his coffee. "It would appear that she is not a figment of my imagination. And," he continued, as he reached into his shoulder bag, removing the cold, lifeless, leaden lump and placing it on the round table, between them, "There is this."

"What is it?" Alan enquired, leaning forward for a closer examination of the object, keeping his arms at his side, as if fearing to touch it, in case it should do him some harm.

Azarias shrugged his shoulders, and turned the cuboid around, and over, like someone attempting to solve a Rubik's cube, affording a view of all sides.

"I don't know. It has done nothing since the noise, and the flashing lights, of last night. I also have this. Came in while I was I driving. Read it."

Handing Alan the Blackberry, Azarias produced a scrap of paper from within his bag, along with a Bic biro, and began scratching out a note. Alan studied the screen on the Blackberry, before speaking.

"Can I come with you? I would like to see where this is going."

Azarias slipped the note across the table, placing the forefinger of his right hand to his lips, signalling silence. Alan turned the scrap of paper 180° and read the following:

'Phone might be hacked or bugged. Careful what you say.'

"Actually," Alan added, immediately taking on the conspiratorial role of the spy, "I'm busy tonight. I can't come with you."

Azarias winked, sipped at his coffee, before scribbling another message, and handing that across the table – to anyone watching the pair, they might have appeared as a newly met couple passing love notes to each other. The paper, though, did not contain words of amour but, merely, a reference to Azarias following Alan to The Rose Tree – he had never been to the public house before, and needed help to find the place. *'Enter separately. Me first. Allow a few minutes. We don't know each other! Wait and observe. Leave separately.'* He felt that Alan deserved the opportunity to be 'in on the kill', as it were. Azarias retrieved his Blackberry and read the SMS again –

*'The Rose Tree. Shincliffe. Monday May 19 2014. 17:35. Sit at table next to radiator, beneath cricket painting, facing entrance door. No other table. Answer the mobile device and follow all instructions. Keep the device with you at all times.'*

"Why?" Azarias sighed. "Why are you doing this?"

"Me?" Alan responded.

"No. Not you. Just thinking out loud," he answered, pointing at the screen of his mobile phone. "Are you okay with that?"

Nodding an affirmative, with his thumbs up, Alan added, "It will only take twenty minutes."

"Well, better get on. People to see, places to go, fish to fry," Azarias said, kicking back the chair with his right heel, and standing, giving another conspiratorial wink, before finishing with, "Busy day?"

\*\*\*

17:21 – Azarias walked in to the entrance lobby of The Rose Tree public house, in Shincliffe. Directly in front of him, a plain wooden door, with a Yale lock, was closed – probably leading to upstairs accommodation. To his left, an open door into a room, with tables set for diners, in darkness perhaps ready for the serving of evening meals. On his right another door, top half glazed, lower half panelled, through which he noticed a few people seated. He pushed this door and entered the bar, scanning the surroundings, much as he did, 'back in the day', when he was 'in the job' – his old life – when he was surveying the scene of a crime for clues, or searching for a face in a crowd. That same old, same old! *'Some things never change. Part of the programming. Remove the human chip and replace it with the, well ...'* Once a copper, always a copper! After all, that was what he was doing – scanning the bar, the people, for anything that stood out from the normal, something odd, threatening, or dangerous, but there was no one in the bar instantly recognisable in his memory bank of faces.

An initial assessment of the situation, the bar, revealed two couples, all in his immediate eye-line, all with drinks to hand, no one evident behind the bar, and a slim glass, containing a fresh drink, on the bar top, closed to the table where he had been instructed to sit – *'Whose drink is that? Someone gone to the toilet? What if they want that table? Get the table. Fast. Follow the instructions. Perhaps drink belongs to person behind the bar.'* As he made his way towards the table he made mental observations about the other customers, one couple, probably in their mid-sixties, occupying a cushioned bench seat, to his right, beneath the front window. *'Real ale for him, white wine for her',* he guessed. Old habits! Old habits were beginning to kick in – a mystery to solve.

The other couple, most likely in their thirties – *'Very touchy feely. Lot of eye contact. Still getting to know each other. Not together too long. Too involved. No threat.'* – They sat next to each other on another bench seat, at a right angle to where the older couple sat, backs to the window which looked out on to the car park. *'Pint and a half of lager.'* He surmised that the two couples posed no threat, and that they were not why he was there. They made no attempt to acknowledge Azarias as he continued on his way to the chosen table, weaving around to the left, alongside the bar.

There was a country farmhouse feel, such was the style, colour, and design of the bar, and the fittings – a touch of the 'Laura Ashley', with the powder blue painted of the three metre long bar, with inset floral designed ceramic tiles above the optics, and below the bar top. At the far end, set back on the bar surface, a frighteningly strange object – a model of a park bench, with a hideous, nightmarish, figurine of Olive Hardy, sat alongside an even more horrendous Paul Robeson/Louis

Armstrong-type model; almost Black and White Minstrel-ish! *'A conversation piece, if nothing else!'*

Opposite the bar, along the length of the wall, three other square tables, apart from the one Azarias was about to occupy. Each of these tables had two chairs, facing one another on either side. The first of those tables hid a brick built fireplace, with an empty hearth. Sitting in the appropriately chosen chair, Azarias studied the print of the painting of a cricket field. And then he remembered why he was there – *'Answer the mobile device. What mobile device?'* he caught movement, behind the bar, out of the corner of his eye. *'No threat.'*

Wearing a crisp sky blue shirt, khaki tie, beige coloured chinos, razor-sharp creases, and brown brogues, a man with well coiffured grey-white hair, and Amalfi tan, was in an alcove, which appeared to separate one bar from the other, housing the till, a telephone, pen, pencils, and restaurant order pads. Space was limited, particularly for anyone above 1.8 metres – confirming the first thought about the closed door leading to upstairs accommodation. *'How many people have cracked their skulls on the underside of those stairs? Must happen. Particularly when they are busy. Tearing here, running there, and taking orders, serving drinks. Lack of concentration. Crack!'* The man behind the bar turned from his task beneath the stairs and greeted his new customer with a porcelain white smile.

"Hello," began, looking first the unattended glass of coca cola, or coke and something, in the event that it had been mixed with alcohol, before looking left than right, and placing a few coins on the bar, close to the glass. "Must have nipped to the loo. What can I get you?"

Azarias had studied the four taps, near the entrance – *'artificial' gassy beers and lagers* – when he had entered the bar. Around the corner, a Coca Cola dispenser, and three real ale pumps. It took less than 30 seconds to make a decision.

"Half of Black Sheep please."

The glass of ale was delivered quickly and Azarias handed over a five pound note recently removed from his wallet. While waiting for his change he claimed the table, beneath the cricket print, placing his Blackberry and drink on the side where he had been ordered to sit – facing the door. He collected his change and, without checking it, buried the coins in his left trouser pocket. Azarias then sat on the chair and took a sip from the glass, making a hum of approval as the ale slipped across his taste buds and down his throat. *'Nice beer. No signal,'* he thought, looking at the screen on his mobile phone. *'Odd.'* A polite attention-seeking cough invited him to look up at the man behind the bar.

"You will be lucky to pick up a signal in here, and in the rest of the village. The village that time forgot," he chuckled.

"Really?" Azarias queried, somewhat surprised, if not perplexed. – *'And I'm waiting for someone to potentially make contact on a mobile phone. Where there is no signal. Why?'*

"Yes," the host continued, even if Azarias was not completely attentive to his complaint, "I own both of the

182

pubs in Shincliffe. The other one is around the corner. To the right. An inn. Bed and breakfast. I have lost potential repeat business because of the poor signal. Well, no signal. If they are trying to conduct business and can't make contact, they go elsewhere next time they need to come to Durham. Why should they come back?"

"Why indeed?" Azarias responded, just to be polite, before mumbling to himself, holding the Blackberry above his head, "So, how does this work then?"

He wondered whether any of the people in the bar might be in on the secret, part of some conspiracy, but dismissed the thought – they all appeared too normal, and ordinary. It was then that he noticed the strange thing about the plate racks above the entrance door and the front windows – no plates, no jugs; none of the usual pub paraphernalia was on display. Instead, the long narrow pelmet shelves contained lines of old mobile phones – a large variety of models, some, perhaps, fifteen years old. Azarias counted them, without making it look too obvious – *'About 70 old discarded mobile phones. Bizarre.'*

"Great," he grumbled, with a sense of irony, nodding with his eyes to Alan, who was approaching the bar, pretending not to know his friend – *"Look. Behind you,"* Azarias mouthed, pantomime fashion. Alan turned, noting the display of unwanted technology, returning to Azarias with a wink and an ironic smile – *'Pretend you don't know him. Get a drink. Normal stuff. Sit there, behind him. Observe. Nothing more. Just observe.'*

Azarias listened to Alan ordering – also a half of 'Sheep', and the manager referencing the woman who had still not returned to claim her drink, or her change. *"Nowhere to be seen. Odd. Cannot still be in the toilet. Must check."*

"Perhaps she has gone for a bus," Alan offered, paying for his ale, admiring the dark coloured liquid, and white froth, settling in the glass sitting on the bar. "I saw the bus stop over the way. Perhaps she came in to kill time. Realised the bus was due. Puff! Gone."

"Perhaps," well-coiffured man responded. "Still, I will leave it there. Just in case."

Alan carried his drink to the table directly behind Azarias, so that he was looking at the back of his comrade's head. He was facing in the same direction, with an eye on the entrance, watching for the unusual; anything out of the ordinary. But nothing much happened for a brief period of time.

The man behind the bar placed the unclaimed drink, and the pile of coins, behind the bar, beneath the optics. The couple in their sixties sipped at their drinks, staring ahead, without a word uttered to each other – their many years of marriage having enabled them to communicate telepathically, and the younger couple seemingly sang, cooed, and, metaphorically speaking, danced their love for each other – their expectations for the future. The anticipated and the expected. Yes, the expected. And anything that might have been expected was shot down in the flames – fourteen minutes after Azarias had entered the bar the unexpected happened.

*The thing about the unexpected is that it is not easy to prepare for, in spite of what any motivational speaker or sales training manager would have people believe. It is possible to prepare for the expected as, by virtue of the term, we may expect the expected. But the unexpected? That is another matter. Can anyone really prepare for the unexpected? Does it make sense if someone tells you to expect the unexpected? Prepare for the unexpected!*

Certainly no one was prepared for what was about to happened but that is what one might expect from the unexpected.

All of the mobile phones, on the strange plate rack display, above the front door and windows, burst into life.

At first the screens illuminated, and then the phones began to buzz, vibrate, and shake, before emitting a variety of ring tones. Those people sitting beneath the display lifted themselves to their feet, surprised, stepping back to view the scene, and avoid a few of the phones that fell, bouncing on, and off, the cushioned bench seats. The older woman gasped, and mumbled and grumbled – something about *'a dangerous and disgraceful trick.'* Perhaps she had not had much to complain about recently, and maybe be she enjoyed complaining. As a contrast, the younger couple appeared to find the situation amusing, maybe wondering if they were being filmed by hidden cameras for some reality *'Candid Camera'* television programme. The man behind the bar stood, hands on hips, safe on his side of the counter, aghast, mouth hanging open. All those dead mobile phones, alive, ringing, vibrating, flashing, some tumbling and falling from the shelf – *'How is this possible?'*

Azarias had also lifted himself to his feet, turning to look at Alan, confused – both shrugged their shoulders.

"What am I supposed to," Azarias whispered. "Which phone? Answer the device. Keep the device. Follow the instructions. Which one?"

Azarias placed his hands firmly on the table as he attempted to push himself to his full height, in order to get a better view. It was then that he felt the vibration coming up through the table, his ears picking up the interment buzzing sound, beneath him. A rattling, steady buzz, with brief intervals between the vibrations. Placing the palm of his left hand flat on the table top Azarias verified that it was not in his imagination – something really was vibrating beneath his hand, under the table. *'Clever. Don't get it. But, very entertaining.'*

Sitting back on the seat, with all the commotion at the front of the bar distracting everyone, Azarias reached under the table, groping for what he imagined might be hiding there, with his right hand.

"Yep, this must be what I'm looking for," he muttered, attracting Alan's attention with a nod of his head, accentuating the fact that something was hidden under the table. Using his fingernails he picked away at some tape, which was securing a solid object in place, eventually producing a ripping sound from the parcel tape as he peeled it away from the wood, catching the vibrating metallic object in his left hand once it had been freed from strictures holding it in place. Bringing his hand from under the table he produced an old Motorola RAZR V3, but not just any old Motorola RAZR V3, but as Azarias recognised, his previous mobile phone – the one thrown into a draw, and no longer used. And it was now vibrating in his hand. He couldn't even remember where he had stored it, so long was it since he had last used the phone. Yet, he now held it in his hand. *'How is this possible?'*

Alan moved from his table, positioning himself behind Azarias, to capture a better view of what had been happening under the table, and observed as he flipped the screen open to read the message:

*'You will find me reflected by The Lady of the North at 23:55 tonight. Bring the mobile device. Alone, this time. Come alone.'*

Acknowledging the final words of the message Azarias snapped the phone shut – *'Come alone. Perhaps every move is being monitored.'* Turning to Alan, who had returned to the other table, Azarias held up the Motorola RAZR, stating that he had got what he had come for, and that it was time to leave. Both men finished their drinks, placing the empty glasses on the bar before heading towards the door, and the bemused couples, muttering in shocked and surprised tones.

"I have to finish this alone," Azarias said, almost apologetically. "The instructions are clear. It is possible that my movements are being monitored."

"That's okay," he replied, feigning disappointment. "At least we know there is something tangible.

Something real. Whatever is going on. At least you are not mad."

Azarias smiled, a little relieved that he was not losing the plot; that he did not need to get a grip – it was real. He placed the old mobile in his right hand trouser pocket, on the opposite side to the Blackberry. As they drew level with the other people, and the publican, and noted that all the ringing, buzzing, and vibrating had ceased, Azarias could not resist having the last word.

"I thought you couldn't pick up a signal in here."

\*\*\*

A strange sequence of events, then, had brought Azarias to the car park of The Snowy Owl at a quarter to midnight – not least the message he had received on his old Motorola. It was as well that he had returned home, to change his clothing – preferring to dress in black for his midnight rendezvous – and taken time to enter *'Lady of the North'* in the Google search engine on his laptop. There would have been little chance of the meeting taking place if he had driven to The Angel of the North – the first thought that had entered his mind rather than heading to Northumberlandia. All this time, living in Cramlington and he had never visited the largest human form landscape sculpture in Europe – Northumberlandia, or The Lady of the North, a reclining female figure.

"A first time for everything," he whispered to himself as he passed through a wooden gate, leading from the car park of the inn to expanse of grass, which allowed access from The Snowy Owl to the car park of Northumberlandia, about 100 metres away. Azarias skirted the edge of a line of trees to avoid being detected by people vacating the inn. No one really had much business visiting Northumberlandia at that time of night – probably the reason for the choice of venue, in that it was closed, yet accessible. There was not much preventing access, low fencing and a low gate, yet he did not imagine many people would think of entering the site late at night; not even courting couples, as there was no access for a vehicle beyond the car park. With all that in mind he did not need any bystanders, or passing drivers, getting overly curious about the furtive looking guy, dressed in black, sneaking around in the shadows at the back of an inn, on the edge of Cramlington, in the dark hours, so he quickly climbed over the low wire fence, disappearing into the trees.

Dark brooding shadows, like creatures of the night, crept through the wooded copse, the trees illuminated by the glow of a half moon, moving behind, and passing, the occasional patches of light cloud. Misty shafts of light, the colour of eau de nil, provided barely enough light for Azarias to pick his way through the leaf litter, avoiding ditches, tree routes, and other trip hazards, until he reached the clearing, at the edge of the trees, beneath the silhouette of Northumberlandia, where the lunar light shone brighter.

Stepping away from the trees Azarias crossed the tailored grass, heading towards one of the many paths circumnavigating, and criss-crossing, the domain of The Lady of the North, reclining in all her resplendent dark and dusky beauty, basking in the night air. To his left, the highest point of the sculpture, her sleeping head, and scanning to the right, the mounds of her breasts, trig-point nipples, along the length of the body, and down her sloping legs, to her ankles, Azarias absorbed the wonder of the sculpture with his eyes. *'Must visit in daylight sometime.'*

A sound! Behind him, in the trees. Rustling of leaves. Straining eyes and ears he focussed all attention, and senses, on the creeping crawling shadows, but nothing stirred. Imagination, paranoia, or a small animal. He heard nothing, saw nothing in the darkness. It was quiet and we was alone, very alone. *'What is the time?'* Azarias struggled to read the time on his watch and turned it towards the light of the moon. *'Another two minutes',* He guessed, assuming she arrived at the designated time, if she arrived at all. *'What if it is a prank? What if ... '*

It was then that he really became aware of the stretch of water, mirror-calm, between him and the earth mistress. A small lake, or a large pond, parted by a grassy causeway, a path leading to the summit of the earthwork – her forehead. The reflection on the surface of the silvery water, when viewed back towards the night sky, resembled a Rorschach inkblot test. Azarias followed the contours of her body, once again, down to the ankle, where the foot melded with the ground, at the edge of the water. And it was there and then that the most unexpected thing happened – so unexpected, that the collection of old mobile phones, batteries without charge, let alone no signal, bursting into life and ringing, simultaneously, might appear quite normal, and expected.

A Lowry-esque silhouetted figure, reflected in the pond, appeared from nowhere, out of the ether, seemingly rising up out of the water. *'Some entrance. Is it her? Surely! Where has she come from? How did she do that? Impressive stuff.'* It had to be her. There was something feminine about the figure. Azarias stood routed to the spot, imagining those cat-like green eyes piecing the dark, searching for him. She found him. Turning to face Azarias, she raised her right arm and beckoned him to join her – to meet, to connect and complete the promised journey.

Even under the luminescence of the moon, against the backdrop of light pollution from the nearby town, at that distance, about 150 metres, her femininity was obvious, despite the slim, almost boyish hips, the figure hugging one-piece suit emphasising her shape. Again, she beckoned and then stood facing him across the water, with hands on hips, the symmetry of the reflection creating a mechanical flywheel effect. Azarias blinked a few times, checking his vision, and refocussing his eyes – but she was still there.

With the rush of excitement came an initial instinct to sprint around the water's edge, though this was tempered by sensibility and the desire to appear a little nonchalant – not a lovelorn teenager on a first date. A compromise brought with it a quick march along the path, by the side of the glistening mercury pool, turning to the left up a rising bank, where they came face to face; and not for the first time, as his memory instantly informed him. Her feline emerald eyes, accentuated by the deep dark pools of her pupils captured and held his gaze, as Saluki greeted him with a warm friendly welcoming smile. This was met, on his part, in return, with a quizzical smile, and a tilt of his head, which expressed a sense of disbelief. *'How did she do that? Where did she come from? A trick?'* She spoke.

"You will want to question many things, but some things you will just have to accept at face value. Some things are what they are, and will remain unexplained for various reasons."

He did not really want to challenge her, at this stage, and responded, accordingly, to her demand for the box, as she held out her right hand.

"This?" Azarias queried, removing the cold metallic lump from a pocket in his black leather jacket. "A box? I thought it was just a lump of metal."

He placed it in the centre of her open outstretched hand, attempting to heed her advice – *'Some things you will just have to accept at face value. Much easier said than done taking into account the fact that she had appeared out of the night air, from nowhere.'* Not something experienced every day of the week, during the course of normal events. Asking too much of the uninitiated, perhaps?

In her warm hand the cold lump clicked, then buzzed, the uppermost part opening like the aperture on an old SLR camera. From the tight confined space within the small object a light illuminated their faces, casting shadows and bright white shafts into the night. Saluki dipped her left hand towards the box, forefinger and thumb pinching at a small item, contained therein, which she lifted clear and held before their eyes. The aperture buzzed, and then clicked, the disappearing light fixed on the retinae for a while, causing a temporary blindness.

*'A chip for a mobile? Is that it?'* Skipped through his mind. *'All this for a mobile phone chip?'*

Then Azarias noticed the black utility-type belt she wore around her waist, with wallet shaped compartments, into which Saluki placed the grey lead lump. Again, she held out her right hand.

"Now, the mobile device. Please."

Azarias never questioned, or attempted to defy her commands, compliance, surely, being far easier at this stage of their 'getting to know each other.' No point in creating a confrontation. She held all the aces and was the one who had appeared out of the ether, and removed a mobile phone chip from a lump of lead. She had written the script, so Azarias was in no position to query the performance or the performer. Azarias obliged, handing her the mobile phone – his mobile phone – his old Motorola, which she had, somehow, managed to tape beneath the table in that public house in Shincliffe. And then 'the penny dropped', and his memory was jogged once again.

"Of course," he muttered, his right hand to his forehead, in the tones of that old TV detective, Columbo. "The drink. On the bar. At Shincliffe. And the change. It was you."

She opened the back of the phone to place the chip into an already empty space. Azarias examined it closely as she replaced the back.

"How come it was capable of receiving messages? Without a chip? *No answer.* "Okay. I'll try another. This is all a bit elaborate. There are easier ways of getting someone's attention. Arranging a meeting. Why?"

"Because I can," was the response, if not an unsatisfactory answer. "Here," she continued, handing the mobile back to him. "You are now ready. Switch it on."

Taking the phone in his right hand he flipped the screen open, ready to depress the power button but paused, giving some thought to potential outcomes. His mind buzzed with questions.

*'What am I doing? I don't know her. What are her intentions? Is this a throw-back to the old job? Do they still want my silence? No. That was settled. All acquitted. I was a laughing stock. An embarrassment. If not that, what then? Is she real? Do this and die? Do nothing, learn nothing? If I die now, right here and now, does it matter? Am I ready to die? Do I have much to live for, anyway?'*

"Shit! Here goes. All or nothing," he hissed, and the Motorola played the start-up tune – *'bloop-a-bloop, bloop, bloop, bloop, bloop.'* The screen illuminated, flashed and flickered – nothing unusual, except that the Motorola symbol had been replaced by the word, Genetikos, the acronym EFRON, on background of blue, with a ring of yellow-gold stars – nothing particularly spectacular, though; not immediately, anyway. *'Different, though fairly insignificant.'* And then, suddenly, for want of a phrase, it all kicked off.

It was probably the most unexpected thing ever – certainly up there in there in the top three of unexpected things – so unexpected, that an emerald-eyed woman appearing from nowhere out of the night air, as if by magic, might appear normal; that unexpected! It was highly likely that Azarias was not expecting it to happen and, therefore, somewhat unprepared; though he could be forgiven for not having any particular expectations, given the peculiar circumstances.

The Motorola snapped shut, without the assistance of Azarias, and began vibrating in his hand. It was not the normal vibration associated with a call or incoming message, but it was the level of vibration expected from an industrial electric hand-held sander. His fingers locked shut around the phone, the muscles of his forearm in spasm and not without some pain. He tried to free the device with his other hand but he couldn't prise his fingers open, and could not shake the buzzing, vibrating mobile phone from his tightening and uncontrollable grip.

"Don't fight it. Accept it. The time is right. Hold it up. Look at it. Trust me," she implored.

Using his left hand to cup his right, Azarias dragged the phone upwards towards his face, seemingly fighting a personal battle against the whole force of all 10 Newtons, as if gravity was pulling him into the centre of the Earth. Saluki just stood and watched. *'An initiation ceremony? What if I am about to die? No. Not like this.'* And when the phone was level with his eyes the events that followed confirmed, without any doubt, that he was alive – very much alive, if not still in some pain. It was an almost exquisite pain – that kind of pain when warmth returns to the extremities – fingers and toes – having been exposed to freezing temperatures, when having made snowballs with naked hands or wearing, perhaps, frozen sodden woollen mitts. The pain of life pulsed through his body.

Azarias let a deep, long moan escaped from between his lips, as he fell to his knees, but almost as a sense of release from the agony, which began to ease. A bright blue light beamed from the screen, the flip-down lid having reopened of its own accord, and it lit up his eyes. It was only for a few seconds, even though it seemed like an age to Azarias, but in that light he remembered everything.

Memories flooded his mind. Memories of everything. Memories of all that had happened to him. Memories of things yet to happen. Memories echoed around his brain – memories of memories. Memories from the inside, looking out, and memories from the outside, looking in, as if a third person was narrating his life story. There were memories of faces, memories of places – memories of everything and everyone he had ever been, memories of everything and everyone that had touched his life. Memories of sun. Memories of rain. Memories of joy. Memories of pain. Such exquisite pain – an agony and an ecstasy, never before experienced, and with those many memories he found knowledge.

A sense of knowledge, knowing the unknown, flooded into his brain. That knowledge was the sum total of everything he had ever learned and remembered, and the knowledge of things he had yet to learn; knowledge received in an instant. *'Wow! What is happening? Weird!'* A sense of knowing, but not knowing what it was he had always known, separating that from what he now knew – the new knowledge. It was all about knowledge, which he recognised. Had he always known this? This knowledge? And as the light of knowledge grew within him, enlightening him, so the torchlight shining in his eyes faded, and the pain subsided; though he felt a little nauseous, and dizzy, as he lifted himself back to his full height.

Azarias blinked rapidly, several times, in an attempt to readjust his eyes, once again, to the darkness, having endured the bright light in his eyes. Shaking his head from side to side he sought to silence the whistling sound in his ears, and sucked in four deep breaths of air; one to stop the nausea reaching a peak, spilling over in the form vomit, the other three to steady himself, and oxygenate his brain; seeking clarity of thought. *'Get a grip.'* The ache in his bones faded.

"Shit!" he whispered, for fear that someone might hear him, "What was that? What just happened?"

"The truth," she purred, emerald eyes gleaming in the dark. "You have accepted and realised the truth."

"The truth hurts," he retorted with a sense of irony. "Now what?"

"Now? Now the education begins," she asserted, her voice dropping to a whisper, as she repeated, "The education begins."

# Chapter 18

"This is up there with the most ridiculous things you have ever done," Alan said to himself, squatting on a folding fishing stool behind a hedge in field, as he reflected on the events of the previous 32 hours, and the trail that had led him to this place. *'An excuse for weird behaviour? I wonder.'* He dwelled on that thought for a few seconds; dismissing it as he checked the time on his mobile phone – 23:31.

Half an hour, he had been sitting on that stool, in that field, the four aluminium legs poking, unequally, into the uneven soil, waiting for Azarias to show. *'But what if he doesn't show? Of course he will. He made it clear that he was to finish this alone. She doesn't want me involved. That's obvious. Too good an opportunity to miss, though. Follow it through to the end. Only fair. Now? Just wait. And observe.'*

\*\*\*

The previous afternoon Alan had found himself sitting on his doorstep, locked out of his home, having pursued Azarias, who had taken off in something of a hurry. Alan has remembered the key words when Azarias had snapped out of the hypnotic state – *"The time is right."* Alan had then watched Azarias speed off into the distance, the British racing green coloured Rover disappearing behind the rows of parked vehicles that impeded his view of the length of the street. He was concerned as to whether that hypnotic state, rather the way Azarias had come out of it, may have caused some psychological harm, though, in reality, doubted that to be the case. Alan was really feeling that he was missing out, and wanting to be part of the adventure – curiosity had the better of him. He wanted to know, and need to know – natural curiosity being part of his trade – and that led to a restless night, and a slightly dishevelled Alan waiting in the college car park, earlier than usual, with a mind to catching Azarias before he had a chance to get out of his car.

Alan had approached the Rover 75, concerned and intrigued. Azarias appeared to be talking to himself, or was he on hands-free? No, it seemed that he was ranting. Perhaps at himself, as he was, seemingly, slapping himself about his head. *'Ouch!'* As Alan approached, he struggled to make out a word of what he was saying, the glass and sound proofing of the vehicle impounding the full content of the tirade. *"The common denominator? You. Fuckwit!"* Alan managed to grasp, before knocking on the side window.

\*\*\*

A feeling of numbness in certain extremities focussed Alan's mind on the present, and his task – to observe Azarias, and to follow his journey, hopefully, to the end. His reflection on earlier events had been distracted by the loss of feeling in his toes, and his penis – not that he was feeling particularly cold; just that certain nerve endings had been constricted. He was wrapped up in a Parka, with a faux fur trimmed hood, and wearing lined trousers and thermal socks.

Sitting on that stool for more than thirty minutes, hiding behind a hedge, in a field, opposite the entrance to Northumberlandia, had not helped. His toes had gone to sleep, and he imagined finding his digits remaining inside the socks when he removed them later. Moreover, the action, or inaction, of crouching on that tiny seat, for that length of time, had placed pressure on the Perineal nerve, causing such numbness of the penis, as for Alan to readjust his position, allowing feeling back into his knob-end – fearing that if he stood up that his cock might drop off and fall down the inside of his trouser leg. As he shifted his position he checked the time again – 23:34.

"Time flies when you are having fun," he moaned aloud, remembering the more recent sequence of events that had actually led him to this place, and point in time.

\*\*\*

Alan had noted that Azarias seemed to be experiencing polarized mood swings – one minute,

200

seemingly, muttering angrily, the next, elated, excited and happy. When they sat down in the college refectory Alan thought Azarias had appeared 'wired', for want of an expression. A cause for concern, perhaps, though he decided to play along, to observe, and follow the conspiratorial tone, particularly when Azarias produced the odd piece of lead, and the text message on the Blackberry, and suggested that the phone may have been hacked or bugged.

"Paraphrenia?" Alan had later queried, noting his thoughts in the voice recorder on his mobile phone. "Appears delusional. May even be creating false text or SMS messages. Believes his phone to have been hacked. Has hypnosis triggered or accentuated this event? I have decided to play along and lead him to the public house in Shincliffe, and observe. Is it possible that he is suffering hallucinations on a number of different levels?" Alan saved the message and placed the phone upon his desk in the communal open plan staffroom, and nothing could have prepared him for what would follow, later, that afternoon.

As agreed, Alan would wait in his Vauxhall Insignia, and allow a few minutes to pass before entering the bar, and purchasing a drink, whilst pretending that they did not know one another. *'Play along. Observe.'* There was some notion that Azarias was going to meet with this woman, *'a potential figment of his delusional mind,'* and that he was expecting to find a mobile phone containing a message, was all a bit too conspiratorial for his liking. Alan had begun to surmise that Azarias was living out some fantasy born of a delusional brain, and a troubled mind. *'Help him. Observe. Offer support. Find the answers to the niggling questions. Diagnose.'*

Upon entering the bar Alan acknowledged the two couples seated near the front windows – accepting, and returning, eye contact – a sign of respect, interest, and agreed acceptance of equality – receiving smiles for his efforts. Turning his gaze to the plate shelves above their heads he noted the unusual pub display – an array of mobile phones, lined up in a row. As he approached Azarias he had motioned, with a sense of irony, with his eyes, towards that display, having remembered the reference to mobile phones in the text message Azarias had shown to him. At the same time Alan played his role to the full, pretending to have never set eyes on Azarias before. He ordered a glass of ale and then pulled up a chair at the table directly behind his colleague – to observe. And observe, he did – the most unexpected event, certainly something for which he was not prepared.

The mobile phones, on that unusual display, came to life. Alan was as surprised as the other people in the bar, who had jumped up from their seats to avoid being struck on the head by falling, vibrating devices, edging their way off the shelf. Alan had moved away from his table, standing behind Azarias, who was also straining for a closer look. *'Answer the phone? Which phone?'* And it was then that Azarias had produced the phone from under the table – *'Okay. Observe. Perhaps not delusional. Say nothing. Continue to observe.'*

Oblivious to the attentions of Alan, behind him, Azarias had focussed on the message on the recently extracted mobile phone, unaware that the message was being read over his shoulder, and Alan had made a mental note of the instructions, particularly the part – *'Alone, this time. Come alone.'*

*'Say nothing. Observe.'*

Had it not been for the fact that Alan had spoken to his wife about meeting up with Azarias, for a drink and a chat, he would have ended up near the Angel of the North.

*'That's not a lady,'* she had shouted through from the kitchen. *'The Angel of the North is based on a man. Anthony Gormley – the sculptor – modelled for it. Google it. That is not called the Lady of the North. Trust me.'*

He did just that – trusted her, and searched for the Lady of the North – and then informed his wife that he was meeting up with Azarias at The Snowy Owl – lads' night out – for a drink and a bite to eat. *'How do you explain going out for midnight, or thereabouts? Better to pretend that we are meeting up for a meal, or a drink. Have a meal. Kill time, then hide out and wait. Wait for Azarias to appear. Observe. Find the truth.'*

The plan – use his wife's Ford Fiesta. Azarias would not recognise that car, parked at the rear of the inn. Then, eat, drink, and wait – hide, wait, follow, and watch. As far as if wife was concerned, it was an ordinary sort of an evening out. She had often encouraged him to make friends, and get out more! *'Why her car and not mine? She has the prepaid disc fitted to the windscreen, affording cheaper access through the toll gates at the other side of the Tyne Tunnel. Good enough reason. Also, lower fuel consumption. That being said Elizabeth never queries such things. Better than setting off about 11 p.m. That might appear a bit odd.'*

***

Another time check – 23:38!

A few vehicles had come and gone from the inn. Alan's proximity, on the stool in the field, to the Snowy Owl was close enough to distinguish the difference between taxi cabs and private vehicles; and he would certainly recognise the Rover belonging to Azarias, should that use the car park. And his viewpoint was, in his mind, secure from discovery – Alan had checked it out, walked along the road, placed the stool in the field, then walked up and down the lane again – he could see nothing behind the hedge. Alan concluded that passing motorists, few though they might be at that time of night, on the Cramlington to Blagdon lane, would not spot him seated behind that hedge, in that field. He was confident that Azarias, also, would not spot him. But he would be able to see Azarias, and follow him, unseen, in the dark. That is, of course, if he does make an appearance. Surely he would. 23:41 – he did!

A vehicle slowed, on the bend in the road, as it approached the Snowy Owl from the direction of the A1068. As it turned right into the car park of the inn Alan first recognised the shape of the headlamps, then

204

the whole of the car as it turned broadside across the road – no doubt about it – his heart beat faster – Azarias!

He was certain. It had to be him. A few minutes, or so, and his curiosity would be rewarded. The truth was all he sought. He felt he was owed that much, and had gone to some to lengths to follow this to the end, much easier to have stayed at home, put on his pyjamas and watched some nonsense on the television. If only he had not read that message on the mobile, across the shoulder of Azarias, he would not be here, at this hour of the night – curiosity! *'And all that business about Azarias coming alone. Who was watching?'*

So Alan had pretended he had not seen that message, over his shoulder, in the public house in Shincliffe, so as not to be deterred from his mission, and avoid disappointment. *"Not an appointment with disappointment,"* he whispered into the night air. *"Maybe stuff doesn't just happen to other people."* And then he spotted Azarias, skirting the edge of the trees, in the field adjacent to the car park. *"Observe. Say nothing. Do not interfere."* He squinted against the moonlit murk and watched the muffled figure of Azarias, blurring and fading with the dark satanic shadows, as he climbed the fence into the wooded copse. And then he announced, softly, to himself, *"Now!"*

Rising to a crouching position Alan turned 180° and scurried, rodent-like, along the field side of the hedge, keeping low to avoid being seen by Azarias, should he decide to check if anyone was following him, or had observed the stranger sneaking about amongst the trees. Alan arrived at a metre wide gap in the foliage, where the wire fence was exposed, directly opposite the entrance to the car park of Northumberlandia. Gingerly, holding down the barbed wire, he lifted his leg over the fence, avoiding injuries to veins and arteries, or the serious scratching of his scrotum. With both legs over, and on to the road, his Parka snagged on twisted sharpened steel. Alan stumbled, almost falling onto the tarmac, as material ripped free under pressure. *"Shit! Explain that one away. Focus. Right. No traffic. How far?"*

Alan estimated that he would have to cover about 100 metres, the approximate distance to the wooden cabin at the entrance gate, the other side of the car park, in about the same time as Usain Bolt, if he was going to keep an eye on Azarias, who had a good head start. *'Don't lose sight of him. Fuck it. Run!'*

He sprinted across the road, exploding breath from his lungs and, failing to inhale air properly, due to his lack of athletics training, Alan struggled to maintain the momentum, and slowed up as quickly as he had started. At least he had made it as far as the drive into the car park. Another push. *'Go for it. The hut. Cover. Shit! That hurt. My foot.'*

Something strained, stretched, a spasm on the top of his left foot. Alan pulled up, a lame horse in the Grand National, and he continued with a half-limp, half-trot, towards the five bar gate – the vehicular access, adjacent to the wooden pedestrian entrance. The wooden hut, at the edge of the woods, was just on the other side, within reach. He climbed the gate, gently, to avoid the potential squeal of metal hinges scraping and screeching in the breathless night air. *'Shit! That hurts. Why am I doing this? Because I have to. I want to. Come on. You can do it.'*

Alan pasted his back against the wall of the cabin, to the right of the wide avenue, leading to the earth monument, through the trees. He melded himself into the fabric of the building, catching his breath in short, painful, gulps – an attempt to cease his gasping and wheezing, for fear of it reaching the ears of Azarias, in the loud silence of the night. He could hear his heart thumping in his chest; feel the beating of it in his throat. Alan retched quietly, but managed to hold the bile and vomit down. Steadying himself he wondered if he dared to look around the side of the hut. *'What if Azarias is there, waiting? What if he knows I am following him?'*

His external anal sphincter twitched – a reaction to fear, excitement, or both. Slowly, surely, he peered around the side, and into the blackness, straining to focus for any signs of movement. All the shadows, under the moonlight, appeared to waver with the whisper of wind, caressing and rustling the treetops. And then he caught a glimpse of Azarias, between the towering pines, as he moved from the copse into the open air. *'Must bring the family here. What now? Don't let him see you. A challenge. What to do?'*

He had lost track of time but thought better of looking at his mobile – he knew it would light him up in the darkness. Alan peeled back the cuff of the left sleeve of the heavy, thick, Parka, and turned his wrist watch towards the light of the moon; any available light to read the time – approximately 11:48. *'Now or never. All or* nothing. *All for one, and one for all, and all that stuff. Stuff! Stuff is happening.'*

Azarias was about 300 metres away, out in the open, maybe at a 30° angle, to Alan, through the wood. Alan intended to shorten the distance by at least half, using the trees as cover, so as to provide him with a good view of what was about to happen – whatever that was. He fumbled in a pocket, muttering as he did so. *"Switch your phone off. You plonker."*

Alan then made his made his move, darting from tree to tree, with a view to keeping three or four lines of the tall pines between himself and the edge of the wood, where Azarias had made his way to the side of large pond. Or, was it a small lake? As he skipped through the wood, gliding in his imagination, across the vegetation, the reality of his heavy footfall, rustling the leaves beneath his feet, reached the ears of Azarias, who turned and looked back towards to the dark foreboding, spectral shadows.

Pinning his body to one of the pines sucked silently at the night air, like a grounded Guppy, in an attempt to avoid being detected. Alan counted to sixty, in his head, before daring to peep around the trunk. *'Safe.'* Azarias was not looking in his direction, and was illuminated by the albedo of the moon, and the reflected light from the glassy still water. He appeared to be waiting for something to happen. Alan was also happy to wait, and to observe. And, so, they both waited, and neither was prepared for what was about to happen – but then nobody really expects the unexpected.

Alan's point of view, through the trees, from behind the pine, from where he observed events, afforded him a wide vista – Azarias silhouetted against the steely water, and the night-glow on the monolithic monumental earthwork. In trying to imagine the world through the eyes of his colleague Alan trained his gaze beyond the right shoulder of Azarias, to a point where The Lady of the North's foot melded with a path on a slightly raised area, at the far end of the stretch of water, backlit by fluorescence of the nearby town. It was in this immediate vicinity that a figure, a person, appeared, seemingly, rising up from the reflection in water, out of the night air. *'Female! Without a doubt. Clever trick. How did she do that?'*

'She' appeared to turn and face Azarias, across the water, causing Alan to pull back, lest she should see him hiding in the trees, peaking out again when another fifteen seconds, or so, had passed. He could see Azarias walking towards the figure, standing with hands on hips, resembling one of those ink-blot experiments Alan had his psychology students explore, such was the symmetry created by the reflection in the mirror of water. And then he saw another reflection and looked upwards – it was Azarias, now on the far side and closing in on his appointment. *'An appointment with destiny. I wish.'* It was then that heard something or, rather, felt something – a presence behind him, in the woods. Alan turned, slowly, and was, again, greeted by the unexpected.

Standing before him, some twenty metres away was a person, someone, dressed from head to foot in white, sporting a white full face crash helmet, with dark tinted visor. *'The Stig? What is he doing here? Where are*

*Clarkson, and his crew?* He attempted to focus his eyes in the mottled murkiness, and shifting shadows. This being had seemingly appeared from nowhere, or crept up on Alan without a sound – he had heard nothing, merely felt a presence. Whoever this person was, they raised their left arm, pointing towards Alan – perhaps as a sign of greeting, but the right hand came across and tapped upon a bracelet-like object worn on the left wrist. Alan took five or six steps forward, inclining his head to the right, in a quizzical manner. *'Who are you? Why are you here?* In his mind he was also attempting, rather unsuccessfully, to carry out a risk assessment on the situation. *'A threat?'* Alan glanced over his right – a quick look – to reassure himself that Azarias had not been disturbed by this meeting in the woods. Azarias appeared to be illuminated, his face lit up, by something the woman was holding in her hand. *'Too far away, and too involved. Perhaps too far away to help, if help is needed. A threat? Why are you sneaking about in the woods dressed like that at this time of night?* A strange thought, given that Alan was also sneaking about between the same trees at the same time of night. The answer to his questions, though, was swift, sharp, and painful.

Thwump!

An unseen, invisible, blast – seemingly moving air – smashed against his torso; a formula one wrecking ball. Alan was lifted off his feet, through the air, smashed, with massive force about two metres up the thick trunk of a pine tree. Alan heard several loud cracks – felt the sharp cracks – and it was not the snapping of twigs. He did not bounce off the tree, nor did he slide down the trunk. A metre long spear-shaped broken branch, on a right angle to the tree, had pierced the back of his Parka, tearing through the thick material, his shirt, and flesh and lung, between the sixth and seventh ribs on his right side; instantly impaled.

"Pah!" he exhaled, spitting and dribbling blood from his lips.

Skewered on the spike, bubbling blood around his mouth, with the pale glow of the moon on his face, Alan hung from the tree, feet not touching the forest floor; a macabre clown-like puppet – a Pierrot miming death! He had never experienced excruciating pain such as this, ripping through his battered broken body – shattered by one massive trauma. An unseen force had fractured bones, smashed like porcelain, and ruptured internal organs – and he could picture all this in his mind; all ripped, pummelled, and spurting blood.

And there followed a wave of exquisite release from the agony, as encephalin and endorphins exploded from his brain, binding to opioid receptors, creating a natural analgesic response to the shock suffered by a system now in shutdown. Then relief would not last long, though, but then neither would his life. A feeling of euphoria and ecstasy pervaded his senses, momentarily focusing the mind on his predicament. With chin on chest, Alan, given his limited medical knowledge, attempted a prognosis, and it was not good; not good at all.

Dark blood, spraying from his breath, like an aerosol, stained the front of the Parka, where the sharp end of the branch pushed the material forward – it had not protruded all the way, but, curiously, the bulge reminded him of a time in his adolescence – an embarrassing hard-on pushing against his shorts, on a topless bathing beach, whilst on a holiday in Spain with his parents. That particular pain, he had exorcised with his right hand in the cubicle of a nearby public toilet but there was only one outcome here. There was no doubt that there was going to be only one release from the pain which was creeping, crawling, back into his nerves, flesh and bones – death. And nature's anaesthetic was wearing off.

Erratic, hurried, uneven breathing from the one remaining, working lung – something was not right. The left side of his torso was inflating and deflating, rapidly, like a balloon when the air is blown in, sucked out, blown in, blown, sucked, in, out – fluttering and irregular, and his fragmented rib-cage was not co-ordinated with the faltering breathing. *'Flail chest? Fuck. I'm fucked!'* Something had read, sometime, somewhere – *'paradoxical breathing.'* He was certain that was the diagnosis. Statistics! *'Half of people with flail chest die.'* Fifty percent chance of survival, then, but that was not the end of it – he was impaled on a spear of wood, dangling in the air; perhaps the thoughts of a man facing death, not seeing images of his life flashing before his eyes, contemplating how he was going to die. But he was not going to die alone, was he?

'The Stig' was standing in front of him, about a metre between them, black visor tilted slightly to the left, as he examined the outcome of his handiwork. And he was singing – singing softly. No doubt about it, he was singing. *'Italian? Latin? Opera? Sadistic bastard!'* Alan had no idea what was being sung, by who he now recognised as male, but he was singing something operatic, and memories of gangster movies, real or imagined, flitted through his mind – mafia hitmen singing an aria at a hit. Maybe he was reminded of that scene in Reservoir Dogs – Michael Madsen, *'Mr Blonde?'* Dancing and singing along to *'Stuck in the Middle With You'* while preparing to kill – *'who was that he was going to kill?'* As blood drained from brain his memory began to fail, though Alan was certain that he was not going to be saved by a dying cop, lying in a pool of blood. There was only his blood. *'Hallucinating? No. He is singing.'* His killer was waiting for him to exhale his last breath. *'Sadistic shit!'*

Alan wanted to cry out to Azarias, or even curse the evil that snuck up on him, and was watching him, waiting for him to expire, but all that escaped his lips was the frothing, foaming crimson life force. And then he voided his bowels and emptied his bladder – death was close at hand. Blood, shit and piss soiled his clothing, the warmth of it all running down his legs. He could feel his heart pumping wildly, compensating for the massive drop in his blood pressure, and his one working lung heaved painfully, desperately sucking at life, which many do not give up without a fight. And then, hypovolemic shock. *'Cold. Very cold.'* One last bid for survival.

In his wildest imaginings, in his mind, Alan had pushed his body free of the spike and launched himself at the 'Stig', ripping the visor from his helmet, and had bitten off the end of his attacker's nose, gouging out his eyes with his thumbs. In reality, in the last throes of life, as a primordial instinct had caused his body to twitch, convulse and thrash. Something had snapped – the branch, or bone, maybe both – and he had fallen to the ground, almost in slow motion, as if the puppeteer had cut the strings. Alan knelt, briefly, before falling face down in the leaf litter, his head turned to the right, puffing blood over the detritus near his gaping red mouth. And the last thing he saw, before there was nothing – nothing at all – was his terrible reflection in the visor of the sadistic singing bastard, who had crouched down for a closer look; admiring the outcome of their meeting.

"You shouldn't have been here," the voice whispered from inside the helmet. "Why are you here? I wonder. No intruders. That is the rule. I had no choice. You do see that, don't you? It is against the rules to interfere with the passing of time. For the sake of the future. You know him? Too late now. Does it hurt? I have never used this before." Le Feuvre showed him the device on his left wrist. "First time, for real. You gave me choice."

*'Fuck you. Fuck...'*

...Life extinct – 23:59!

# Chapter 19

Side by side they stood – Damarov and Le Feuvre – staring silently across the Territories and Provinces de la Belgique; the La Meuse River shimmering in the afternoon sun like a snaking diamond necklace, carelessly and, full of promise, sensually dropped upon the floor of a lover's boudoir. The summit, the roof terrace, of La Tour de la Croix bleached beneath the naked 42°C azure sky, yet the artificial intelligence of the Nanotechnology in their clothing and footwear insulated their bodies and feet, providing comfort and preventing perspiration. Gabriel released a deep discontented sigh from the depths of his diaphragm, and the very cellar of his soul, before speaking with such a tone that reflected his status and authority.

"We do not have a body. Or evidence of a body. Yet. It may have disintegrated on impact with the water. Like hitting concrete from this height." He waved his right hand in a dismissive – *it is not your turn to speak yet* – fashion, silencing any potential interruption, before continuing. "However, there are pipes drawing water into the complex, for the cooling system. And, pipes recycling the water back into the lake. It is possible that we will find some evidence to confirm his suicide.

Something of him may be found, in the lake, the pipes, or filters, which will leave no doubt as to the outcome. Yes? And. You saw the body fall. Correct? You may speak."

A drop of sweat tickled the tip of Le Feuvre's nose, and this was brushed away with his right hand as he gesticulated in the direction of the edge of the roof terrace. He opened his mouth to speak, but the Superus cut him off before there was any chance to utter a word.

"Never, never answer that question. Whether I ask, or anyone else asks. You were not here. Remember? Life has been recorded as extinct. A body was seen to fall in the lake. Accident? Suicide? That is for the investigating team to decide. But we do not have a body. Let us hope that the divers find something. Some evidence of death. One does not reach such positions of authority without a little healthy paranoia. I would hate to think we might have been tricked. Evidence of death is a solution to that problem. So, tell me about the other problem. What happened?"

Augustin was wearing his white uniform, but was minus his crash helmet – he did not shift his gaze from the distant horizon while describing events in the wooded copse, where he had been assigned to observe the meeting of commandant Saluki Damarov and the emergent, Azarias Tor. There had been an intruder at the scene. It was someone who should not have been there, in those woods, watching from the cover of the trees. Ask no questions. Shoot first. Eliminate the threat.

"I believed him to be an associate of the emergent," Augustin said, obsequiously seeking approval for his actions. "So I thought it better eradicate him, in order to protect our position. The status quo. It was possible that he knew too much anyway. I believe the emergent to be a threat. But this person? He should not have been there. It is the first opportunity I have had to use the Subsonne Mark II in a situation, against a human. I have tested the prototype on live animals, and carcasses. First time on a human, though. Silent, but deadly. If only my grandfather had lived to see such technology. Sub-sonic sound used as a weapon?"

"So," Damarov began, boredom creeping into his voice, "what was it like? I am aware of the potential. This makes you the first to use the Mark II in the field. We cannot share the information, though. We will recalibrate the weapon. And ensure that no one else has knowledge of your illegal time leaps. We share the secrets for a purpose. To do the right thing. Preserve and maintain. Protect the future. Our future. To do that, we must control the past. Unorthodox but necessary. I digress. I need details. A report. Your observations. I am also interested in the length of time that elapsed between discharge of weapon and recorded death. And then you can bring me up to speed with the activities of my daughter. Yes? Good. And I trust you have disposed of the body in such a way that it will not be discovered. Anyway or any time."

A long silence, as they stood side by side, staring out across the Territories and Provinces de la Belgique, and Le Feuvre considered and planned the delivery of his report, wherein he would recall the events in that dark wooded copse, with cold, calm efficiency.

\*\*\*

*"In the event of my death, or arrest for any crimes associated with the mission, this message will be released to the appropriate bodies in conjunction with attached incriminating evidence,"* Augustin Le Feuvre began recording, speaking into the device on his left wrist, as he walked alongside the Lake beneath La Tour de la Croix, alone, in secret, away from curious ears, CCTV or other listening devices, *"to prove that I was following the orders of Superus Gabriel Damarov. The mission, I was informed, was to flush out corruption. The Vice-Superus has been implicated with corrupting time to meet his own needs and desires. The Superus has evidence, so I have been told. However, the mission is a covert operation. Observe the Vice-Superus. Eradicate, if necessary. And the order was given. I do not know why but following the orders of Gabriel Damarov I carried out an unauthorised time-leap, under cover, and went back two weeks to meet the Vice-Superus on his roof terrace, having observed his movements over a period of time. The mission. Eradicate the Vice-Superus. Secrecy must be assured. I was told. I was supposed to be the assassin but he jumped. Why? Perhaps he did not wish to feel the force of the Subsonne Mark II. I have been promised promotion for my compliance and my vow of silence. I have ambitions. But I have to track and observe his daughter. Fine but eliminate her, also? Damarov has sanctioned this action. His command. Use my judgement, he said, if not directly commanded. Why?*

218

*Does he fear her? I have no problem with killing that Azarias Tor, or that office boy, Lamont. What is a code delta one-five? Is that what he fears and why he is concerned about the lack of a body? But I saw him fall from that rooftop. Tipped backwards over the edge of the 580 metre drop. I did not see the body hit the water. I did not wish to be seen. Witnesses, in the shopping mall, saw a body hit the water. He could not survive that fall. Possible disintegration on impact. Body parts may be found in time. The search continues. And then I had to follow and track his daughter, Saluki Damarov. Observe her meeting with the emergent. Act on my own initiative, he said. And so I had to deal with the intruder in the woods"*

The thing about having friends in high places – at least being in favour with superiors – does mean that access is granted to higher levels of security, that certain protection is afforded, and that allowances are made when it comes to fulfilling the objectives of secret missions, particularly when tracking compatriots without their knowledge. Saluki Damarov was unaware of the fact that her father had set in place a covert operation with the aims of receiving reports about her movements. *'Why?'* That unanswered question, again. *'Something to do with the emergent, perhaps,'* was a possible answer. The greatest shock, though, was that the Superus had mooted the idea of sanctioning her eradication – the death of his own daughter – should it prove necessary; in the event that her actions might have a profound impact on the natural order of things – that same old mantra! She could not be allowed to do anything, particular where the emergent was concerned, to jeopardise the present by interfering with past events – no one could be allowed to do that, and he was apprehensive regarding any potential influence that Azarias Tor may have on her decision making, given that he may wish to change events in his personal history. The task, for now, was to *"follow, track and observe."*

Le Feuvre, with the assistance of the *'dark side'* InfoTech team had 'hacked' into Saluki's uRAPP, and could therefore track her through time and space, with pinpoint accuracy. He could then call up a satellite view, or map, of the surrounding area, where she had chosen to meet with her assignment. A view of the immediate vicinity, captured in daylight, on the same day was always going to be appropriate – it could prove fatal, landing on a top of a tree or within the fabric of a solid structure. He had selected an area close to the wooded copse for the landing from his time leap, maintaining a discrete distance in the shadows, some 400 metres away from the action – *'follow, track, observe and report.'* Augustin, though, had not been prepared for the intruder, the stranger in the woods.

Having landed, as planned, at the right time, in the right place, shortly after Commandant Damarov had arrived, on the outskirts of the tall pines, Le Feuvre adjusted his view of the world, using the night vision facility in his visor. The dark tint worked the same as a two way mirror – he could see out but no one could see his face or eyes; only their own reflection. A little intimidating, as no one could guess what he was thinking, or prejudge his actions – he liked it that way, but he did not like what he saw in the dimness of the forest. Some distance away, in an easterly direction, leaning against a tree, in the murk of the night, he saw a figure, wearing a green hooded jacket. *'Who is this? Male? Female? Definitely male. Doing what?'*

Creeping forward, carefully, quietly, with a soldier's stealth, he found a tree some twenty metres away from where Augustin could follow the stranger's line of vision, through the trees, out into the open, and across the mercuric water. And there he saw Saluki, waiting on a small mound of grass – Azarias heading towards her, following a moonlit path around the edge of the lake. *'Small lake or large pond?'* A movement closer to hand. The figure in the trees had heard a sound, or detected a movement – perhaps a feeling – and was now facing Le Feuvre. *'Why is he here? An intruder. Spy? Shoot first, ask questions later.'* He laughed, inwardly, having the knowledge that this person was not going to be in a position to answer any questions, once the Subsonne Mark II had been discharged; the first time against a human. Raising his left arm at a 90° angle to his body, pointing at the intruder in the woods, he gave another quite laugh as the 'spy in the woods' started to walk towards him. *'He thinks I am raising my hand to greet him. How wrong. How ironic.'*

*'Engage. Prime. Release.'* – Using the index finger, and middle finger, of his right hand, Augustin applied pressure to the appropriate buttons on the device on his left wrist. A telescopic aerial-like object protruded about 15 centimetres across the top of the clenched fist of his left hand. An invisible pulse was released, causing a slight jerk of the wrist. Le Feuvre had read the manual, the 'spec', and had taken part in the testing of the prototype, observing the results of autopsies, describing

the effects on live animals, and seen the damage inflicted upon animal carcasses, and then imagined, in a split second, what was about to happen to the man dressed in green, as he watched the body flying backwards, and upwards, smashing against the trunk of a massive pine.

The man in the white suit, scanning the dark wood through the night vision enhanced dark visor, walked gently through the leaf litter towards the body, which appeared to be impaled to the tree, some two metres off the ground. *'How bizarre. How unfortunate for you. I have the task of getting you down. How does it feel, I wonder?'* The attack had been silent but deadly. Saluki was too occupied, too far away to hear what was happening in the woods; unaware of the noiseless slaughter in the cover of the foliage, and unaware that one of her own was only some 400 metres away – *'the dark side'* had blocked his signal, so that Saluki would not pick up a fellow time traveller on her device. As he moved, quietly, a little closer to his quarry, thoughts of prey and hunter running through his mind, Le Feuvre prepared himself for the destructive power of this weapon.

*'I am death, my friend. Powerful. Deadly. Creeping through the trees. The hunter. The prey? You. The first time I have used this in anger. Anger? No. Cannot say I am angry. But you shouldn't be here. No. Not anger. For the hell of it. Because I can. Not good for you. Death hanging from a tree. Meat for carrion. Wrong place, wrong time? No. Right place, right time. For me. A good testing ground for the Subsonne. Do you want to know how it works? This small tube delivers a silent subsonic pressure shock wave. Concentrated. 343 metres per*

*second. Speed of sound, yet silent. I know. Amazing! A cone of silent air pressure, slamming into the target. Unseen. Thumping the life and oxygen out of crushed lungs. I have been informed that it is like being hit by the shock wave from a high order explosive, in such a range as to receive primary blast injuries. Broken bones? Yes. Look at your chest. Ruptured organs? You are spitting blood. Shattered spleen. Lacerated liver. And, impaled. Ouch, ouch, ouch. Not long, then no pain. What is that you say? Bubbling, frothing blood, or attempting to speak? You want to kill me? I don't blame you. But I am the bringer of death. You are death. Soon you will sleep the long sleep. Reminds me of a song. An opera. How does it go? Yes. I remember.'*

Standing beneath his victim, admiring the crucified figure, staked to the tree about two metres off the ground, Augustin brought to his mind an aria from the opera, *'Gau Batean Basoan.' Roughly translated, A Night in the Forest. Like this.'* In his imagination the dying man could hear his thoughts; a telepathic connection between the killer and the killed.

"I am not so lacking in culture," he whispered into his visor, the words not reaching the ears of his victim. "Damarov thinks that I am nothing more than a hired thug. Not so clever, he thinks. But he does not really know me. Do you like opera? Perhaps you do. I am not so stupid. I have to tell someone. You will not tell anyone, will you? All those meetings, in secret, I have recorded. Insurance? Evidence, certainly. Leverage, perhaps. A guarantee of securing promises that have been made. Blackmail? No. Career development. I will have his job. Yet he will move upwards, also. But I will always be able to hold this over him. Even in death. That is my plan. It is not me that is the fool. Damarov is the fool. He talks too much. I am clever. Look simple, act smart. And you? What of your plans? None. I will sing to you. While you die. A lullaby, perhaps. The aria. The opera. A story of unrequited love, and unrecognised national identity. Two heroes of the Basque region, at the turn of the century. My century. Not yours. One man's love for another. Their shared love of their national identity. Keep up. Don't die yet. They were rebels. Hunted down. One of them mortally wounded. The other sings this lullaby of death."

Touching the feet of the impaled body, with a certain reverence, Augustin looked upwards with awe. The man above him knew when he was going to die, on this very night, and he almost envied him. That aside, he took a couple of steps back and began to sing, quietly, to the best of his knowledge, learning, and understanding, in the language of the Basque.

*"Lo goxo, lo goxo, amets sakon, pentsamenduak ilun saihestu, goxo, goxo, segurtasunez, gauaren basoan. Zure ametsetan gero hiltzen baduzu, zure hilobira etzan izango duzu."*

Which, in his mind, roughly translated to *"Sleep sweet, sweet sleep, dream deep, dark thoughts avoided, gently, gently, safely, in the forest of the night. Then if you die in your dreams, you will lie on your grave."*

"Appropriate, don't you think? I would like to talk with you a while but you don't have much time. I have things to do. Do you hear me? See me? Feel me? Your last fight for life. All that is precious – survival. Don't

224

struggle. No! Look what you have done. You have messed yourself. The stench of death. No dignity. And now you rest on the forest floor, with all the other insects. I crush you. I am the bringer of death. Sleep sweetly, in the forest of the night."

Le Feuvre checked the time on his device, satisfied himself that life was extinct, depressed a button on a touchscreen, and then moved away from the corpse for a better view of Saluki and Azarias. *'Observe and report.'*

***

"And you can guarantee that you have dealt with the body accordingly?" Damarov enquired.

"Disposed of carefully. Another time, another place," Augustin answered, thoughts of the death in the forest drifting from his mind, as he passed a wallet and mobile phone to his superior. "I found these. It would appear that he is a colleague of the emergent. Look. A pass and an identity card for the same college. They work together. There is cause for concern. No? How is it that this person has been allowed to observe their activities? He must have been aware of the situation. Perhaps the commandant has failed in her mission to maintain absolute secrecy."

"Perhaps," Damarov snapped. "As you were. Observe and report."

With the wallet and mobile phone in his hands, Superus Damarov, without a further word, turned and marched towards the rooftop elevator, happy in the knowledge that witnesses appeared convinced that Raphael Antinori had, seemingly, committed suicide.

Le Feuvre had not been observed in the vicinity around that time, and that then did not incriminate Damarov by association. Augustin was left alone, muttering under his breath, staring out over the Belgique countryside, so lost in concentration, regarding recent events, that he was unaware that Damarov was no longer at his side.

"Strange, don't you think? That a man should purchase such a grand apartment then not live in it. Why has he used it for such a short time? Did he have a plan? To throw himself from the roof? Not much of a plan. Still strange. Why bring me here? Why?"

Augustin turned to Damarov for a response but he was not there. Spinning on his heels, Le Feuvre was in time to watch the Superus disappearing in the glass elevator as it sank into the roof, towards the apartment below.

He clenched his fists, feelings of anger frothing and foaming to the surface, boiling over as, once again, he was reminded of his place in the scheme of things, in spite of the promises guaranteed for his loyalty to the cause. Spittle dribbled from his lips, the venom in words spat out with force.

"Fuck you, too," he hissed. "One day. One day. You will see. You will meet someone you have wronged and you will be on your way down when they are on the way up. One day. If you live that long."

*Newton's third law – 'for every action, there is an equal and opposite reaction.'*

To that end it was highly likely that Damarov had not attained his position in life without considering every action on his part, and every potential opposite reaction from those from whom he sought fealty; such being garnished with references to career advancement and financial rewards; and it was just possible that Gabriel already had plans in place to counter the plans of others, who might pose a threat to him – *'you cannot kid a kidder!'* Not sure that what was in the mind of Isaac Newton when he developed his third law but it did mean that a person's life could be endangered if they messed with Damarov.

# Chapter 20

Azarias was buzzing, his mind in a muddle, attempting to comprehend the situation – *'The truth? Laughable. Surely? Who is going to believe me? I'm not sure I believe it. Perhaps I am under the influence. Maybe she has slipped me something? Saluki. Some trip! Maybe I'm dreaming. In a coma? That's it. Like that TV series. Shit. What was it called? Something about Mars. But it's real. Fucking hell. Time travel. How? Why? That's the education bit. Some learning curve!'*

\*\*\*

"On a need to know basis," she began. "I will tell you most what you need to know, when you need to know it. There may be some questions to which you will not receive answers. Some things you do not need to know. Some things you should not know. And there are restrictions. Rules."

Azarias invited her to sit on the smaller of his two brown leather sofas – her pacing around was only adding to the confusion. His head was hurting and his nerves jangling – a mixture of the effects of the physical assault upon his person, and the information he was struggling to absorb, and yet he took time to note her accent – perhaps French, or Belgian, or an amalgam of the two. Strangely sexy, too, the accent, and *'not unattractive.'*

Far from it. Those haunting, hypnotic, emerald green eyes, and that young Elizabeth Taylor, *Cleopatra,* captivating look, and the ever so shiny jet coloured hair, shaped in a tidy pixie cut, and the slim hips, small firm breasts. Yes, he was taking notice. A pang of guilt tortured him as he was reminded of his vows of old, his eyes catching a glimpse of the two wedding photographs on the dark wood faux mantel, surrounding the electric faux 'coal' fire, set against the party wall.

"She was beautiful," Saluki said softly, with a sympathetic tone, refusing the offer to sit on the large sofa. "You must have loved her very much."

"Still do. Never stopped," he snapped at himself, the guilt growing into self-loathing, for taking even the slightest sexual interest in another woman – a stranger in the home he shared with his wife.

"Please excuse my insensitivity," she responded, apologetically, before adding, "But is it not 'till death us do part'?"

"I'm not dead, though. Yet."

Sensing the deepening mood, and that Azarias's darkest moments were being dredged to the surface, Saluki accepted the offer to take a seat, seeking an opportunity to move away from the current topic.

"I like your furniture," she added, an attempt to divert his thoughts.

She sat in the corner of the two seater sofa, close to the party wall of the semi-detached property, which was set at a 90° angle to that side of the house. There was an uncomfortable silence, as Saluki stroked the high-backed sofa, feeling the quality in the caress of her fingertips. In front of her a larger rectangular rug – a creamy colour, with a thick chocolate edging, upon which rested a stocky, low, dark wood coffee table, inlaid with thick glass. Saluki quietly admired the surroundings, looking around the room, waiting for Azarias to fill the silence.

*'This self-loathing. Will it ever go away?'* Azarias thought, his misty eyes focusing on the large canvas wedding photograph in the corner, above the Panasonic flat screen television.

He was perched on the edge of the three-seater sofa, a larger copy of the other one, where Saluki relaxed, in silence, her eyes flitting from him to photographs, artwork, furnishings, and back again, as if she might be building up a profile based on his goods and chattels; though it was nothing she did not already know. The longer high-backed, roll-armed, sofa sat at a right angle to the other, both strategically aligned with the rug and the table, with space enough between them to allow ease of access to the enclave – a living area within the open plan design.

The furnishings in the dining area, a table with six upholstered chairs, and chest of drawers, with central wine rack, of light rubber wood, sat on the pine laminate flooring, which dominated the whole of the downstairs,

230

even in the conservatory, and up to the front door. Saluki's eyes traced every line, every angle, of the walls, windows, doorframes, and the wooden rails of the varnished wooden stairs. And then she studied the wall art and his photographs on canvas – the orange setting sun on St. Mary's lighthouse, the monochrome of the Sage and the Tyne Bridge, and the lilies on Rydal Water – a take on Monet.

"Delcor," Azarias muttered, almost absent-mindedly, shifting his eyes from the wedding portrait. "The furniture. Sofas. Hand built to our specification."

*'Our specification. Our Delcor. Mierde. Change the subject,'* she pondered, developing the idea that she was, effectively, sitting in a mausoleum – a shrine to the dead wife. He was still suffering, these years along the line, and she had scratched the widower's wound. Time to change the tune. *'Time for business.'*

"Listen," she began, preparing for a monologue, "and listen carefully. Please save questions until I have finished. And, remember, I may not provide answers to all questions. Yet. I will tell you what you need to know. The first thing to take on board. There is no such thing as aliens. Beings from beyond the clouds. From other planets. I am an alien. Time travellers are the aliens. The stereotypical view of the alien has been created through contact with people like me. But not me. I am careful. I have been careful. There are no travellers from outer space. We come from inner space. The time traveller. This will become clear. You are an emerging time traveller. But you are not from my time."

231

She raised her right hand to silence Azarias, as he made a move to interject. Saluki could sense scepticism, even though he had appeared to accept the truth. *'Why should he accept everything at face value? I have informed him that he is a time traveller. Why should he believe me? Crazy woman! He is not from my time. Why should he believe a seemingly impossible truth?'* And then she revealed a seemingly impossible truth.

"I was born in 2158."

It was probably not unlike one of those Alcoholics Anonymous moments, or similar, when a new visitor truly acknowledges their condition for the first time with the announcement, *"My name is ... and I am an alcoholic."* The difference, though – the emphasis on the word 'was', suggesting that an event in the future had already happened; yet for Azarias it hadn't happened – not by a long shot. *'Hi. My name is Saluki. I was born in 2158.'* The truth? The truth.

Adrenaline pumped around his body, fear of the unknown, and his arms and legs felt weak, as if all blood and life-force had been drained from those limbs. *'2158?'* Yet he knew it was the truth, with every fibre, nerve ending and blood vessel. He knew. He could feel it in his bones and there was no reason to doubt her version of the truth. She had been born the year 2158, in the future, and she was a time traveller. And, he was a time traveller, so she had told him. The truth? Of course. And then he asked the question that a gentleman is not really supposed to ask of a woman, because, in reality, he was somewhat at a loss for words.

"How old are you?"

"I am 40 years of age."

"Wow! An easy paper round!"

"An easy what?" Saluki probed.

"Never mind. I am 42."

"I know."

"Of course you do. You would. You have an advantage over me."

"I do. And I will do something about that. You have a right to certain knowledge. The history of time travel."

From his point of view, his point in time, that term, *the history of time travel,* sounded bizarre, yet Saluki set about unravelling a series of surprising truths during her brief lecture, and history, of time travel.

Time travel was developed over a period of 170 years, initially, at the CERN laboratories, before a larger replica of the underground facility was built deeper into the terra firma of the Territories and Provinces de la Belgique – there was more to the project than smashing sub-atomic particles together at the speed of light. The titanium-zirconium-vanadium alloy lining of the Large Hadron Collider had been developed with the idea of exploring the potential of time travel and teleportation. The magnets, injected with helium, cooling the machine to 4°Kelvin had not just been designed to produce the Higgs boson sub-atomic particle. And that was all he needed to know about that for the moment. Enough theory! Oh, and there was some stuff about hacking into satellites through the decades, to pass signals through time, and that involve using churches, cathedrals, abbeys and historical monoliths, where the technology did not exist. *"Stonehenge might look like a circle of large boulders, but* "But why me?" The burning question, among the myriad of other questions. "What? Why me? How? What is my part in all of this? How am I connected to this? To this, what did you call the underground thing? The device?"

"I didn't call it anything. It is the Nebogipfel Project. Also known as the History Maker. And that is all I can tell you. At this stage. As far as your part in this, and your connection."

An anomaly – that was how she described him. He shouldn't exist, not in his time zone – in 2014. There have been others – there are others, scattered throughout time, and history. Products of corruption from her time. Why? That is the question – part of her investigations, which involved him. Azarias was special, though, because he was unstable. There was a problem with the chip, most likely – the chip that had been implanted at birth. *'Chip? Unstable?'* He mused. Saluki moved quickly from that topic and began to talk about the rules and regulations of time travel, but she would return to that other topic later.

The instability of the embedded chip, causing unplanned, uncontrolled time leaps during sleep would now be managed by the mobile device. *'Some sleep walking, that!'* All those dreams that had seemed so vivid, so real. That was why. Then the intervention, where Saluki and her team had to step in, to prevent harm to himself, and damage to the very 'fabric' of space and time. It had proven necessary to maintain the illusion of the dream, sedating Azarias to ensure that he awoke in the appropriate place, where he been sleeping, and that he had not interfered with any of the mechanics of the course of history, whereby he may have disturbed the equilibrium of the future – the distant future. And, there had been meetings, a number of meetings, regarding his readiness to be made aware of the situation – Saluki neglected to mention the part where they, the deciding committee, had referenced the choice that was available; *'educate or eradicate.'*

*'The future?'* At that point Azarias could not have known what the future, any future, held for him, nor could he even begin to guess at the possibilities that life held for him.

"You are what is termed as an emergent," Saluki continued. "Detected only due to your instability. It has happened to others. No one, though, has jumped around through time, out of control, in the same way that you have. As long as you have this mobile device you will be able to control time travel. Stay with me on this. You will experience it soon. But there are rules. I know that I repeat myself but it is important. There are terms and conditions."

And these rules, regulations, and terms and conditions, she shared with Azarias. She handed him a printed sheet of paper with the title, The Ten Rules of Time Travel –

1)   Travelling forward in time from the point of origin is forbidden – the consequences of such a time leap may prove fatal.

2)   Time travellers must not interfere with people and events in the past, so as to change the course of history, without good reason, and without the permission of the directorate. Such actions have been forbidden without consultation with the aforementioned directorate.

3) Time travellers shall not attempt to gain pecuniary interest or material benefit when visiting the past, and must not transport, or move, any artefacts, of any type, to any point in their future where such artefact may be deemed as relics, antiquities, or vestiges of immense value.

4) Time travellers must not, under any circumstances, eradicate human life, or attempt to extinguish any family line or ancestry, when visiting the past, unless such acts are sanctioned by law, and endorsed by two appropriate signatories of the Directorate, with such good reason as to protect the status quo of the point of origin.

5)   Time travellers are forbidden to fraternize with 'past lives' in an attempt to create progeny where it should not exist, thereby producing their own alternative lineage, as such an intervention may infect the genetic pool, thus impacting on the Guardian class, at the point of origin.

At this juncture, looking across his shoulder, from behind, and judging by the way his forefinger traced the words, and realising the point he had reached on The Rules of Time Travel, Saluki raised a relevant, probing question – *"What do you know of you father?"*

"Very little," he replied. "Why do you ask?"

"I am interested. Do you have, umm, any images, likenesses, photographs or digital recording of him?"

"No. Nothing," he lied. I have no idea what he looks like. Should I say, looked like. I have no recollection of ever having met him." He hoped that she did not possess the ability to read minds, as well as travel through time and space, but then, maybe she already knew the answers to all the questions – from her perspective it had all happened, surely.

Saluki had her limitations, though, and did not know everything. She did not have all the answers, just most of them, and it might prove difficult tracking someone who was abusing their status, position, authority, or abilities, if they also had the wherewithal to leave no trace of their movements; ensuring that no record of their visit or activities was left for anyone investigating time crimes. And all she had to go on, at this point was rumour and conjecture; an unsubstantiated reference to names, and some biblical connotations which could be purely coincidental –

*'Azarias and the Archangel Raphael. Possibly nonsense but must be considered. Perhaps there would be no record of him, if he wanted to conceal his activities and relationships. Would he allow images or*

*memories to be collected and stored? An angel? Perhaps a long time ago – angels. Time travellers. One and the same? Superstition and fear of then unknown. Angels – time travellers leaving a legacy. Who? Why? To what end? At what cost? Have we already paid the price for corrupting history and time?'*

Azarias spoke, snapping her out of her reverie. "What about my father? Why the interest?"

"Never mind. Later, perhaps. Continue reading the rules. Please."


6)   Time travellers should not attempt to commit to a time leap if connected or attached to a fixed or permanent structure or object. Such action could prove fatal, resulting in partial removal of the time traveller from a point in history, followed by partial arrival at the point of origin, that point of origin being the place in time from which any such time leap originated.

7)   Time travellers should always ensure they have a safe point of arrival at any point in time and space – planning and preparation is paramount.

8)   Time travellers must procure a number and variety of safe places to which to return at the point of origin, where safety and security are guaranteed; particularly the event of any emergency.

9)   Time travellers should adopt the mode of dress, customs, language and currency appropriate to the time. Planning and preparation are paramount.

10) Time travellers must, at all costs, in all actions, endeavour to protect the integrity of the point of origin.

Azarias carefully placed the document on the coffee table, on the edge of the inset glass, so as to align the paper as if he was laying it in scanner or photocopier; such attention to detail, perhaps a little OCD. His eyes remained focused on the paper for a while, in contemplative silence, and he could sense Saluki, behind him, slightly to his right, her eyes searching his profile for a glimmer of a reaction, perhaps to the rules – to anything. A lot to take in, and accept, but he had accepted the truth. He knew it was the truth. *'What next?'*

"Questions," she broke the silence. "You must have questions."

"Many," he replied. "Where do I start? Please. Sit down again. I am trying to understand. All of this," he gestured towards the document.

She sat on the same sofa, crossing her legs, right over left, reclining back into the corner, her right hand coming to rest on the arm of the sofa, he left palm coming to rest on her lap. She fixed her emerald eyes on his face, with a confidence that suggested she was more than comfortable, at home here. Azarias returned her gaze, smiling the sort of smile that invites more than just a conversation between friends, offering all sorts of potential promises of romance and seduction. *'Attractive? No doubt. But I am still married.'*

"Number six on the list," he began. "Point six. And number ten. Surely ten covers points two, three, four and five."

"Bureaucrats!" she sniffed. "One hundred words when one will suffice. Justification of importance. However, such rules must be observed. I will explain."

Saluki clarified the terms and conditions – the rules of time travel – and reinforced the fact the any breach carried heavy penalties, and could prove fatal. The document had been born following the advent of time travel, and adjusted over time. It had proven necessary to police the corrupt, those individuals who had sought to use and abuse time travel to suit their own needs, to meet their own ends, and ambitions. Azarias was a product of such corruption – the product of a breach of rule 5 – and there are many more examples of this crime having been committed throughout time. A few had been brought to task, and dealt with accordingly, where crimes have been committed, driven by greed and the desire for power.

"Point six on the document," Saluki stated, "Was not merely written with a view to the safe return of travellers to the point of origin, but with consideration to as rescue, or extraction, from any time zone, any epoch in history, and time, where those who are in breach of the rules may face justice. Unfortunately, some have found themselves facing the justice appropriate in that time. On more than one occasion a time traveller has returned incomplete, having been shackled in medieval irons, locked in stocks, or in the process of being crucified or hanged. Some have abused their position and attempted to change history. I will attempt to summarise," she continued. "Many people are frightened of the truth. They do not want to hear the truth. Certainly not accept what I am about to tell you. It undermines many belief systems and does not help to explain the great variety of creeds and religions that have existed." She correct herself – "That exist. History is not what it seems." Saluki studied his face, again searching for a reaction. There was none, so she delivered the punchline.

"Your past, and your present, all of which is my history exist, and are made, in the future. My present. My world. Your history. My history. Our history is made in the future. Everything that we are, everything that is, starts with the Nebogipfel Project. The History Maker."

# Chapter 21

Side by side they stood – Damarov and Le Feuvre – staring silently across the Territories and Provinces de la Belgique; the La Meuse River shimmering in the afternoon sun like a snaking diamond necklace, carelessly and, full of promise, sensually dropped upon the floor of a lover's boudoir. The summit, the roof terrace, of La Tour de la Croix bleached beneath the naked 42°C azure sky, yet the artificial intelligence of the Nanotechnology in their clothing and footwear insulated their bodies and feet, providing comfort and preventing perspiration. Gabriel released a deep discontented sigh from the depths of his diaphragm, and the very cellar of his soul, before speaking with such a tone that reflected his status and authority.

"We do not have a body. Or evidence of a body. Yet. May have disintegrated on impact with the water. Like hitting concrete from this height." He waved his right hand in dismissive – *it is not your turn to speak yet* – fashion, silencing any potential interruption, before continuing. "However, there are pipes drawing water into the complex, for the cooling system. And, pipes recycling the water back into the lake. It is possible that we will find some evidence to confirm his suicide.

Something of him may be found, in the lake, the pipes, or filters, which will leave no doubt as to the outcome. Yes? And. You saw the body fall. Correct? You may speak."

A drop of sweat tickled the tip of Le Feuvre's nose, and this was brushed away with his right hand as he gesticulated in the direction of the edge of the roof terrace. He opened his mouth to speak, but the Superus cut him off before there was any chance to utter a word.

"Never, never answer that question. Whether I ask, or anyone else asks. You were not here. Remember? Life has been recorded as extinct. A body was seen to fall in the lake. Accident? Suicide? That is for the investigating team to decide. But we do not have a body. Let us hope that the divers find something. Some evidence of death. One does not reach such positions of authority without a little healthy paranoia. I would hate to think we might have been tricked. Evidence of death is a solution to that problem."

As they stood there – side by side – each with their gaze fixed on the distant horizon, a loud noise ripped through the cloudless sky, like a single clap of thunder or a jet breaking the sound barrier, and it echoed around the countryside. Damarov shook his head, briskly, as if the sound had caused his ears some pain. Both searched above, and around, seeking the source of the interference but nothing was evident or visible. Nothing! They both returned their gaze to the far distance, beyond the La Meuse.

"So, tell me about the other problem. What happened?"

Augustin was wearing his white uniform but was minus his crash helmet – he did not shift his gaze from the distant horizon while describing events in the wooded copse, where he had been assigned to observe the meeting of commandant Saluki Damarov and the emergent, Azarias Tor.

"Nothing out of the ordinary. Observe and report. You said. I observed. I am reporting. I remained hidden and ensured that I could not be traced. I would suggest that it was a carefully selected location. On the part of the Commandant. And the time. No other persons were evident at the chosen site. I could see enough by the light of the moon. How much larger the moon was back then. I digress. Nothing unusual. He now has a device to enable him to control time travel. All that we anticipated. I am of the same belief that the device will now link to the chip, which was implanted at or close to birth. Perhaps we will discover the identity of his father, in time. They departed together in his vehicle from a nearby parking place. An inn, I believe. The Snowy Owl. Later, that same night, they engaged in a controlled time leap. November 1999. They remained at that point in the past no longer than 15 minutes. Nothing remarkable or out of the ordinary, as I previously stated."

"Good. Good work," Damarov enthused. Let us hope things remain that way. Nothing remarkable. No cause for concern. Nothing out of the ordinary. Excellent. Perhaps, one day, you will be able to report on the effects of the Subsonne Mark II. One day. Stay close. Covert. Observe and report. Take action where necessary."

Damarov turned to leave but was stopped in his tracks when Le Feuvre said, "Strange, don't you think? That a man should purchase such a grand apartment then not live in it. Why has he used it for such a short time? Did he have a plan? To throw himself from the roof? Not much of a plan. Still strange. Why bring me here? Why?"

"Perhaps we will never know the answer," Damarov pondered. "As you were. Observe and report."

Superus Damarov, without a further word, turned and marched towards the rooftop elevator, which would return him to the apartment that was once the home of Raphael Antinori. Le Feuvre was left standing alone, staring into that same distance, lost in thought, muttering to himself.

"One day it will all be mine," he scowled. "I will be Superus."

The Superus was out of earshot, descending in the elevator, sinking through the roof and into the apartment below.

"And," Augustin continued. Hissing with venom, "You will be nothing more than muck that I may scrape from the sole of my boot. You will be nothing. Soon. I promise you that. One day. Soon."

*Newton's third law – 'for every action, there is an equal and opposite reaction.'*

To that end it was highly likely that Damarov had not attained his position in life without considering every action on his part, and every potential opposite reaction from those from whom he sought fealty; such being

245

garnished with references to career advancement and financial rewards; and it was just possible that Gabriel already had plans in place to counter the plans of others, who might pose a threat to him − *'you cannot kid a kidder!'* Not sure that what was in the mind of Isaac Newton when he developed his third law but it did mean that a person's life could be endangered if they messed with Damarov.

\*\*\*

Azarias scoured the open plan office space, searching for Alan but he was not to be found in the usual places. His Vauxhall had not been immediately obvious in the car park, yet he would normally be in place, at his desk, a little after 8 a.m. It was 8.40 a.m. Azarias had arrived later than usual but then he had had a busy night, what with meeting with Saluki, the revelations that followed, the introduction to the terms and conditions, and taking part in his first controlled time leap; yes, a busy night! He felt tired, yet exhilarated, and wanted to share the details with Alan. He owed him that much, he thought. He had obeyed the diktat, and denied Alan the opportunity to witness that moment when Saluki had appeared out of thin air, from nowhere, beneath Northumberlandia, like a spirit in the night. Azarias had not stopped to enquire with any members of Alan's team as to his whereabouts, assuming that he might be in his classroom, or attending to his morning constitutional in the men's room. He might have parked his car elsewhere on the site − but why? Heading towards his own desk, Azarias considered catching up with his colleague and friend later in the day. Arriving at his desk, he found on the lid of his closed laptop, a scribbled message on a yellow post-it note – *'A.T. Phone Liz. Urgent. 07974898581.'*

"Strange," he murmured to himself; his colleagues were too otherwise occupied to take notice of him, reading emails, sending messages, making last minute adjustments to PowerPoint presentations and lesson plans, perhaps discussing student discipline issues. Some tutors, from various work stations, began heading towards their teaching objectives, dragging plastic wheeled trollies, containing student files, behind them.

Azarias was going to be late for his first lesson of the day – one hour and thirty minutes of Functional Skills, English – but it did not appear to be a coincidence that Liz had called, and that there was no sign of Alan around the college. In retrospect, given the circumstances, he did think it a little odd that Alan had not been waiting with bated breath for an update on the events of the previous day. He pressed the numbers into the keypad of his Blackberry Pearl – 0-7-9-7-4-8-9-8-5-8-1.

Leaving the office, Azarias headed to the landing at the top of the stairwell, before pushing the green handset symbol. He had connected with the number, which rang out four times before it was answered. Liz spoke, breathlessly – panic in her voice.

"Azarias? Thanks for calling."

"That's okay," he said expressing the concern in his tones. "What's wrong?"

"Alan," she sobbed, uncontrollably. "He didn't, didn't come home last night. I haven't seen—seen him." Liz was struggling to get the words out, repeating herself as she tried to gather some dignity. "Where is he? Have, have, you seen him? I can't reach him on his phone."

Azarias urged her to take a few deep breaths, to slow down and start again; he had no idea what she was talking about. What had it got to do with him – Alan not returning home? And, as she continued, the proverbial 'penny dropped.'

"Yesterday," Liz said, composing herself. "He said he was going out to meet you. A drink and a meal. The Snowy Owl. I phoned them. He was there. But he hasn't come home. They said …"

"…What time?" he interrupted, repeating himself. "What time?"

"He said that you were meeting about half-seven. Eight. The Snowy Owl. A meal. He said. Time with a friend and colleague. He doesn't get out much. Very much a home bird. But he hasn't come home. I haven't seen him since last evening. I'm worried."

"I understand," Azarias offered, pausing to think, for what seemed an age, but was probably only a few seconds, before continuing. "Leave it with me. I will call you back in a few minutes. And don't worry."

"What is going on?" she probed. "Do you know something?"

"Trust me," he urged. "I will sort this. A few minutes and I have a feeling that everything will be just the way it was." And then he finished the call.

In a cubicle, in the 'gents', Azarias locked the door, and removed his Motorola from a trouser pocket. Remembering the lessons he had learned from the previous night, his first controlled time leap, he entered the approximate time, the correct date and location and pressed enter, just at the very moment someone opened the main door to the men's room. He heard whoever it was pull up the urinal, and the sound of piss splashing on the porcelain, but it was too late – Azarias would have no idea that his colleague would splash all over his shoes when a flash of 'electricity', and a crackling sound, filled the room. Too late. *'Shit, fuck and arseholes! Here we go!'*

Azarias experienced the same sensation as he had done during the first controlled time leap, the previous night – that feeling when a pilot pulls back on the throttle as the aircraft begins its descent towards the airport. A sense of floating, suspended by magic in the air, as if the hovering might cease and end in a crashing fall from a great height. The same feeling experienced on a stomach churning fair ground, or theme park, ride, with that same threat of nausea and vertigo – he had been informed that would improve with time, and experience.

A short journey – less than 24 hours, unlike the earlier trip to 1999, and this meant that the tunnel of light, with its images, was so much shorter. At the culmination of that journey Azarias had vomited in the alley at the side of the Tyne Cinema – he had never suffered with travel sickness before, in his life, but this was different; time travel sickness. It would cease, Saluki had assured him, and he would become accustomed, in time, - *"No pun intended," she had said* – and that he would move through the pain barrier.

He arrived, as planned, in the field adjacent to The Snowy Owl Inn. Azarias was certain that no one had seen him meld out of the air, the earth, appearing from nowhere, kneel on the grass retching, this time without vomiting. And no one was around when he rose to his full height, and walked towards the car park of the inn – nobody had noticed anything out of the ordinary. Azarias scoured the area, searching for that particular model of car – the one belonging to Alan but could not find what he was looking for, and returned to the gate, that would take him back into them field leading towards The Lady of the North. *'Surely not,'* he thought. *'The old dog. Having an affair? No. Where is his car? Hang on. No.'*

A change of mind caused him to about turn and walk towards the main door leading into the inn. Upon entering he passed a couple – male and female – *'early thirties',* he thought, for no apparent reason; only that old habits die hard, those traits and skills developed in his other life, when he used to be in the job. Azarias almost felt like he was on the job now, on a case. The couple were standing outside, smoking cigarettes – that pointless exercise of not smoking inside the building, yet wafting the smoke inside every time the door opens and closes, not to mention the pile of dog-ends surrounding the immediate vicinity. Looking to his left, closing the door behind him, he noted that the place was busy, and his eyes scanned the faces of the people seated, and those standing at the bar – ordering food and beverages, sipping a beer or wine, stuffing the occasional fork full of meat or fish, and vegetables into gaping mouths – but

250

there was no one he recognised, and the restaurant and bar space extended beyond the end of the serving counter, around a corner, to the right, and into smaller rooms. Azarias had eaten in here, with his wife, and knew the layout of the inn. *'Alan could be anywhere, if he is in here.'*

He worked his way through the building, searching every nook and cranny, exploring every face in some uncomfortable detail. And then he caught sight of an area of the car park, to the rear of the building, through a window, and noted that smaller cars could be hidden from view by larger models – *'how often have people attempted to turn in to what appeared to be an empty parking space, only to find some little Tonka-type car hiding behind a Range Rover?'*

"Of course," he mumbled to himself, causing one woman nearby, sitting alone, to look up at him from that seat near that window.

"Sorry," he said, smiling apologetically. "Talking to myself. First sign of madness."

Azarias turned and retraced his steps to the main door. Beyond the entrance lobby, at the other end of the building, another area – a smaller section, with four tables, surrounded by chairs. Three of the tables were occupied – a couple, most likely in their sixties, empty plates in front of them, on another table, a family – two adults and two children, all in the throes of shovelling food into their mouths. At another table, near a window, a single male, head buried in a large menu. Walking towards that table, upon reaching it, Azarias tipped the menu forward, enabling the reader and the inquisitor to make eye to eye contact.

"Doctor Livingstone, I presume," Azarias said, much to Alan's surprise.

"Ah. I didn't expect you this early," Alan mumbled, placing the menu flat on the table. "What I read over your shoulder suggested you would be here much later. I was going to wait and watch. But you are here. Now."

"I saw the car. Your wife's car," Azarias stated. "She called me."

"When?" he asked.

"Ah. Now that is difficult to explain," Azarias responded.

At the very moment they made contact people in the bar, and the smokers outside, physically jumped at the sound of a loud bang – somewhere outside, echoing across the sky and rattling the windows. Startled drinkers and diners looked out of the windows attempting to track the sonic boom-stroke-thunder-clap in the heavens. And when the sound ceased it was replaced with a cacophony of mumbling voices, as people returned to their food and tables, each, possibly giving their own version, account, or theory as to the source of the noise –

*"The open cast mine." "Not at this time of day, surely." – "Fracking, I think." "Not around here." "How can you be sure?" – "Aircraft? Sonic boom, maybe." – "An explosion, I think." "Where?" – "I'll Google it later. Someone will have reported it."*

A few pairs of thumbs were busy tapping on mobile phones with internet facilities, searching for any information relating to ear-splitting, sky-splitting sound, in spite of their actions being so immediate to the event, such was the competition to be the first to report the cause – Azarias had his own thought.

"What was that?" Alan asked, craning to look out of the window himself, then back to Azarias. "Coincidence?"

"I'd like to know what happened before," Azarias said, thoughtfully running the fingers of his right hand through his hair.

"What do you mean? Before?"

"I'm not sure," he responded, "But I think I now know what it sounds like to breach one of the rules of time travel."

\*\*\*

Superus Damarov was surprised to encounter Saluki in the apartment of the deceased Vice-Superus, as he made his way from the elevator to the door. She stood to attention, clicking her heels together, and bowing her head before him – official business, not mere father, daughter personal issues. Three other officers, two male and one female, appeared to be busy searching cupboards, drawers, and moving artwork – looking for something, perhaps.

"What are they doing?" the commandant asked, casually, glancing at each of the officers in turn.

"Looking for clues, as to what might have happened here," Gabriel answered, cutting a sweeping arc with his right arm.

"What has happened here?"

"Walk with me," he urged, opening the door to leave the apartment, giving a visual sign for her to take the lead, which she did. As they walked side by side the Superus side-stepped the moving walkway, preferring to use the time to is benefit.

"Walk," he repeated. "And talk."

Damarov maintained the same lies, and remembered that Saluki had her mind on other things, involved elsewhere in space and time, and may not yet be aware of the death of the Vice-Superus. *'Why is she here?'* He said nothing for a while, wondering what might be going on in her mind.

Even though Saluki had returned to the point of origin and at the time she had departed, she had not been kept up to date with news. She was a little confused, there having been no such drama before travelling through space and time to fulfil her obligations towards the emergent, Azarias. Saluki looked back over her shoulder at the closed door, a sense of dread tingling inside her chest, and she knew something was wrong, terribly wrong and Saluki could sense, almost hear, Raphael Antinori speaking to her, warning her that things were not as they first seemed. *'No. This cannot be,'* she thought, shaking her head.

"It appears that he jumped," Gabriel interceded, regaining her attention , possibly attempting to read her thoughts through those inscrutable emerald green eyes. "Witnesses saw a body fall from the top of the building into the lake. And his life is registered as extinct." Again, he searched her eyes for a sign – something that might betray her allegiance, or reveal knowledge of the truth, but he saw no 'tell'.

"But why? Why would he do that?" Saluki asked, adjusting her steps to match the timing of his feet, as they proceeded along the cathedral-like corridor, passing the doors of other apartments.

"Guilt, perhaps," he offered, with a conspiratorial tone. "Evidence has been mounting to suggest corruption on his part. We have a file. It is possible that he is linked to your emergent. Azarias Tor."

"But that is easy to prove. Surely. DNA. I am sure Azarias would oblige if it meant he could discover the truth about his father."

"That will not be necessary," he growled, stopping them both in their tracks. "We have enough evidence to make the link. We must not interfere with the past or its people."

"Of course. I was not thinking." She paused, and Gabriel did not make a move to fill the silence, allowing Saluki to tentatively offer a thought; "There may be another way. It is just a thought. I asked what he knew about his father. Had he ever seen him? He said, 'he knew very little about him and had not seen him.'

"Your point?"

Her uRAPP began to vibrate on her left wrist, buzzing audibly, as she attempted to answer his question – *'The point? What was the point?'*

"The point," she began, maintaining a poker face as she read the message displayed on the central screen – *'Delta one-five! D1-5! For your eyes only. Mierde. Serious stuff.'* Saluki noted, with some concern, that her father did not appear to have received a similar message – at least, his device was not attempting to gain his attention – and she could not discuss it with him, the Superus, until she knew the contents of the message. And then, maybe not at all. The receipt of a Code Delta One-Five meant that she was sworn to secrecy and worse still; she was in a state of personal lock-down.

"The point," she repeated, silencing the buzzing sound at the same time. "Like I said. I asked him if he knew anything …"

"Do you need to deal with that?" Damarov interrupted, pointing at her uRAPP, with a sense of interest, as if he was fishing for information regarding the message she had received.

"No, no. It can wait," Saluki responded, a little distractedly. "Back to my point. I think he lied. Azarias. Lied about his father. Think about it. His mother was an artist. Of sorts. She might not have been allowed to capture an electronic image, or photograph, but would she not be able to produce images from memory? Sketches? Drawings? A painted portrait, perhaps? A sketch of her lover. The father of her son. What do you think?"

And then her father said something, which she would never forget – a few words that caused the hairs on the nape of her neck to bristle, though she hid her thoughts. Buried them deep inside – at least, that was what she hoped to achieve.

"Of course. I should have remembered," he said, almost as if his thoughts had drifted away to some distant memory of a long lost past – another past in another time. And suddenly, he snapped himself back to his senses.

"His name," he continued, having regained his presence of mind. "Have you given much thought to his name? Azarias. What it stands for? What it might mean? No? You should do. A little research might enlighten you. Anyway. Enough. Is there anything else?"

Again, the belligerent and bullying Damarov controlled and directed debate and discussion, with a dismissive wave, particularly if he had lost in the subject matter, or it was an issue he wished to avoid – ever the politician. But there was something else bothering him.

"There has been a breach," he stated, as they reached the elevator of the central tower. "You heard it too?"

She nodded.

"Your mission?"

"I don't know."

"It is your place to know," he added. "I will visit Nebogipfel. Discover if there have been any repercussions." He held out his right arm out, so as to prevent the elevator door from closing. "Are you getting in?"

"No. No. You are right. I should investigate the breach," she partly lied – there was the small matter of the Code Delta One-Five, though that would have to wait. First she was going to have to discover if Azarias was responsible for the breach. And, if so, why?

Damarov pulled his arm in and the door hissed as it closed, and he immediately engaged with his uRAPP. Le Feuvre's face appeared on the central screen.

"Superus Damarov. What can I do for you?"

"I need you to carry out a mission for me. A small task. We must remember that you are certain for promotion. Soon. In the meantime I want you to locate some papers for me in the home of the emergent. I have an idea that we will find something that could prove incriminating in the wrong hands. Avoid contact with him. He must not come to any harm. I will tell you what I am looking for. Can you do this?"

"Consider it done," Augustin answered.

***

Azarias arrived back at the cubicle in the cubicle, in the staff toilet, as if he had never even left the building – same time, same place. It was as if he had just closed the door behind him. The evidence of the time leap, though, was in the fact that he was retching, again, and again, heaving but not vomiting. It would wear off, in time. He had never suffered with travel sickness before, but then he had never *knowingly* travelled through time and space, until the previous evening. Azarias did not include his 'sleep travelling' episodes. *'A little knowledge is a dangerous thing!'*

"Are you okay in there?"

He had forgotten that someone had entered the men's room at the very moment of the time leap. Sensing that the unseen person was approaching the cubicle, Azarias thought it prudent to reply, and depressed the flush at the same time.

"I'm okay. Thanks. A touch of morning sickness," he joked.

Whoever it was, out there, turned and stomped away, seemingly put out by the light-hearted response, muttering – *"Ask a bloody civil question. Don't know why I bother."*

Upon hearing the main entrance door open, then close, Azarias vacated the cubicle, and located a wash basin, where he washed his hands with the due care and diligence of a surgeon, and then splashed cold water on to his face. Someone else entered the men's room. Azarias allowed the water to fall from his face, and drain from his hands, and then turned and looked up. Alan greeted him, chattering excitedly, like a playful capuchin monkey, leaping from one tree to another, as Alan flittered through a range of subjects and issues surrounding the past 24 hours or so.

He raved about that *"boom"* – the window rattling noise. It had made the early morning news – *"Police received numerous calls regarding the sound of an explosion yesterday evening heard in the Cramlington area. Some callers had described hearing a loud noise which was a cross between a sonic boom and a very loud clap of thunder. There were reports of windows rattling and, in some cases; the vibrations which followed the sound caused objects to fall from shelves. A search of the area revealed nothing and a spokesperson for Newcastle International Airport stated that there was no reason to link the sound to flights arriving and departing from the airport. The sound remains an unexplained mystery.* Alan also referred to the fact that he had taken the advice of his friend and colleague and returned home to his family. *"Nothing out of the ordinary."*

Then he had arrived home on one piece, unharmed, the passage of time having been altered; but he did not know that – Azarias had guessed that something sinister had been avoided. He did not want to discuss it though. *"Better not mention this again."* But Alan could not help himself, and ranted about the fact that he witnessed Azarias vanishing before his eyes – the leap through time and space ending in the men's room, as promised. He had failed in his original mission, to hide in that field and wait for Azarias to arrive. Alan had hoped that he would get to see this woman – *Saluki* – who was sending the text messages, and giving him the run-around. He never got to witness that meeting. Azarias had found him in the Snowy Owl, before the event. *'Damn. Didn't plan for that.'* Still, Alan had been privileged to watch Azarias meld into the evening air, in that field, with the promise that they would meet again in this place, at this time. *'Mind-boggling. The point of origin! He must have met with her. Never mind. Perhaps another time.'*

Azarias opted against informing Alan that they could now possibly be on an alternative time-line, or that he, himself, was now experiencing a second and different start to his Tuesday morning, with no change for Alan and everyone else – one person was in on the secret, that there were, potentially, *'two different same days! Does that make sense? I am aware of two different mornings. Or is it just the same one, but different?'* He kept his thoughts locked away. No one needed to know, not that anyone would believe him. But it was a different outcome – Alan had returned home to his family and his wife, Liz, had not missed Alan, and had not cause for concern, or reason to phone Azarias. In this time and place Alan was not missing. Whatever had happened to Alan hadn't happened due to intervention – another time, another reality.

*'How many other things have turned out differently, or not happened? Happened, even? Due to that shift in time,'* he pondered as he turned his hands beneath the drier. *'Maybe it is insignificant. Had no noticeable impact on anything or anyone. Too localised, perhaps? Such a short space of time. But the sound? No. What could have happened? What could have changed? And would we know any different? Shit happens. Que sera, sera.'*

"A penny for them," Alan said, his mood having calmed somewhat.

"What teaching do you have this morning?" Alan questioned, removing himself from his deepest thoughts.

"Nothing until after the break," he replied, adding in an *Are You Being Served* John Inman style, "I'm free!"

"Okay. I promised. And I feel I owe it to you. You will be sworn to absolute secrecy. And you may be complicit, if you know what I mean? Meet me in G62 at …" he looked at his watch on his left wrist … "Nine-twenty. Give me time to send my group away on along breakfast. No point in kidding myself that they will go and study in the library. Is there? And, taking recent events into account my days here are probably numbered."

"Why. What have you done?"

"Discovered time travel."

\*\*\*

As Le Feuvre arrived at his prearranged coordinates, more by luck and guesswork than judgement, he froze, having neglected to consider the possibility that the property might have an intruder alarm; a movement detector. Augustin waited, statue-like, prepared to return to his point of origin should any alarm in the home of Azarias draw attention to this intrusion. No point in attracting unwanted attention. The instructions had been clear – *'Avoid contact with him. Take that to mean avoid contact with others in the locality, also.'* – Nothing happened. Silence. Le Feuvre moved his left arm, waving his hand by the side of his helmeted head. Still nothing. Silence.

"Of course," he said to himself, removing the helmet, placing it carefully upon the inlaid glass of the coffee table, "A safe place to return from a time leap. You would not want to set off your alarm. You may not enter the code in time. Until you get used to it and no longer suffer the effects. You don't want to attract attention either, do you? Date and local time," he continued, reading the data from the central screen on his uRAPP, "Tuesday May 20th, 2014. 09:25. Good. We have all the time in the world. Now. Where do we start?"

Le Feuvre collected his helmet from the table and headed up the varnished wooden stairs, turning at the top to face the door to the third bedroom – the study. A few steps forward and he opened the door, entered the room, setting his helmet down on the larger office-style desk, situated to his left.

"Yes. A good place to start. Don't you agree?"

There was no one present, no other person in the room, and no colleague listening on the end of any communication device, to answer his question, other than himself.

"Yes. This a very good place to start."

***

It had taken about 25 minutes for Azarias to give a potted account of the events of the previous evening; that meeting with Saluki, the rules and regulations of time travel, and the first controlled time leap. He had ensured that his fifteen students had lost themselves around the college, so that he could share the information with Alan, without interruption. Somewhat irresponsible, perhaps, but the speed at which things were moving for Azarias led him to conclusion that he was not going to be in the employ of the college much longer, and it was highly unlikely that any senior members of staff would venture into the is part of the building; too busy fulfilling their roles of self-importance, pushing data round and round in circles, and far removed from the realities of teaching in the classroom. He had had enough, anyway, but never expected, suspected, or anticipated his escape route would be so dramatic.

He sensed that he was on the cusp of a life-changing event, and he was going to need an ally; someone he could trust – someone he could trust with his slowly germinating seed of a plan, which was growing in his fertile mind, following the two controlled time-leaps. It was the first journey that Azarias was keen to share with Alan, the second having involved finding his colleague in The Snowy Owl and that was the journey from which the plan was being hatched. Something had been altered. He was not prepared to explain too much, not yet, until he was certain that his plan would work, and he began by sharing the details of his first controlled time-leap.

*** 

Having proven to Saluki that he could remember, and recite, the 'ten commandments' of time travel, she

264

decided it was time to prepare Azarias for his first controlled time-leap.

"Well done. You have passed you theory," she joshed, standing and moving behind the sofa, to the space between the bottom of the stairs and the lobby door.

"Join me here," she commanded. "With the device. The Motorola. You will need it. This is your first practical."

His mood changed from the slough of despond, having spent some time wallowing in the misery of the shrine to his wife, and his own self-pity, to an Everest of anticipation, at the thought of his first controlled time-leap – *'Surreal!'* Azarias stood beside her and flipped open the mobile phone, noting that the keypad had been altered to include *date, time and location* buttons.

"Question," he commenced. "I have a concern. What if the battery runs out, or is low in power, and I find myself stuck somewhere in time? And, I can't recharge? Two questions, really."

"And good questions," she enthused, pleased with her student's progress and attitude. "Very good questions. It will only ever cease to operate if you cease to exist …"

"… Excuse me?" he interrupted. "If I cease to exist?"

"Yes," she smiled. "Your life force provides the power. You are, as you so quaintly put it, the battery. Remember? I told you. The chip. Embedded at or near your birth, you are at one with it. The chip connects you to the device. The device connects you to the most powerful force developed by physicists. You will learn. Now, switch it on. Feel the power."

Azarias switched the Motorola on with the corner of the thumbnail of his right hand, just as he had done so in the past, when he used it. But something was different. His body buzzed, tingled, from the feet upwards – not like electricity but more like a static charge, and a feeling that he was connected to everything; aware of the very planet upon which was he standing, the life-force pulsating and vibrating through him. *'Whoa!'*

"Feel it?" she asked, before ordering Azarias to place the mobile phone on any step of his choice.

He moved forward, unquestioningly, and placed the Motorola on the fifth step up from the bottom, then looked to Saluki with an inquiring expression on his face. She pulled him back, some distance from the stairs, and told him to hold out his right hand, and focus his mind on the device.

"Picture it in your mind. Focus. Call to it. Command it to come to you. Focus. Believe in the unbelievable. See it. In your mind."

*'Weird! Daft! Am I going mad?'* he thought, holding out his right hand, as instructed, thinking the requested *'mad'* thoughts.

"Dismiss the negative thoughts," she whispered. "It is only natural. Focus. Good."

*'Come to me. Come on. For fuck's sake,'* his mind screamed. *'To my hand. Come on.'*

And then an unexpected thing happened – something that Azarias did not expect, and something many people would not expect to happen. That is the thing with the unexpected – it is not usually expected but Azarias was now starting to accept the unexpected; expect the unexpected. The mobile phone rattled on the step, as if it was on a tray that someone was shaking, before hovering, repelled by some unseen magnetic force. It wavered for a few seconds and then glided through the air directly into the outstretched right hand of Azarias. He clamped his finger around it, feeling a connection – something that was part of him, a device, linked Azarias to planet Earth and its history, perhaps all of known time and beyond.

"Wow. Shit!" he exclaimed. "There are more things in heaven and Earth, Horatio, than are dreamt of in your philosophy."

"Who is Horatio?" she enquired.

"Me," he replied. "Me, the ignorant. Without a doubt. I could never have imagined such things were possible. Never. Not in my wildest dreams."

"Yet where have your dreams taken you? In your past? Now you have a chance to be in control. Yes? But you must obey the rules. Now, choose a point in history you wish to visit. I will show what you need to do. Then we travel. Okay?"

Azarias had already given this some thought, and reached a decision regarding the point, and place, in time he wished to visit. An easy choice, for him.

"19.11.1999," he erupted. "A few minutes before 11.19 in the morning. Near the Monument, in Newcastle."

Saluki wanted to know why, of all the moments in history that he could have chosen, he had picked this one, though she suspected that it might have something to do with his prepossession with his dead wife. Having received confirmation of the meeting for their first date together, beneath Grey's Monument, on that day, and at that time, she deemed it necessary to remind him of the 'ten commandants' of time travel, and the potential consequences should he interfere with past events.

"I know. I know," he snorted. "Observe. I promise. I just want to see it. Capture the memory. That's all. Just a memory I had taken for granted."

"Okay," she said, demanding attention, hands on her hips, turning to face him. "Listen very carefully. I do not want to cause any upset. I know the scars are deep, but it is important that I share this knowledge with you. From my point in time, 2198, we are able to observe potential variables for past lives. What would have happened if this had changed or this had been different? In the case of your wife, should you prevent her death in the automobile crash, she will meet her end in a coach accident, and ten other people will die. Again, you will live. Avoid the coach crash; the next possibility is an explosion aboard an aircraft. No survivors. Except you. You always survive. Your wife was connected to you by an undercover operation you were involved with. A case you were investigating. You are now part of my investigations. Trust me. Maybe we can bring these people to justice. But you must trust my judgement. If you attempt to save her life many others may – will – die. I have seen the many potential paths because you are now living them. Have lived them. Some things could be changed. Some things should never be changed. And some things must never be changed. Make of that what you will. Do you understand?"

Azarias deigned to understand what was required of him, and agreed to whatever she wanted him to understand – he was bored with the rules and the regulations, and commandments – *'Get on with it!'* – Time for the important stuff.

"Show me," he said, offering her the Motorola. "What now?"

Saluki gave him a brief guided tour, and introduction, to the alterations to the keyboard, and any changed usage. The globe – internet/web tab – was now used to find any given location. Press that, and then enter location using the normal processes – address, town, city, county, state, country, zip code, post code, district number, and map coordinates. Then again, the screen would supply a satellite view of the chosen area, at the chosen time.

Landscapes change, edifices fall and rise, and cities and towns grow, while wars move boundaries on maps. Populations increase, cultures merge, and peoples move from one place to another, for a variety of reasons – whether through choice or as refugees. That is why timing is everything, absolutely crucial – where do you want to be, and when? That is why the text message tab and the envelope have been changed to assist with calendar dates, and the asterisk to a clock.

"When entering the date," she stated, "be sure to enter it in the order of day, month, and the year in full. Like this." She showed him an example. "Okay? Good. And then there is the use of Gregorian and Julian calendars. Just don't travel further back than 1582 until we discuss that in greater detail. The differences may be slight and the device will compensate, but you must take once step at a time. Are you ready?"

"Ready," he said. "Maybe I have been ready all of my life. And haven't I travelled in time already?"

"You have. By accident. Now. Enter the data. I will lock on your destination. You lead. I follow. Why the hesitation?"

A trickle of fear crept up and down his spine. *'What if this is the last thing I ever do? What have I to lose, other than my life? What if? Do or die. Live and learn. Nothing ventured!'* He tapped in the date – 19:11:1999, then the time – 11:14, allowing five minutes to position himself, to ensure a good view of the event. The he typed in the venue – 'Grey's Monument, Newcastle upon Tyne, UK.' It was enough – location and time coordinated, the screen produced a satellite image.

"Take care not to leap into a building, into something you do not have a visual for," she warned. "If you get the coordinates wrong you could become part of the fabric of a building, or tangled in some mechanism or other structures. Finito. And avoid crowds. Your sudden appearance out of the ether may cause shock to some. It is not the norm."

"I suppose not," he smirked.

Saluki provided guidance as to how to navigate on the screen, using the 'compass' arrows on the outer circle of the mobile fascia – the very centre should only be depressed once Azarias has the landing target locked in the sights. He moved the green 'cross-hairs around the area, adjacent to Grey's Monument, on the Google Earth-type view, searching for a safe landing place, away from people, down an alley between Pilgrim Street, behind the Tyneside cinema. Azarias knew the area well enough to take a chance that few people would use that cut-through, from one street to the other.

"And you?" he queried, finger hovering above the central button. "You need these coordinates?"

"I am locked into you. Where you go, I go. I will always know where you are. Ready?"

"Ready as I will ever be," he answered, grimacing as he pushed the button.

The full force of this giant blue white globe, our planet, spinning endlessly in the vast blackness of space, held him fast like a powerful magnet. Azarias imagined, felt, that he was in contact with the very core of the planet, and he was unbalanced by the journey around the sun; the rotation, as day turned into night, into day and back to night. He was freefalling through time, and space, and there was no turning back, no changing his mind – too late – until the chosen destination had been reached.

The world before his eyes, his world, his front room, the furniture, all solid matter, unseen atoms, and the air itself, appeared to dissolve around him, as if folded, crumpled, and poured into funnel. All light, all colour, gone. That sensation of an airline reducing speed, releasing the throttle, as it prepares for its final approach to the airport – that hovering feeling as the plane descends. Spots of light flashed in front of his eyes, as he also spiralled in that same funnel.

Nothing. Blackness. Disorientation and nausea – travel sickness. Not just any travel sickness – time travel sickness. The landing, arrival, was sudden and abrupt; like running into a mesh wire fence and bouncing off it, before coming to rest upright, safe and sound – all substance, matter, colour and sound, seemingly, unfolding from inside the funnel. *'Oh God!'* Not so safe and sound.

Retching, heaving guts – hands on knees. No vomit, just dribbling, stringy saliva, trailing from the mouth to the floor. A cold blast of near freezing wind, and a warm trickle of blood from his right nostril, shook Azarias to his senses. As he straightened himself to his full height, the realisation that appropriate clothing had not been considered, with regards to the time of year, suddenly dawned on him. *'May to November. Must remember that one in the future.'*

"It will not always be like this," a voice said. "It gets easier. Take a few deep breaths."

Saluki was rubbing his back, between his shoulder blades. Azarias focused his eyes on the new surroundings. *'Wow!'* He was at the end of the alley,

272

closer to Grey Street to avoid appearing out of thin air in front of the booking office, and café, belonging to the Tyneside Cinema. No one had witnessed their genie of the lamp appearance, though two male youths turned the corner, into the alley, from the direction of the Monument, just at the moment Azarias wiped blood from his nose, on to the back of his right hand.

"You need our help, pal?" a spotty pizza-face lad, jested.

"Looks as if ye getting a hiding," his comrade added, "Sad alkies!"

The two fairly unmemorable, easily forgotten, blend-in-with-the-crowd, lacklustre, tactless, thoughtless adolescents, lacking style, social graces and, most probably, female contact of any kind, laughed as they continued on their way, in the direction of Pilgrim Street. Azarias was now leaning against the wall of the bank and also laughed, as he thought to himself, *'Yeah, we probably do look like a couple of winos, fighting in an alley. Ignore them. Ah, that's better.'* And Saluki? Was she going to let it pass? No, she was not going to let their remarks pass, without comment.

"Hey boys," she called, provocatively, her hands clenched fists by her sides. "You want to find out what I can really do when I am mad? The nose bleed? Nothing. Just a gentle tap."

The two lads turned to face Saluki, and Azarias pushed himself away from the wall, checking his nose for further secretions, still slightly dazed.

"You what?" spat the youth, the one with the face most resembling the Hawaiian variety of pizza. "You talking to me?"

His friend remained silent, uncertain, and seeking guidance from his pal, perhaps lacking the confidence to make such a verbal challenge, yet prepared to provide support in a fight where the odds were in their favour. Saluki cocked her head to the right, boring into them with her unflinching green stare. She made a scorpion-tail shape with right arm, her hand raised above her head; her left hand outstretched, fingers beckoning them to step closer, if they dare. The youths lost the bottle and the alpha male dropped his gaze, withdrawing from the staring competition, with a nonchalant laugh, and shrug of the shoulders, as if to suggest that this was a challenge not worthy of pursuing. If the truth be known he was probably scared, fearing a humiliating kicking from this woman in front his comrade. To save face he was trying to make it appear as if he was doing her a favour.

"Forget it. She's a psycho case and they're a couple of sad alkies. Leave them."

As the two adolescent turned and walked away, the leader covering his uncertainty and fear with his mocking laughter and faux hard man swagger, Azarias joined Saluki.

"So much for *thou shalt not interfere,*" he teased. "This way," he motioned to the Grey Street end of the alley.

"Those two will have no major impact on history or time," Saluki added, "And I will have caused no great harm."

"And you know that for certain? I suppose you do. Here. Look around this corner. See. Up there. On the steps of the Monument. That's me. In few minutes Theresa will come out of there."

Azarias gestured towards the gaping walled hole, which disappeared into the ground; highlighted by the yellow Metro signs. Beyond the entrance, standing beneath the monument, a 27-year-old Azarias, huddled against the cold of the November day, his Irish tweed shin length coat, lapels pulled up around his ears, hands thrust into the pockets. Perhaps he thought he resembled that iconic image of James Dean walking in New York in 1955; perhaps he was just cold.

"Why?" Saluki prodded him in the top of his left arm with her right forefinger, as she surveyed the scene. Of all the things we could visited in time – why this?"

"Memories," he muttered, gulping down a ball of emotions that had threatened to manifest as tears. "I want to remember the memory. Not just remember. I want observe it from the outside. And remember the feeling. Do you understand?"

She thought for a few seconds, focusing her eyes on the younger Azarias, before answering.

"I don't think I do."

She'll be here soon," he enthused, turning to Saluki. "Do you know what is significant about date?"

"Today?" she asked. "Here?"

"Yes."

"No. What? I don't understand."

"What is the date?" Azarias urged, a little impatiently.

"Why do you ask?"

"Humour me. Please," he beseeched her. "Please. If only to learn something about this situation."

"Okay. 19.11.1999. Correct?"

Azarias used his fingers and thumbs in an exaggerated fashion to announce and reinforce each number.

"Yes. One – nine – one – one – one – nine – nine – nine. You see?"

"See what?"

"There she is," he announced excitedly, turning his attention back to the matter of ultimate importance – the reason for being there – and became distracted from the point of the conversation. "There. The Metro. Coming up the stairs. Look."

Memories flooded into the dark abyss of his tortured soul, as his undead wife – undead wife-to-be to be precise appeared to rise from the dark gaping grave of the Monument Metro entrance, protected from the cold by the plum-coloured quilted Parka-style, faux-fur trimmed, jacket. The garment was fitted to the waist and she wore skinny black jeans, tucked into brown leather ankle boots, with a fold over cuff. Atop her thick black curled shoulder length hair, a purple crocheted fascinator-type cap, which matched her long scarf, wrapped around her neck, and the fingerless mitts.

Azarias remembered her face, framed by that hair – the small band of freckles bridging her nose beneath those dark brown almond shaped eyes, and those large jet black discs of the pupils, into which he fallen, time and again. She had known how to use those eyes to her best advantage, to get her own way and to express her feelings. He had been captivated from the first time he had looked into those eyes. And then he noted that his younger self had waved and begun to move away from the Monument, at the moment Theresa made a right hand U-turn at the top of the steps. His older self – in the alley – wanted to call out, to warn her, save and protect her life but the potential consequences, and the 'rules', prevented him from doing so, though the seed of an idea began to germinate in his mind. *'Perhaps there is a way.'* And then he was distracted, again, this time, by events unfolding in the alley, and failed to notice the hooded figure peering around the corner on the other side of the piazza-style area beneath the monument, near the entrance to the Eldon Square shopping centre – someone watching. Saluki had also failed to spot the watcher on the corner, also distracted by sounds behind them – pizza face and his friend, and three similarly pock-marked youths, all dressed in loose fitting leisure bottoms, wearing hoodies. *'Trouble!'*

"Lads, lads, lads," Azarias said, repeating the word in an affable advisory tone, "I would seriously advise you not to do something you will later regret. Go home. Trust me."

"Fuck off," the gang leader whined. "What ye ganna de, like? Divn't take nee notice of him. He gets slapped about by his missus."

"Aye," his lieutenant added, "A couple of alkies up an alley. Reckon they both need a slapping, like."

The newly recruited gang members shuffled their feet, awkwardly trying to look like real gangsters – 'hard' – but lacking brain cells, playing 'follow the leader' aimlessly, blindly, without thought, like sheep – potentially, sheep to the slaughter.

"Are you sure you want to do this, boys?" Saluki asked singling out the ring leader. "I will make you cry for your mama."

"Bollocks!" he spat, signalling to his friends to make a combined attack.

"I did warn you," Azarias said, putting his hands up in mock surrender. "I have a really bad feeling about this."

"And what ye ganna de aboot it?" the feckless youth asked, squaring up, ready to make his move, as part of the gang.

"Me? Nothing," Azarias laughed. "I intend to do nothing. I don't think I have to do anything."

"I thank you, sir," Saluki joked, saluting Azarias. "I will remember that, when the time comes. When you are up against the odds."

"I have a feeling a feeling you don't need my help."

At the moment the crew started to make a move –
somewhat lacking an organised plan, though in unison –
the sound of Santana's *Smooth* leaked into the cold
November air from a bar, or a nearby open window.
Azarias could have been forgiven for thinking that
Saluki had picked up the swaying rhythm, and was about
to show them how to salsa – how wrong!

From the split second Saluki sprang from a standing
start, spinning 360 degrees, two metres above the
ground, to the moment the last of five had learned an
embarrassing salutary lesson, less than two minutes
elapsed.

*'Bruce Lee? No. Jackie Chan. Or that tiger, dragon
thing. Crouching dragon? Sleeping tiger? Can't
remember. I know what I mean. Impressive stuff.'*

And there she was, spinning through the air,
delivering a nerve jangling blow to the neck of the gang
member farthest to her left, with her right foot, causing
cranium to crash into cranium as his head, carried by the
force of the blow, clattered against the skull of his
adjacent companion. Like two professional football
players challenging for a missed header, they both went
down in a heap, holding their temples and brows, with
an agonising tooth ache-like pain. Completing a full
circle, Saluki dropped to her haunches, her left foot
acting as a pivot as the right leg, outstretched, swept like
a scythe, behind, and under the legs of the next in line,
causing him topple backwards, as feet flipped skyward,
right wrist screaming out in agony, as it impacted with
the tarmac under the full weight of his body, cracking
like a snapped plastic ruler.

A fourth member of the gang felt the full force of her right fist rising at speed into his gonads. An excruciating exhalation breath exploded from his gaping mouth, eyes bulging, as the earthquake of pain pierced his kidneys. In a Michael Jackson crotch clutching pose, he fell in slow motion to his knees. Azarias winced, comically empathising with the 'brotherhood of pain' the lad was experiencing, yet he was not prepared for what happened next; then none of them were. Saluki was obviously not ready for the punch that the gang leader delivered because he managed to get a punch in as she was rising from the crouching position – splitting her lower lip against her teeth. Azarias made a move to step in, as she appeared to fall backwards under the force of the blow. And it was the next part that he and the gang member were not prepared for, as Saluki turned a back-flip somersault, immediately adopting the scorpion pose, right arm arching above her head. With the back of her left she wiped away a trace of blood with the back of her left hand. Examining the red smear Saluki then turned her hand into that *'come and have a go if you think you're hard enough'* beckoning gesture and something really unexpected happened – not just unexpected, but strange and weird.

Azarias and the youth looked on in disbelief as the cut on her lip healed before their eyes, in a matter of a few seconds, the only memory of the wound being the swipe of blood on her chin. Her assailant was freaked by this and, as his crew began to crawl away, embarrassed, battered and beaten, he turned to make good his own escape, having first exclaimed, "Fuck you. Fucking freak."

In spite of Azarias's plea to let them go, it was obvious that Saluki had not yet finished with the ring leader – she had made him a promise, which she was prepared to fulfil. No escape! As the adolescent attempted to make his way towards Pilgrim Street Saluki held out her left arm and, with the forefinger of her right hand, stabbed on the central screen of her device. A black cord ejected in a straight line from the device, like a chameleon tongue, wrapping around the right wrist of fleeing assailant, locking, stopping him in his tracks. Like the recoiling plug of a vacuum cleaner he was pulled towards Saluki, unable to loosen the offending restraining cord, which unravelled once she had grip of his right arm.

"I want to hear it," she whispered with menace, forcing his right arm up his back, and his face to the ground. "Cry for your mama. It's all you have left. Your friends have deserted you. Look. Gone."

She pulled his hair back, so that he might witness the final retreat of his gang, as they turned right at the end of the alley, without looking back. He tried to struggle, he swore and he cursed, but to no avail, and a little more pressure and he gave in to her demands.

"I want my mama," he muttered.

"I can't hear you," she pushed, taking his elbow close to breaking point. "I have a hearing problem. Louder," she demanded.

Mama! Agh! Mama," he screamed. "I want me mam."

"See, that wasn't so difficult, was it?" she mocked, releasing the snivelling wreck; wriggling on the ground, holding his limp arm, which had just escaped serious injury. He dragged himself away. A crowd had developed behind them – the curious attracted, and drawn, from Grey Street buy the commotion.

"We need to leave," Azarias urged. "I used to be in the police. Remember? If I had seen a crowd like this I would have investigated."

The crowd was beginning to disperse, and Azarias could only hope that his younger self had not been distracted by the rumpus, and had continued on his date, as he did all those years; in that coffee shop where he started the first date with Theresa. And then it occurred to him that he had no memory of any such distraction, adjacent to the alley, when they first met; what could have ever distracted him?

"Did you think not to offer any assistance?" Saluki probed, pulling focus on his distant thoughts.

"From where I was standing you were managing quite well without any interference from me," he replied as they walked together towards the Pilgrim Street end of the alley, away from his former self, his other self, with a need to find a quiet place where they could vanish from view, and make good the return trip, without being observed.

"And that lip thing," he continued. "It was cut …"

"Sshh," she interrupted. "One day. One day soon, I will tell you."

***

"I didn't miss much, then," Alan joked.

Azarias still could not bring himself to mention the fact that he had lived the same morning twice – one with Liz crying down the phone because Alan had not returned home the previous night, and the other sharing details of the first controlled time leap with a man he thought might otherwise be dead. *'What had happened? Why was he missing? Where was he? Alive? Dead? What have I done?'*

Alan had confessed to reading the phone text message over his shoulder, in the Rose Tree public house, and his plan – to hide in the bushes and then observe Azarias – had been thwarted when they met inside the Snowy Owl; something Alan had not anticipated. *'Why had Azarias shown up so early? Did he know? How did he know?'* He was disappointed that he missed out on the action, though grateful for the small crumbs of the adventure that Azarias had fed to him.

"Anyway," Azarias began, "I had better go and round up this crew. Do my job. While I am still here. I will keep you posted. I promise but I think it is not in your best interests to get to close to me, or these people. Put your family first. I have seen her in action. I imagine there are others out there and they are probably dangerous. They mean business."

They exited the classroom together, walking the corridor towards the main atrium in silence, where Alan turned right to head up the stairs, while Azarias searched for familiar youthful faces in and around the restaurant and communal areas. As he established eye contact with different students he gave a five-fingered "five minutes" salute, gesturing towards the classroom. It would not be unusual for students to be outside, smoking, so Azarias headed for the main entrance, and it was just as he reached the sliding doors that he felt someone grab his right elbow, quickly guiding him towards the football pitches, over to the right, before he had a chance to raise an objection.

"You have done something," a recognisable foreign female accent barked – it was Saluki. "What have you done?"

She led Azarias along the edge of the football pitches, far enough from the crowds not to be overheard. Just for a moment a thought entered his head – *'This will do my street cred no harm, being dragged off by her like this. Are you watching lads?'* – Her emerald eyes blazed at him, accusingly, bringing him back to Earth with a bump – *'Not a social call, then?'* The normally ivory cheeks were flushed the colour of rouge – she was angry. *'What have I done? Shit. Of course. Act dumb. Play possum.'*

"What have you done?"

"What do you mean? What have I done?"

"There has been a temporal disturbance. A breach of the rules that we discussed. It has reached my time. I have heard it. I am as yet unaware of the implications. So, tell me. What have you done?"

"Heard?" Azarias queried a slight nervous edge to his voice. "What do mean, heard? You said, *'I have heard it.'*

A gentle breeze caressed Saluki's face, causing her fringe to flutter on her forehead, like black silken threads brushing across porcelain. She paused, biting her thick red bottom lip, as she considered how she might respond.

"Pachakutiq Profondo!"

"Packet what?" he quizzed.

"Pachakutiq Profondo," she repeated. "The sound. You heard it?"

He nodded an affirmative, adding, "Like thunder? But not thunder. Like the sky splitting open?"

"You have heard it. Damn. It is a space time disturbance pulse. That you have heard it means that it originated here. What have you done?" she asked again, this time with her hands on her hips, staring at her own reflection in his eyes.

"Good question," he offered, not dropping her gaze. "Though I would like to know what it is that I have undone. Perhaps that is more to the point. What have I undone? Surely you know."

"You tell me," she demanded.

Azarias gave an account of the two versions of the same morning; the first where Liz announces that her husband is missing, and the second, where he is alive and well, and in the college.

"And Liz? Well, she said Alan, her husband, was meeting with me at the Snowy Owl. Close to where we met. Where I had parked the car. Yes? Good. But no such meeting had been arranged. I travelled back and met him. My question is what had happened before I travelled back? Shit. Listen to me. What would have happened if I hadn't travelled back? Doesn't sound better, whichever way I try to say it. He was killing time, with a view to hiding out and observing our first meeting."

"But how did he know about that?" she cross-examined, her hands now clasped behind her back, in full inquisitor mode. "How did he know about that meeting?"

"Okay," he began, deflecting any blame from himself, referring to events of the previous evening in The Rose Tree public house, "I admit to allowing Alan to lead me to the pub and to wait to see what might happen. I had my reasons. Don't look at me like that. You weren't the one who thought he was losing the plot. Anyway, what a bloody fantastic trick that was. Setting off all those dead phones. Talk about attracting attention. And then, the phone under the table. Okay, I admit, I was a bit impressed. But I did not know he had read the contents of the message over my shoulder. I'll know better in the future. But that does not explain what happened to him in the Liz phoning scenario. If you know what I mean?"

"I do," she smiled. "You look …," she hesitated, suddenly a little embarrassed …, "interesting when you are angry. You are right. It does not explain that.

Something is wrong. Very wrong. Something is wrong in the Province de Belgique. Something is very wrong. Someone else must have been there. Someone from my time. And seen your friend. But why? Why was someone tracking my movements?"

"And that person, from your time, might have harmed Alan? If he found him spying on us."

"Harmed him?" she disputed, questioningly. "Killed him. He would most certainly have been killed. You saved his life. Intervened. Prevented him from being there. Changed the course of history. Such a brief moment, though. It might not show. I can't be sure. Perhaps a very limited local impact."

"I have no idea what you are talking about," Azarias interjected, but at that was the moment that the germinating seed of his plan sprouted in his mind, and he could not share those thoughts with anyone. And, he considered the consequences – it could cost him dearly; perhaps cost Azarias his life but he knew what he had to do, and it would only be a matter of time before he put his plan into action.

Saluki was concerned, though, on the verge of paranoia, because if an agent from her time was in the same location, vicinity, even in the same time zone, the device on her left wrist should vibrate and flash red, around the edge of the central screen. If there had been someone, one of her kind, in that copse, she should have known but didn't. That doesn't happen unless it is sanctioned by a higher authority. And there is the death of the Vice-Superus. And the Delta One-Five.

"You've lost me," Azarias confided, scratching behind his right ear. "You lost me at Vice-Superus. As for Delta One-Five."

She apologised for thinking aloud, spewing her fears out of her mouth, and on to Azarias. And there was another matter giving her cause for concern; an issue she had raised before with the man standing in front of her, checking his watch, and expecting the worst if a member of senior management was to walk by his empty classroom at that very moment.

"Your mother," she started, breaking his train of thought. "She was an artist. Yes?"

"Of sorts," he nodded.

Saluki had surmised that she might well have sketched him when he was a boy, and at very stages of his life. And, would it not be likely that something of such sentimental value might be passed down from mother to son? That being the case, she suggested, was it not also possible that she might have sketched portraits of the father of the boy, from memory, at a later date?

"Why would she not use her talent to create such memories?" she asked, again, looking deep into his soul, through his eyes.

"Okay. You've got me there. I have some sketches. Some may be of my father," he said, raising his hands in surrender. "I had never met him. Face-to-face! So could swear that it is my father. Could be anyone, so did not think it important enough to mention."

"I need to see them," she ordered. "Now.."

Azarias pointed out that it would take about forty-five minutes to drive home, and that he should really get back to work. His students were loose around the college, if they had actually bothered to remain on the site, and then there would be the return journey of another forty-five minutes, back to the college. *'Couldn't it wait?'* Saluki gave a satirical snort, realising the humour of the situation, smiled, and shook her head.

"I think you may be missing the point. Have you forgotten who you are? Forgotten what you are capable of? Have you not yet grasped the concept? No. I don't believe you. You are playing games," she laughed, shaking her head in mock disbelief. "Because we would not be discussing a temporal disturbance. Would we?"

The penny dropped!

"Right. I get it," he acknowledged. "We can leave here now, visit my home, and return to the now, like we had never left. Right?"

"You have done it already. As long as you are not still there. Yes? Timing is everything."

\*\*\*

Le Feuvre surveyed the room from right to left, anti-clockwise, starting near the door to the study, which he had closed behind him.

"Sketches. Drawings," he muttered, fingering the spines of books on the shelves of the large IKEA

289

bookcase. "Where to start? Where would he keep such stuff? Does it even exist?"

He marvelled at the pristine condition of the antique literature – paperbacks, fiction, non-fiction, dictionaries and magazines – all of which would be of great value to collectors in his world, in his time. Augustin thumbed through the authors and titles, zig-zagging up and down the shelves, reading out loud wherever his finger stopped for a moment or two.

"Lee Child. Maybe. Jeffery Deaver. Not sure. Isabelle Allende. In Spanish. Dan Brown. Okay. *Catch 22*. Don't know it. *Men are from Mars, Women are from Venus*. What is that? Ah. Phillip Pullman. The complete trilogy. In excellent condition. A prize, indeed. If only I could take you with me. Rules. Ha!"

He shifted his attention to the tall free-standing unit, immediately next to the bookshelf; three deep shelves above a double-door cupboard, packed, seemingly, with academia. On the very top of the unit, and arrangement of strange objects – mementos and tourist gifts – tat, for want of a word – a bronze-coloured metallic miniature of the Tour Eiffel, a thumb-sized doll-like statue, set on a tiny plinth, with the words, *'Sio Niño Dios Gaucin'* engraved on a brushed steel plaque, and a Burj Khalifa, complete with faux diamond set in the pinnacle of the tower.

In front of a tiny wooden bookshelf, stood a Spanish gift-shop donkey, with a basket of 'olives' hanging on either side of its flanks. In the miniature bookshelf, probably once a container for gift-wrapped chutneys, the top four compartments each contained one tiny book. Le

Feuvre scanned from left to right, mouthed the titles to himself.

"*A Special Wife.* Ha! What is this one? *A Book of Love.* Oh dear. And this? *I love you.* Sentimental slush. And, another. *Grow old with me.* Mierde. You expose your weakness, my friend."

Set on a lower shelf, to the left, in the tiny library, two gaudy red painted flamenco dancers – one male, one female – and in the middle, two champagne corks. To the right of that, something resembling a small crystal bird's nest, two birds perched on the side, beaks touching, and two eggs in the bowl of the nest. He pulled down and adjacent wedding photograph and examined the bride.

"A pretty catch. Very nice. What if I was to meet you somewhere in time? I wonder. You are his weakness. Look at your shrine," he said, lifting the photograph, as if she might be able to take in the view, before replacing it carefully from the point it had been removed from, before continuing his search.

"Okay. Sketches. Images. Where would you keep them?"

Augustin opened the double doors at the base of the unit, looking briefly inside, before closing the doors, having seen a range of folders, in a range of colours – '*undoubtedly academic essays and work*'. Muttering and mumbling to himself he then turned attention to the scarlet-painted metal four drawer filing cabinet, in the corner, by the window, and thumbed through files and other objects contained therein, eventually resigning himself to the possibility that he was not going to find what he was seeking in those drawers – in truth, he was now getting bored, and could not be bothered to search for these imagined items with too much effort. If they came to his fingertips easily, so be it, but he was not really up to digging too deep for something potentially inconsequential.

"Why would you keep such things in here, anyway?"

He stopped and looked through the voiles, framed by the red tartan curtains, at the silent suburban scene of the quiet cul-de-sac. On the other side of the tarmac road, an area of grass, the size of half a football pitch, beyond which lay a footpath and three small blocks of apartments, each containing four separate domiciles, the farthest of these to the right disappearing behind the high hedge belonging to the garden of one of the detached houses at the end of the road. He studied the vacant spaces in the parking bays, and the empty drives of surrounding properties – all was quiet, very quiet, even for the black and white cat, paws padding softly on the tarmac, as it followed the instinct to stalk and hunt prey, in spite of the full bowl of food waiting in the comfort of a neighbouring home.

"Small town. Small people. Small lives," Le Feuvre hissed, returning his attention to the interior and the large expansive desk-cum work station, against the outside wall of the semi-detached property. And then he caught sight of his destination, beyond the clutter on the desk – the laptop, lid open, scattered pens and pencils, two hole-punches, a stapler, a few loose staples, random 'spider-scribbled' post-it notes, three elastic bands, some unopened mail and a pencil sharpener, in juxtaposition to the order, almost anal retentive neatness he had encountered downstairs in the house. Ignoring the other images, photographs of Azarias and Theresa in graduation gowns, on the bridge across the desk, between the two towers of drawers and shelves, Augustin headed for the dark veneer cupboard door, situated above the stairs.

"In here, perhaps?"

And then he paused, holding his breath – sound. *'Someone there? No. You are hearing things. Nothing. No one there.'* He opened the door and his gaze immediately fell upon the 'Jacob's Crackers' tin. "What do we have here?" Le Feuvre removed the container and took over to the window ledge, where he would be able to use the natural light to view the contents. Noting some woman in the street, holdall slung over a shoulder, going from door-to-door, pushing bundles of folded paper into letterboxes, Augustin lifted the lid clear of the tin, exposing the innards, and grunted at the moment the letterbox rattled on the door beneath. He watched her walk away to the top of the short drive and turn right, the next pile of papers already gripped in her right hand – she hadn't noticed him, hadn't even looked up, but then why should she. After all, even if she noted the shadowy figure behind the foggy voile, the woman would have no reason to suspect that he did not live in the house. Augustin watched as she turned from the road onto the drive next door.

"Ah. I see," he muttered, placing the age-battered, scratched lid to one side. "This must be what I am looking for. How's that? Thirty one minutes past nine. Six minutes. Not bad. Not bad at all. Time to leave."

***

Azarias staggered and swayed, steadying himself, and used the back of the sofa for support following the sudden arrival in his lounge. Dizziness! At least he was not experiencing that feeling of nausea, the retching and heaving that had threatened to tear his stomach from its internal moorings, and his nose was not bleeding. But the house alarm was bleeping, with a view to resounding loudly around the neighbourhood, drawing unwanted attention, if he did not manage to enter the security code in the next twenty seconds. Their movement had been detected in the room, within moments of completing the time leap, having not entered the house by the traditional method – through the front door.

"I've got it," he shouted, leaning against the wall beneath the stairs, where a load bearing wall me with the slope of the stairs at a 90 degree angle – where the alarm keypad was attached.

"I've got it," he repeated, mouthing the numbers as he entered them, ceasing the high-pitched beeping. "That's better. I might leave that off. For a while, anyway. Until I get used to this time travel stuff. I don't want to disturb the neighbours every time I pop up here. And, I don't have my keys. Left them in the car. Right. Upstairs. After you."

Azarias ushered Saluki up the stairs, finding himself, not for the first time, distracted by her femininity; the curves of her firm pert buttocks, clad in the tight material of her slacks, dancing provocatively, yet with innocent intent, in front of his face, as she made her way up the stairs. And, not for the second time did he dismiss what he considered to be inappropriate thoughts from his mind; that guilty feeling of the imagined betrayal of his marriage vows – *'Till death us do part. But I'm not dead.'* That same old tune! He tried to look somewhere else – up at the ceiling, anywhere, other than at the temptation that transfixed him.

"In there," he said, once they reached the top of the stairs, pointing to the door at the end of the landing.

"You didn't tell me about that date. The significance of the numbers. You started to tell me," she said, opening the door and entering the room. "Nineteen, eleven, nineteen, ninety-nine. You didn't tell me."

"I didn't," Azarias replied, flatly.

"Well?"

"In here," he said, ignoring the interrogation, closing the door behind him and opening the cupboard above the stairs. "In this tin. Here."

As he placed the tin on the desk, moving a few of the objects to make room, Saluki took a note of the surroundings – the old style clock – *'eleven minutes past nine; those same numbers'* – the collection of memorabilia and the photographs. *'Another shrine'.* Azarias removed the lid from the tin.

"You will tell me. You will want to tell me. Soon.."

295

"Maybe," he quipped. "Maybe not. These five of me. Various stages of my formative years.."

Azarias laid out the sketches over the desk, and on top of the laptop, laying the other three on top of those. The green eyes stared up at him, from the coloured pastel portrait, causing him to do a double-take with Saluki and the image, and back again. *'Those eyes. No. Can't be. Coincidence. Surely'*.

"Raphael," she said, without a trace of emotion, running her forefinger lightly across the name on the sketch, as if reading Braille. "Indeed. Is that really your name?"

Saluki stacked the collection of portraits back in the tin, carefully replacing the lid. She handed the container to Azarias.

"Thank you. That is all I needed. Put them away," she ordered. "Your mother was quite the artist. She captures the essence of a person."

"Yes. I believe so."

"I have seen what I needed to see. Now I must leave. I have work to do.."

Without any further ado, or discussion, Saluki prodded the central screen on her uRAPP, and was sucked into the air before his eyes, without a bye or leave. Gone. Evaporated.

"And goodbye to you," he sniffed sarcastically. "And I was just about to raise the point that I am now in two places at once. Is that right? You must have more important stuff to deal with."

Azarias placed the tin in the cupboard, closed the door, and then flipped open the Motorola screen – 09:15 – and pressed the return button; he, too, evaporated into the ether.

# Chapter 22

"I have these," Le Feuvre stated, as a matter of fact, handing the sketches to Damarov. "I found them in a metallic container, which I returned to the cupboard. I placed some blank pieces of paper in the tin. Perhaps he will have no reason to look at them."

"Perhaps," Gabriel droned, laying the images out in a line across his white desk, in his polar white office. "Is this all of them? Six?"

"All that I could find," Augustin lied. "Four of the boy. And the other two? Well, they would appear to be of you. I found nothing else."

The Superus studied the images, with a certain obvious admiration, as if he was remembering something special – a moment, perhaps – or maybe he was just admiring the skill of the artist, and how she had captured the likenesses of both subjects. *'A good choice. She was a good brood mare. Shame I had to end it that way'.* Shifting the artwork into a neat pile, he placed it all in a white drawer, close to his right leg, in his white desk.

"Now to the matter of your promotion," Gabriel said smoothly, with a conspiratorial edge. "You are an invaluable field agent. Perhaps a promotion there? Or maybe you would consider the role of Vice-Superus? After all, there is a vacancy. As well you know. Would you miss the action, though? The cut and thrust. Go away and think on it. Don't give me your answer now. You are due some leave."

Le Feuvre clicked his heels together, and stood to attention, and dipped his chin, by way of salute, suggesting that this meeting was now adjourned. As he had done, many times before, in similar situations, he held his protective white headgear under his curled right arm. Thoughts whirred around his mind, regarding the offer of promotion – *'Equality with your daughter. That would be a start',* the thought rumbling loudly in his head.

"I have thought, sir," he revealed, causing Damarov to raise his brows in surprise; that he was daring to speak out of place.

"I am listening," he offered, moving around from his desk, raising his clasped hands as if in prayer. "Have you thought this through carefully?"

"I have, sir. I am ready to take on the role of commandant. I would like promotion to commandant. Sir.."

A short silence followed as Gabriel approached Le Feuvre, and he clasped his hands behind his back as drew close to his subordinate, circling him like a wolf tracking prey, finally stopping just behind the left shoulder of Augustin.

"Why?" he breathed into his ear. "Why not Vice-Superus?"

"The action, sir. I prefer to remain in the field. I have been given the task of investigating your daughter" – he paused, reconsidering the use of words, before continuing – "investigating Commandant Saluki Damarov. Would it not be more fitting to be investigated by someone of equal rank, sir?"

"Or senior rank," Damarov added. "Imagine that. Being of a superior rank. Give it serious thought. And be reminded of two things. One. In the role of Commandant you would have to transfer to another region. There is not a vacancy for Commandant. Yet. And this region only supports one commandant. But there is the obvious vacancy for Vice-Superus. And, two. Remember. Secrecy at all times. We keep this to ourselves. Trust no one."

Le Feuvre agreed to take three days leave and then departed the office at that point where the wall melts away to reveal the long corridor. Once outside the office, the opening was replaced by the digitally created image of the entrance. Augustin pulled two pieces of paper from inside his jacket and, hidden from the view of cameras, looked at the images of the young Azarias Tor, and the colour sketch of the younger Gabriel Damarov. He replaced them, holding the images under his jacket beneath his armpit, and smiled, swaggering along the corridor, swinging his helmet by the chin strap, talking quietly to himself.

"Insurance. Why would I want to be Vice-Superus when I can be the Superus? When I can be anything I want to be? If only you knew. If only you knew.."

\*\*\*

Saluki sat silently in the darkness, the only available light emitting from the permanently backlit wall-art in the penthouse apartment, the home of Raphael Antinori – the home of a dead man. She was deep in thought, focussing her attention on the potential outcome of the Code Delta One-Five she was about to exorcise – good choice of venue to uncover the truth. After all she entered the apartment under the guise of continuing investigations into the recorded death of the Vice-Superus. *'Maybe they have missed something'.* She had a feeling about this whole affair, and had been up to the roof, alone, and studied the point from he was supposed to have fallen – no evidence of a body had yet been found. *'A mystery'.*

Saluki had been somewhat preoccupied, with Azarias Tor. He was beginning to intrigue her – more than that; Saluki was starting to develop feelings running beyond that of mere professional interest. *'Why? Because he knew how to love? She was a lucky woman. Focus. Focus on the task in hand. Here and now. Here and now? Is that significant? Here and now? No'."* Whatever it was, lost in her mind, some forgotten memory, it would not bubble to the surface. She was tired. *'Here and now? No. It's gone. Stop thinking about it'*. Having searched the roof terrace, and the depths of her mind, for a clue that would help her locate the body – anything to indicate what might have happened – Saluki sat brooding on the black four seater sofa, staring at the reflection of the night sky, which poured in through the large window and onto the glass table in front of her. She had been out on the balcony, directly beneath the point where he was supposed to have fallen – nothing there, either. Her mind was almost as dark as the lake far below, where ripples of light from nearby homes broke the shoreline, like slow-motion lightning bolts in black starless sky. *'Nothing. Is the answer here?'*

Holding her left arm out in front of her, Saluki touched the screen on the right side of the uRAPP. A beam of bright light cut through the thick blackness of the darkened room, culminating in a holographic-type image two metres away. The message flickered before eyes, illuminating Saluki's face, reflected in the Pilkington Twenty-Two triple glazed glass walls, and sliding balcony door. *'A message?'*

*<File: ZX541221052148. Vice-Superus Antinori, Raphael. EFRON. Life extinct: 20.06.2198/ 17:35:15 seconds. Anomaly. Evaluate. Anomaly. Error report. Anomaly. Investigate. Life extinct. 20.06.2198/17:35:18 seconds. Anomaly. Final report. Ground zero impact: 20.06.2198/ 17:35:48 seconds. Life extinct: 20.06.2198/ 17:35:48 seconds. Anomaly.>*

"Anomaly? What anomaly? What does this mean?"

The image flickered, dissolved, and reformed to show an image. At first Saluki did not understand what was happening, unfolding before her eyes and her fatigued brain. And then she recognised the landscape – an aerial view from a satellite showing the immediate surrounding countryside, zooming in on the Celtic cross-shaped 'La Tour de la Croix complex. In the top right corner, the date and time – 20.06.2198 – 17:31:32. And then she heard a sound, just outside the apartment.

She switched off the device, cancelling the bright image, which left coloured lights dancing inside her eyes, and then made her way, swift and low, in the direction of the kitchen beneath the mezzanine, where she secreted herself in a dark corner. Now she had the element of surprise; at least that was her hope. The main door to the apartment opened, flooding a wash of trapezoid light into the room. Saluki did not want to give herself away, just yet, so remained hidden – she could not see the one elongated shadow cast by the intruding light but could sense the presence of one person; only one person. If she moved her reflection might be seen in the glass wall and windows. *'Wait.'* The door closed and the world around her was once again thrown into darkness – soon there would be nowhere to hide. And, then, the lights came on, temporarily dazzling her. *'Mierde! Now'.*

"Halt!" Saluki shouted, leaping from her hiding place, arms in front, right hand over her left wrist. "Halt or I will fire."

\*\*\*

Azarias had returned to his place of work – the college – but, at that very moment, it seemed unimportant. His world was undergoing a huge change, and his life had already changed. *'Shit. Time travel. Who'd have thought it?'* His life was fading away, melting; even those threads of his marriage which he refused to let go – slipping away from him. Yet he was seeking for his group of students, to whom he felt an obligation; those who had failed their GCSEs, or who had been failed by an education system more interested in league tables than enlightening young minds, enabling youth to take its rightful place in society. Now, those young people needed to either re-sit GCSE English and/or mathematics or obtain appropriate certificates in functional skills in those given subjects, if they were to have any chance of following a career, let alone finding any decent paid work. And Azarias cared, he really did, but things were different – his life was not going to be the same old same old anymore, now that he could now travel through time.

"Excuse me. Azarias," a '40 a day habit' smoky female voice called above the cacophony of white noise in the air-hanger style atrium.

"Shit," he whispered, turning to greet his line manager – the painfully thin 40 year old, going on 60, shrivelled, prune-face sour-puss of a woman. *'Caught! Banged to rights'*.

"Azarias," she squeaked, once again, catching up with him, breathless and wheezing, brushing a curl of wiry grey hair away from her eyes. "Where have you been? I have seen some of your students out of class.

Told me they had been sent away. Said you were in a meeting. You know you can't do this. They have to be in class. You know that."

"I know, Pam," he shrugged, coming across as if he really didn't care anymore.

"That's not the attitude I expect," she rasped. "What is going on? You do realise that this will involve a disciplinary. I will have to check my diary. Arrange a meeting."

"Don't bother."

"What do you mean," she wailed, her ire stirred. "Don't bother?"

"To be honest. Nothing against you. I respect you. I've enjoyed working here. You've been good to me. But my heart isn't in it anymore. There are more important things than you could ever dream of out there. Give the job to someone who needs it. Here.."

Azarias handed her his identity swipe card, hanging from the corporate lanyard, and the classroom key. Silence! No more words, just action. He did not need anything from the office – his bag and jacket had been left in the unlocked classroom. Pam stood, mouth agape, unsure how to deal with the situation – this had never happened to her before. Azarias collected his belongings, saying a few goodbyes to some surprised students, and then he left the premises, and did not look back.

*'Azarias Tor is no longer in the building'.*

During the forty minute drive home his Blackberry rang about ten times, announced six voicemail messages, and the receipt of four text messages – all connected to the swift departure from the college, he surmised. The behaviour, out of character for Azarias, had likely caused confusion. *'Welcome to the confusion club. Confused of Cramlington'.*

When he arrived home the first thing he noticed, upon entering the lounge, was the red light '05' flashing on the phone, in the corner, near the television. On and off. On and off. *'Five messages. The college. Tough'.*

"The alarm!" he exclaimed, checking the keypad when he realised it had made not sound. "Tit! You left it off," he rebuked himself, "Earlier. Ignore it," he continued when the ringing of the phone caused him to start.

Azarias removed the phone connector from the socket on the wall, silencing the offending noise, and then made his up the stairs, two steps at a time. A change of clothes was needed for what he had planned – all black, perhaps. Camouflage might draw too much interest. First though, he wanted to check a few dates in the past, and the days upon which they had fallen, and the weather on those same days in specific locations. *'Necessary research'.* And he was about to switch on the laptop when he noticed that something was amiss; something was different.

"I thought I had closed this," he mumbled to himself, pushing shut the door to the cupboard above the stairs, which he found slightly ajar. "I did close it. Definitely.."

Azarias opened the door and closed it again. *'Definitely closed it'.* Opening the door again, he searched for the cracker tin – it was there, but not quite where he had left it after showing the sketches to Saluki. He remembered things like that; mild OCD, or just anal retentive, call it what you will, but if something was not in its rightful place, where he had put it, Azarias would twitch, mentally, and had to rearrange and straighten the offending article. That tin was not where had left it, aligned with the inside wall of the cupboard – parallel, not at the current angle it was resting. *'Who had moved it?'* And then the image of the coffee table, downstairs, flashed into his mind's eye.

"Of course," he said, placing his right hand to his forehead, spinning in circle away from the cupboard. "That sheet of paper. The commandments. That's been moved, too."

It was very subtle but the paper had moved. Azarias had lined it up on the glass of the coffee table and the wood precisely in the right angle, where the two elements joined, just as he might when using a photocopier. He hadn't registered it immediately but it had obviously been moved. *'Someone has been here'.* He listened intently, checking if anyone was still in the house, hiding in another room, waiting to pounce – to attack him. Nothing – just the distant hum of the traffic on the 'Spine Road'. *'Who has been in here? Surely not'.*

Azarias returned his attention to the cupboard and removed the cracker tin. He placed it on the desk and prised open the lid, which clattered on the varnished wooden floorboards, having slipped from fingers at the moment of realising that the sketches had been replaced with blank sheets of paper – each of these he turned over in his hands, as if expecting the portraits to be on the other side, even though he could clearly see this was not the case, and these, in turn, also dropped to the floor. *'She hadn't shown any interest. Why sneak back, steal them, and replace them with blank sheets? Why?'*

"You only had to ask," he said, looking up at the ceiling – perhaps time travellers fall from the sky – "You only had to ask," he repeated, a tone of disappointment in his voice, feeling unexpected betrayal from a person he was starting to trust.

\*\*\*

Lamont lowered himself to his knees, his arms raised in a sign of surrender.

"Don't shoot," he cried. "I am unarmed."

"Place your hands behind your head," Saluki ordered, "And keep them there. Don't move. I will fire my weapon."

He obeyed the command, and lowered his eyes towards the floor. Saluki moved quickly, patting him down – *'Weapons? Recording device? A trap? Why is he here?'* She removed his uRAPP from his left wrist and, backing away slowly, placed it some distance from him, while still maintaining her defensive attacking stance. *'Harmless? Perhaps. Check. Make certain'.*

"On floor," she barked, moving back towards him leaving his device on the table. "Face down. Spread your legs. Now.."

Again, Lamont obliged and followed orders, not wishing to discover the consequences of disobeying Commandant Saluki Damarov. He laid down, his right cheek pressed to the floor, his body in the shape of a starfish. But he was calm, suggesting that he had nothing to fear. Lamont was there for a reason, yet Saluki was not aware that they were linked by a recent communication she had received. She stood over him, kicked his legs further apart, before questioning him.

"Why are you here?"

"Probably the reason as you," he replied. "Code Delta One-Five. Yes? You know what I am talking about."

She relaxed her stance, stepping away from his prone body. Ordering him to rise slowly to his feet, she positioned herself between Lamont and his uRAPP – she did not want him to have access to that device, just yet. Rising to his full height, he brushed himself down, quickly returning his hands to the surrender position in case Saluki might misunderstand his actions, even though she had searched him for hidden weapons.

"You have not yet used the Subsonne Mark Two in anger," Lamont uttered, pointing to her left wrist. "No?"

"No. Not yet. But there is always a first time."

"Trust me. I do not need to be that first time. I believe we are on the same side."

"Are we?" she queried, waving her right arm in arc towards the sofa and chairs. "Sit over there. In that chair. On the left. Walk around the back of the sofa. Good. I will sit opposite. Where I can see you. Just in case.."

They sat facing each other, in silence, both composing their thoughts, for what seemed an age but was in fact no more the 30 seconds, before they spoke at the same time.

"Okay ..." Lamont stuttered ...

"I have ..." Saluki cut in ...

"After you," he offered. "You first.."

"How do I know that I can trust you?"

"Good question," he returned. "How do we know that we can trust each other? Your father. Superus Damarov ..."

"Not him," she interrupted. I can't trust him. I can't trust my own father. The Superus. Can I trust you enough to tell you why? I can't tell anyone. Not yet.."

"You need to see the Delta One-Five. Perhaps you have seen it."

"I was," she continued, "Starting to watch it and then I heard you. Outside. You need to attend the 'stealth training'. You have heavy feet."

Lamont suggested that they witness the contents of the Delta One-Five together. He gestured towards his uRAPP but she remained unmoved with regards to returning it to him, in spite of the reference to him not having the appropriate clearance to enable him to be armed with a weapon.

"Not yet," she said. "Sit back in the chair. Cross your feet and tuck them under. Good. Now place your hands, palms up, flat on your legs. Excellent. We will watch this together. But remember. My reactions are fast. I don't need to inform you of the consequences of making the wrong move."

"So, best to sit still," he added.

"We understand each other. Good."

Saluki raised her left arm, pointing slightly skywards, steadying it with her right hand after she tapped the screen again. The hologram image reappeared, starting at the beginning again. As before, the pictures floated some two metres away, in the air, projected by the beam of light extending from her left wrist. They read the contents in silence, which she then paused.

"Are you seeing what I'm seeing?" Saluki probed, answering her own question before Lamont had a chance to draw breath. "The repetition of the word, anomaly. And the anomalies?"

Lamont studied the hologram, the sentences, that hung in mid-air, for a while, before giving a considered answer.

"He appears to have died twice. Three times. If you count impact with the water. Is that what you see?"

Saluki did not give an answer. She tapped the screen, causing the message to continue from the point at which she had originally turned the message off – the satellite view of La Tour de la Croix, and the surrounding territories. The powerful lens, aboard the geostationary Ptolemy ZX5412 zoomed in and focussed on two figures on the rooftop terrace, above where Saluki and Lamont were sitting. It appeared as if the two figures were dancing together – some macabre sort of tango; a dance of death – ending with one of them falling backwards over the edge of the 580 metre high building.

"Mierde!" Saluki exclaimed, pausing the report again. "Le Feuvre!"

"So it would appear," Lamont said, leaning forward, to gain a better view, in spite of the warning not to move. "Following whose orders?"

Saluki then did something rather extraordinary – she removed her uRAPP from her left wrist and set it down on the table next Lamont's device. This caused the image to drop but it was still visible; held on pause, at the moment where Raphael appeared to fall backwards from the top of La Tour de la Croix, and Augustin Le Feuvre looked on, having just wrestled with the dead man. Her action had made it clear that she was prepared to place her trust in Lamont.

"Are you ready to make an unauthorised time leap?"

"Where? What time? Date? Why?" he fired off in rapid succession.

Saluki reminded Lamont of the position that Raphael Antinori had taken, regarding his sign of surrender, but with the right over his left wrist. *"Unusual."* She considered the potential for the Vice-Superus having had

312

a plan in place all the time – and he had anticipated this moment; may be even created it. *"Perhaps better to be dead."* Odd, that he had purchased the penthouse suite two years before, yet had only move in a few weeks ago. Lamont shrugged, perhaps not fully grasping the point she was trying to make.

"He brought me here. Two years ago," she whooped, realising her eureka moment. "He knew. He was preparing me. And you. I thought he was just showing me around. There was still some work going on. Automated systems. Finishing touches. Here and there. They are expensive units. Finishing the roof terrace. Here and now. That's what he said. The balcony."

"I have no idea what you are talking about."

"Trust me? Here," she offered, handing him his uRAPP, and replacing her own, clasping it around her left wrist, switching off the hologram as she did so.

He nodded. "Nothing to lose, I suppose."

"Then follow my lead."

# Chapter 23

The young boy awoke with a start, rubbing his eyes with curled fists. On the bedside cabinet, to his right, a travel alarm clock lay snapped shut, like a square clam. A small pool of water, formed like a bead of mercury, had found its natural level on the white gloss painted surface, having been accidentally tipped from an upended plastic beaker during the night – the scene of crime the likely result of some nocturnal thrashing of the arms, or somnambulistic activity. He carefully opened the clock, into its triangular position, avoiding the puddle, which he silently vowed to mop up later. The luminous dots and numbers glowed in the heavy gloom; thick curtains, with sewn black-outs reducing the majority of external light from entering the room through the window.

"Twenty minutes to nine," he mumbled, sharing the information with some invisible third party, who only existed in his mind. "You shouldn't have gone back to sleep."

Peeling back the sheets and top blankets, the young boy exposed himself to the mid-winter chill, compensating for this by quickly wrapping his pyjama-clad body with his warm, luxurious, dressing gown. Sitting on the edge of the bed he then edged his feet into his wool-lined slippers. Switching on the ceiling light at the wall he stopped to collect his final prize from the advent calendar, hanging on a hook on the inside of the bedroom door. Behind the number twenty-five, a red and white Santa, obviously covering similarly shaped milk chocolate. With the gift clasped in his right hand he opened the door and walked out onto the landing.

Standing at the top of the stairs he listened for signs of life, briefly debating whether he should use the toilet – he had been earlier – but there were more important things to attend to. The theme from the 'All New Pink Panther Show', muffled by a closed door, and distance, reached his ears. His feet padded softly down the carpeted steps, moving along the passage with the stealth of a cat stalking prey until he reached the door to the lounge. Suddenly, he pounced and grabbed the handle, throwing the door open, bursting into the room.

"Happy Christmas," he announced loudly, the hem of his gown flapping as he span circles in the lounge, heading towards his mother, who was sitting at the dining table.

"Whoa horsey. Not so fast," his mother said, raising her right like a traffic police office directing traffic. "It isn't Christmas yet. Haven't you forgotten something? Your job."

He gave a knowing look and did an about turn and headed towards the other end of the room, in the direction of the front bay window. On reaching a brown bureau-style unit the boy pulled up by a large rectangular A3 sheet of paper, fixed to the side of the unit at his head height. The sheet contained a number of sketches of heads and faces, in charcoal and pencil. They were of members of the Watford football club; John Barnes, Kenny Jackett, Luther Blissett, Steve Terry and, the club chairman, Elton John. At bottom centre, beneath the portraits, a small calendar, from which each month had been removed, leaving only December – all hand made by mum!

She followed him, switching off the television, caressing his thick dark brown hair as he marked a cross, on the 25th day, using a pencil attached by string and Sellotape to the homemade calendar.

"Look at that," he said, tracing his fingers along the remaining days of the month. "Not many days and it will be 1983. And I will be eleven, and going up to the big school after the summer. Can I stay up to see the new year in with you?"

"Shall we do Christmas first? After all," she added, pointing at the X he had just struck through Saturday December 25th, 1982. "It is now officially Christmas Day."

"Hooray!" they both shouted, jumping up and down, around in circles, gowns and arms flapping like a flock of seagulls seeking to steal the food from a child's hand on the seafront. And when they stopped, they held hands and danced and sang in slow tempo, *"Save Your Love"*, a one-time hit by Renée and Renato.


"You tricked me. You tricked me," mother repeated twice, tears of laughter rolling dance her cheeks. "Reddest rose! Not reddest nose."

Regaining her composure she guided him through an 180° turn, her hands on his shoulders. Before them, two armchairs, in the bay window, laden with colourfully wrapped packages, were glistening with shiny bows and ribbons – of various shapes and sizes. Both had spent a great deal of time and care with their prospective purchases, having only each other to dote on, and one parcel stood out above all the others.

"What is that?" the boy asked, pointing at the large trapezium shaped brown parcel – almost his height – propped up against 'his' armchair.

She didn't know – could only hazard a guess as to its contents – having responded to a card found on the doormat, referring to the parcel that had been left near the back door. She suspected it was from his father.

"Open it," she urged.

"Did you see him?"

A brief silence followed as she gently bit her lower lip, sucking air through her clenched teeth, attempting to keep her emotions in check. *'Breathe. No tears. Not today. Smile'.* He sensed something was wrong and turned and hugged her around the waist, making a solemn promise –

"I won't leave you, Mum. I'll look after you. And when I am a police officer, I will find him."

"I know you will. I know you will," she whispered, ruffling his hair. "Now come on. Open it first. Let's see what it is."

As the boy placed his left hand on the large, oddly-shaped, carton his left knee knocked against it, causing a low gentle boom, and hum, to resonate within. Tentatively, feeling the weight of the item, he moved the package to the sofa, where he sat, and begin picking at the glossy parcel tape with his fingernails. Small sticky pieces of the tape wedged themselves beneath his nails, and he eventually ripped the brown paper open, tearing and shredding it, as it fell to the carpet, revealing the gift contained inside.

"Wow!" he shrieked.

\*\*\*

Azarias exhaled a cloud of breath in the cold winter air, inside the shed, in which he had hidden himself for a number of hours. It had been dark when he had arrived and propped the package up against the back door of the house. Having posted a card through the letterbox, while the house was asleep, Azarias had then secreted himself in the shed at the bottom of the back garden, and watched from afar as the lights of that Christmas morning flicked on and off around the house. The window of the bathroom was illuminated and the not-so-tall figure of the boy appeared to be attending to call of nature, then washing hands, before the room fell dark again, and the house remained in darkness for some time before a crack of light bled through a gap in the curtains of the back bedroom – Azarias knew the house well; his mother's bedroom. He then chose that moment to look away for a while, feeling a little awkward at the thought of watching the frosted figure of his mother going through her motions in the bathroom – Oedipal voyeurism. When he looked back the bathroom was in darkness again, and the crack of light has vanished.

Some minutes passed – the reading of the card, discovered on the doormat, he surmised – and then the opening of the large heaving drapes on the inside of the back door, splashing harsh light onto the cold, dark, patio; the package leaning against door sliding downwards as the door opened inwards. For a moment it looked as if the parcel might fall off the step, but she was able to grasp the neck of the package with both hands before it had a chance to slip any further. The strange shaped box disappeared inside the bright Yuletide warmth of the house, though the back door remained open, sucking the winter air into the warm confines of her home.

Azarias ducked down, balancing on his haunches, peering through a knot-hole in the larch-lap wall of the shed. He watched holding on to his breath, fearing that he might give away his location in a cloud of exhaled breath, as she stepped out on to the patio, wearing her long 'Queen of Sheba' dressing gown. She appeared to be looking for something, or someone, and for a second it appeared as if she might walk down the long garden path towards the shed, where Azarias was hiding. He froze, in more than one way; his cold-numbed fingers poised over the Motorola, in the event that he would have to make good his escape back to his own time but she stopped, turned around and went back inside the house, closing the door behind her. And then the fluorescent light in the kitchen flickered into life.

Standing up, and stretching, Azarias turned, refocussing his eyes in the gloom, searching for something in his memory – and it was there, where it had always been, hanging on a hook affixed to the wooden wall – a red, yellow and orange striped deckchair. Taking it down, he set it up in the middle of the floor and lowered himself into it, carefully. It was an old deckchair – no, it wasn't, not here, anyway, in 1982. He settled down, to wait a while, discover if his plan would come to fruition. Azarias wanted to be where the action was, so to speak, and it was still early in the morning, and some time before any of the presents would be opened. *'Some things are worth waiting for'.*

***

Le Feuvre sniffed at the air, his head jerking from side to side – a meerkat sentry on the lookout for intruders or predators on the prairie – and his listened intently, holding his breath momentarily. Something was not quite right. Not desperately wrong, not just quite right. All the lights were on throughout the apartment that once belonged to the now deceased Raphael Antinori. *'Why? Is someone here? Who would leave the lights on? Why? Focus. Approach with care'.* He scanned the apartment, remaining motionless, but ready to pounce should the need arise. *'The kitchen? Nothing. The Mezzanine? No one there. No sound. Nothing'.* He satisfied himself that he was the only one in the apartment, concluding that some fool from forensics had left the lights on as they vacated the property. There was only his reflection in the black glass, which separated him from the warm humid night.

Augustin had returned to the apartment with a purpose, and that meant going up to the roof – the scene of the crime – into the sultry suffocating night air, in a bid to cover his tracks, just in case there was something that had been missed; in fact he was certain that there was some minute detail that even the most eagle-eyed investigator might have missed, would not have considered, if was not for the fact that the death was being treated as a suicide. He had good reason to visit the scene, having remembered, clearly, the events leading up to the demise of the Vice-Superus; *'his fall from a great height'*. Le Feuvre had departed the scene quickly, without checking that he had left not signs of having been on the roof at the same time that Raphael had fallen to his death. *'Very remiss'*. He was still concerned as to why all the lights were on, yet no one was at home.

*'Who has been here? Why not turn off the lights? Recently? Who?'*

In the heat of the night, on the terrace, Augustin Le Feuvre shone a powerful beam of light from his uRAPP, illuminating the rooftop around his feet, searching for that tiniest of clues that he suspect he may have left at the scene – evidence of the scuffle between himself and the Vice-Superus. *'Most undignified. A waste of energy on his part. Pointless.'* But the pointlessness of the attack on a trained soldier was exactly the point.

"Why did you do that?" he asked himself, scouring the surface in great detail. "I could easily have snapped your spine. You were trying to leave clues. Yes? Not so clever. I am not so stupid. You kicked my crash helmet for a reason. Ah. Yes. Here. Not as clever as me. Ha!"

In the beam, on the surface of the terrace, Augustin detected a slight abnormality – a glint, a sparkle; a trace. Not much to the untrained eye but enough evidence for a forensic crime scene investigator to process, in the event that suicide was ruled out; as unlikely as that scenario was. The Superus had received a Code Delta One-Five – a digital recording from a satellite, showing slightly distorted images, in close-up, of Raphael Antinori toppling backwards off the building, arms raised above his head. There had been a slight break in the transmission, a glitch, but the body was then seen to hit the surface of the water; an impact akin to hitting concrete from that height. No one survives a fall like that. It was fortunate – perhaps planned – that the recording of the demise of Antinori was cropped in such a way as to show no evidence that anyone else was present. *'Surely part of a plan. The Superus. Must be. Covering our tracks. He has connections. Switch that off. Switch that on. Delete that. Save that. Evidence. I am learning the tricks. All part of your plan. Yes?'* – He could not have been more wrong.

***

The cold grey dull December filtered the glistening particles of dust through the beams of light which pierced the cracks, holes, and window, of the shed. Azarias shook himself into wakefulness, having drifted into an uncomfortable, bone-aching, toe-numbing, joint-stiffening sleep – the type of half-sleep experienced by a weary traveller subjected to dozing in a bus depot, railway station, or airport lounge, in the early hours. He stood up and stretched, grabbing at handfuls of air, as he curled his fingers into fists.

"What is the time?" he rasped across his dry tongue, holding the Motorola up to his rheum-encrusted eyes – '09:38. Saturday December 25 1982'.

"Soon," Azarias sighed, clasping the mobile device in his left hand, and crouching before the knot-hole again.

The icy-cold air chilled his right eyeball, peeping out through the hole in the shed, stimulating the blink reflex; tear welling in the lower lid, trickling down his cheek. He could make out no discernible movement in the house, so returned to the deckchair, and sat back with his hands in his lap, closed his eyes, and searched for memories of a Christmas past.

Warm salty tears streamed down his face, and between his lips, the memory of a special time, long since passed, focussing the attention of his mind on that particular Christmas morning, from the moment when he opened the door and burst into the lounge, greeting his mother. The events of that morning – this morning – were recalled through the eyes of the boy.

'*His mother's face – smiling from inside the dark frame formed by her long cascading hair. The Milky Way of freckles beneath her eyes and across the bridge of her nose. – "Should have taken the time to count those freckles." – His task. It's not officially Christmas until it has been crossed off the calendar. 1982. The year his beloved football team, Watford, were promoted to the First Division. The sketches of the players, upon which the calendar had been glued. Making the X though December 25. Christmas day. Then dancing and singing – "The reddest nose!." Laughing together. And then the gift. From his father? Revealing the surprise. – "Wow!"*'

"Wow!" he blurted, sitting upright in the deckchair. "It worked."

There was no loud bang – no single crack of thunder splitting the sky and shaking the shed. Nothing. Just the quiet of a Christmas day morning and the beating and thumping of his excited heart. And there was a feeling – no, not so much a feeling – more an awareness of a significant and subtle change, yet not a change. It was something that he had been developing since he was 10 years old, though it came to him like a new memory – '*weird*'! A sense that something had just happened, yet had been that way for some thirty years, since the moment he received that gift – the gift from himself. '*Very weird!*'

Raising his hands to his face, still clutching the Motorola, Azarias examined the fingers on his left hand. The nails had been cut very short, and the tips of the finger were hard – calloused, yet it was nothing new. They had always been like that, as long as he could remember, yet they hadn't. At the same time he was aware of the impact he had made on his own life – *'Bloody weird!'*

"Soon," he whispered, laughing under his breath. "Soon. It is just a matter of timing."

He tapped a button on the Motorola and faded into the cold December day, leaving a swirl of dust in the empty shed, and a deckchair on the floor, which no one would lay eyes on until the spring of 1983, and pay no heed to it; mother and son simply thinking that the other had set it that way. Hardly worth a mention!

Azarias took with him, back to his own time, the knowledge of the change he had made to his life. There was no going back but he felt the need to discover the impact that he may have had on others, and the future. None that he was aware of, but would he be aware? Would he recognise change or would it just become part of his experience – the norm? He knew because he was responsible for the change – *'confused!'* And Azarias could have had no idea of the impact on his future, and others around him, that his main plan would have – no idea!

\*\*\*

Saluki raised the forefinger of her right hand to her pursed lips, gesturing, signalling with the other hand for Lamont to adopt a crouching position, with the minimum of fuss, without making a sound. The apartment was in near darkness – not the way it had been when they had left it – the only available light spilling over the edge of the mezzanine, perhaps from a bedroom. Other than that, only moonlight penetrating the glass wall illuminated furnishings – furniture which neither of the recognised. The artwork on the back wall was different – more animal than intergalactic. Something was wrong – very wrong.

A sound from the mezzanine – a low groan, a female emitting a sensual animal-like sound – and it caused them to start. They scrambled for cover behind one of the four white curved two seater sofas, which formed a circle. A woman's clothing, and undergarments, was strewn across two of the sofas; a pair of red patent leather high heels, carelessly discarded, a metre apart, lay in a line leading towards the access to the upper floor. The groaning sound again – rhythmic and repetitive, coupled with small yelps, animal-like barks, and cries of *'yes, yes, yes, oh yes'*, building towards a crescendo. Saluki and Lamont both felt each other's panic rising – amidst confusion.

"What is happening?" Lamont whispered his hushed sounds barely audible above the cries of the continuing coital climax. "Where are we? Are we in the right place? Right time?" He dared to look over the sofa, which concealed him, towards the mezzanine, searching for answers.

"Right place. Right time," Saluki hissed, grabbing his left forearm and pulling him down. "But everything is wrong. Listen. I need to find out what has happened.

You should return to him. Stay with him until I return. It is too dangerous to stay here."

And then they heard the words that confirmed their fears; that they had returned to an alternative present. *'An anomaly!'* Saluki thought. *'He must have changed the course of history. Changed the past. That date'.* The unseen woman, in the bedroom, on the mezzanine, in the throes of her ecstatic, frenzied, love-making called out the name of her paramour.

"Yes, yes, yes. More. You are so generous. So big. You fill me, Augustin. Don't stop. Oh yes. Now, you, Vice-Superus. Come. Come. Oh yes. That is good. Yes? Fill me up. Oh yes."

Saluki's face flushed slightly, most likely with embarrassment; perhaps because in this alternative future Augustin Le Feuvre was Vice-Superus at Genetikos.

"I must try and make this right," she disclosed. "This is not good. I will come for you both. When the time is right. Go. Now."

\*\*\*

Saluki peered over the edge of the rooftop, down into Blackett Street, close to where numerous buses delivered passengers and shoppers into the heat of Newcastle, the same buses collecting those same shoppers, and students and workers, and transporting them to outlying areas in Tyne and Wear, Northumberland, County Durham, and beyond. As destinations go, the rooftop above the

327

shopping mall proved as good as any place to materialise out of thin air, away from prying eyes.

"Now find a way down," she murmured to herself, skirting the edge of the building, in a westerly direction, observing the St. James's Park football stadium rising proud above the surrounding skyline. "Too busy down there."

She checked the date and time on her uRAPP – 19.11.1999 – 11:05 – and then tapped the central screen, purposefully; her white two-piece outfit flickered, appeared to move and twitch, and changed to the colour black from the hem of the trousers, upwards to the collar of the jacket. *'Better to blend in with the surroundings. Meld into the shadows. Police officer. That's me. Who would question the activities of a police officer?'*

"Timing is everything," she whispered, admiring her new police uniform. "Catch him before the event. Prevent it from happening. And not too soon. Don't want to draw attention from his other self, in the alley. And me. Wait for the fight. A distraction. Of course. But what is his plan?"

Tapping the screen again Saluki produced a map of the immediate area, in which she was the slowly throbbing blue focal point around which everything revolved. Her view of Newcastle included a square bounded by John Dobson Street to the east, Strawberry Place and the football stadium to the west, High Bridge to the south, to the Civic Centre at the top of Northumberland Street in the north. On the map, two red dots also throbbed rhythmically, like tiny heart monitors – one at the Monument end of Blackett Street, the other on the corner of that alley between Grey Street and Pilgrim Street. Her other self was also a throbbing blue disc. Saluki could see where everyone was – two people in two places at once! Now, she needed to be on the pavement below, in Newgate Street.

Again, the utility device on her wrist proved invaluable, as Saluki fired from it a black cord – of the type used by climbers – and aimed this at the flat rooftop, where it adhered to the surface, fingers and veins forming roots and an anchor, conjoining with the fabric of the building. With the cord firmly attached, and feeding from the uRAPP as she made her way to the edge, the Commandant stepped backwards testing the tension of her rope. She then positioned herself on the low parapet and leaned out backwards, knees slightly bent and feet against the corner of the top of the shopping mall, and then abseiled down the side of the building, towards a quiet service road at the rear of the mall, feeding the cord, like spider silk, from the uRAPP; unseen and unexpected.

"Well done girl," she praised herself, collecting the cord in a heap at her feet which, following further instructions from her device, had detached from the roof, and been tugged over the edge. Another tap to the screen and the matter that made up the cord bonded, blended, and reshaped itself into the design of a female police officer's hat – not just any police officer's hat – a Northumbria Police Constabulary female police officer's hat; appropriate to the time.

"Attention to detail," she breathed in hushed tones, picking up the hat and placing it on her head, reassuring herself that no one had observed her activities – no one had seen anything – *'Unobservant people. Tiny thoughts focussed on their tiny lives. The immediate impact of the next tiny task on their uninspiring tiny lives. Their meaningless existences. If only they could see the future."*

Saluki made an attempt to tie her black hair in a sort of a tail using, of all things, an elastic band secreted about her person from the study at the home of Azarias. *'Might not look right hanging outside the hat'.* Readjusting the black and white hat and a glance in the mirrored screen of the uRAPP confirmed the outcome.

"Yes! Attention to detail."

Moving away from the service road Saluki joined the human traffic on Newgate Street, a police officer on the beat around the city centre – nothing more, nothing less. She was confident that no one had seen anything out of the ordinary – all too busy with their insignificant lives; the majority unable to focus on more than one thing at a time, using their yet undeveloped brain. Science had not yet evolved enough for the human brain to even begin to realise its full potential, and it has nothing to do with that myth about the percentage of the brain used; it is about focus. *'In another 120 years, or so, you will realise your potential. Spot the gorilla in your midst. Time check – 11:11'.*

Saluki was in the belief that Azarias would not make a move, or intervene, until such a time the 'other selves' were distracted with the skirmish in the alley – only then could he potentially approach his younger self, who would have started to walk from the steps of the

Monument towards Theresa, and maybe this is the key –
*'If he diverts her from that path that would likely cause a huge anomaly. One small change in her life, one huge change to the future. Must stop him'.*

Turning right into Blackett Street, beneath the dim, dingy, light-absorbing enclosed footbridge, linking the separate parts of the mall across the busy bus lane, Saluki walked on, mingling with the scattered crowds at the numerous bus stops, once she passed through the dark corridor and back into the light. And then she spotted him, could see it was Azarias, without having to confirm the fact by reading the signal emanating from her device. He was leaning against a store window, near the Monument entrance to the mall, the window displaying a range of electrical goods. Azarias appeared to be watching and waiting, hiding his face beneath a dark coloured hooded sweatshirt.

Saluki knew nothing of MTV, featured on the variety of television screens, of differing shapes and sizes, displayed behind the glass of the long showroom window. And she knew nothing of the performers – *The Eurythmics* – who were moving on the screens in sepia-tones; an androgynous lead singer, with spikey-cropped hair, wearing square sunglasses, booming out bass-enhanced lyrics from the song, *"I saved the world today"*, which struck an ironic chord, as Saluki stalked her prey:

"Hey hey I save the future today," she sang, adding her own lyrics.

From the uRAPP Saluki withdrew a metre length of black cord, somewhat thinner in structure than that she had used to lower herself from the roof and cutting it from the device, she wrapped it three times around her wrist, pulling it taut, like a garrotte – Azarias was too preoccupied to notice.

\*\*\*

*A letter to myself*

*In the event that someone else is reading this letter – whoever you maybe – it is possible that I have lost my life, or my mind. If it is the latter then this letter has been written with the intention of reminding me who I am; recovering my identity should my plan have some catastrophic impact on the passing of time, my life, and the world around me. Bizarre? I would have thought so, not so long ago, but now I know different – it is possible that I can make the dead undead – bring them back to life; but at what cost, I do not know. And what follows now is the why, the how, and the wherefore – for you and for me, should I have forgotten.*

*My name is Azarias and I have recently discovered that I am a time traveller. Strange but true, yet difficult to explain and hard to understand. But it is the truth. I am a time traveller. And, in spite of the rules – 'the ten commandments of time travel' – I have devised a plan and this plan involves great sacrifice on my part, in order to preserve the life, or lives, of those I love and loved. I have no idea what the outcome will be, for me, and the entire human race. For you or me, whoever is reading this letter, this is/was the plan. Forgive me if it goes wrong. I mean no harm – meant no harm.*

*Having realised that I may have already saved one life – that of my friend and colleague, Alan, – through accidental intervention, meeting him before another event, which in theory had happened before (heading him off at the pass), and then I had assisted my younger self my presenting a guitar as a Christmas gift, and have since developed musical ability I had not previously acquired – it is confusing but, yes, I can now play guitar because I gave my younger self a guitar, having travelled back in time.*

*Now, I intend to prevent the first meeting between myself and Theresa – prevent that first date from ever taking place. I have engaged the services of a pretty young escort, for which I apologise (needs must!), having settled on a fee of £100 – I obtained cash appropriate to the time (£177.00) through three different lottery wins, 4 numbers being enough in each case, on Saturday 20th November 1999, using correctly dated 50p pieces. I purchased the tickets at three different locations around the region. I did not wish to draw attention to myself by going after a big win. I have now given consideration to hiding clothing, identities, money and belongings at safe points throughout history, should I survive this current escapade. And if I do remember who I am and survive, will I be the same person – will I have same identity?*

*Anyway, the young woman has to greet me, meet me, the younger me at the right time, presenting an intimate relationship in such a way as to prevent Theresa from making the contact with 'me' – she should be surely be horrified by the unknown woman pretending to already to be in a relationship with 'me'. Enough to put her off and drive her away! Timing is everything. This is the ultimate sacrifice that I am making – preventing her from ever meeting me and thus saving her life, because she will not marry me and, therefore, live a long and happy life, by virtue of having not been connected to the time when I was involved in that undercover operation.*

*My ultimate sacrifice is that I may never know such love, ever again, yet a very special person, a precious life, may live and thrive, and that wonderful, beautiful, person may live and have an amazing and positive impact on the lives of many people. Should I survive I may never realise what it is that I have lost, and this letter may help me to remember. In the event that I lose my identity would you, the reader of this letter – whoever you are – be so kind as to tell me what became of the greatest love of all; Theresa Flores?*

*Regards, and thanks, Azarias Tor.*

# Chapter 24

"Saluki? Saluki? Can you hear me? Saluki. You are safe. All is well."

A reassuring, familiar male voice, in the darkness. She was unaware that she was drifting in and out of consciousness, just that she was lost in the darkness and someone was calling to her, and rubbing, patting the back of her left hand. But she could see no one. *'Why? What was happening? Where am I? Who is that? I know that voice'.* The voice grew fainter, more distant, and images flashed before her – Azarias, wearing a hooded top, leaning against a shop window. That song – *'I saved the world today'* – and catching up with Azarias, and that woman who should not have been there, and then crashing around from one place to another, through space and time, banging into furniture, then – then, darkness. There was that voice, again, much closer than before.

"Saluki? Can you hear me? Saluki? You are safe. With friends. Saluki. Stay with me. Try to open your eyes," coaxed the voice that she recognised.

The blackness slowly developed a red hue, like heavy drapes illuminated from the other side, and she could make something moving – shadows or ghosts. One shadow appeared to loom over her, bearing down through the dark crimson fog. The source of the voice was much closer, clearer and, most certainly recognisable – *'But how is that possible?'*

That's it Saluki. Come back to us. Trust me. You are with friends."

The calmness was suddenly pierced by a shrill scream – continuous, long, and high-pitched; panicked cries, thrashing about, she found herself breaking out into the dazzling daylight. Breathless and panting, she felt as if her thrashing limbs were being restrained and she was blinded by the light, crying, screaming and shouting.

"Get off me. Leave me alone. No. Let me go. Stop. Let go – of – me. No. No. Let – go. Stop."

Another familiar voice – her voice, protesting, demanding to be set free and left alone. *'Breathe, deep. Relax'.* She was panting, puffing, getting control, and breathing gradually slower, as she looked up into the face of the man restraining her, stopping her punching, slapping hands from causing any damage or injury to herself and others. She remembered that benign expression on that recognisable face. *'Not dead? Alive? How is this possible?'* Saluki finally relaxed, the veil of confusion lifting from her face.

"You remember?" Raphael Antinori urged, concern sounding in his voice. "Do you remember? Do you know where you are? What year it is? How many fingers?" He held up his right hand, waving the fingers in front if eyes.

"One question at a time, please," she responded, crumpling the sheet covering the sofa, as she sat up, before carefully lifting herself to her full height. "I'm okay," she continued, waving away the offer of a supporting hand, as she stretched and flexed her limbs.

"I know. I remember. I remember everything," she said, walking over to the large glass window wall, peering out onto the balcony.

"The safety netting around every floor of the building. Still in place when you purchased the apartment. The developers protecting their assets. The finishers. They don't want a few grands worth of robot falling and crashing into the lake below. Or landing on anyone below. Imagine the law suit. And that is why you did not move in for two years. You created a safe place in the past. You had suspicions. You were right. So you planned for your own death. And a fall from the roof turns in to a time leap. Here and now, you fall into the netting. Yet, a body was seen to fall into the lake. How? And, why? And then there is the Code Delta One-Five. Me. Lamont. And the Superus. My father. A different message for him. And then the stuff I saw. What is happening?"

"Now who is asking all the questions? Yet there is one question you are failing to ask," the Vice-Superus suggested. "A very important question." He nodded in her direction, drawing attention to the current choice of clothing.

"Mierde," she barked, noting the 1990s Northumbria police uniform, which adorned her trim body. The hat lay on the floor, adjacent to the sofa.

"Where is he?" she asked, both hands cupping the sides of her face, mouth agape – a recreation of Edvard Munch's scream, frozen in the time, on the realisation of the gravity of the whole affair. "No. No, no, no. What have I done? What has happened? What have I done?"

"Please," Antinori pleaded, "sit down."

"I don't want to sit down. I just want to know. Tell me."

"All I can tell you is that he is alive," he responded, "And that he is here."

"How is that possible?"

"I thought you might have the answer to that question. Can you remember? Try? Lamont is with Azarias. Doing his best, but it is touch and go. We can't seek outside treatment. We cannot afford to draw attention to ourselves. I need you to remember what happened. It is important."

Saluki remembered a letter. In his home. But she was struggling to remember why they were there, or how they ended up there, but she remembered a letter on the coffee table in his house. Now, she could not remember what had happened to the letter.

"Here," said Raphael, holding up a piece of scribbled-upon lined A4 paper. "You were clutching this."

"Now I remember," she said, tapping the side of her head with her right forefinger. "He is smart. I remember now. I see it clearly. It wasn't what I was expecting."

Saluki revealed the details of that November morning, in 1999. She had tracked Azarias and found him close to the point where his younger self met for the first date with his future wife. He was watching, waiting and watching, and Saluki had crept up on him unexpectedly, so she had thought but Azarias had not appeared the least bit surprised when he found his left wrist connected to her right wrist – handcuffed together – by a length of black Nano-carbon fibre cord. Wrapped around each his wrist and her wrist, about three times, the cord had formed a cement-like flexible bond – he wasn't going anywhere, but he hadn't appeared concerned in the slightest. And it became obvious why he hadn't shown any concern – it soon came to light that his plan involved the minimum of interference on his part.

"I have been expecting you," he had said, before asking, "Why have you come dressed as a stripper-gram?"

"A what?"

"Never mind."

And then she had asked that question, again – *What is so special about this date? This particular day? You haven't told me.*

"And you still haven't told me about your self-healing lip," he had responded.

Impasse!

"But he wasn't going to be in a position to intervene," Saluki explained to Raphael. "Attached to me. Or so I thought. And then, when it happened it was too late. The woman. Young. Blonde. Pretty. I hadn't seen the letter at that point. I don't know where she came from. But she placed herself between the younger Azarias and his future wife. I could see the intent. I tried to run. To stop her. But we were tied together. I fell. Twisted. Banged my head hard. I must have been briefly concussed. He was doing this thing. Touching my neck. Like this. Then he has his hands on my breasts. *'What are you doing? I ask'. 'You had no pulse. No detectable heartbeat. C.P.R, he said.* I wanted to tell him about my life-style choice. Pump. Not heart. Instead I did a strange thing. I grabbed him by the back of his neck. There was a crowd. Watching. Police officer, as far as they were concerned. And I kissed him. Full on. Why did I do that? Knowing what I know? But he recoiled. And then I knew. It was all about her. He sacrificed the love of his life, their marriage, so that she might live. They never had that date. Never married. She turned and walked away when the other woman threw her arms around his neck kissed him. The younger Azarias. I never saw any of this. Earlier. It might not have happened if I had not been showing off in that alley. So, she lived. I think. I must check. Then there was the loud bang. Like the sky splitting. A loud crack. Bang! And a flash. Like lightning. People stopped and looked into the sky. Buildings and windows shook. It was like an earthquake. And then we were in his home. It was different. Black leather. Not brown. No photographs of her. No shrine on the mantel. Different. Why? Why was I or, why am I aware of the difference? And there was broken glass.

Blood. Not mine. His. I think. Smashed furniture. The anomaly. We must have crashed into that room. And some things were the same. Maybe some things are always the same. And I found the letter. It was not on the table. It was stuck to a door. Of course. He knew. The door must have been an original feature. There when the house built. He took a gamble on it having not been changed in the alternative timeline. The other life. In this world he chose the furniture alone, so could not chance leaving the letter on any furniture. Was the letter for me or for him? He hoped that someone would find it, perhaps himself. So he would know what had happened to him. Would he believe it, though? Surely he would be a different person? I wasn't expecting that. I had thought that he might attempt to intervene. I would stop him. But to pay someone to do it. I wasn't ready. I did not expect that. The planning on his part. Clever. His manipulation of time. But at what cost?"

"Exactly," the Vice-Superus added, once Saluki had finished her lengthy report. "At what cost? What cost to his future? Our future."

"And what about him? Azarias? She probed. "Can I see him?"

"Soon. I don't know what we can do for him. If he will survive. His system has possibly suffered a massive shock. He shouldn't be here. Now."

"I had nowhere else to go. I couldn't leave him there. It was a mess. How could that be explained away? As for the Superus. My father. I can't take him there."

"Indeed," Lamont offered, having exited the elevator from the mezzanine, joining them by the sofas. "He must remain here. For now, at least."

"How is he?" Saluki and Raphael echoed in unison.

Lamont informed them that he may have stemmed the bleeding, but could not be certain. It was difficult to ascertain the severity of any internal injuries and whether he had suffered any broken bones. His heart, unlike the modern choice of a replacement pump, was beating erratically, fast and uneven.

"We take much for granted," Lamont advanced. "If we bleed, we heal. It is our birthright. Nanotechnology and nanoscience. At work in our systems throughout the whole of our lives. Prolonging life, to the extent that there are now reports of people requesting that their pumps be decommissioned so that they can rest the eternal sleep. When some people have achieved everything, done everything, they get bored of living for so long. And we self-heal, in most cases. Azarias doesn't have that ability. And I. We, I should say. We don't have the old knowledge, or the wherewithal to put it into action. We don't need to know. Do we? We can't help him …"

"We need to help ourselves Antinori cut in. "If we are attempting to maintain the status quo. You both have work do to and it will be dangerous. That I don't doubt. But we need to know what the future holds for us. We dare not even go outside this apartment at this moment in time. We can have no idea what awaits us. I will come when the time is right. We must stop him."

"My father?" Saluki queried, without any hint of emotion in her voice.

"And others," Lamont added. "The anomaly created by his actions," he pointed towards to the mezzanine, "means that Le Feuvre is Vice-Superus. That much we do know. We have seen him. Well, heard; to be accurate. Two years from now, in an alternative time and universe, Augustin Le Feuvre is living in this apartment."

Raphael considered the view that it might all be part of a greater plan. Perhaps Gabriel Damarov has arranged the past, and history, to meet his own needs – his desire for ultimate power. He had made secret of the ambition to attain the top post in EFRON – President. And, Le Feuvre? Greedy for his own slice of the pie; his share of the winnings and the action? Selling his soul to the devil, perhaps, for his gain. But what of Helling? He has been quiet and unassuming. Dutiful! *"Can he be trusted?"*

"And what if," the Vice-Superus continued, "What if we have all been manipulated from the start? What if Azarias is the key to all this, and Gabriel had already known the consequences of his actions? He has set each of us on our individual tasks with a view to achieving his goals by keeping us in separate compartments. Flattering us, caressing our egos. And with the knowledge that each of us would set different things – small things – that would culminate in him attaining that seat of power. Each of us unwittingly helping to build his castle and his empire. He knew that I had my suspicions. I wanted to see how far he would go to silence me. And that is the reason for my escape plan. My death, as it were," he raised both hands, fashioning fingers in the shape of inverted commas. "Make myself dead. Allow myself time to regroup. It appears to have worked. So far. And you, Saluki. I believe. No. I know that there is something that you are not telling me. And it has something to do with me. Yes?"

Saluki looked straight into the eyes the Vice-Superus, unflinching, and assured him that she would share any appropriate information with him when the time was right. She needed more proof, in order to be more certain. And then she would fully support, and serve him, in his role as Superus at Genetikos. But Saluki was frightened, very frightened. She looked at Lamont, then Raphael, before asking the all-important question – the question she feared as much as the possible answers.

"What is the worst case scenario?"

An uncomfortable, stress-filled, silence followed, while Raphael weighed up all the possibilities inside his mind, looking skywards for a more pleasing answer – but none came. It was not the best of times; it was the worst of times.

"There is no easy way to put this," he began, "But I believe that there are some things that have been done that cannot be undone. Somethings will always be the same. Regardless. Unchanging throughout time. Will always be the same. But some things should never have been changed."

Saluki and Lamont looked at each other, faces screwed up with mutual confusion, shrugging their shoulders and admitting they did not understand too much of what he had just shared with them. Antinori then sought to simplify his explanation by using a number of *'what if'* scenarios surrounding the same imagined plane crash – *'for the purposes of the exercise set in or around 2014, to reinforce the time traveller intervention'.*

"The first scenario involves a plane crashing into the sea. 250 passengers and 8 crew are all lost, presumed dead. Scenario number two. Someone with prior knowledge of the crash – someone from the future – decides to intervene. All with good intention. To save 258 lives. No small feat. But this person gets it wrong. Instead of splashing into the ocean the jet smashes into an inner city tower block. Good intentions, bad mistake. Some things are meant to happen. 250 passengers, 8 crew, and another 800 to 1,000 people dead. Number three scenario involves the time traveller intervention allowing the plane to arrive safely at its destination, all passengers alighting without any problems, including that one person making their way through customs unhindered, luggage unchecked, carrying heroin, a powerful narcotic of the time, and this has a street value of one million dollars. A lot in those days. But hey, 258 lives have been saved."

"Okay, okay. So what happens to this person with the heroin in their luggage," Saluki asked, a measure of impatience in her voice.

"That is the question," Raphael nodded in appreciation. "That is indeed the question. And the answer. Well, my answer. Yes. What happens to the courier? Well, it would appear that the courier was shot dead by the person they were meeting. Gunned down by their contact. Greed! Corruption. So, are we counting? Death number one. The contact arrives safely at the point of delivery. No problems. Collects the money. Now has double the money. Never had to pay the courier. This person is followed by two gang members seeking easy takings. Bang, bang. Death number two. The two gang members cannot believe their luck. Double the money. Double the greed. A knife fight ensues during which one of them dies immediately. Death number three. But our friend, the other gang member, was also injured in the affray. Mortally wounded. Bleeds to death in his car. Death number four. Another six deaths are associated with the money alone, the bag of cash being lifted from the corpse by a young boy. Greed is a great motivator. So, where are we up to? Ten deaths. Somewhat slower, I grant you. Bear with me. I am getting to the point."

"Please do," Saluki pleaded' looking to Lamont for support.

"Yes. The point," Lamont pressed. "What is the point?"

"Yes. The point," Raphael sighed, resigning him to a quicker than anticipated conclusion to the scenario eh was enjoying painting in his mind, before he spoke again. "The point? Greed. Greed breeds and encourages corruption. Start adding impurities to the heroin. Chalk dust. Not so bad. Makes it go further. More money to those selling the product. But let's add some toxic contaminants. Add then we throw a bit of gang warfare into the mix. Add a pinch of police corruption. Okay? With me? Keep up. From that one delivery of heroin from that aircraft that landed safely, instead of crashing into the sea, there will have been around 700 associated deaths over a period of about two years. Not to mention the misery, muggings, robberies, child abuse, and other linked crimes."

"And your point?" Saluki asked, somewhat more impatiently than the last time.

"The point is the answer to your question," Raphael offered. "What is the worst case scenario, given all the variables regarding the manipulation of time for one's own benefit – to serve one's own needs?"

She nodded, and Saluki and Lamont leaned forward, moving closer to Antinori, in anticipation of the answer, possibly fearing that they may not hear his words; not that either of them wanted to hear the word that spilled from his lips.

"We could be facing the beginning of the end," Raphael uttered with a certain solemnity. "The beginning of the end."

"The end of what?" Saluki coughed nervously.

"The end of everything," Antinori responded bluntly. "Everything"!

\*\*\*

"Tomorrow and tomorrow and tomorrow," Damarov started, pacing around his office, Le Feuvre and Helling In attendance, both seated in chairs fabricated from the polar white material of the room. "This is why we are here. For tomorrow. The future. We are in a position to shape and design tomorrow, and the future, to suit and serve our desire and our needs. We have that power, and if we can make a difference, why shouldn't we?"

Vice-Superus Le Feuvre, his right forefinger resting across his philtrum, thumb on his chin, appeared attentive and thoughtful, listening to his superior. Augustin's eyes followed Damarov's every move as he continued to justify his actions; reasons for manipulating time for his own benefit. Helling, on the other hand, expressionless, sat with his hands in his lap gazing at the floor, as if he would rather be somewhere else – perhaps he was just bored.

"I am the Nebogipfel Project," Damarov boomed, raising his arms above his head – an almost biblical, 'Moses from the Mount' moment. "I am the History Maker and, in the fullness of time, all will revere me and respect me when they see how I have manipulated the reality of the past in order to improve the present. The true reality. The now. Look at us. We are living proof. Le Feuvre. Vice-Superus today. Tomorrow? This office could be yours. And Helling? You could jump numerous places to fill the vacancy left by Augustin as he moves up the ladder. I aim to hold the ultimate office in EFRON. President of the European Federal Republic of Nations. And all, because we made history work for us. For the better of our kind, while maintaining our superiority."

Damarov's enthusiasm was brought crashing down, bipolar in the extremes of mood change, upon the realisation that two other bodies had appeared in the room, materialising out of the air. Not there one second, then there the next second. A direct contravention of the permissions allowed in this particular office – a breach of security and the time travel firewalls; in place to prevent unauthorised entry via a time leap into the offices of those with a higher authority – a safeguard against attack and assassination. Paranoia! But then, Damarov was not the only one possessing the ability to manipulate the past to suit their own needs.

"How is this possible?" Damarov raged, looking in turn at Saluki then Lamont. "How have you entered this office, in this fashion, without authority? Without the given permissions?"

"I have a good teacher," Saluki suggested, "Do I not?"

"Be that as it may," Gabriel continued, "Rules are there to be observed. It is a breach of security but I have been expecting you. Not you, though," he growled, curling his top lip into a snarl at Lamont. "I had thought that you might use the door. Like everyone else."

"I am not everyone else" she stated defiantly, adopting her usual hands on hips posture. "Am I? In fact, why don't you tell me who I am?"

A tension filled silence ensued while Saluki waited for an answer to her question – she was not prepared to break that silence, to be the first one to speak, and allow Damarov the opportunity to evade the question. No one else spoke, either, and then no one else knew the answer to the question. Lamont appeared a little uneasy, on his guard, and Helling fidgeted, possibly uncomfortably, where he sat. Le Feuvre moved from his seat, placing himself in a corner at least two metres away from anyone else in the room, sensing a developing situation, which may require the soldier within to react in the blink of an eye; and all this in spite of his newly appointed office and position in the corridors of power.

"You want to know who you are," Damarov sighed deeply, moving back to his desk.

Helling remained seated, his head turning to follow the direction from which the conversation sprang, as each spoke in turn. He seemed to be in a more heightened state of unease – almost twitching – perhaps feeling trapped, unsure of his place in the scheme of things; uncertain of how we might respond to any given orders he might receive in the next few minutes. The atmosphere was tense and he sensed that it was not going to improve in the near future; he was guarded, but feared making any sudden movements, taking into account the fact that Le Feuvre was already on his feet, and Helling didn't trust him; had never trusted him. He suspected that the new Vice-Superus would shoot him down, given the slighted excuse, just for the sport – to learn the true capabilities of the new weapon. *'Better not to make any sudden moves, just yet'.*

"I have seen the pictures," Saluki articulated, lowering her hands to her sides. "Sketches. Portraits. Of you."

"Really?" the Superus enquired, with more than a hint of sarcasm.

Gabriel motioned for Le Feuvre to prepare himself to stop Saluki and Lamont from making any moves towards the desk, Augustin dutifully obliged, raising and supporting his left arm, his weapon primed and ready to fire. A look of surprise revealed itself upon her face, and Lamont jolted with fear. Both stood very still. Damarov produced several sheets of paper from within his desk, holding each one aloft, letting each sketch flutter to the floor one by one, following a brief exposure of his unmistakable visage, each having been captured in pencil and charcoal.

"You mean these? Vice-Superus Augustin Le Feuvre removed these from the home of the emergent. I had hoped you would not see them. Unpredictability of time travel. You were obviously there before Le Feuvre. Yet he must have thought he was the first one there. Yes. Timing is everything. Why did you not take them? No. Don't answer that. It is not important now. I had hoped it would not come to this."

"Come to what?" Saluki petitioned.

The Superus coolly examined his fingernails – in his usual fashion – hand outstretched, then closed, nails in the palms of the hands, while he paused for thought and for effect; amplifying the drama of the moment, forming a triangle with both hands beneath his nose. If such actions were designed to create and enhance tension it seemed to be working; Lamont was visibly shaking, the scent of fear almost oozing from his pores, and this was only made worse by the words that Damarov uttered next.

"I have not yet observed the damage that a Subsonne Mark II can inflict upon the human body. Augustin has but he doesn't remember. It happened, and then it didn't happen. Your emergent intervened. Before the event. Remember? And he is not really to blame. He wasn't aware. But he is now, and that is your problem. You failed to control him. I have studied the anomalies and different timelines on the Parmenides programme. It has worked in my favour. And still, I have not yet witnessed a good death caused by this device," he concluded, pointing at the outstretched arm of Le Feuvre.

Saluki regained her composure, the professional cool that came with years of military training. She needed to play for time. *'He will be here. He will come. Soon. Play for time. A father intends to kill a daughter. Why? Questions. Questions. Think. Stall for time. Questions. Answers'*. Time to pose some well thought out questions. If she was about to die, he surely owed her answers to a few questions. *'What will it be like to die?'*

"If I am about to die would you at least answer a few questions?" she pleaded. "Is that asking too much?"

"Helling," Damarov brayed. "You have not yet had an opportunity to test your loyalty. In the event that the Commandant or Lamont, the office boy, make any moves to cause us problems I want you to despatch them. Augustin. Any false moves. You know what to do."

Helling hesitated, studying every face in the room, seeking confirmation that this was not some joke. No joke – not according to the expression on the face of Lamont; fear and panic. Le Feuvre; a neutral dead-pan look, finger ready to depress the 'kill' button. Saluki's fine, bone china features were set with a steely determination. *'Is she not afraid? Where is her fear? I do not want to execute – no – I do not want to murder these people. For what reason? Questions. She has questions. Listen to her'.* He returned his nervous gaze to the Superus, in the hope that he might be able to read his thoughts if he could look deep enough into eyes.

"Questions, questions," Gabriel mused, bowing his head to his clasped hands, as if he was about to offer up a prayer. "I imagine you have many questions. I wonder if all the questions have answers. I can give you some answers, I suppose. I envy you. You are facing death and you have the opportunity to prepare yourself for that very moment. I cannot deny you a few questions. Continue."

"The first that springs to mind," she commenced, "Why would you kill your own daughter?"

"I could answer that with; *'I gave you life, therefore I can take it away'*, but that would not really be the truth. But I will start by thanking you for your services and loyalty across the years. And, thank you for reminding me of the artistic skills of the mother of our emergent. We would not be facing this dilemma if you had taken the portraits away. Instead you left them for Le Feuvre. I had hoped that you would believe that the father of Azarias was Raphael Antinori. But he is dead. Only the people in this room know the truth. Some I trust, others I don't. As for killing my daughter? That would make the emergent your brother. Half-brother, perhaps? My son. Certainly. Your brother? Sorry to disappoint you. How to put this! No. No other way. Just say it as it is. You are not my daughter. Helling. Now it is your time. I have tired of this. Execute them. Use your Subsonne. I have waited for this moment."

***

A loud silence filled the room.

A loud deep moan – like a bovid in an abattoir, clinging to the last vestiges of life before being sliced into a number of steaks and cuts of meat – and the sound filled the apartment. Raphael feared the worst as he entered the bedroom, where Azarias wrestled with the final throes of the fight between life and death. *'What happens if he dies here? Out of his time? 2196, instead of 2014? Wrong place, wrong time. What to do with the body?'* In the event that he should die the blood stained, sweat-drenched bedding would make for a fitting shroud, for any funeral – very dramatic. Raphael felt helpless, somewhat useless, and decided to sit with the dying man, until he breathed his last breath. *'Why? Comfort? For whom? Him or me?'*

Antinori pulled an armchair closer to the bed and, sitting down, focused his attention on his 'death-watch'. *'How much longer?* And he watched, and then a number of strange, and unexpected, things happened; the unexpected being amongst the last thoughts that would have ever entered his mind, given the circumstances.

"What is this?" he, Raphael asked, excitedly, leaning forward, to confirm it was real and not imagined. "How is this possible?"

*\*\**

"Why is this happening?" Helling mumbled, breaking the silence, perhaps also stalling for time, seeking some intervention, which might prevent him from being in the position where he has to carry out the orders of his superior. "Will you not listen to her questions first?"

Sensing some dissent in the ranks, with Helling seemingly refusing a direct order, Gabriel muttered incoherently, and angrily, as he tapped instructions into his uRAPP. Helling was straining to listen, cupping his right hand behind his ear as an aid to improve his hearing. The Superus displayed a sinister sardonic smile, gazing, in turn, at each person in his office.

"I said," he growled loudly, deliberately accentuating every syllable – the whole soft and loud thing being played out for the best effect – "I do not take kindly to disloyalty. So, officer Helling, we have reached the end of the line. I am sorry to say."

Tasting the fear of imminent danger Helling attempted to move, perhaps to attack, rather than defend, but found himself immobilised in the seat – clamped at the ankles and wrists by the very material from which the chair was manufactured. And with a motion not dissimilar to that of a car-crushing machine in a

355

breaker's yard, and applying massive forces upon his human form, the chair began to fold around Helling, as the Nano-particles set about reforming the article of furniture into the fabric of the building, from which it had grown. It, again, became the office floor, making flesh and bone part of the same, the method of death and torture, not by accident but by design.

Le Feuvre appeared physically sickened, yet transfixed, while Lamont shielded the view with his hands, as the Nanotechnology attempted to erase and eradicate the foreign body with which it had fused. Bone cracked, internal organs popped and burst as they were squeezed, and small fountains of blood hissed and splashed, as the solid, heavy, dense mass – capable of forming furniture and other objects upon request – rose and fell, writhed and boiled as it dealt with Helling the way antibodies deal with any bacterium invading the human body.

Saluki opened her mouth to speak but words failed her, locked inside her brain, as the office 'quake' settled and calmed; the only remaining evidence of Helling, a brown and scarlet smear embedded in the white surface of the floor, and a rank smell clinging to nostrils, suggesting that someone had voided their bowels – the stench of death. And as white particles, and matter, moved – 'white blood cells' erasing any infection – the stain also vanished, leaving only that bad smell, and the taste of death; with Damarov hungry for more.

"My design," Gabriel announced proudly. "All my own work. The first time it is has been used on a live subject. Impressive. Don't you agree? Once you realise that it is possible to control the particles, make furniture and other mundane objects you can do anything you put your mind to. See. The floor is about half a metre thick. Body crushed and now part of the structure. Any sudden moves. You know what to do, Augustin. So, Saluki. Saluki, Saluki, Saluki. How do I solve a problem like Saluki?"

***

"What are we going to do with you, Azarias?" Raphael whispered, leaning closer, suspecting that Azarias may well be able to hear him. "I have never witnessed such a thing as this. I had thought you might die. You should be dead. But," Raphael was caught unawares when Azarias inhaled a deep breath – and not his last – and opened his left eye; the dark pool of pupil set in the hazel coloured surround, constricting with the first look at the light. And then the eyelid snapped shut. For a few seconds silence reigned, Raphael holding on to his breath, and Azarias as still as stone, and suddenly he gave two deep gasps, in and out, and the displaced time traveller dragged himself, slowly, into an upright seated position, in sheets that would not look out of place in a busy accident and emergency department on a Saturday night, in many cities. Another sharp intake of breath, before finding a more controlled and regular pattern of breathing, and then focusing his eyes on his immediate surroundings.

"Your eyes!" Antinori exclaimed. "Look at me. Please."

"Who are you?" Azarias quizzed, studying the stranger's face in great detail. "What is this place? Where am I?"

"Raphael. My name is Raphael," he paused, searching for a reaction. "Raphael Antinori. Does the name mean anything to you?"

"I think I have heard it," he responded with caution, somewhat guarded, and uncertain about his whereabouts. "What happened to me? Am I in a hospital? Where am I?"

"Now. There is a question. Where are we? *Where do I start*," he whispered, seeking a way to best explain the situation, without causing any sudden and unnecessary shocks, particularly in light of this person having been near to death a few minutes before. *'There is no easy way'.*

"Okay. Before I start. Can I ask? How do you feel?"

"I feel okay" Azarias replied. "But it's strange. Weird. I feel different. But different to what? I feel like I know stuff but don't remember how I learned it, or where I learned it. I think I can do things that I couldn't do before, but before what? And when? What is happening to me? In fact, I don't know who I am. You called me Azarias. Unusual name. Tell me. Who am I?"

\*\*\*

"Tell me who I am," Saluki demanded, the smell of death still lingering in the office. "That is what you can do with this problem. Tell me who I am. Tell me about my parents. Then Azarias. And then you. Who are you? And why this? You didn't have to do that. At what cost, power? Answer me. If I am about to die I feel that I have a right to some answers."

"Maybe you do. Yes, maybe you do," he opened, before weaving a tangled web of deceit and treachery – not everything, but enough to satisfy the minds of those about to die.

He confirmed that Azarias is his son, and Gabriel admitted to fathering many offspring throughout time – the development of his own private army – part of the greater plan, which involved shaping the present and the future, by making history; leaving nothing to chance, and using his children where and when necessary. Generally, they were loyal, as were his many concubines; the women who bore him children, much further back in time, treated him as if he were an angel, or a god – superstition and fear, and balance of mind, were important , when choosing time-wives.

"Manipulation of the mind is crucial," he continued, seemingly pleased with his control of the mind, as well as events throughout history, space and time. "Each woman is led to believe that they are the special one. The only one. And, I never explain. Never make excuses. I provide for them. Protect them. For as long as they useful to me. In each infant I embed a chip. When the time is right I activate them. I will activate them and control their movement through time. Just as I did with

Azarias. All part of my plan. As were you. But your services are no longer required. Is he dead? Azarias. What has happened to him? At the very least, his mind will be scrambled. But it all worked out for the best. I will realise my goal. I will be president. And all thanks to you and Azarias. You helped to reconnect the desired timeline. For that, I say thanks."

"And Raphael? And me?" she probed further. "What are we to you? What were we to you?"

Damarov coolly informed Saluki that she was not his daughter but was in fact the child of a government minister, whose whole family had been lost at sea when their yacht sank without a trace. *'A tragic accident!'* Damarov explained that the infant Saluki – *which had not been her name* – had been replaced with a baby girl, which had been taken from some place in time, from one of his many wives, to make up the numbers, as it were, should the wreck ever be discovered. He couldn't tell Lamont the name of the woman – he was disgusted with this disregard for human life, yet Gabriel made it clear that he was only interested in anyone when they were of use to him.

"You see," he rambled on, as if he was reasoning with himself for his actions. "My wife. You will not remember her. I am talking about my real wife. She was not well. Not sound of mind. Something genetic, we later discovered. A malfunction. A very rare reaction to the very Nanotechnology that makes our lives better. It seems she did not really belong in our time. Very delicate. Never went anywhere. Never saw anyone. So, when I produced you no one suspected anything. Our union produced no children. I needed a child. Guaranteed loyalty. Particularly a female child. Most likely to be loyal to the father. I had transported a young girl from the past. She died. Brain was probably scrambled. That was when I had the idea to exchange the dead child for you. I knew your family. You fitted the profile, so I disposed of them in order to gain access to you. If the yacht should ever be found then the requisite number of remains will be found. I doubt anyone will find them. No one will be looking now. If they were found I doubt they would bother much with post mortem examinations. I have enjoyed watching you grow and flourish. And you have enjoyed an excellent career to date. Shame it has to be cut short. Now you have outlived your usefulness. And, Raphael? He was getting too close to the truth. Far too clever for his own good. But then I was using his identity as a calling card throughout history. I tried to be careful. Cover my tracks. Ensure that no one had a likeness or image or photograph. I did not give much thought to an artist sketching from memory. Again, I thank you for that. At least his demise will most likely be recorded as accidental, suicide or misadventure. End of story. Doubt whether any parts will be found. Probably disintegrated upon impact. Sucked into the cooling system of the complex. Perhaps the sludge will be cleaned out one day. And he will be fondly remembered. I will see to that. A memorial service. I shall prepare and deliver the eulogy. A great man, I will say. Anyway, I have tired of this."

"One more thing," Saluki interrupted, never getting a chance to inform him that he did not have all of the sketches, and that if he did not, who did? Too late!

Damarov had nodded in the direction of Le Feuvre. He, in turn, nodded his head.

At that point Saluki realised that time had run out and threw her arms out at right angles to her body, forming a crucifix shape, screaming, "Come on. Do it now. Do it now!"

***

"Now," Raphael said. "Look in the mirror."

Azarias stared, for what seemed an age, at the reflection in the A4 sized mirror. It was strange, on more than one level, notwithstanding the fact that he did not readily recognise the face, somewhat in a state of confusion, looking back at him. More than that, though, his mind could not come to terms with that fact that he was watching a wound – a gash – on his forehead, and several scratches on both cheeks, heal – knitting together – in front of his eyes. On top of that he could feel internal injuries to his limbs and torso tingling and itching, during healing processes, which he was struggling to comprehend. And then there was the issue with his eyes; he could not remember what colour they should be but he doubted that he had always had eyes of different colours – hazel, he supposed, in the left eye but the right eye; well, the right eye was emerald green. *'Bizarre!'*

"Your eye," the stranger – Raphael he had called himself – said, handing a sheet of paper to Azarias. "I

362

will attempt to explain. First, though, read this. If you can."

"I can" Azarias started, reading from the top of the hand-written letter. "A letter to myself."

Silent minutes passed slowly as he read the letter through, from start to finish, twice, and then the main points once more, mouthing words and muttering to himself, with a sense of disbelief at the contents. And, suddenly, his expression changed as some memories breached a dam of amnesia inside his head.

"What is happening to me?" he asked, looking into the mirror again. "Those cuts and scratches have almost disappeared. And this letter. I wrote it, didn't I? I have some memories. But they are scrambled. It doesn't make sense. I remember Theresa. She wouldn't listen. I tried to tell her. I had never met the woman before. But I had. Rather, I did. Later. Luciano, her brother, told me I was a tosser. No one would listen. Thought it was a dirty trick, having set up a double date. Something like that. But it was what I wanted, wasn't it?" He paused, holding the letter up, as if offering as evidence in criminal proceedings. "I did this?"

"You did," Raphael acknowledged, handing over a pair of white trousers, and a white T-shirt. "Successfully. To a point."

"To a point?" Azarias checked, doubting his own eyes, while turning his nose up at the clothing on offer. "I would prefer something a little darker."

"That can be arranged. You'll be amazed. I think. Yes. Successful to a point," Raphael declared, giving

Azarias a pair of plimsoll-like slip-on shoes, also in white. "You saved her life. Should I say, preserved her life. That is certain. But you changed the course of your history. Your future. I have no idea, yet, as to the full impact on all of space and time. Oh, and her brother. He lives. I should say, lived. This is the year 2196."

Azarias fell backwards on to the bed, one leg in trousers, one out, losing his balance upon hearing those words and numbers – *'the year 2196. Yeah. Some joke'* – he laughed. He managed to pull the trousers up, and then slip the T-shirt over his arms and head, before slipping his feet into the slip-on shoes, which, to his surprise, self-adjusted to fit each individual foot, moulding to compliment the size and bone structure of both. And the he stood and marched out onto the balcony of the mezzanine floor, taking in the vast expanse of the penthouse apartment and the sparsity of furniture; a large black sofa, two armchairs, a low glass table, set on what resembled a tree trunk and a dining table, with six matching chairs – all covered with thick sheets of polythene.

"Okay. Okay," he laughed. "You've had your fun. Joke's over. What's going on? Where am I? You haven't answered that question."

Raphael joined him on the balcony, grasping the rail with both hands, without uttering word.

"Now. I think I know who I am," Azarias advanced, turning to look at Raphael, searching for a response in his eyes. "What have I done? It's coming back to me. The letter. Saluki. Where is she? Theresa. And then my mother and the guitar. That Christmas. A gift from me to me. I didn't know that then but I know that now. How does that work? I thought it was from my father. The guitar. I had never met him. Never seen him. Only the sketches. Raphael? You are Raphael? She called him Raphael. The face in the sketches. Who is that? It's not you. Do you know him? What is going on?"

"Please. Follow me," Raphael countered, sweeping his right arm in the direction of the elevator. "It is time to bring you up to speed. There is much work to be done."

***

"Our work is done," Superus Gabriel Damarov sighed, rubbing his hands together. "Time clear up the mess. Time to move on and take up our rightful positions in society. Do you have anyone in mind for the role of Vice-Superus?"

Le Feuvre did not reply, attempting to maintain a neutral expression, fearing that he might reveal his deepest, darkest thoughts. *'I could take you out now. But how would I cover it up? At least I have you to help cover this up. It never happened. I have to make it so that what I do to you never happened. Not now. Patience'.* They both stared for a while at the heap in a far corner of the room.

One pile of twisted cloth, bones, flesh, blood, faeces, matted hair, and internal organs – broken and mixed to a pulp – two bodies, once recognised as Saluki and Lamont; life extinct. Above this heap of destruction, which appear to give off steam in the cool air-conditioned room, on two walls, in that corner, and on the ceiling, dripping in blobs, running in rivulets, the splattered viscera of something resembling the detritus and throw way remains in an abattoir.

"Remarkable, don't you think?" Damarov inquired of Augustin Le Feuvre, pointing at the putrid mash on the floor. "Now, imagine that on a larger scale. Capable of destroying an entire army or city with one pulse. There would be no hiding place from such a weapon."

Le Feuvre stood motionless, arms at his side, and said nothing. Instead a sadistic wry smile crept into the corners of his mouth, as he began to admire his handiwork – the art of killing.

The Superus punctuated events when he stated, "Many valuable lessons have been learned here today."

# Chapter 25

"A good start," Raphael announced – teacher pleased with the progress of the student – "That's two valuable lessons we have learned. Who you are. And, what has happened. We have identity and history. Well, some history, at least."

The Parmenides programme proved a useful tool for tracking the timelines of Azarias – *"It does what it says on the label"* – and Raphael produced a three-dimensional holographic image adjacent to the sofa and chairs, and removed the polythene covers, so that they may sit without developing a sweat, and to prevent them from sliding around – Saluki had not looked too comfortable when she had been lying on the sofa earlier; not that that had been the worst of her problems and concerns at the time. The holographic image resembled an underground or metro railway map, with various coloured lines sprouting from each other, but all heading in the same direction – upwards; there was no Circle Line. Raphael drew his finger skyward, pointing towards a purple line, which he traced, as they sat down on separate chairs. The line started with the birth of Azarias and remained in one vertical path until it reached a date, clearly marked December 1982.

"And this is where it gets complicated," Raphael revealed. "And this is the abridged edition. We don't have much time."

"I thought we had all of time," Azarias hypothesised, studying the lines, which appeared to move and shift. "And when do I die?"

Raphael Antinori attempted to make something easy which was in fact complicated, involving matters of life and death. At that very moment, in that very room, in the year 2196, Azarias Tor was very much alive, and the Parmenides programme proved that to the case. But the timeline was a web of contradictions, and a set of problems to be solved. It was like a living organism – other lines grew from it, branching outwards, upwards, and inwards, away from and towards the main line, then out again; and in places gaps had appeared, disconnecting the main line and some subsidiary lines from their chosen courses.

"Why is it doing this?" Azarias scrutinized, drawing attention to a line sprouting – a small twig – from the month of January in the year 2015. "And this? June 2196! But it is detached from anything. And the rest are growing and moving. Why? What does it mean?"

"I don't have all the answers," was the best that Antinori could offer, his focus still on the Christmas of 1982. "I will be exploring more than I will be explaining. Certainly to start with. I have never encountered such as this before. You have created a number of anomalies throughout time, from your birth until the present day. You are, yourself, an anomaly. Quite unique. See? This is the branch where you

368

intervened in 1982. And now you have two different memories of the same event. One where you think the guitar is a gift from your father, and the other where you know that you gave the guitar to yourself as part of your experiment. Testing the waters, no doubt, for the big event. Preventing your younger self from meeting your potential future wife. And that changed so much. Now, it is the fact that you are here that creates a great deal of interest and intrigue. You should be dead. But here you are, and I am attempting to understand all of this as much as you are."

Raphael attempted to explain what might be happening in the brain of Azarias, using the graphics as a visual reference. It was not Antinori's field of expertise but he had enough knowledge of the subject to surmise that new synapses were forming in that very brain, even as they spoke, taking into account that Azarias had now lived more than one life, or different parts – additional parts – of the one life, and this could be observed, looking back from a projected point in the future, far removed from his own timeline. And the timeline was fragmented, branching out in various directions, all with no ending, then starting up again, somewhere completely detached from all the other lifelines – no death, either. He had not died; no evidence of death in the Parmenides programme. The last piece of information gave some cause for concern; Raphael hoped that was something that would not fall into the hands of the wrong people; better to be thought of as being dead, the same as himself, for the present.

"So, you learned to play the guitar," Raphael started, by way of a recap. "Here. This additional loop. It

369

branches out from the point of intervention. Christmas 1982. Because it had not happened before you intervened. Stay with me on this. You had already lived your life right up until this point," had added, pointing to May 2014, "Before travelling back in time to give yourself the guitar. Back here. 1983. You start guitar lessons but you do not have that much impact on your timeline. Music still played a part in your life but not so that you chose it as a career in any form. Ah! Apart from that tribute band you formed in 2013. IB40ish, you called yourselves. What does that mean? No? It will come to you. And then that line curves back in here. See. Merges back into the main timeline. Not much difference. A short space of time. Because some things will never change. Perhaps pre-destined, if we want to believe that. Looking from here we might argue for that being the case. Anyway, you still became a law enforcement officer. And the undercover operation was part of that life. And the deaths of Luciano and Theresa. And then here, you went back to 1999. The rest, as they say, is history. Your history. Or rather, your histories. Am I making sense?"

"It is starting to make sense," Azarias affirmed. "It's like the time before the first time leap. A feeling of knowing stuff that I've not known before, yet have known it for all time. I have lived all of those lives and have all this knowledge. I feel it."

He had lived it all – was living it all, and together they watched events unfold at various point on his many timelines because he was there, and there, and there – 2015 – 2014 – 1999, then there, and there, and there, far from, and detached, from the original timeline – 1935 –

1962 – 1974. From the original time, two branches from 1999, one of which was broken, disconnected from any future. And then that line began to move. Other lines, branches formed, fracturing the hologram, like the cracks in the windscreen of a car, caused by someone perhaps firing a powerful air rifle at the toughened glass. Many disconnected lines continued to fracture before their eyes. Raphael had seen enough, and closed the programme.

"I envy you, Azarias Tor," Antinori enthused, looking into the different coloured eyes. "To be able to see your future in the past. This means that you live. Beyond whatever happens next. That is certain. You are living. You may not make full sense of it yet, but you will. And I would love to be inside your head. I believe that this is going to be the start of an amazing adventure. For you. The rest of us may be lucky enough to enjoy the crumbs."

"The rest of us? Of course. Saluki. I need to find Saluki," Azarias demanded.

"Yes. I think you are ready" Raphael confided. "You are ready. I need your help. We need your help. And it is time for you to learn the truth. Time for you to meet your maker."

\*\*\*

"Augustin. We have much work to do," Gabriel Damarov celebrated, clinking his glass of amber whisky against Le Feuvre's tumbler. "It is time to prepare ourselves for higher office. You like your new apartment? Yes? I was able to pull a few strings. He had no heirs. Remember, it is not always about what you know but about who you know. I called in few favours. People anticipating my rise to power. Fear is a great motivator. Anyway, now all this is yours."

They were standing on the balcony of the penthouse suite that once belonged to Raphael Antinori, sipping the whisky and admiring the view, gazing at the distant shimmering horizon, bathed in afternoon summer sun, beneath a cloudless ultramarine sky. Gabriel sighed deeply.

"President! Imagine that. Soon. Very soon. Timing is everything."

***

"Okay Azarias. Remember. Timing is everything," Raphael Antinori pressed. "It will be risky. No doubt. But necessary. Do you think you can do it? You are sure? Good. Let's go over it again."

Raphael had reminded Azarias that he thought it a miracle − an anomaly − that he had survived the time leap in to the future, and that the serious wounds, received when he had crashed around through space and time, and his home, when cuffed to Saluki, had healed so rapidly. Antinori put it down to a number of potential reasons − *during the time leap, locked together, something had passed between them.* That might possibly explain the colour change in one eye but it could also have been a genetic thing; passed from father to son, and triggered by the same time-travelling events. Perhaps they would never know, for sure. *"It is what it is!"*

"And, if it is a genetic thing, we have a limited time to learn how to take advantage of any inherited attributes," Raphael reminded Azarias. "On the job training."

Raphael Antinori had exchanged the old Motorola with an up-to-date uRAPP, and fitted it to the left wrist of Azarias, his latest recruit, and injected a microscopic chip into his left arm, bringing him up to speed with current technology. Azarias was as ready as he ever could be, given the limited amount of time they had, in which to plan and act, and find his father; to fulfil the promise he had made to his mother when he was a boy.

Between them, they had devised a plan, of sorts, with a view to arriving in time to prevent Damarov from killing Saluki and Lamont – an outcome that Raphael had considered most likely – and to avert the complete corruption of time, which Antinori feared would benefit the few over the many, further widening the gap between the Haute Monde and the Vulgus. Raphael promised to explain but, first, they had to execute the plan – a plan in theory, only, and not in practise, as there will only one opportunity to get it right. Azarias, for his part, was not quite sure why he was involved with such activities some 180 years ahead of his time, in Belgium. *'No time for such questions'.*

"Are you sure you want to do this? You don't have to."

"I want to do this. I need this," Azarias declared, moving some distance away from Raphael, perhaps fearing that he might cause injury to the bystander at the moment the time leap was activated.

The risks were reinforced – *'this is a first – never attempted before – okay for someone of this time, but ...* no explanation was necessary, though according to the Parmenides programme this could not the be the end. Azarias knew he was going to live. He had seen his future, in the past.

"Okay," Raphael continued, moving towards a countdown, and lift-off. "Stick to the basics when using the device on your wrist. We want to avoid full-scale destruction. Coordinates have been programmed. Just press the green disc when instructed by me."

You don't get to rise through the ranks, one step behind the Superus, without learning a few tricks along the way; acquiring the knowledge of how to breach security, and bore through firewalls.

"Remember the important stuff," Antinori urged, mentally carrying out final prelaunch checks. "Act quickly. Know your enemy. Disable your enemy. Secure the site. Keep one thing in mind always. Timing is everything. Are you ready?"

"Ready as I ever will be."

Raphael was standing between the sofa and the low table, holding his uRAPP up to his face, as if awaiting contact or a call to arms, and Azarias was just below the edge of the mezzanine, poised, ready to go, a finger hovering above the device on his wrist, muscles tensed in advance of the final instruction, which came suddenly.

"Do it – now!"

***

"Come on. Do it now," Saluki screamed, realised that time had run out, and threw her arms out at right angles to her body, forming a crucifix shape, "Do it now!"

Le Feuvre was caught totally unaware, legs kicked from under him, nose and teeth smashing on contact as his face hit the floor. No chance to execute the final command, to despatch Saluki and Lamont – no chance to do anything. It has all happened so rapidly and only because he had been taken by surprise. And then an excruciating, screaming pain shot through all the limbs of his body, as a heaving weight pressed down on his left elbow, and a strong pair of hands pulled his wrist backwards, sharply, snapping the joint, forcing bone and gristle out through the other side. *'Know your enemy. Disable your enemy'*. A dull thud cracking the back of the skull, face bouncing again off the hard surface, a bright white flash, a myriad of dancing, flickering spots before his eyes, followed by blackness, then nothing.

Somewhere, beyond the walls of the office, a loud thunder-like boom split the air, rattling the structure of the building – an anomaly!

375

"Stop!" Damarov commanded. "Stop and stand away from him. Or, I – will – kill – them," he said slowly, with meaning. "Believe me. I will."

"I believe you," Azarias said, standing upright, moving away from the recumbent body of Le Feuvre whose blood formed two different pools – adjacent to his face and his shattered arm, in spite of the nanoscience working overtime to repair the damage. Azarias raised his arms, palms facing outward, as a form of surrender. "I know you will. I have a question. Actually I have many questions. Hey. But, one at a time."

Azarias lowered his arms, slowly, directing his left hand towards Gabriel Damarov, placing his right hand over his left wrist, index finger hovering above the central screen of his new toy. The Superus focussed his gaze upon Azarias, and the changing facial expression revealed the truth about the changing shift in power – Damarov was not really in a position to make demands of anyone. His 'son' spoke again.

"Yes. My first question. I have been told to press this button. Should the need arise. What does it do?"

"How did you get that?" Gabriel barked.

"I have my contacts," Azarias continued, peering down at the screen on the device. "Amazing. This. Like Batman's utility belt."

"Who is Batman?" Gabriel growled, refusing to admit to any sense of fear, or that he was losing control of the situation; such was the arrogance and self-realised superiority of the man.

"Of course. Forgive me," Azarias laughed. "I keep forgetting. Somewhat before your time, I think. So, my second question. Let me see. This screen. See here."

Again, Azarias peered at the device. Damarov became a little agitated but did not lower his aim from Lamont and Saluki; both standing, motionless and silent, their watching eyes flitting from Azarias to Damarov, and back again – spectators at a tennis match, waiting for an ace to be served; hopefully by Azarias Tor. They watched as he mentally bounced the metaphorical tennis ball, setting his sights on the imagined puff of white chalk dust, which would knock his opponent out of the tournament. Aside from deep-thinking tennis analogies there was a plan, of sorts. There had not been enough time available to practise, prepare for all the variables. Then how do you prepare for the unknown, in a time and place in which you do not belong?

"Get to the point, boy," Damarov snapped, in an attempt to regain the control that was slipping through his fingers. "You are wasting my time."

"Boy?" Azarias mimicked with a quizzical tone. "That is the first time I have ever heard a fatherly term used you. Dad. And you use it to chastise me. I am disappointed. I had thought we might share some father, son stuff. Perhaps play football together. Help me with my homework. Just ordinary stuff, really. But then, you were never real. Oh yes, the point. Yes. It says here, SS Mark Two. And here, primed. And, Execute Command. So, that is the question. What happens if I touch that? I don't even know what it is. Not really."

"Don't. Don't touch anything," Gabriel pleaded, panic and fear now definitely evident in his voice. You don't know what you are doing. You have no idea what they thing is capable of doing to the human body. You are out of your depth."

"I imagine you know its capability. Don't you?" Azarias probed. "Did you plan to use it on these two?" he asked, nodding in the direction of Saluki and Lamont.

"They are expendable," he replied, sensing an opportunity to flatter Azarias by elevating his status above the others present in the room. "But you? You could be someone. Here. In this time. This place. You could be at my side. The world at your feet."

"Tell me more," Azarias prompted, lowering his arms slightly, seemingly to the consternation of the other Lamont and Saluki, whose facial expressions revealed a sense of treachery and betrayal. "What is in it for me? Tell me, Father, why should I trust you? You were prepared to kill your own daughter."

"No. No, my boy. My son. She is not my daughter. Not your sister. But you are my son. My heir. Which is why I wanted to have these," he motioned to the sketches and portraits of himself and Azarias, which lay on the floor where he dropped them. "Memories."

"Well, that's all right then," Azarias said in mocking tones, which appeared to go unnoticed. "Memories? So, tell me about my mother. You and her. See, that is another question. Something I have had time to think about, recently. Knowing that I was going to meet you. You and my mother."

"What do you want to know?"

"I wanted to ask if you had any real feelings for her. If you loved her. But I see that you are incapable of love," Azarias menaced, raising his hands again, taking up his original stance with the Subsonne Mark II. "You see, what I really want to know is, were you in any way responsible for her death?"

There followed a brief silence, broken by Saluki, who pleaded with Azarias to lower the weapon; that it was necessary to make Damarov answer for his crimes through the proper channels, in a court of law. Azarias did not lower his aim or his gaze.

"I take your refusal to speak as the answer I suspected," he roared, preparing to depress the appropriate button. "So, what really does happen if I press 'Yes'?"

Damarov flinched, curling the upper half of his body into a sort of ball. "Please," he pleaded. "Don't. How do you know how to use that, anyway?"

Azarias lowered his aim, once again, and smiled, winking at Saluki, who, in turn, attempted to return a wink, which became two blinks.

"How do I know how to use this?" he asked in almost corybantic fashion, which disturbed Damarov and Lamont, but not Saluki, who had now had some idea of what might be about to happen – she would not be disappointed.

"I have had a good teacher," Azarias almost drooled, for effect; which worked, as Damarov was now definitely unnerved.

"Teacher?" Damarov bawled, nodding in the direction of Saluki. "Who? You?"

"No. Me," a voice from behind Damarov grunted. "Me."

Raphael Antinori was now in the room. Gabriel Damarov, surrounded and outnumbered, resigned himself to taking a less aggressive stance. Saluki and Lamont relaxed, any threat to their lives, or well-being, having been reduced dramatically. Saluki approached Azarias, a questioning look in her eyes, and Lamont joined his immediate superior, Raphael, who produced a document, an important looking letter. He handed this Damarov, who noted the signature at the end of the dictate – *President Carrick Juan-Hill.*

"You are now relieved of your post," Raphael Antinori announced sternly. "I am now acting Superus. It is written. See?"

"You still have written documents then?" Azarias quipped.

"For legal matters," Saluki answered, drawing closer to him, her emerald eyes ablaze with feelings she was struggling to control. Touching his right forearm, gently, with her right hand, she added, "Look at you. When I left you I never thought I would see you alive again. Look at you now." And then she punched him, on the top of his arm.

"Hey!" he exclaimed. "Why did you do that?"

"For, for, for," she stuttered, in mock anger. "For making me think – making me believe you were going to side with him. I thought. I thought. You—"

"—I know," he interrupted. "I look like an old fashioned gymnast. White is not my colour. Not my choice. Look at these trousers."

"Is that all you've got to worry about? Come here," she offered, taking hold of his left hand. "Look at the screen. Here. Press there. There you go. Easy. Now choose."

She had produced an application, which connected to the Nanotechnology, the material and fibres, from which the clothes were manufactured, and changed all, or part, of whatever was being worn at the time, and altered the clothing to suit specific needs and desires throughout history; where necessary blending in with the surroundings like a chameleon, creating the ultimate camouflage. All that Azarias wanted to do was change the colour of the outfit he was wearing.

"Black?" she asked, sliding a finger around the screen. "Don't know what you have against white. There you go. You even have choices of shades of black. That's it. Better?" she concluded, with a question, taking two steps back , watching the footwear, trousers, and T-shirt, merge from white to black, starting at the bottom and spreading upwards.

Gabriel Damarov broke up the pleasantries, growling and snarling, unprepared to relinquish his grip on power, if at all possible.

"You fools," he barked. "You treat this like it is a joke. You have no idea what you are interfering with."

Raphael remained unmoved, by the outburst, demanding that Damarov remove, and handover, his uRAPP. He was being decommissioned and an arrest was imminent. Police were on their way to the office. Enough evidence had been presented to the prosecuting office to enable charges to be brought against the deposed Superus. He would soon be in custody.

"Evidence? What evidence?" Damarov challenged.

"We could just start with everything you revealed to Saluki. It was recorded," Raphael started. "I never divulged my full capabilities and skills. My escape route. The link through time to Saluki. I played you at your own game. We will need details of your interventions through history. Your children. How did you phrase it? Your own private army. Loyal concubines. Every rule broken. Add to that murder. Conspiracy to commit murder. And treason. How were going to become president? I am curious. Still, it is finished now. Take care removing that. You are outnumbered."

"I see that," he replied, making slow, cautious movements, towards removing his uRAPP. "Heed my advice. Take it or leave it," he continued. "Take great care about who you trust."

"I have learned that already. Still, sound advice. Thank you," Antinori said with sarcasm. "No doubt I will learn more, as part of the investigating team. I will be involved with interviews, where I anticipate that you will share more pearls of wisdom, and advice."

Suddenly Lamont lifted his left arm, towards Azarias, and stabbed at the screen with his right forefinger. There was a pop, a whooshing sound, and a 'thud', followed by an electrical short-circuits buzzing crackle. Azarias flinched, a look of surprise in his face, but felt nothing. He examined his arms and torso – nothing. The he realised that the attention was focussed behind him – all eyes on Le Feuvre.

Agustin Le Feuvre, with his smashed nose, broken teeth poking through his split lips, and badly broken arm, swayed like a sapling in a gale, before his legs finally gave way. In his chest, a dart-like object flashed, crackled and buzzed. The wounds to his face, and arm had begun to heal, though the open fracture at the elbow was making hard work for the nanoscience that was attempting to repair the damage. Now, he collapsed to his knees, falling to his face once more.

He had been ignored, almost forgotten, and Le Feuvre had risen to his feet with a view to killing the man who had smashed his face into the floor, trying to point his distorted arm in the right direction. Azarias Tor had only taken him down using the element of surprise – on any other day, face to face, one on one, Le Feuvre was convinced he would have killed the opponent with his bare hands; ripped his head from his shoulders. *'Punish him. All too busy. Ha! Mierde. Office boy!'* The dart shot by Lamont had fired electrical impulses into the chest, shorting out the pump – the electronic heart having its power supply cut. He was dead when his head hit the floor, and it quickly became evident that the interruption had created a brief distraction from Gabriel Damarov.

Azarias spotted Damarov tapping at his device on his left wrist, and reacted by firing a two-metre length of black cord, which wrapped around the right wrist of the

Superus. He tugged, pulling the hand away from the uRAPP.

"Too late," Saluki shouted. "He has entered travel coordinates. Let go. Cut the cord. You will be dragged with him."

But Azarias had another idea. He fired the other end of the cord at the floor, where it cemented to the fabric of the building, pulling tight as Gabriel tried to fight against it, dark tree-like roots spreading inside the solid white structure. There was a rushing sound, like a whirlwind whipping up in the room, as the time portal struggled to close – Damarov still being attached to solid fixed matter. Then other four dug their feet into the ground – there was nothing to hold on to – as they fought to avoid being dragged into the same time leap, a potential tangle of flesh and bones. But suddenly it snapped shut, leaving behind an ear-shattering yell, and the right arm of Damarov, which clunked on the solid surface, as he vanished, only to reappear in some different time and place, of which no one had an immediate record; Gabriel Damarov had covered his tracks, and escaped – at the cost of losing his right forearm. The fingers twitched for a few seconds, trying to grip some unseen object, then died.

"Ouch!" Azarias rasped. "I bet that smarts"

Raphael Antinori was in no mood for jokes, though, and snapped, "Damn. Damn. We have lost him. This is not good. Not good at all."

"We can track him. Surely," Azarias remarked, offering a more serious tone to proceedings, his attempt at levity, a nervous reaction, seemingly inappropriate. "And what of his arm? He must be in a bad way."

"Look at it," the acting Superus suggested. "Look closely. What do you see? Or rather, what do you not see? What is missing?"

"Blood," Saluki declared, standing over the limb. "No blood. No wounds. No exposed bone. A perfect severing of the limb, with skin covering the area where it has been cut from his body."

"I was asking Azarias," he moaned. "He needs to learn. But you are correct. A clean cut between time zones. Very little blood loss. If any. One arm, but he will be back. If we don't find him and stop him. As for tracking him. I managed to hide myself until I wanted to be found. He can do the same. Now, he is more dangerous than ever. Somewhere in time. And he will try to find a way to destroy us. Erase our very existence by making history suit his needs. We don't have much time."

"Train me," Azarias suggested. "Prepare me. Send me to hunt for him. Surely he will go after me and my ancestors. I am there. Aren't I? The Parmenides programme? It is already happening. How did you put it? Predestined?"

"You are right. Of course," Raphael concurred. "You are the key to this. Perhaps you are the only one who can find him. I am not so sure, though, that he will go after you. I think he needs you to live. If he removes your ancestors from history you will not exist, and I think he needs you. My concern is that he will go after other

385

people associated with you. People whose lives you saved, through intervention. They may be in danger. Or their ancestors. And I have a theory that he will want to kill the *'you'* that is in the here and now. Then there is the small matter of the alternative worlds and lives which now exist. Saluki, you are also in danger. Your ancestors. Lamont. Me. It is a mess. A tangled spaghetti. People, who died, lived. Against the natural order of things. Different timelines have sprouted. It's complicated. But we have to bring Damarov to justice."

As Raphael was speaking Azarias became increasingly aware of new memories growing within – he was remembering, with clarity, two different lives; yet lives that had separated and grown in different directions. And there was feeling of having lived a life that had come to an abrupt halt, though he had not died – yet he must have died, somewhere, sometime, in the other world; the other life. There were now so many memories – two homes, but one house. The same house but a different home following the intervention. The life that included Theresa, and then the life without her. Luciano did not die because they were never involved with any undercover operation; in another life, though, they were trapped in a burning warehouse. He could see all this, and had developed the memories, because he was looking back from the year 2198, two years on from where he had arrived with a crash in his own far-distant future. And that left them with the major conundrum – the Azarias who was now in this distant future had originated from the year 2014, having gone back to intervene in the life of his younger self, the day of *'that first date'*, in the year 1999; the problem being that the

Azarias living at that time was still moving along that timeline, oblivious to the fact that his older self was living over 180 years in his future – there were two Azarias Tors in the world; actually, the same one but in two different places in space and time.

"Definitely complicated," Saluki agreed. "Where do we go from here?"

Raphael Antinori had the makings of a plan, spinning around in his head, but decided that everyone needed some *'down time'* before reconvening in the office, prior to a meeting with the president; the affair was going to take some explaining, and Raphael suggested that it might be better if he was in the office alone when the police arrived and found that Damarov was nowhere to be found; had escaped, even when he had been surrounded. That was not going to go down well with the law enforcement officers, expecting to make a high profile arrest, and President Carrick Juan-Hill, whose reputation had just been preserved, due timely intervention – the probability being that his life had been also protected – was not going to be impressed with the idea that his potential usurper, potential assassin, was still at large, plotting his return, somewhere in space and time; and time was the weapon of choice of their enemy.

"Take some time to gather your thoughts," Antinori continued. "We have to discuss strategies and share ideas. Difficult times lay ahead of us. And we need to consider the roles that each of us will play. Saluki, would you consider taking up the position of acting Vice-Superus?"

"I'd rather be in the field, with Azarias," she responded, without hesitation, having possibly already considered that such an offer would be made, given that Raphael was now acting Superus.

Sitting himself in the chair once occupied by Damarov, Raphael clasped his hands and rested them on the desk. Reluctantly, he agreed to Saluki continuing in her role as Commandant, and then began deliberating the role that Azarias was going to play. Raphael considered that they were not yet fully aware of the impact that Azarias had made on history. But there was no doubting that he was no longer the same person who was transported into the future, far from his own time.

"You no longer belong to your time," Raphael proposed. "Yet you do not really belong here. You cannot go back, though. Adjustments may need to be made. If you are prepared. Do you understand?"

"I can't go back?" Azarias queried, receiving a shake of the head from Raphael by way of a short response. "In that case I will need that arm," he declared pointing at the limb that was once attached to Gabriel Damarov, which still lay where it had fallen.

There were puzzled looks from Saluki and Lamont, regarding the acquisition of that severed limb, though it appeared that the acting Superus was on the same wavelength, and strange things had happened, and all of it in a relatively short space of time, or throughout a vast expanse of time, depending from where events have been viewed.

"It is now 14:51," Raphael announced. "You have a few hours, or the whole of time, depending on how you use the time, before we meet back here at 18:00 hours. This is just the beginning. I don't have the answers to all of the questions. The best advice – no, order – I can give is to not attempt any heroics until we have considered all options. I imagine that Damarov will be taking stock, consolidating his position and preparing his soldiers for the battle of time. Preparing to send his children to war. And, there is a thought to finish on. Sending his children to war. And, we have no idea how many are out there. 18:00 hours, then? Remember, whatever you do now, in the past, and in the future – timing is everything."

# Chapter 26

The tall lean man stood naked, before the full length mirror, admiring his manhood. He was clean shaven, face and head. The dark hairs on his chest fell in a thin line towards his navel, on his flat board-like abdomen. His erect penis jutted forth from a bush of greying pubic hair, swinging with the movements of an elephant trunk, the beast marching across the plains of Africa, as he began to stroke his right arm with his left hand. In the reflection, behind him, a woman, thick black hair splayed across a white silken pillow, knees up, legs apart, and wrists tied to the metal bedhead with her stockings, craving further attention.

"Ven aqui," she purred. Peering over her voluptuous breasts, nipples erect, opening her legs wider, exposing her pink, moist vagina, amidst jet black curls of pubic hair. "Y cogeme duro. Me gusta cuando me follas de perrito bien duro."

He flexed the fingers on his right hand, tracing a line from the wrist towards the elbow with the fingers of his left hand. Just below the elbow, a seam, around the arm, where the texture and colour differed either side of the join. *'An excellent prosthetic. Ahead of its time. Just like the real thing. With added extras'.* Smiling at the woman in the mirror, he shaped his right hand like a child making an imaginary pistol, and pressed an area on the wrist with fingers on his left hand. Two fingers, and the thumb, on that right hand, vibrated and buzzed softly.

Turning from the mirror he padded towards the bed, which blended with the dark wood Spanish colonial furniture. His bare feet slapped on the cool tiles of the floor, and his erect member swung with the motion of his passage across the room. Kneeling on the bed, between her legs, avoiding knocking his head on the slowly revolving ceiling fan, he probed her hot wet vagina with the vibrating fingers, deeply, so that the thumb buzzed on the swollen, tingling clitoris. Her long black hair thrashed from side to side, her head banging around on the pillow, her open mouth emitting animal-like cries, as an intense orgasm exploded through every fibre of her body.

"Cogeme. Cogeme duro," she howled, thrusting her hips upwards, grinding and writhing, unaware that her carnal and bestial aria carried beyond the closed shutters, through which slits of light cast stripes upon their nakedness, echoing in the narrow Valencia calle, on that sultry July afternoon – siesta time. She gave little regard to her neighbours and the potential disapproving looks she might receive during the course of the coming days; it was probably the furthest thing from her mind, and didn't give a damn.

Untying the stockings restraining her wrists, as he rolled her over on to her stomach and lifted her on to her knees, it became quickly apparent that there was something she did care about, as he pulled her curvaceous hips towards him – that Jesus was watching her commit this carnal sin; *'Voy a ir a confesión'*. The woman reached up to the dour framed image of Jesus Christ, hanging on the wall above the bedhead, and attempted to turn it around, so that the son of God would not bear witness to her lustfulness. Instead, as he pulled her onto his large throbbing cock, in the throes of passion, she wrenched the icon and the picture hanging hook from the wall, throwing it, crashing, off the bedside table and on to the floor, as she made to grab hold of the shaking bedhead. The falling Messiah knocked a diary to the floor, as the framed picture scattered items as it skidded towards the tiles, where the glass shattered on impact. The diary fell open, on a bookmarked page, revealing the date – Domingo Julio 28, 1974. On that page, in large capital letters, was written, *'GABRIEL'*. And he began thrusting hard, his testicles slapping around, left hand pulling her head up, using her long hair like reins..

"Dios mio!" she screamed. "Dios. Oh Dios. Dios mio."

"Si tan solo supieras," Gabriel Damarov grunted, as his hot seed spilled into her depths. "Si tan superias!"

\*\*\*

"This is where you mother has been laid to rest?" Saluki enquired, as she followed Azarias along the winding, interlocking paths of the North Western Avenue cemetery. "It is not like this in the future," she continued, cutting herself off realising that it might seem inappropriate, sharing details of a far distant future when focus was on his own past.

"Not far," he said, thrusting his hands into the pockets of the brown and tan mixed hide calf length trench coat. "I visited her for some years."

"I never knew my mother" she mused, her breath forming a white cloud in the cold grey damp morning air. "Nor my father, it would appear. I was cheated of that. By Damarov."

A brief silence followed – Azarias uncertain as to how he should respond to a woman who has recently discovered that the man-who-would-be-father was most likely responsible for the murder of her real parents – and she adjusted her scarf, woollen gloves and bobble hat. She attempted to pull the zip on the navy puffer jacket beyond its natural limit, in a bid to protect her face from the biting January cold. Saluki cocked her head to the right.

"Do you hear that?" she asked. "Music. Strange. Don't you think?"

"Disrespectful, perhaps. Depends," he offered.

They followed the sound of the music to its source, purely out of curiosity, until they found an Afro-Caribbean male, of middling years, kneeling before a gravestone, muttering beneath the volume of a popular song, which resounded from iPod, with attached speaker, propped up against the headstone. Azarias recognised the song, singing the lyrics, *"Who Do We Think We*

*Are,"* in his mind, before the man realised that he had company.

The music ceased abruptly, twitching fingers finding the pause button, as he turned to face Azarias and Saluki. Both noted the details on the headstone –

*'Leon McGonagle. Born January 21 1994. Died January 21 2014. Beloved son, brother, nephew and grandson. Forever a star'.*

"I am sorry," the man murmured quietly. "It is disturbing you? You want something?"

"No," Azarias answered, reading the grief in the man's dark brown eyes. "No to both. Not disturbing me. Us. And, I want to help."

"How? How can you help? Too late for that. My son needed help a year ago. But he was alone. That night."

"His birthday?" Azarias enquired, noting the corresponding dates, between headstone and birthday. "Where did you say it happened? When?" he probed, ignoring Saluki and her elbow jabs to his ribs.

"Don't you dare" she hissed. "You can't."

"He was studying to be an actor," the man whispered proudly, tears welling in his eyes. "At Central School of Speech and Drama. He was gonna be someone. A movie star. He was home for his birthday. Out with friends. It wasn't that late. He sent a text message when he got out of the taxi. Last message I had from him. About half eleven. He would have been home before midnight. Do you know the service road? Behind the BMW showroom? Took the short cut along there, rather than

394

walk in the light. Racially motivated, they said. I went looking for him. Called Rob. Half past midnight. Said he had got out of the taxi an hour before. It wouldn't take more than 6 or 7 minutes to walk from there. I took the dog out. Legend. That's the dog. The music you heard. John Legend. My son loves his music. Legend found him. I found him."

The man was bereft, broken, racked by massive sobs, and he turned to continue arranging some fresh flowers in a vase. Saluki shook her head, even though she realised that she might be wasting her time attempting to prevent Azarias carrying out the plans she sensed he was about to undertake; interfering with time, or attempting to '*make history*'.

"Your eyes. Your eyes are different colours," the man commented detaching himself, momentarily, from his grief and staring at Azarias. "I apologise. I just noticed. One eye is the colour of emerald."

He had not intended to cause offence – none taken – but he did not anticipate the response. The grief-ridden man had returned his attention, again, to the flowers, and tending the weeds that had grown around the grave, until he heard Azarias speak – a somewhat insensitive choice of words – and he stood to face him, confused and angry. But no one was there. They had, seemingly, vanished. All that remained were the fading clouds of breath, in the cold January air, and the words that Azarias had uttered –

"None of this ever happened."

"I am glad that we are not related," Saluki whispered, as they merged into the darkness of the unlit service road, between the garages and gardens of homes on one side and the rear of the car showroom and service department on the other.

Azarias and Saluki were waiting. He was on one side, behind a wooden fence, Saluki the other side of the narrow tarmacked lane, hiding beside a garage belonging to a house at the far end of a long suburban garden. It was dark; any artificial light bleeding from nearby homes, and the duplex apartments, behind Azarias, situated above shops on the St. Albans Road, obscured by curtains and drapes. Many people would be in bed, asleep, with a view to rising early; potential commuters to and from London, aside from those working in their home town.

"I said ..."

"I heard you the first time," Azarias cut in, checking the time on his recently acquired uRAPP – the gadget that did almost everything a person could need. "Shush. You'll spoil the surprise."

Azarias checked the date and time on his wrist – January 21, 2014 -

'23:31! Why would you choose to walk along this unlit alley? You could have – should have – walked along the main drag,' Azarias thought, as he peered through a small gap in the fence, towards the western end of the lane, some 300 metres away, where the orange-yellow lights of Beechwood Avenue flooded in as far as the first of the white striped road humps. And there he was, as expected, and anticipated, turning left into the alley from the direction of the main road.

"He's coming," Azarias hissed, focussing on the strutting silhouette heading in their direction.

"I cannot see him," she replied. "Not without revealing my position."

"Trust me. You'll know. Let him pass. He doesn't need to know," Azarias suggested. "Now I see the others. Behind him. Hanging back. Five of them. Why can't he hear them? About 50 metres between him and them. Okay? Ready?"

Pulling the hood of his trench coat up over his head, Azarias attempted to blend in with the dark of the night, and the murky surroundings. Saluki lowered the dark woollen bobble hat over her ears, lifting the collar of the navy puffer jacket, so as to conceal as much as her pale skin as possible. Black gloves hid her hands, and she disappeared into a corner, where the garage adjoined to a brick built wall. Silence, as both held onto their breath: silence broken, only, by an approaching tinny rhythmic sound – music played through headphones, or earphones, loud enough to scramble the contents of the skull.

'John Legend', Azarias guessed, remembering the words of the man in the cemetery. 'Probably never heard them coming'.

As the target drew nearer Azarias and Saluki dropped down on to their haunches, holding a collective breath, melding with the shadow of the night. The initial aims and objectives were met – the adolescent male; 'mixed race', Azarias made out in the gloom; passed by, unaware of his would-be protectors hiding in darkened corners, and unaware of those behind him, intending him harm. And, he was singing along, somewhat out of tune – unable to hear his own voice, due to the sound thumping through the ear pieces.

The off-key singing became a mumble as the young man continued on his way home, oblivious to matter unfolding, or about to unfold behind him. He was probably close to the point in the alley where his cold, beaten, lifeless body would have been found by his father walking their dog, Legend, searching for the son who had not arrived home, but for this timely intervention.

"Oi! Mate," one of the gang rasped, "I'm fucking talking to you. Don't ignore me."

*"He can't hear you. Prat,"* Azarias hissed, silently, in his brain.

The pattering of feet – two pairs – breaking into a jog; perhaps size eight – probably not big lads. They would be relying on outnumbering their prey – five to one, by the time the others had caught up with their lead party. Between the ages of sixteen and eighteen, Azarias guessed, and not unlike those he used to teach at the college; that was already another lifetime ago. As the youths drew closer, their panting and wheezing breath became audible – smokers!

*'Timing is everything'!*

And their timing was perfect. Azarias and Saluki pulled the cord tort, snapping it from the concealed camouflaged position on the tarmac to what they judged to be about shin height. Their judgement was also perfect. The cord pulled against their effort to hold it rigid, on contact with legs and ankles, but Saluki and Azarias held fast as two shadowy figures flashed through their field of vision – one flailing his arms like a windmill, the other diving towards the solid surface of the service road, arms outstretched in a bid to save his face from crashing onto the tarmac.

'Windmill arms' lost his balance but was able to lower his body into a fall, and roll, in stages, lessening the final impact. His comrade, though, hit the ground palms first, crying out like a cat in a fight as at least one bone cracked in one of the wrists, and tiny pieces of grit forced their way into the epidermis. Both stayed down, writhing, sucking air through their teeth – the one without the broken wrist mainly due to the swift kick to the testicles from Saluki, which shot a shattering, screaming pain throughout his lower abdomen. One holding his left wrist, the other his balls, and the other three standing motionless, fear-ridden, and uncertain what to do next, standing before two nightmarish figures; a reality to the similar situations faced in the world of computer and video games, or in movies.

A loud bang, a mix between a thunderclap and a sonic boom, echoed around the surrounding low rise apartments. A few lights flickered on, curtains twitching, as curiosity won over some people, though others probably slept through, oblivious to the fact that the course of their future lives may just have been altered.

"What was that?" one youth asked. "That sound?"

"A life saved," Azarias said in a hushed voice, an ecumenical tone to his voice, as he was about to preach a sermon. "We only the ring the bell when an angel gets its wings."

"You what? Who the fuck are you?" the same youth hissed through the dark gaps in his yellow teeth, his comrades having seemingly lost the power of speech.

"Angels. We are angels," Saluki teased. "You do believe in angels, don't you?"

While the group let out snorts of derision, mixed with the nervous laughter of uncertainty, Saluki tapped on the device in her wrist – she vanished, before their eyes, and reappeared, a few seconds later, a metre behind them.

"Angels. Or demons. You decide," she added, causing the adolescents to strain their necks, following her as she walked from behind them back to where Azarias stood.

"Shit, man," uttered the one holding his injured left wrist, to one in particular. "We've had some Lipton Tea. And that vodka. This is a bad trip."

Azarias assured them that it was all real, their eyes were not deceiving them, and it was not a trip. Angels had been sent to offer them a second chance – choose a different path from the one that they would have taken; the path that would have led to the unnecessary beating, and kicking, to death of a young man with a bright future ahead of him. An opportunity to consider their own futures.

"We will be watching over you," Saluki stated, peering over her shoulder, as she and Azarias turned to walk away. "We will always be there."

"And get yourself to the hospital," Azarias advised. "You might have suffered a fracture to the scaphoid bone."

The five youths stood motionless, in silence, mouths on spotty faces agape, as the two 'angels' walked slowly away towards the light at the other end of the service road, where the lone figure of the young man, headphones booming in his ears, turned left in the direction of the safety of home.

"Leon lives," Azarias whispered.

"What about them?" Saluki asked.

"They are crapping it. They'll not tell anyone. Might be the end of that gang. Would you want to explain that away? I used to live along here," Azarias continued.

"I know."

"Of course you do. So, what now?"

"We shouldn't have done that," Saluki sighed.

"So people have told me. Why did you?"

"It felt good. Because it felt good," she replied. "It made a difference. And, you know, I would like to see my parents. We didn't get to your mother's grave."

"Another time. Perhaps."

"Perhaps."

"So, what now?" he repeated, not having received an answer the first time. "What about me? Where do I belong? Who am I?"

"Look at me," she demanded, as they entered the yellow/orange glow of the avenue at the end of the darkened back lane, stopping Azarias opposite the quiet gardens of the nursery school on the corner of the main road.

"This is beyond my experience. Now both of your eyes are green."

"And that is my point. What do I do now? I don't belong here anymore."

"But one day, you will be here. The other you," she said softly, as they proceeded up the hill into the sleepy housing estate. "Here will do. It's quiet enough. We have a meeting with Raphael scheduled. We can time leap from here."

They set a predetermined date, time and location into their devices, and a brief uncomfortable silence ensued, which was broken by Azarias.

"I know," he asserted.

"What do you know?"

"That I probably have to die."

She nodded her head, and they both tapped the screens, and then they vanished, together, somewhere in time and space.